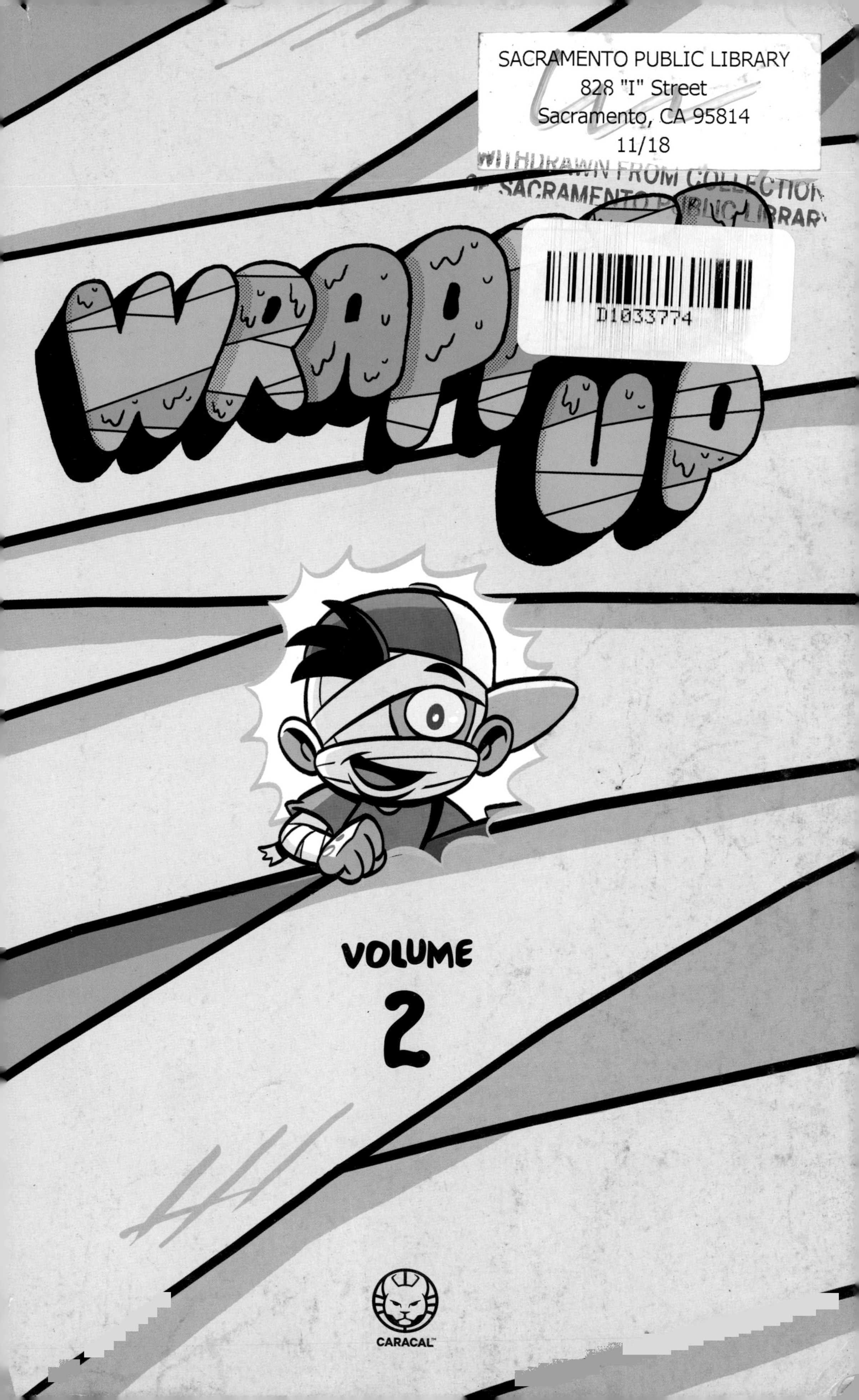
VOLUME
2
CARACAL™

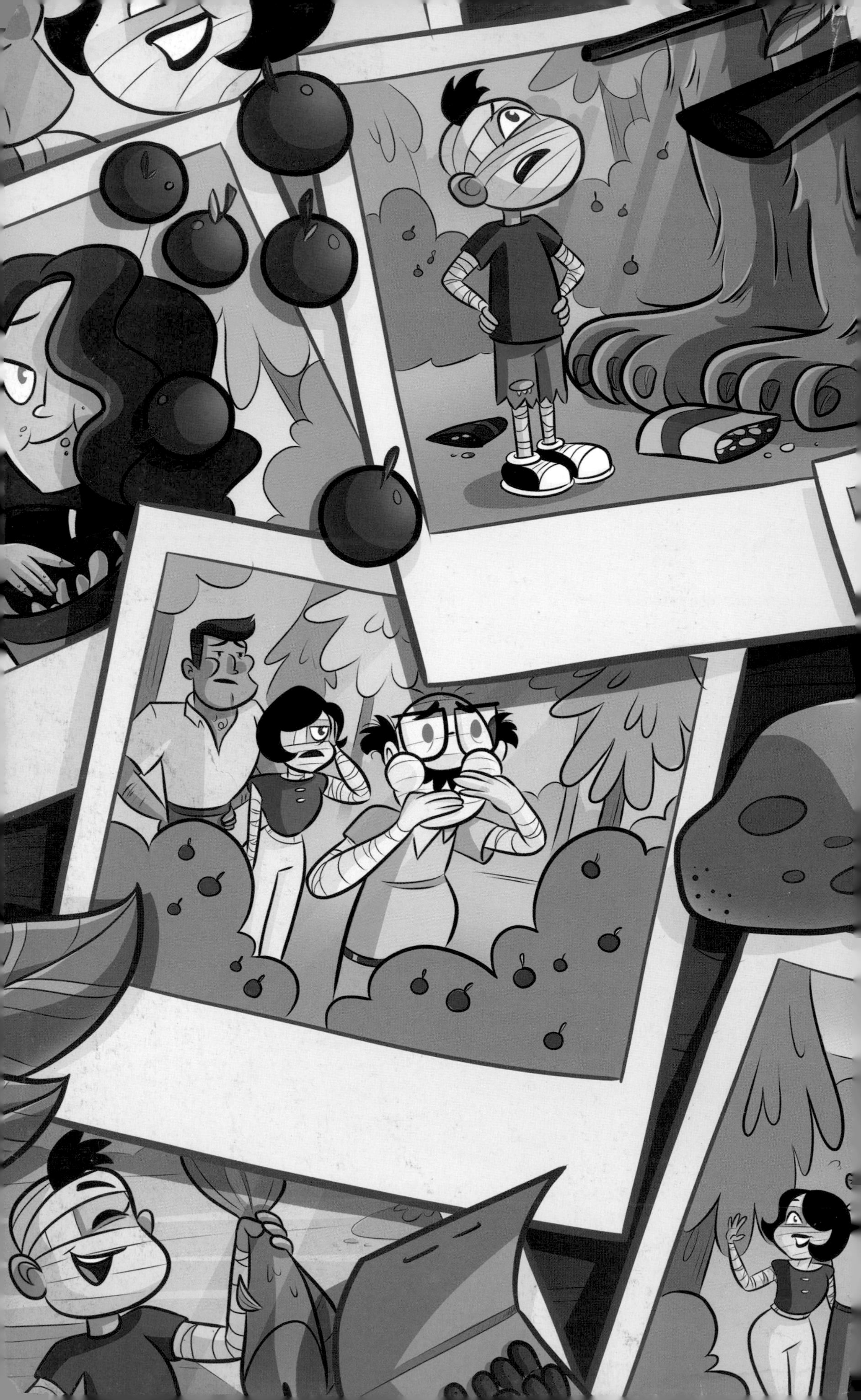

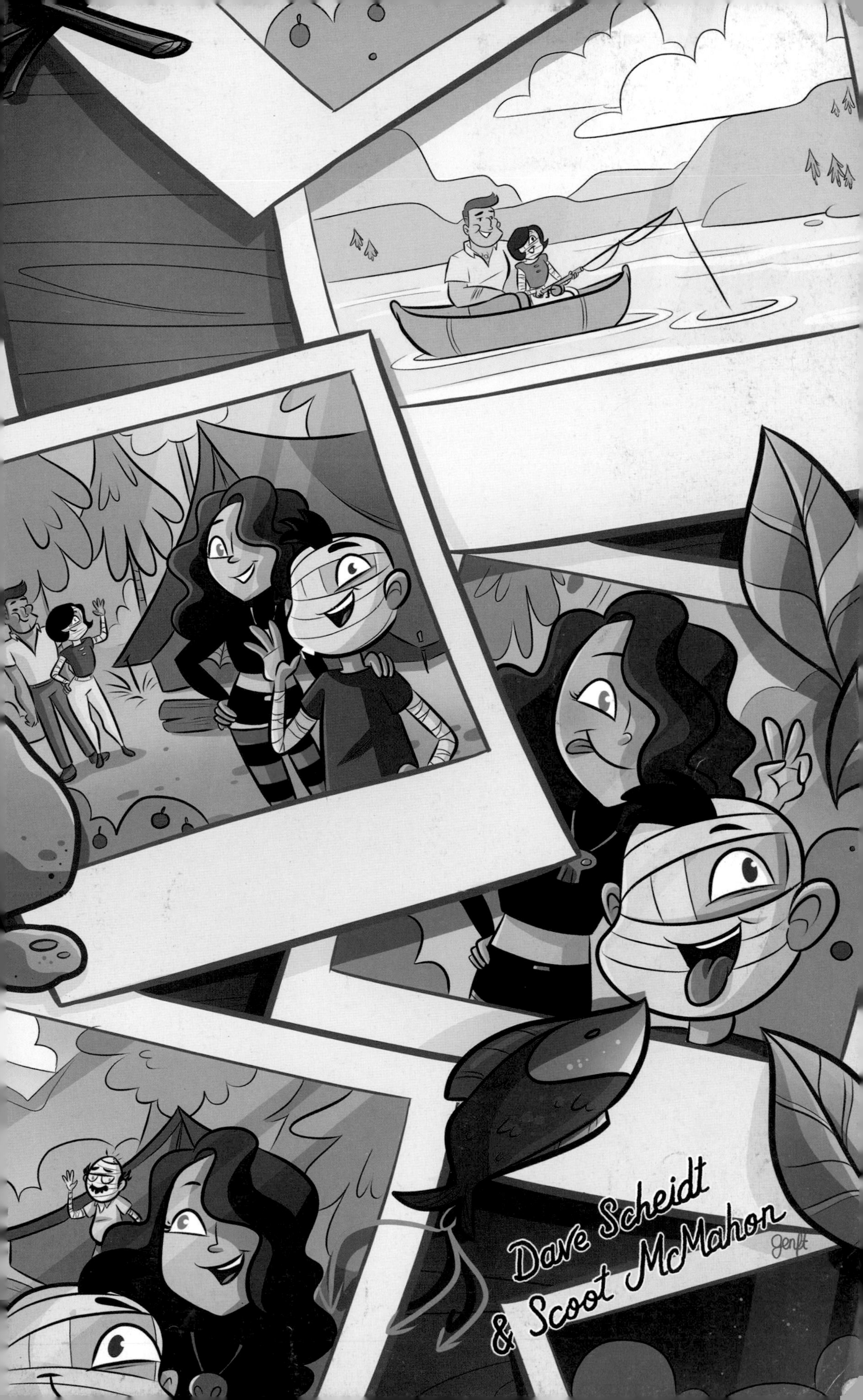
Dave Scheidt
& Scoot McMahon
genlt

WRAPPED UP

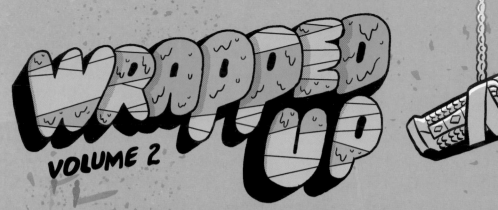

VOLUME 2

WRITER
Dave Scheidt

ARTIST
Scoot McMahon

COLORIST
Sean Dove

ASSISTANT COLORIST, ISSUES 6–8
Andrea Bell

BACKUP STORY ARTISTS
Yehudi Mercado   Mason Dickerson
Sean Mac   Aaron Pittman   Shan Murphy

EDITOR
Hazel Newlevant

ASSISTANT EDITOR
Amanda Vernon

ISBN: 978-1-941302-70-5

Library of Congress Control Number: 2017955348

CARACAL™

Wrapped Up, Vol. 2, published 2018 by The Lion Forge, LLC. Printed in China.

10 9 8 7 6 5 4 3 2 1

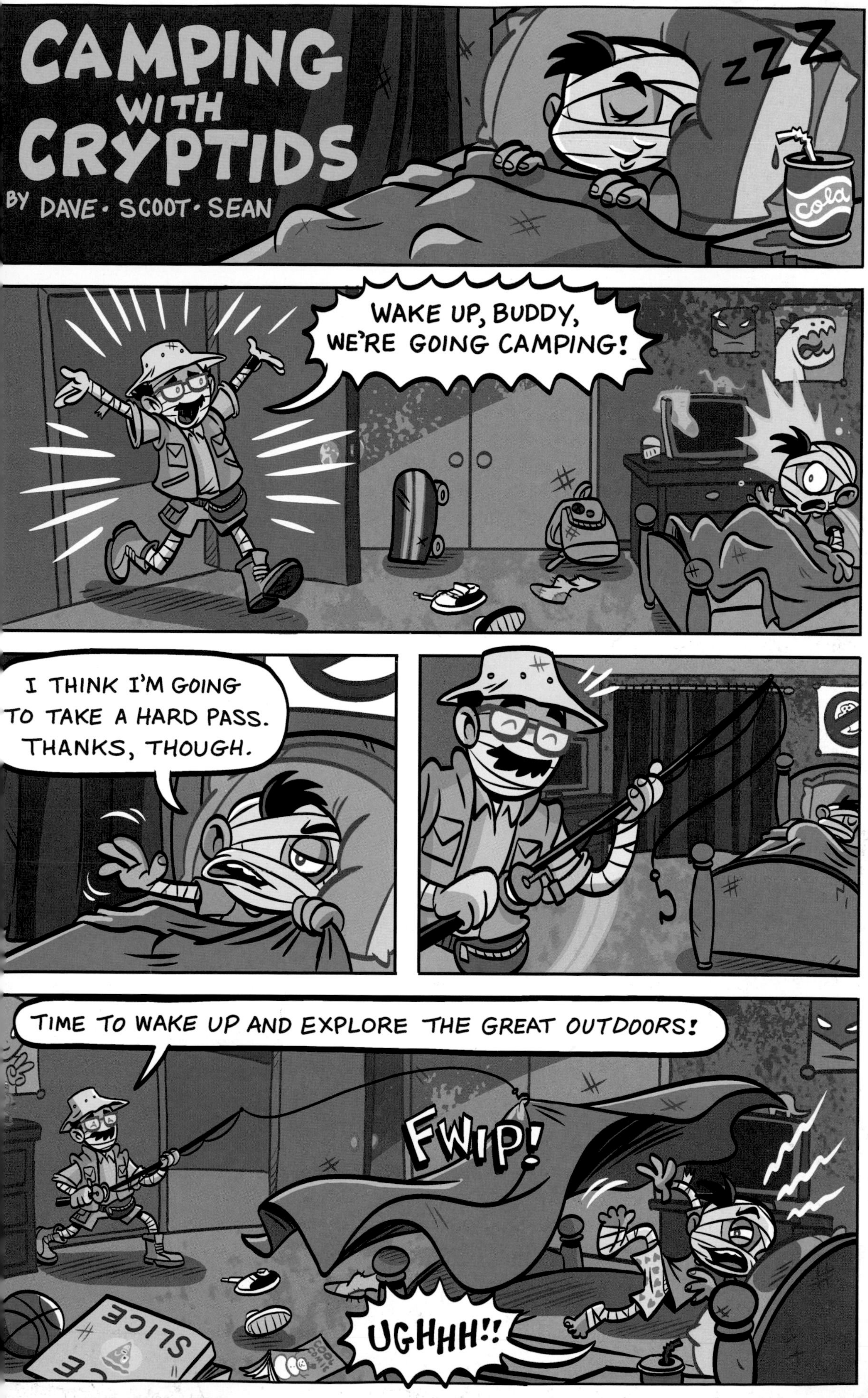
CAMPING WITH CRYPTIDS
BY DAVE · SCOOT · SEAN
ZZZ
COLA
WAKE UP, BUDDY, WE'RE GOING CAMPING!
I THINK I'M GOING TO TAKE A HARD PASS. THANKS, THOUGH.
TIME TO WAKE UP AND EXPLORE THE GREAT OUTDOORS!
FWIP!
UGHHH!!
SLICE
COOL COMIC

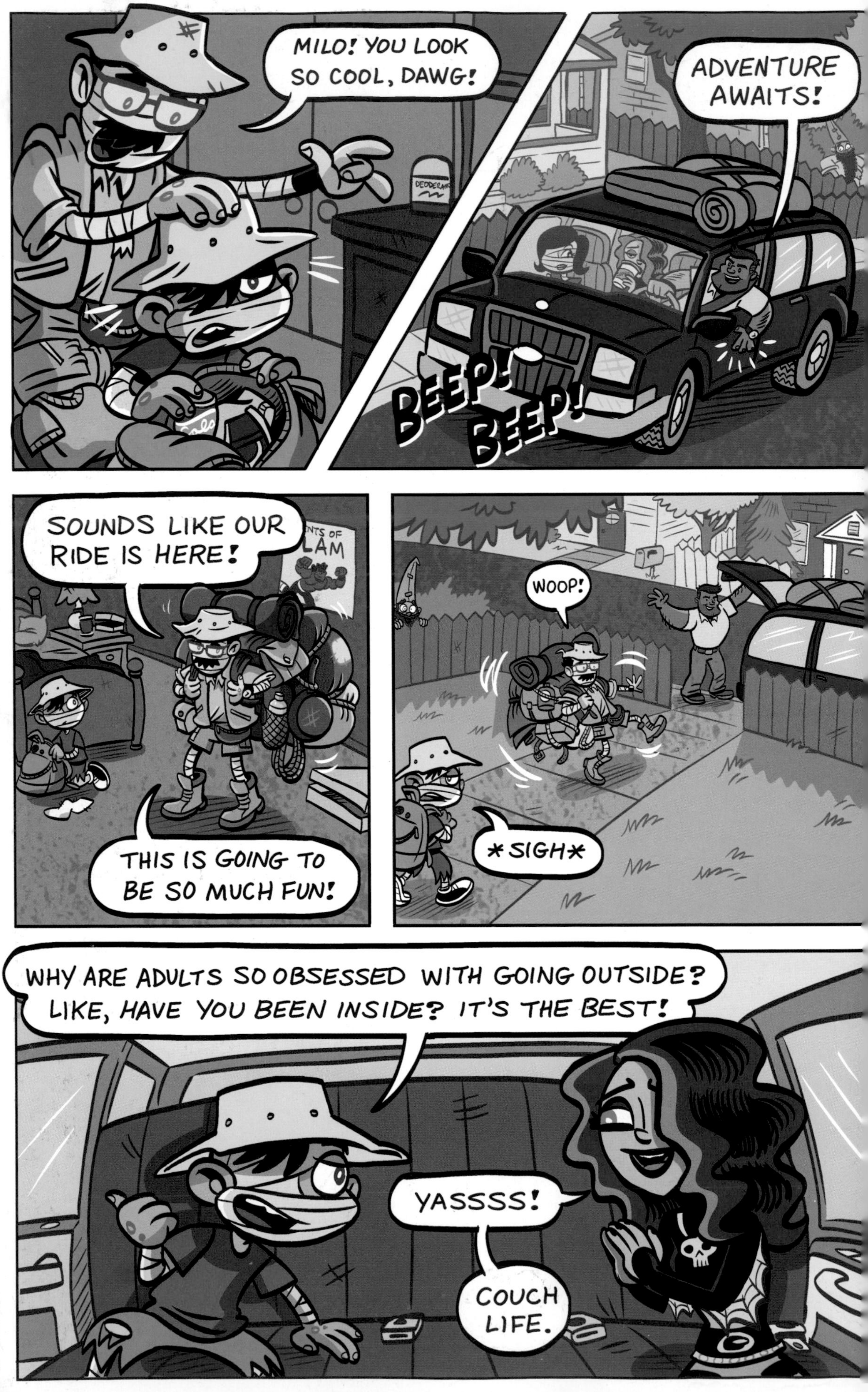
MILO! YOU LOOK SO COOL, DAWG!
ADVENTURE AWAITS!
BEEP! BEEP!
SOUNDS LIKE OUR RIDE IS HERE!
THIS IS GOING TO BE SO MUCH FUN!
WOOP!
SIGH
WHY ARE ADULTS SO OBSESSED WITH GOING OUTSIDE? LIKE, HAVE YOU BEEN INSIDE? IT'S THE BEST!
YASSSS!
COUCH LIFE.

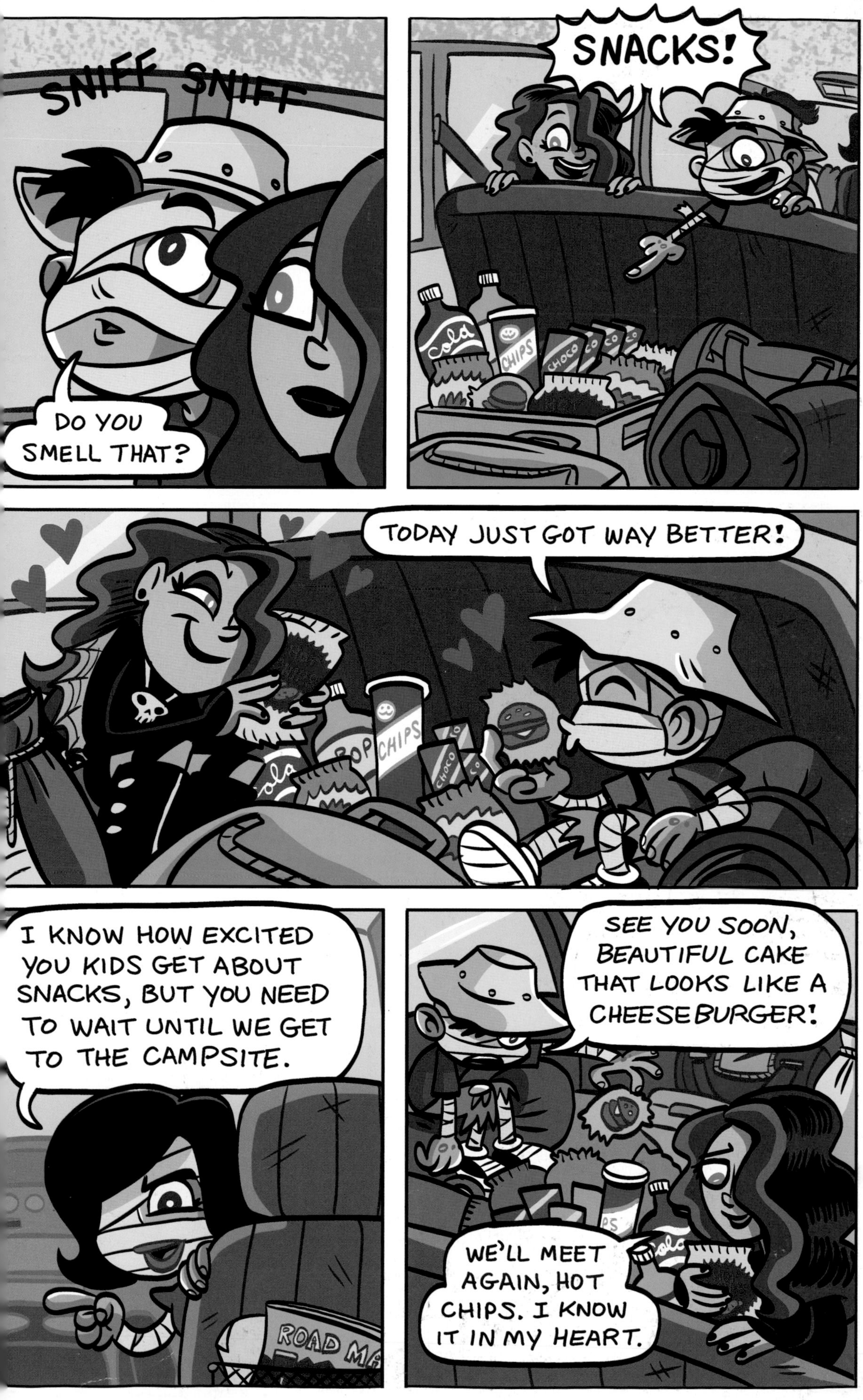
SNIFF SNIFF
DO YOU SMELL THAT?
SNACKS!
COLA
CHIPS
CHOCO
TODAY JUST GOT WAY BETTER!
POP
CHIPS
COLA
CHOCO
I KNOW HOW EXCITED YOU KIDS GET ABOUT SNACKS, BUT YOU NEED TO WAIT UNTIL WE GET TO THE CAMPSITE.
ROAD M
SEE YOU SOON, BEAUTIFUL CAKE THAT LOOKS LIKE A CHEESEBURGER!
WE'LL MEET AGAIN, HOT CHIPS. I KNOW IT IN MY HEART.

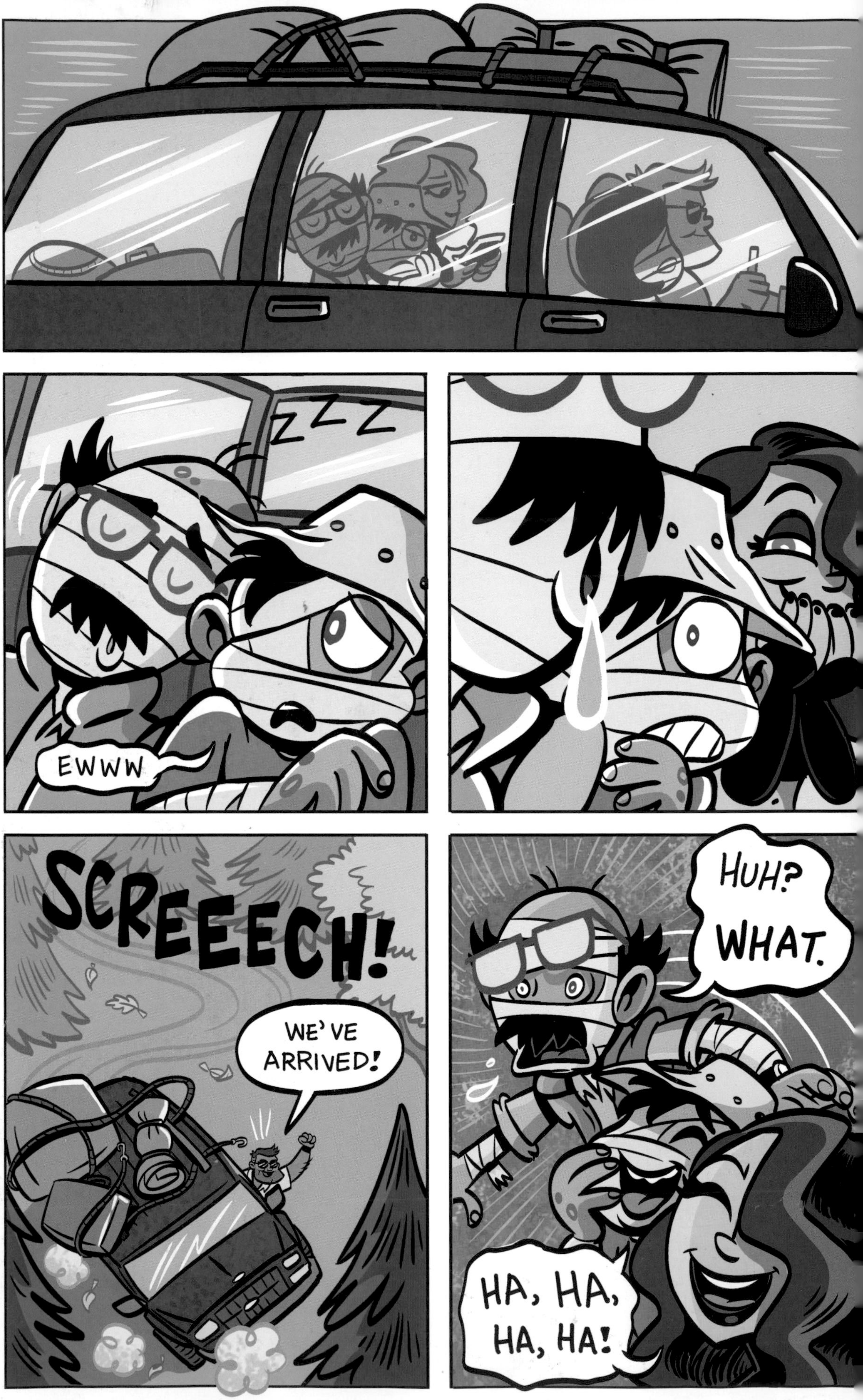
ZZZ
EWWW
SCREEECH!
WE'VE ARRIVED!
HUH? WHAT.
HA, HA, HA, HA!

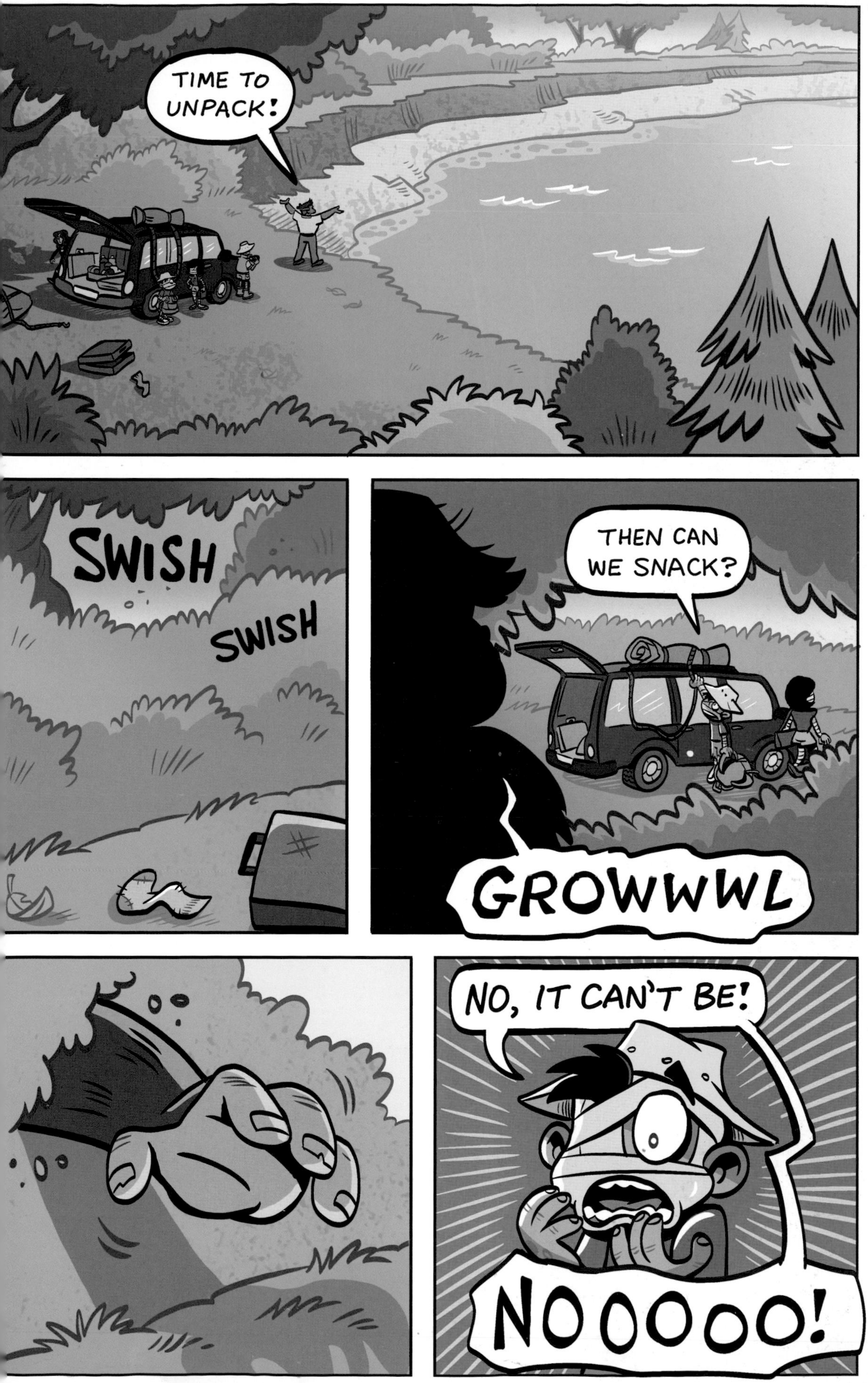
TIME TO UNPACK!
SWISH
SWISH
THEN CAN WE SNACK?
GROWWWL
NO, IT CAN'T BE!
NOOOOO!

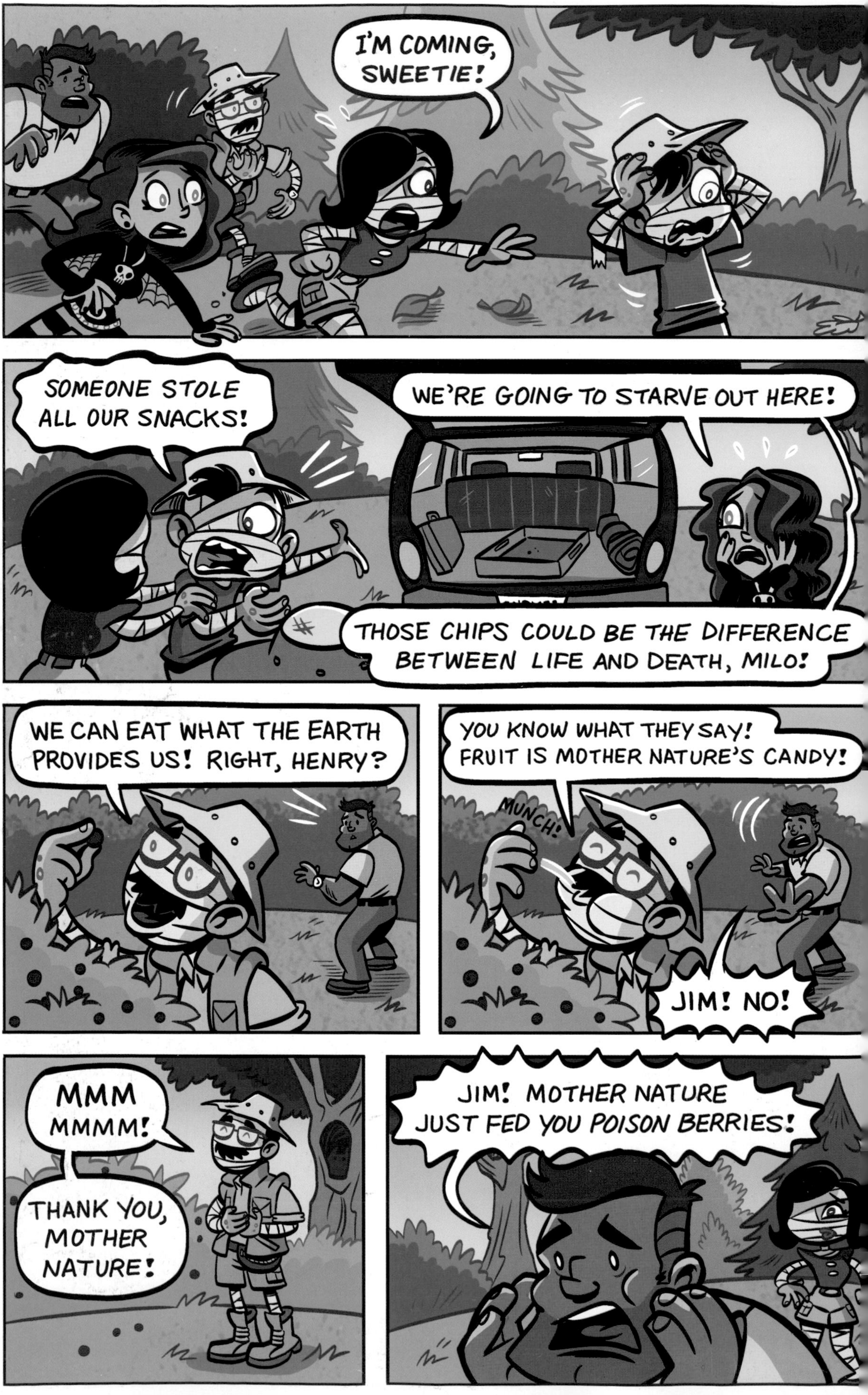
I'M COMING, SWEETIE!
SOMEONE STOLE ALL OUR SNACKS!
WE'RE GOING TO STARVE OUT HERE!
THOSE CHIPS COULD BE THE DIFFERENCE BETWEEN LIFE AND DEATH, MILO!
WE CAN EAT WHAT THE EARTH PROVIDES US! RIGHT, HENRY?
YOU KNOW WHAT THEY SAY! FRUIT IS MOTHER NATURE'S CANDY!
MUNCH!
JIM! NO!
MMM MMMM!
THANK YOU, MOTHER NATURE!
JIM! MOTHER NATURE JUST FED YOU POISON BERRIES!

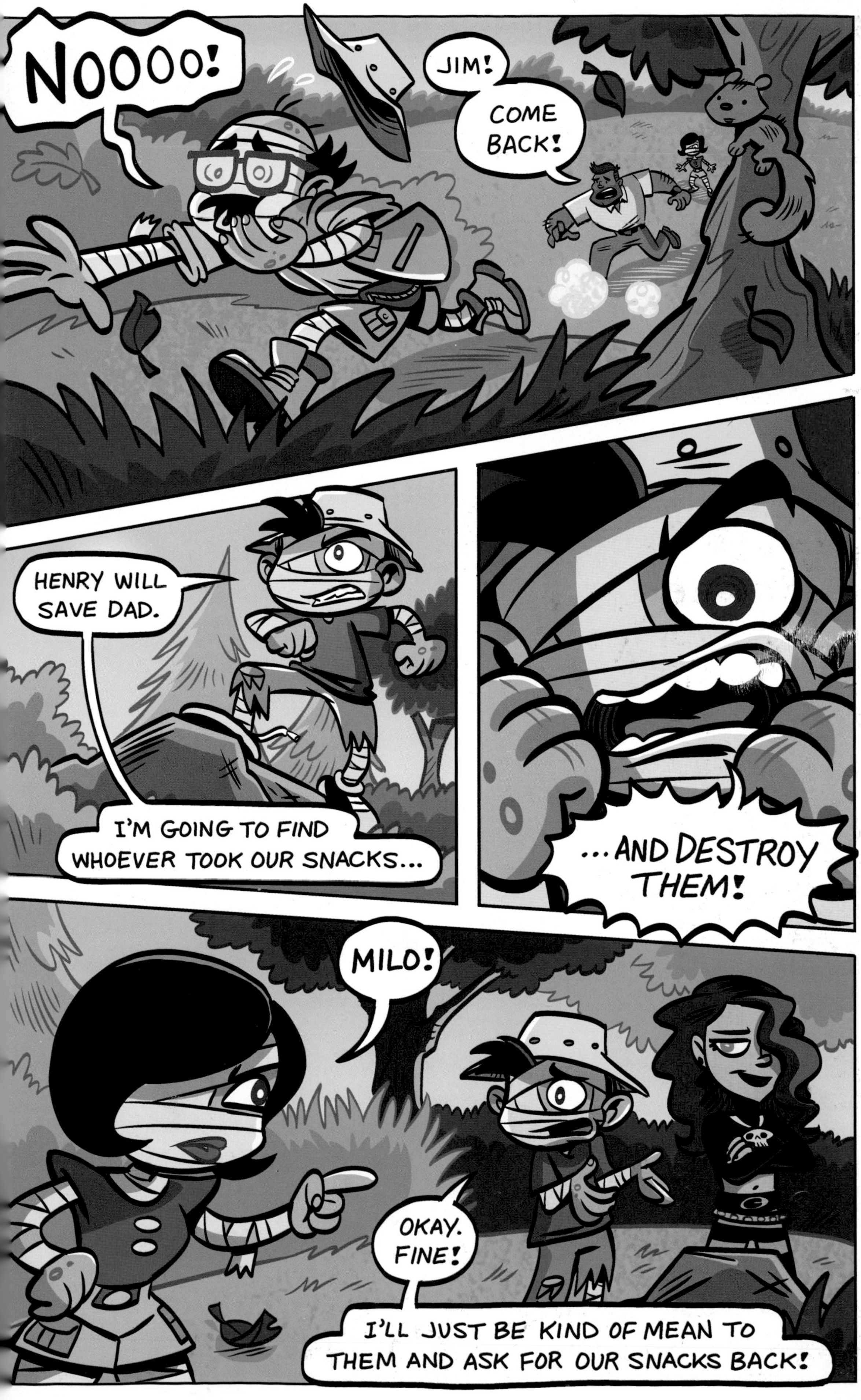
NOOOO!
JIM!
COME BACK!
HENRY WILL SAVE DAD.
I'M GOING TO FIND WHOEVER TOOK OUR SNACKS...
...AND DESTROY THEM!
MILO!
OKAY. FINE!
I'LL JUST BE KIND OF MEAN TO THEM AND ASK FOR OUR SNACKS BACK!

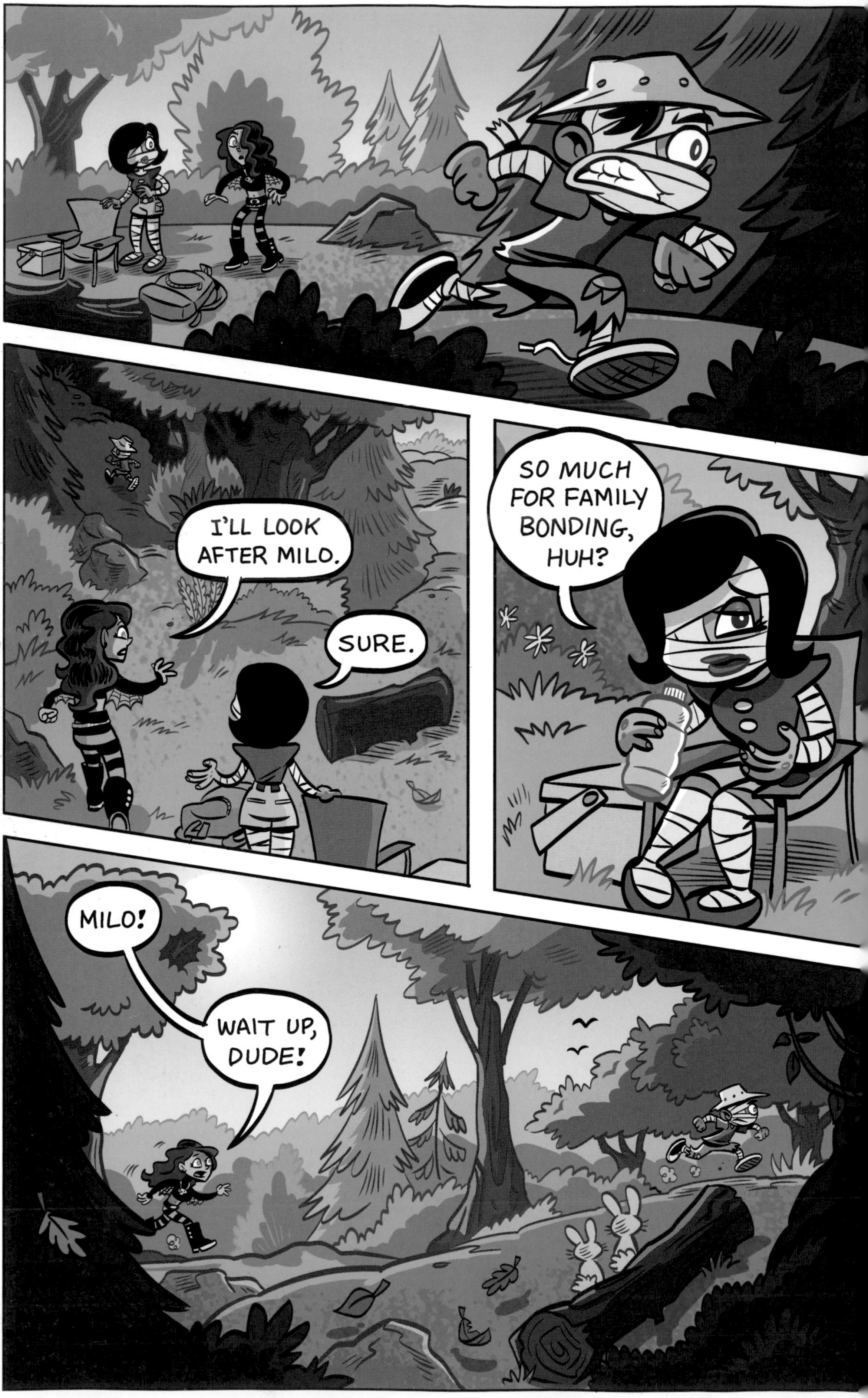
I'LL LOOK AFTER MILO.
SURE.
SO MUCH FOR FAMILY BONDING, HUH?
MILO!
WAIT UP, DUDE!

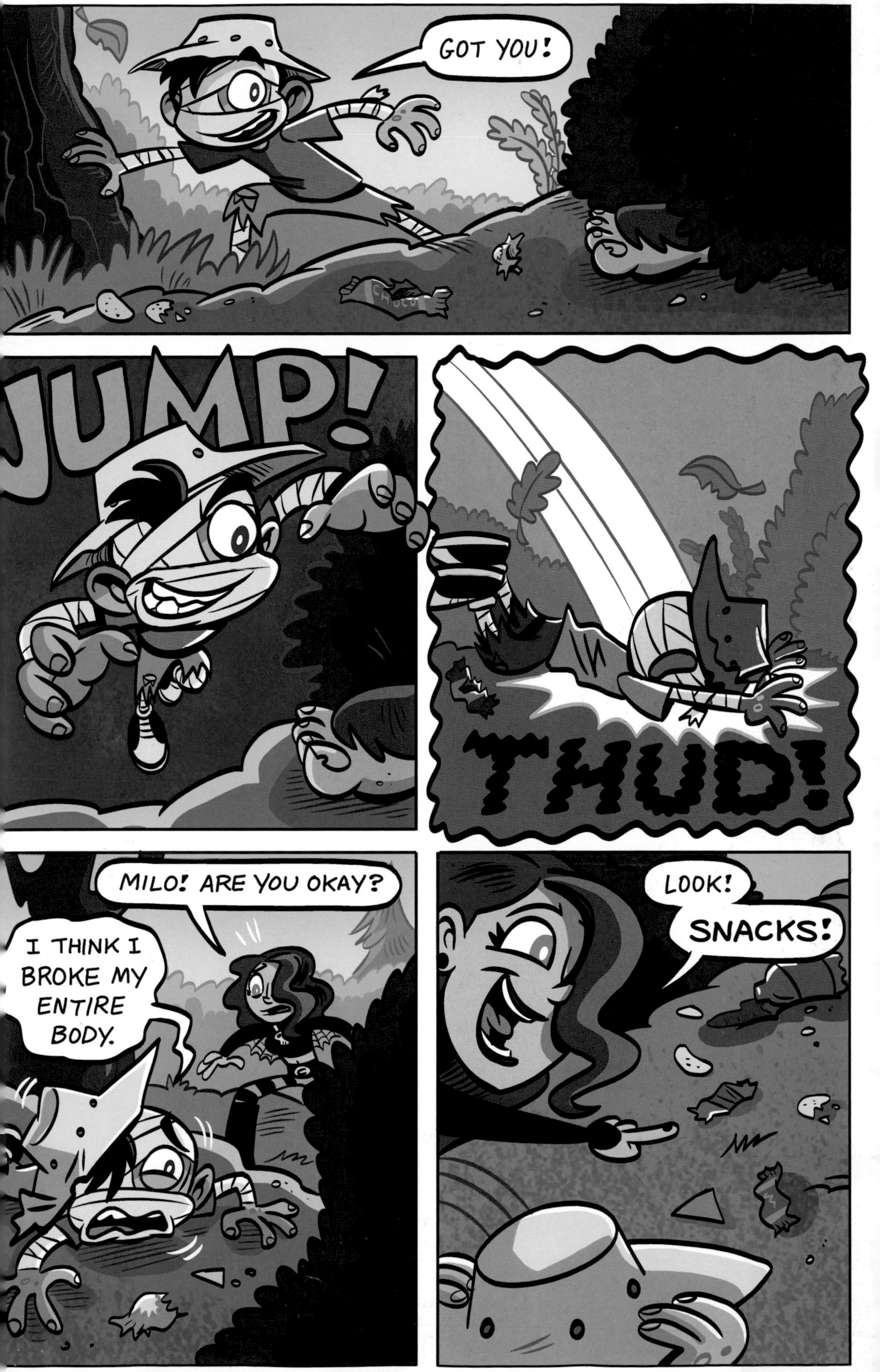
GOT YOU!
JUMP!
THUD!
MILO! ARE YOU OKAY?
I THINK I BROKE MY ENTIRE BODY.
LOOK!
SNACKS!

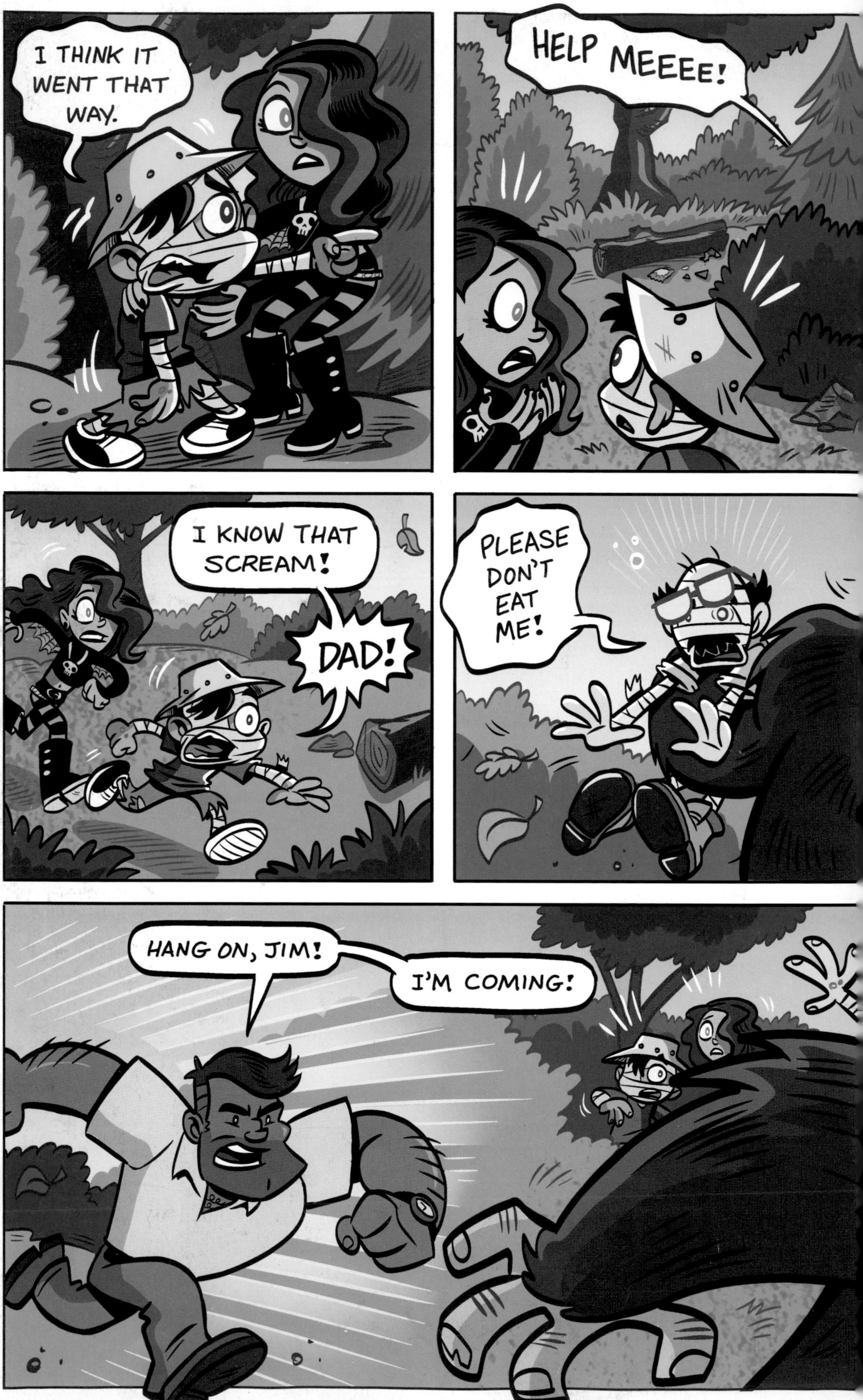
I THINK IT WENT THAT WAY.
HELP MEEEE!
I KNOW THAT SCREAM!
DAD!
PLEASE DON'T EAT ME!
HANG ON, JIM!
I'M COMING!

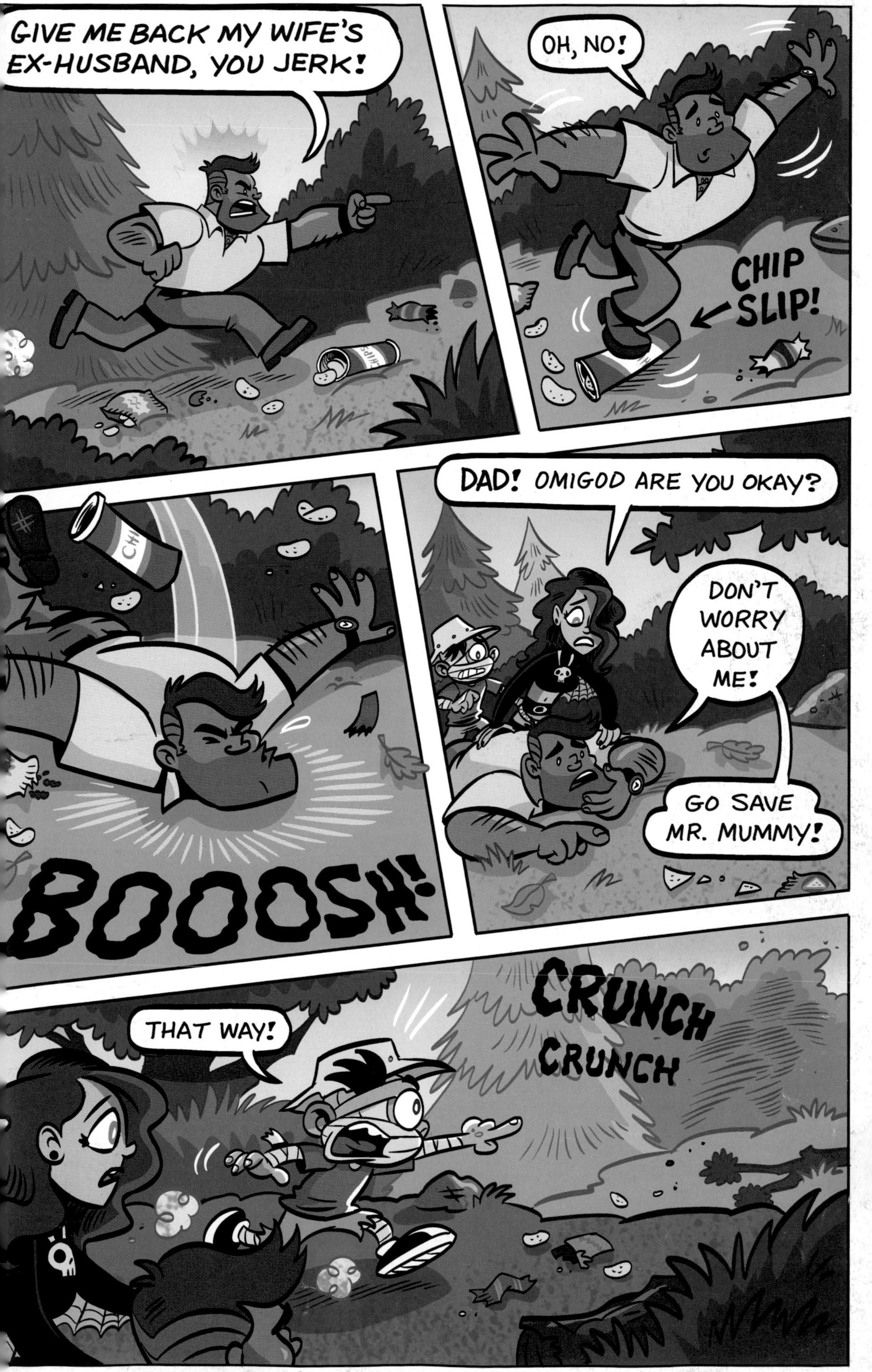
GIVE ME BACK MY WIFE'S EX-HUSBAND, YOU JERK!
OH, NO!
CHIP SLIP!
BOOOSH!
DAD! OMIGOD ARE YOU OKAY?
DON'T WORRY ABOUT ME!
GO SAVE MR. MUMMY!
THAT WAY!
CRUNCH
CRUNCH

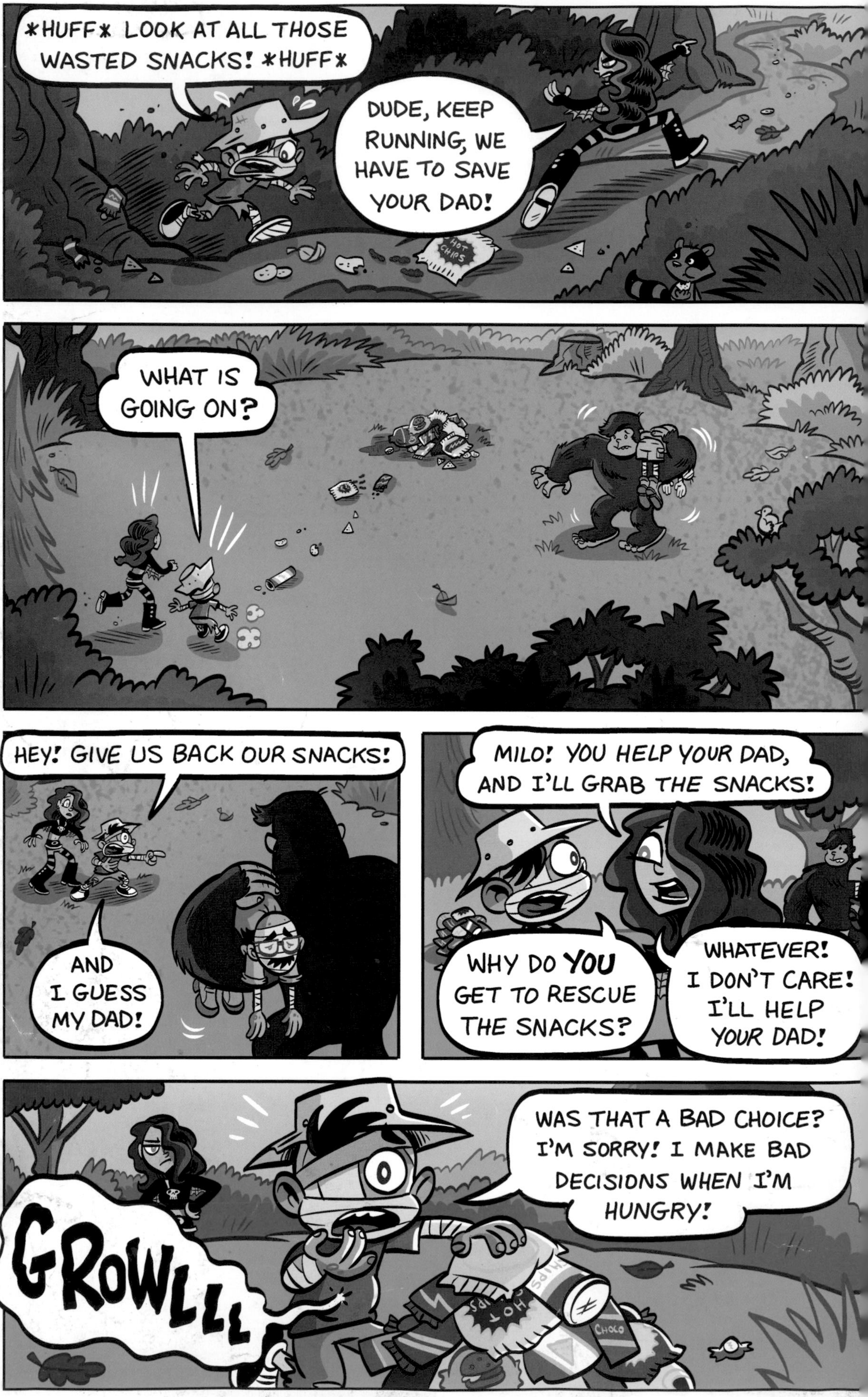
HUFF LOOK AT ALL THOSE WASTED SNACKS! *HUFF*
DUDE, KEEP RUNNING, WE HAVE TO SAVE YOUR DAD!
HOT CHIPS
WHAT IS GOING ON?
HEY! GIVE US BACK OUR SNACKS!
AND I GUESS MY DAD!
MILO! YOU HELP YOUR DAD, AND I'LL GRAB THE SNACKS!
WHY DO YOU GET TO RESCUE THE SNACKS?
WHATEVER! I DON'T CARE! I'LL HELP YOUR DAD!
WAS THAT A BAD CHOICE? I'M SORRY! I MAKE BAD DECISIONS WHEN I'M HUNGRY!
GROWLLLL
HOT CHIPS
CHOCO

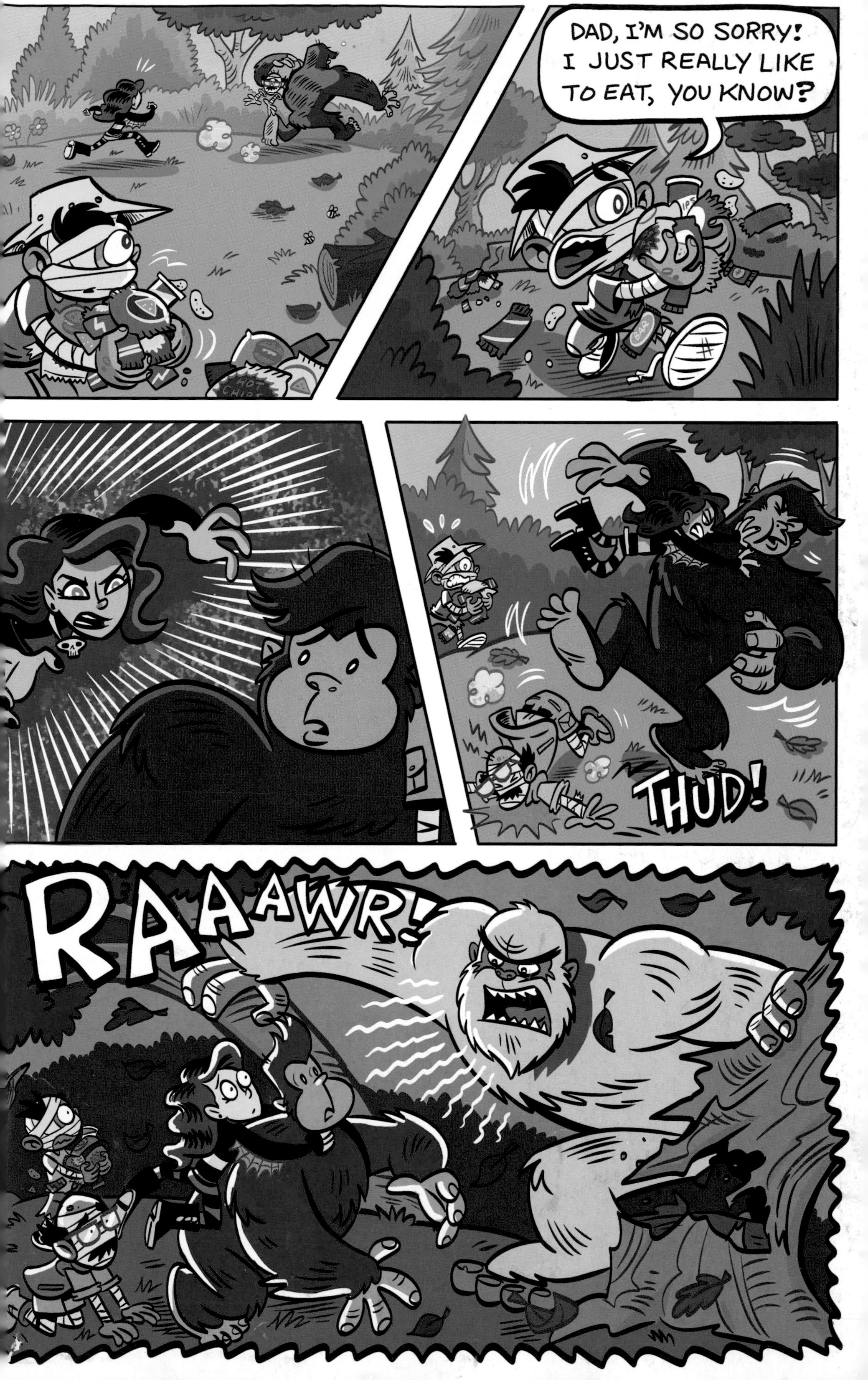
HOT CHIPS
DAD, I'M SO SORRY! I JUST REALLY LIKE TO EAT, YOU KNOW?
BAR
THUD!
RAAAWR!

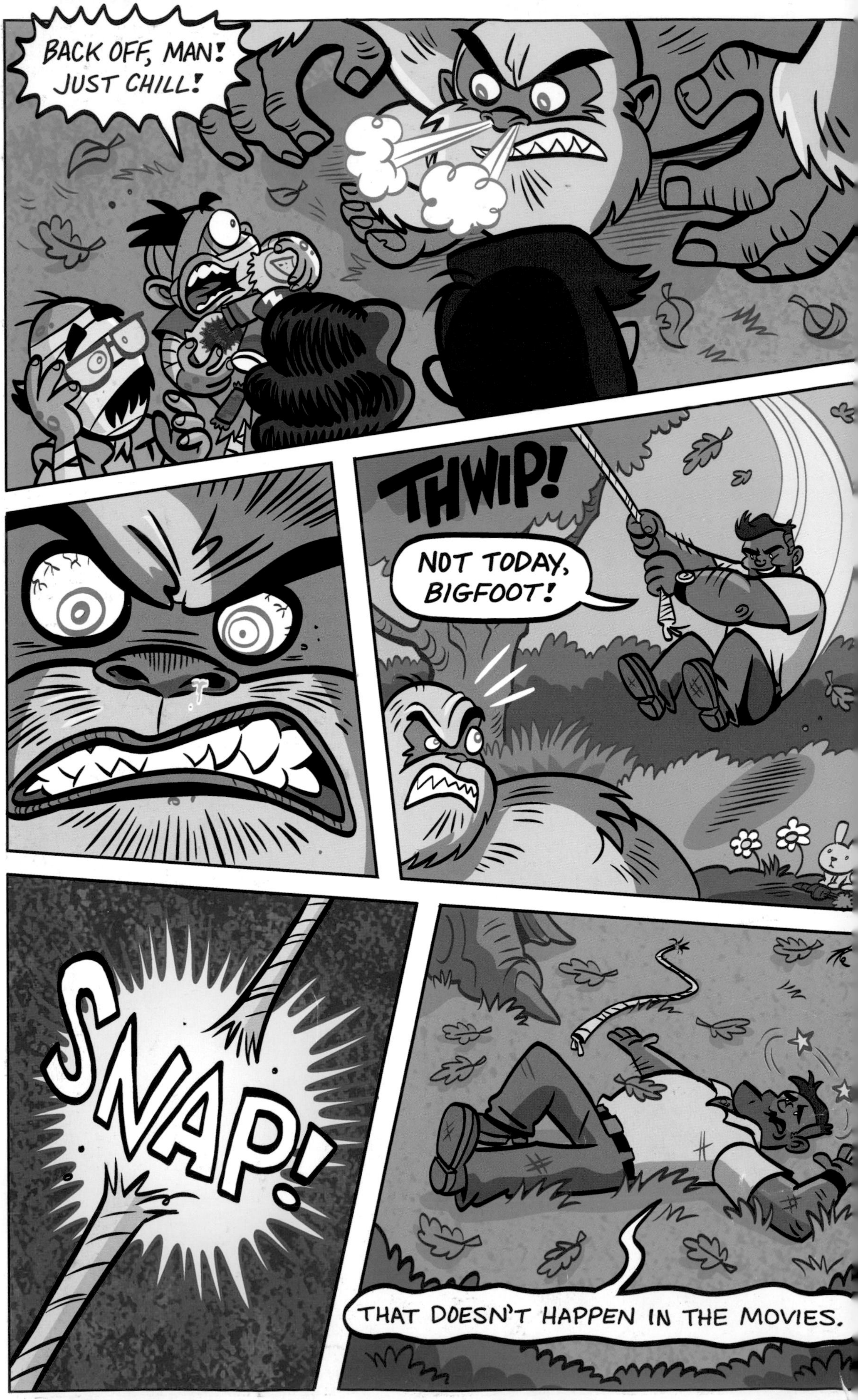
BACK OFF, MAN! JUST CHILL!
THWIP!
NOT TODAY, BIGFOOT!
SNAP!
THAT DOESN'T HAPPEN IN THE MOVIES.

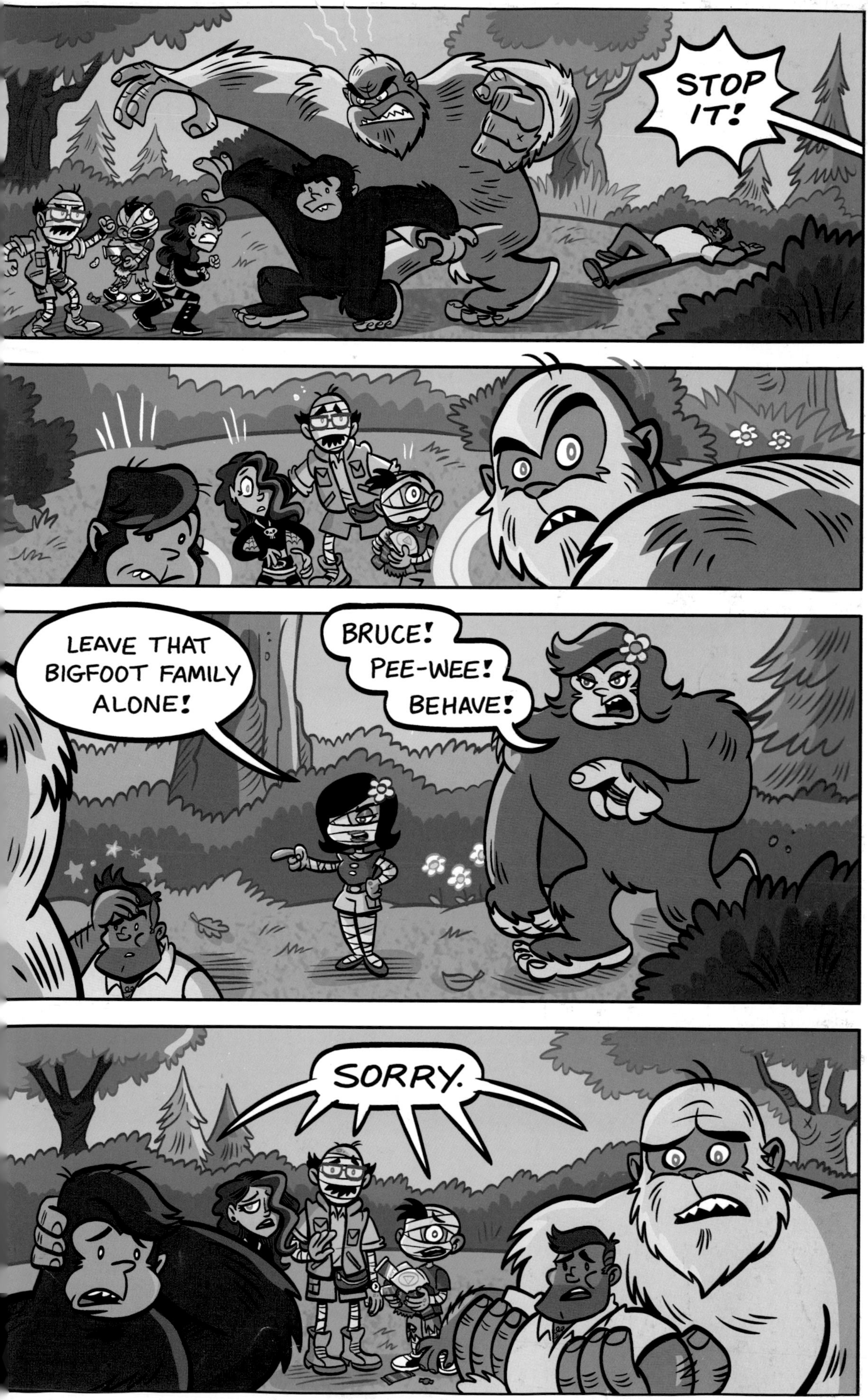
STOP IT!
LEAVE THAT BIGFOOT FAMILY ALONE!
BRUCE! PEE-WEE! BEHAVE!
SORRY.

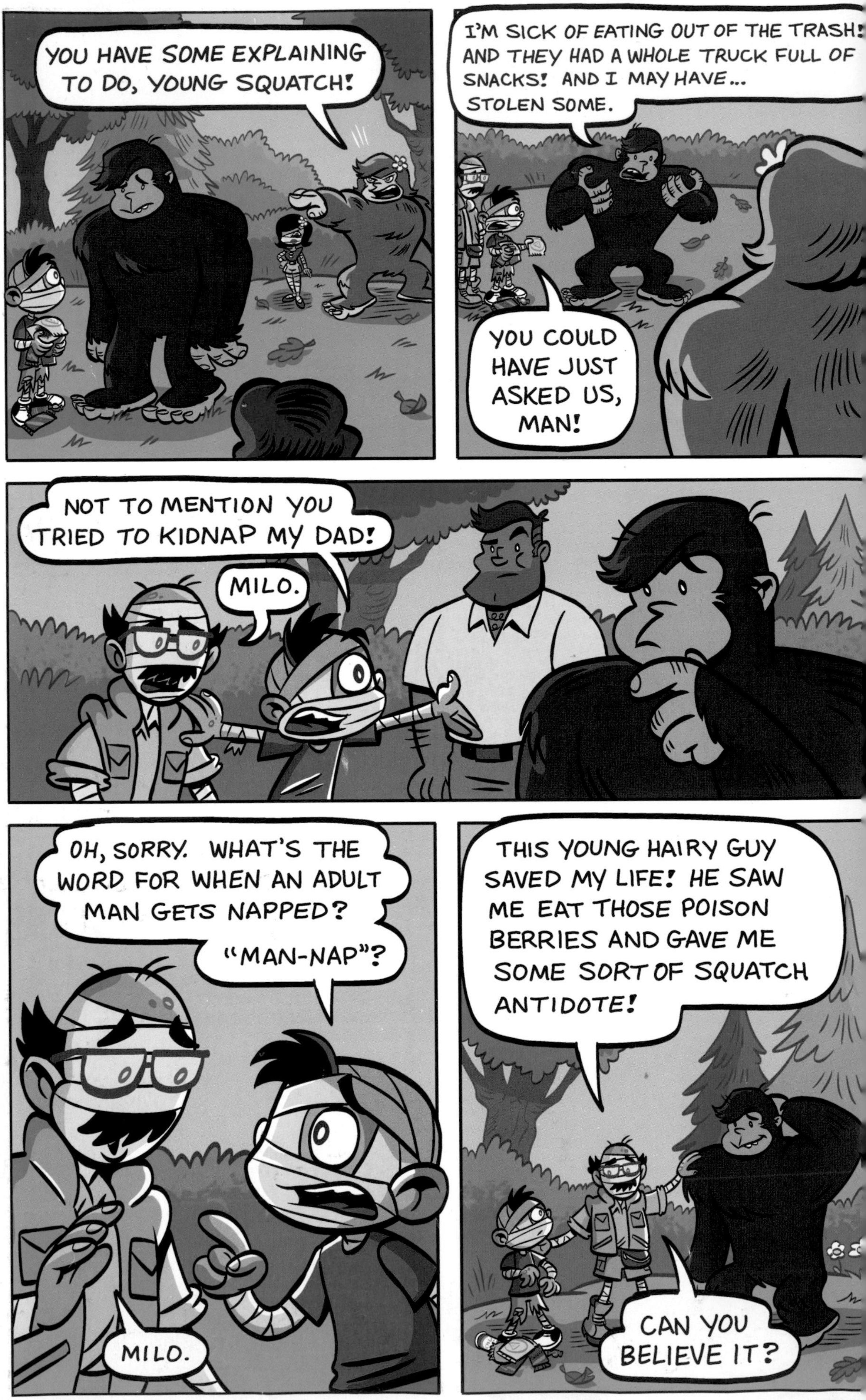
YOU HAVE SOME EXPLAINING TO DO, YOUNG SQUATCH!
I'M SICK OF EATING OUT OF THE TRASH! AND THEY HAD A WHOLE TRUCK FULL OF SNACKS! AND I MAY HAVE... STOLEN SOME.
YOU COULD HAVE JUST ASKED US, MAN!
NOT TO MENTION YOU TRIED TO KIDNAP MY DAD!
MILO.
OH, SORRY. WHAT'S THE WORD FOR WHEN AN ADULT MAN GETS NAPPED?
"MAN-NAP"?
MILO.
THIS YOUNG HAIRY GUY SAVED MY LIFE! HE SAW ME EAT THOSE POISON BERRIES AND GAVE ME SOME SORT OF SQUATCH ANTIDOTE!
CAN YOU BELIEVE IT?

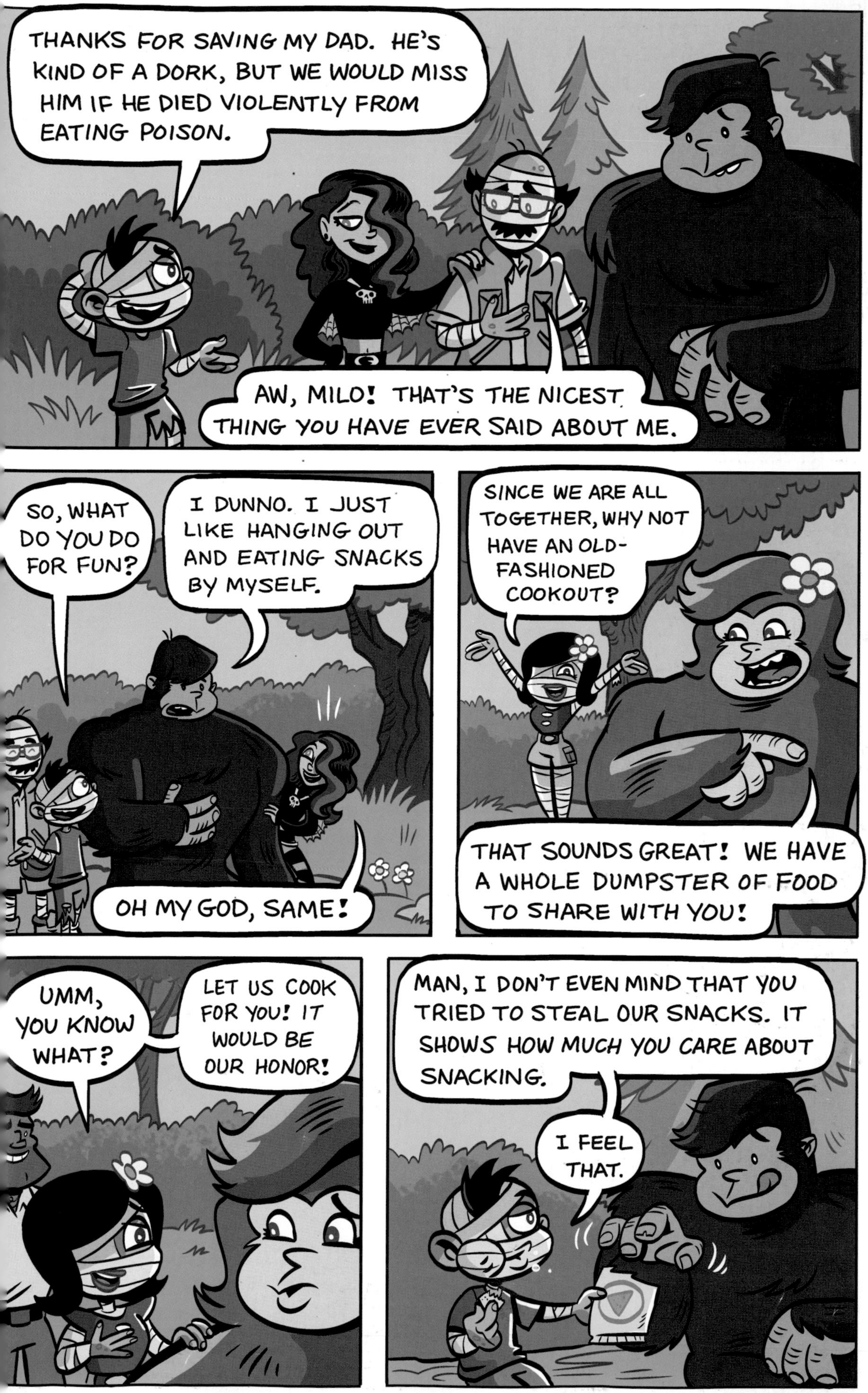
THANKS FOR SAVING MY DAD. HE'S KIND OF A DORK, BUT WE WOULD MISS HIM IF HE DIED VIOLENTLY FROM EATING POISON.
AW, MILO! THAT'S THE NICEST THING YOU HAVE EVER SAID ABOUT ME.
SO, WHAT DO YOU DO FOR FUN?
I DUNNO. I JUST LIKE HANGING OUT AND EATING SNACKS BY MYSELF.
OH MY GOD, SAME!
SINCE WE ARE ALL TOGETHER, WHY NOT HAVE AN OLD-FASHIONED COOKOUT?
THAT SOUNDS GREAT! WE HAVE A WHOLE DUMPSTER OF FOOD TO SHARE WITH YOU!
UMM, YOU KNOW WHAT?
LET US COOK FOR YOU! IT WOULD BE OUR HONOR!
MAN, I DON'T EVEN MIND THAT YOU TRIED TO STEAL OUR SNACKS. IT SHOWS HOW MUCH YOU CARE ABOUT SNACKING.
I FEEL THAT.

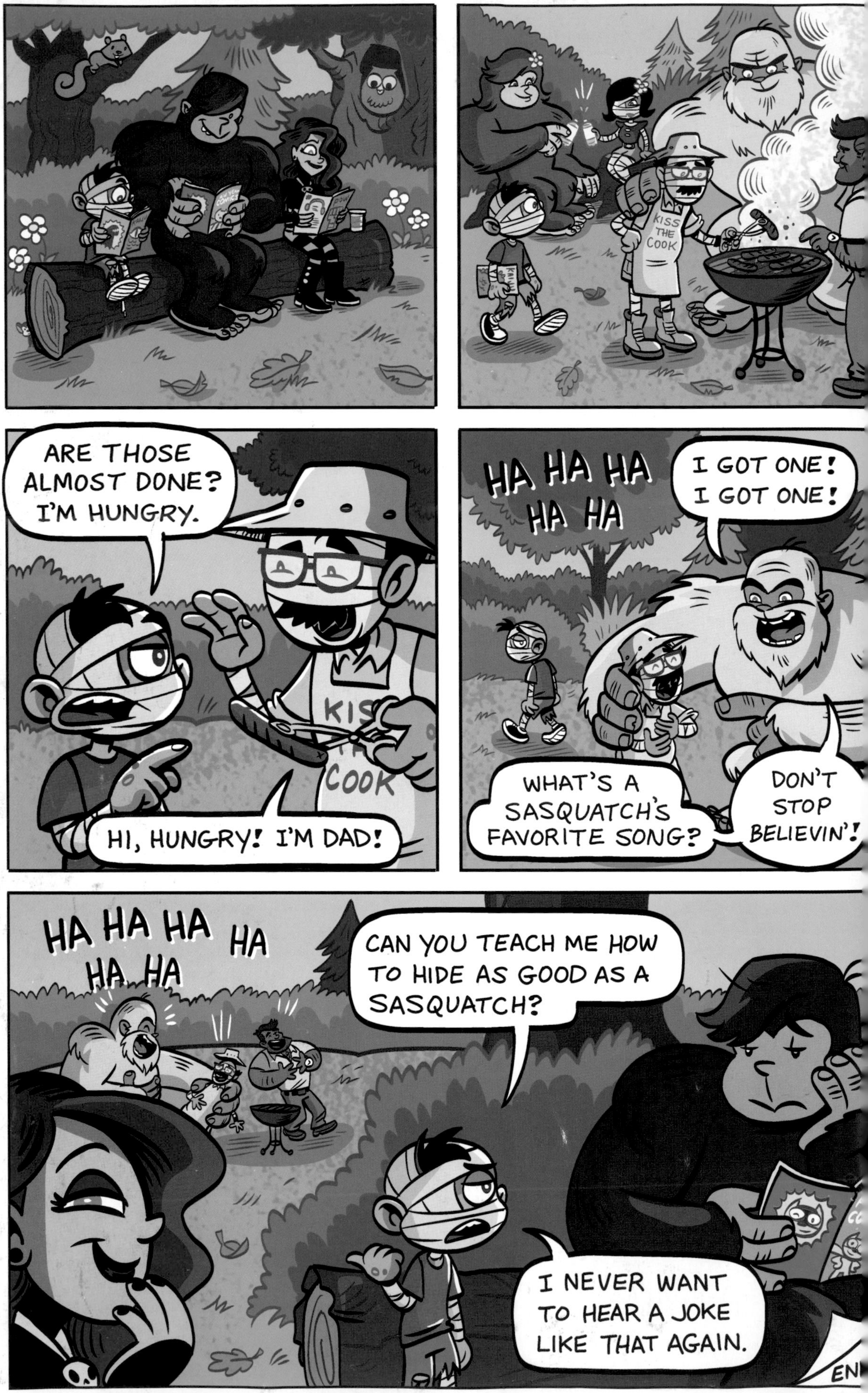
ARE THOSE ALMOST DONE? I'M HUNGRY.
HI, HUNGRY! I'M DAD!
HA HA HA HA HA
I GOT ONE! I GOT ONE!
WHAT'S A SASQUATCH'S FAVORITE SONG?
DON'T STOP BELIEVIN'!
HA HA HA HA HA HA
CAN YOU TEACH ME HOW TO HIDE AS GOOD AS A SASQUATCH?
I NEVER WANT TO HEAR A JOKE LIKE THAT AGAIN.
KISS THE COOK

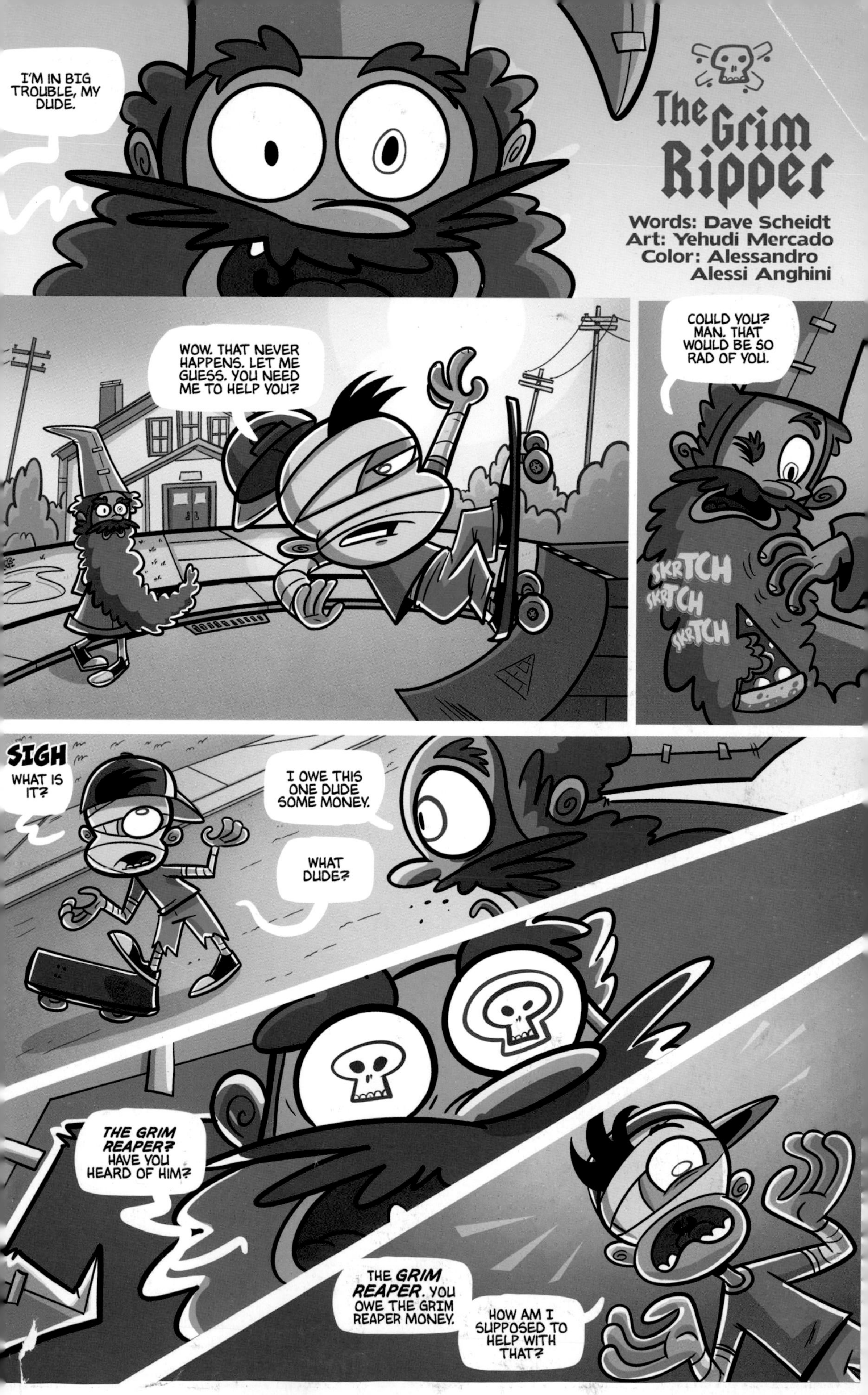
I'M IN BIG TROUBLE, MY DUDE.
The Grim Ripper
Words: Dave Scheidt
Art: Yehudi Mercado
Color: Alessandro Alessi Anghini
WOW. THAT NEVER HAPPENS. LET ME GUESS. YOU NEED ME TO HELP YOU?
COULD YOU? MAN. THAT WOULD BE SO RAD OF YOU.
SKRTCH SKRTCH SKRTCH
SIGH
WHAT IS IT?
I OWE THIS ONE DUDE SOME MONEY.
WHAT DUDE?
THE GRIM REAPER? HAVE YOU HEARD OF HIM?
THE GRIM REAPER. YOU OWE THE GRIM REAPER MONEY.
HOW AM I SUPPOSED TO HELP WITH THAT?

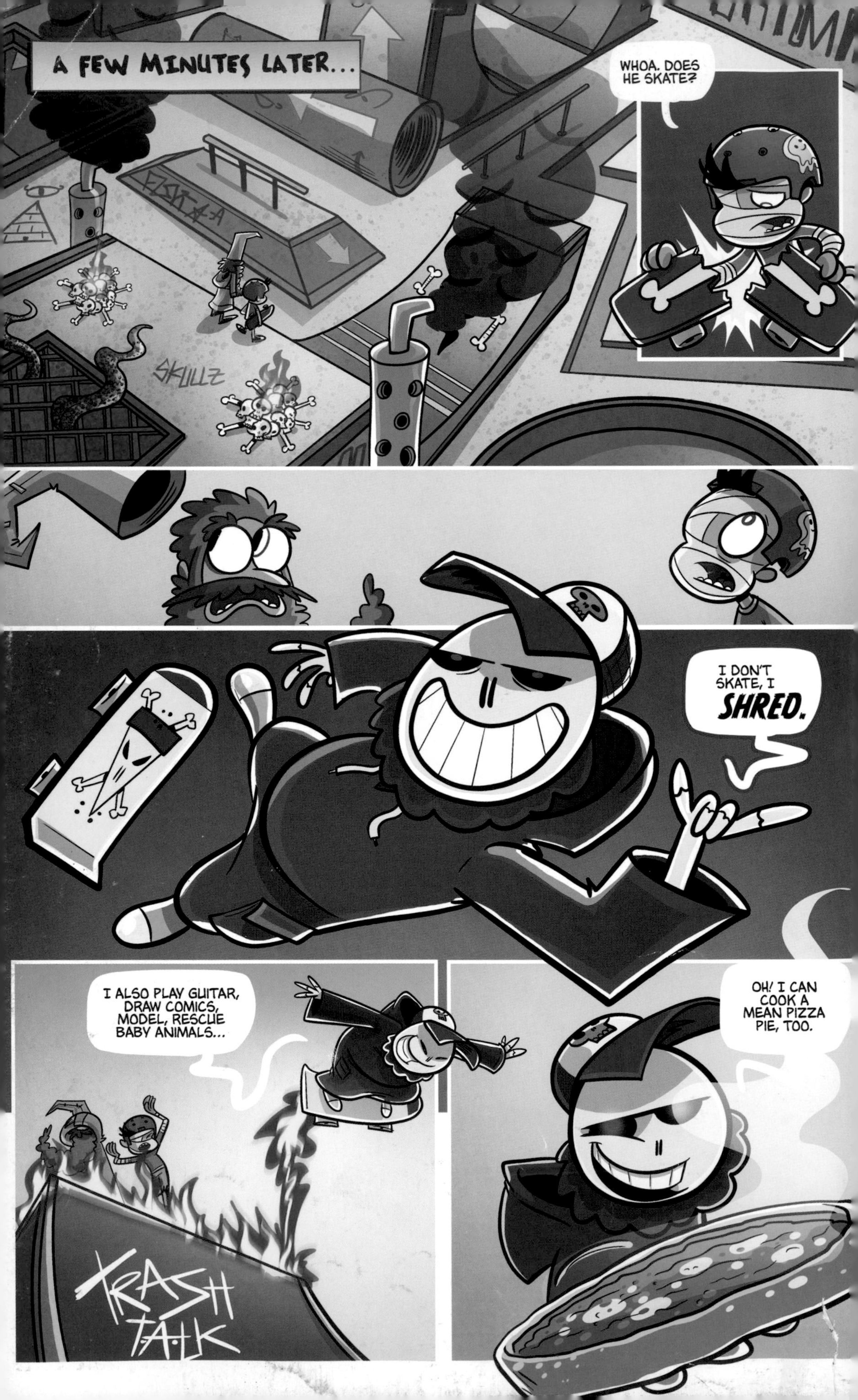
A FEW MINUTES LATER...
WHOA. DOES HE SKATE?
SKULLZ
I DON'T SKATE, I SHRED.
I ALSO PLAY GUITAR, DRAW COMICS, MODEL, RESCUE BABY ANIMALS...
TRASH TALK
OH! I CAN COOK A MEAN PIZZA PIE, TOO.

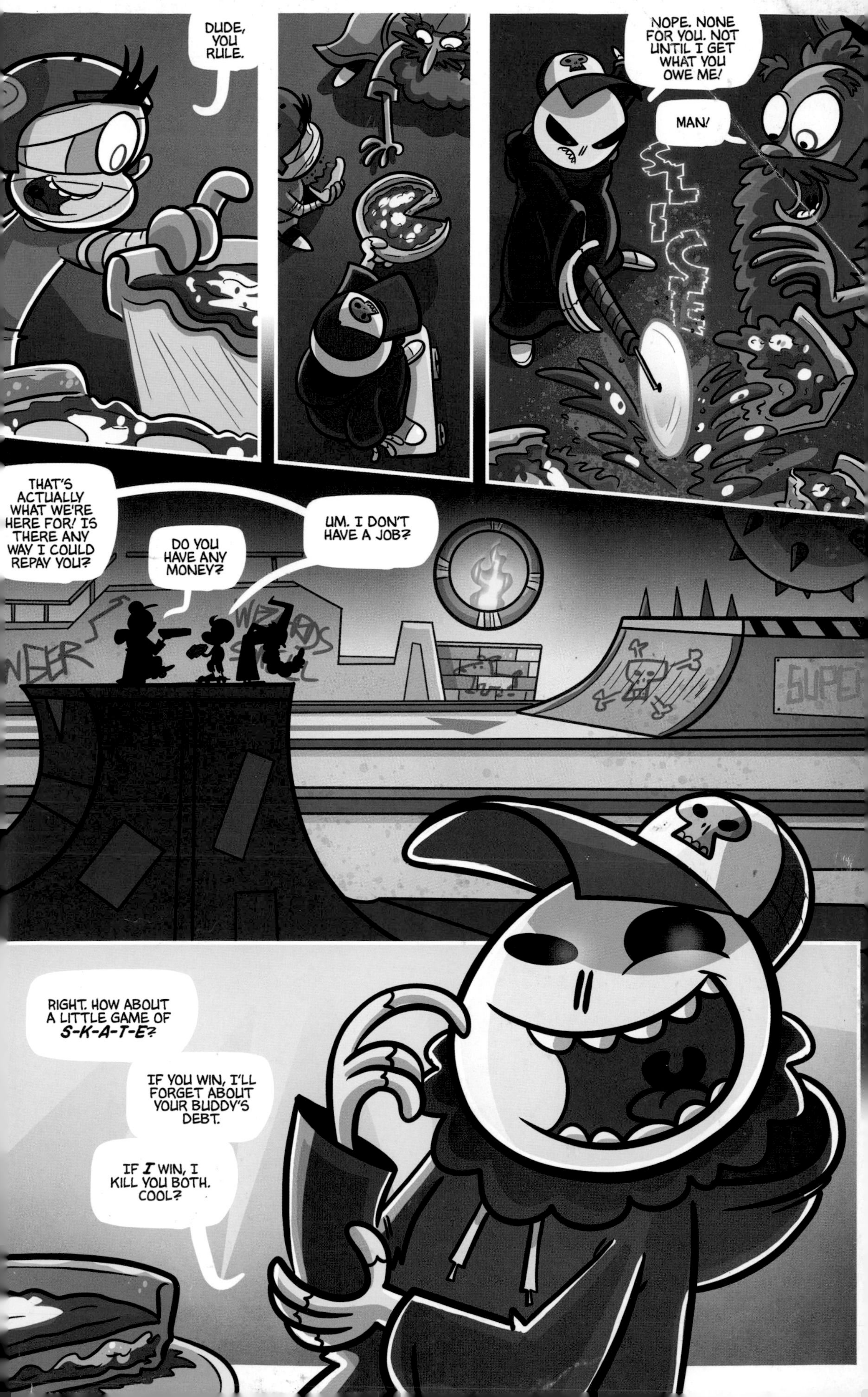
DUDE, YOU RULE.
NOPE. NONE FOR YOU. NOT UNTIL I GET WHAT YOU OWE ME!
MAN!
THAT'S ACTUALLY WHAT WE'RE HERE FOR! IS THERE ANY WAY I COULD REPAY YOU?
DO YOU HAVE ANY MONEY?
UM. I DON'T HAVE A JOB?
RIGHT. HOW ABOUT A LITTLE GAME OF S-K-A-T-E?
IF YOU WIN, I'LL FORGET ABOUT YOUR BUDDY'S DEBT.
IF I WIN, I KILL YOU BOTH. COOL?

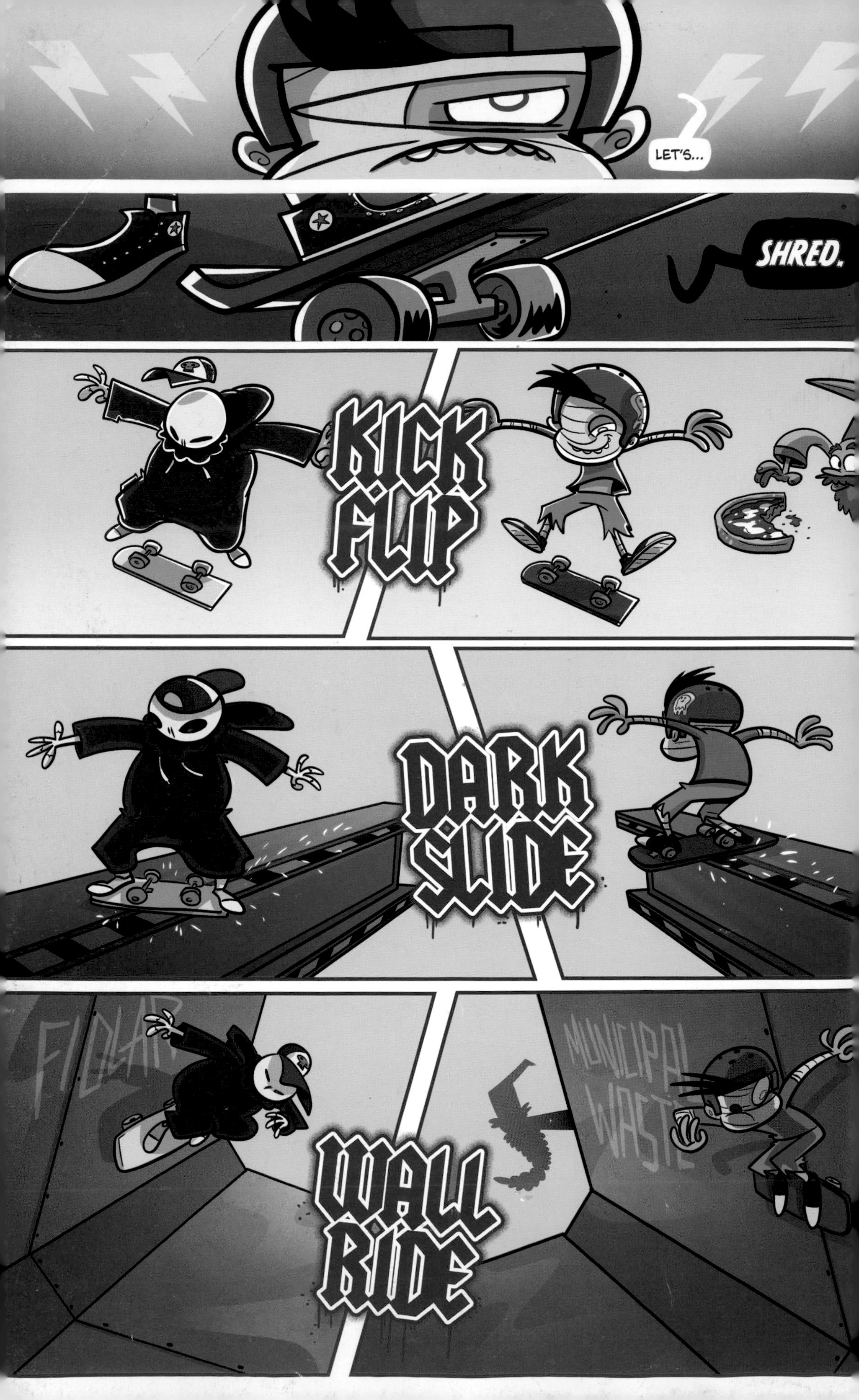
LET'S...
SHRED.
KICK FLIP
DARK SLIDE
FIDLAR
MUNICIPAL WASTE
WALL RIDE

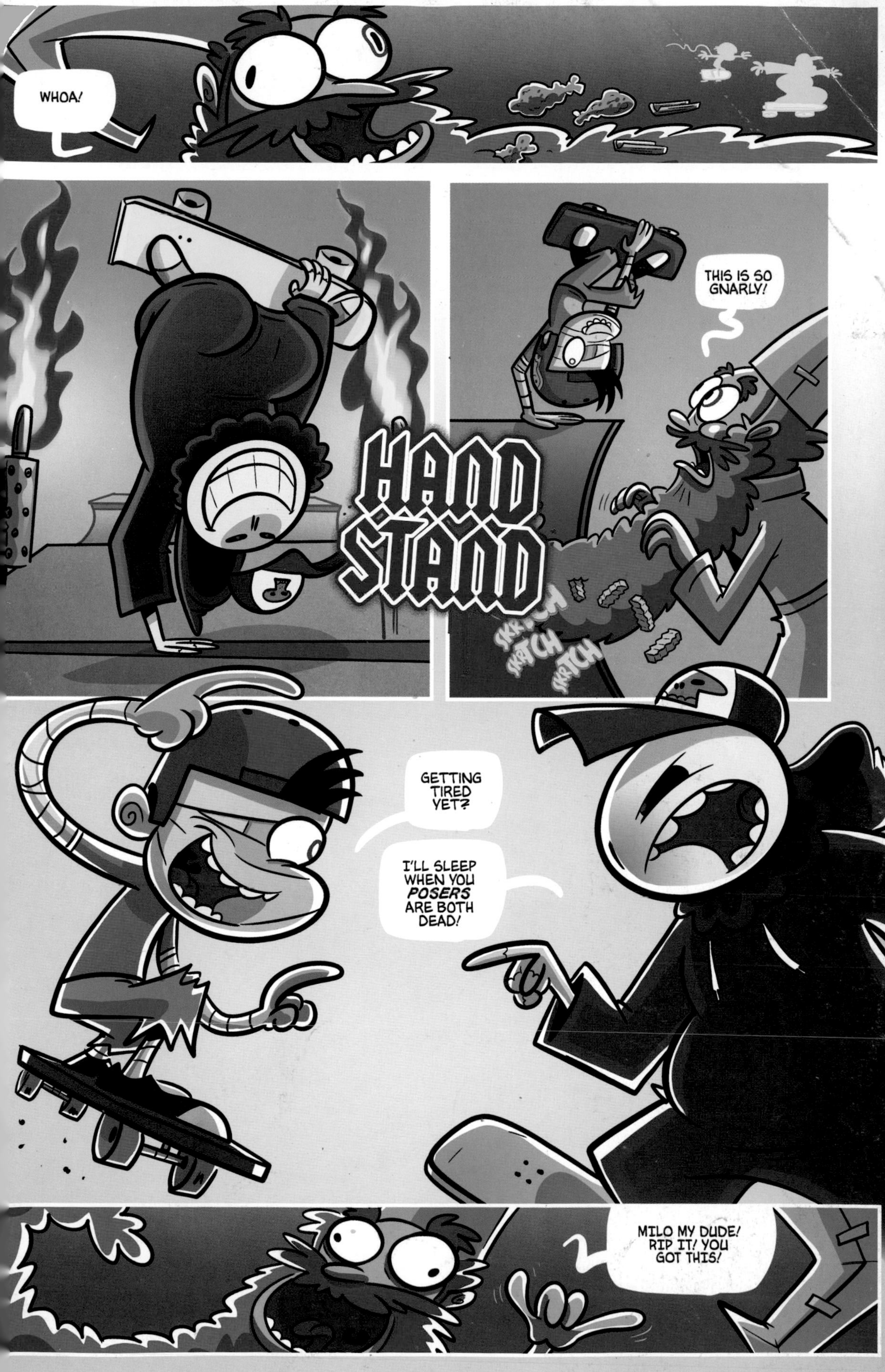
WHOA!
HAND STAND
THIS IS SO GNARLY!
SKRTCH SKRTCH SKRTCH
GETTING TIRED YET?
I'LL SLEEP WHEN YOU *POSERS* ARE BOTH DEAD!
MILO MY DUDE! RIP IT! YOU GOT THIS!

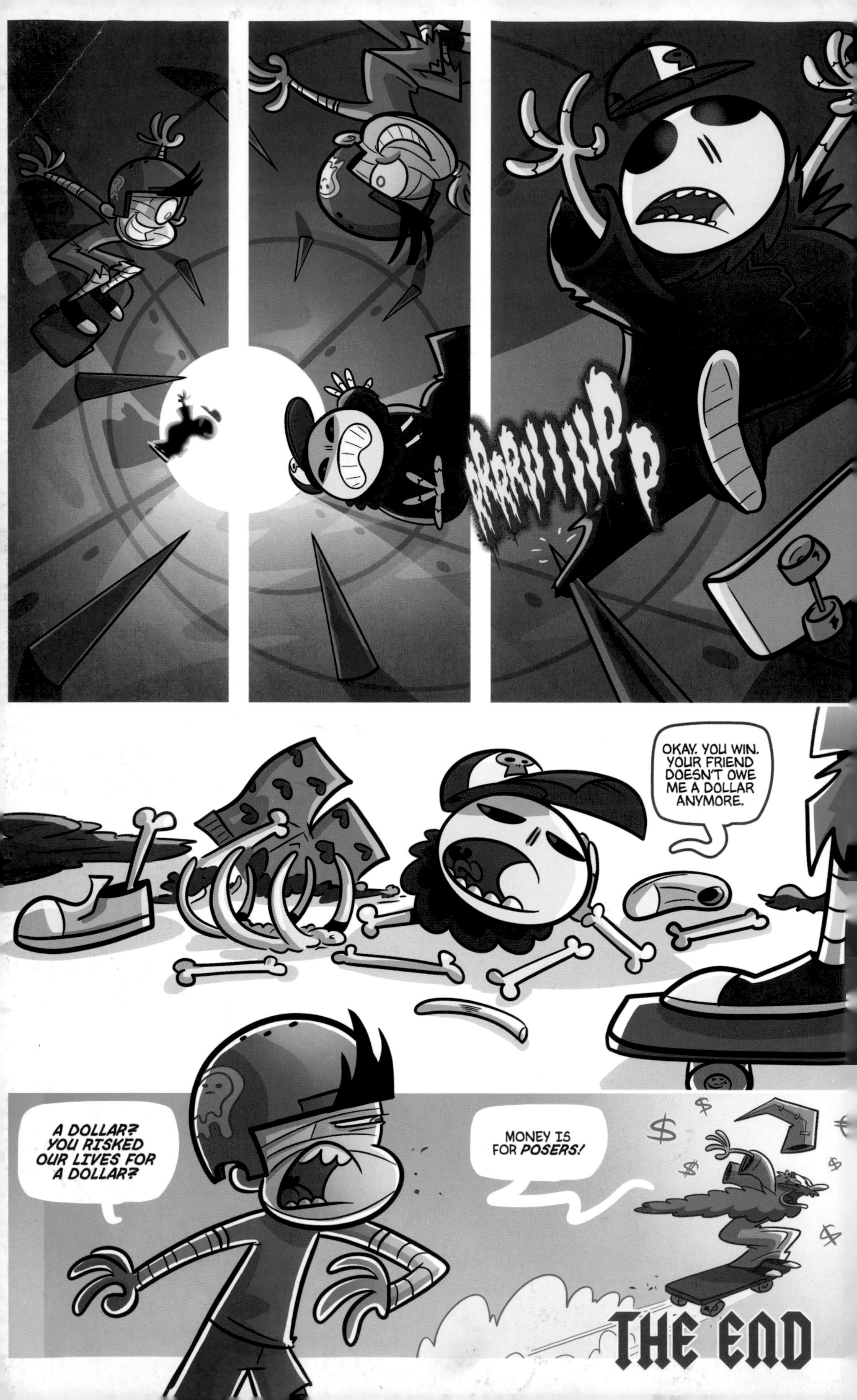

BRRRUUUPP
OKAY. YOU WIN. YOUR FRIEND DOESN'T OWE ME A DOLLAR ANYMORE.
A DOLLAR? YOU RISKED OUR LIVES FOR A DOLLAR?
MONEY IS FOR *POSERS!*
THE END

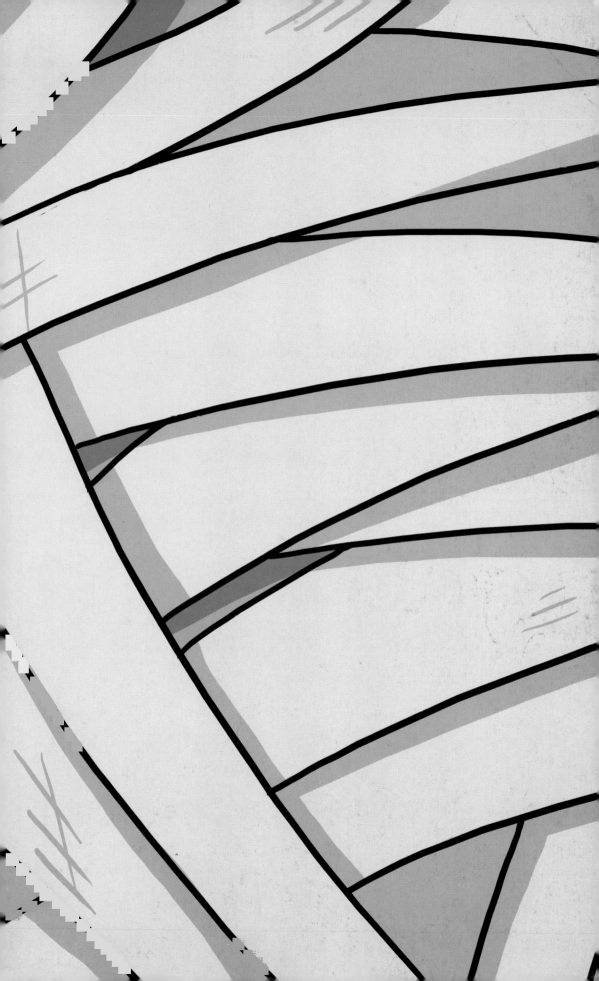

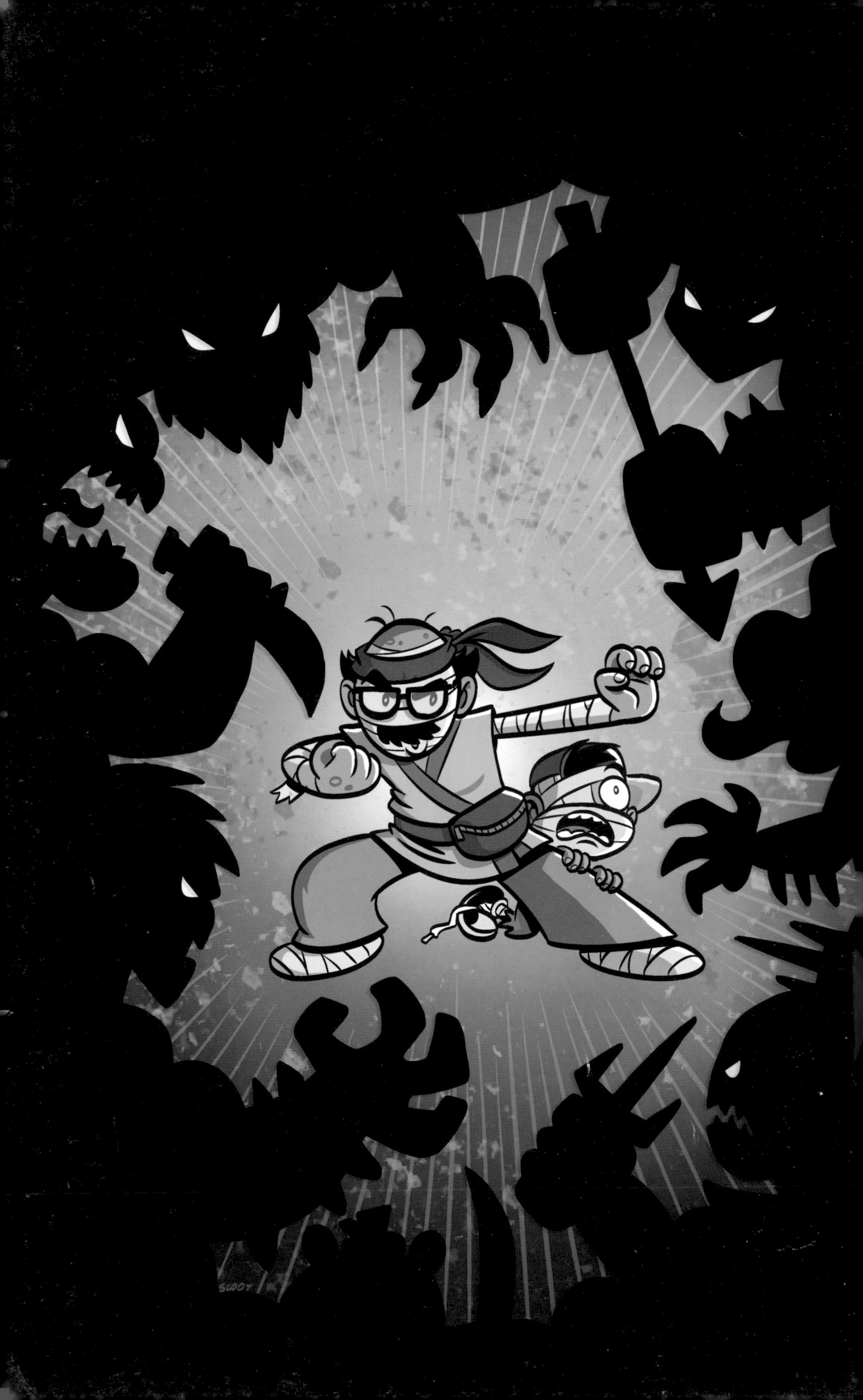
SCOOT

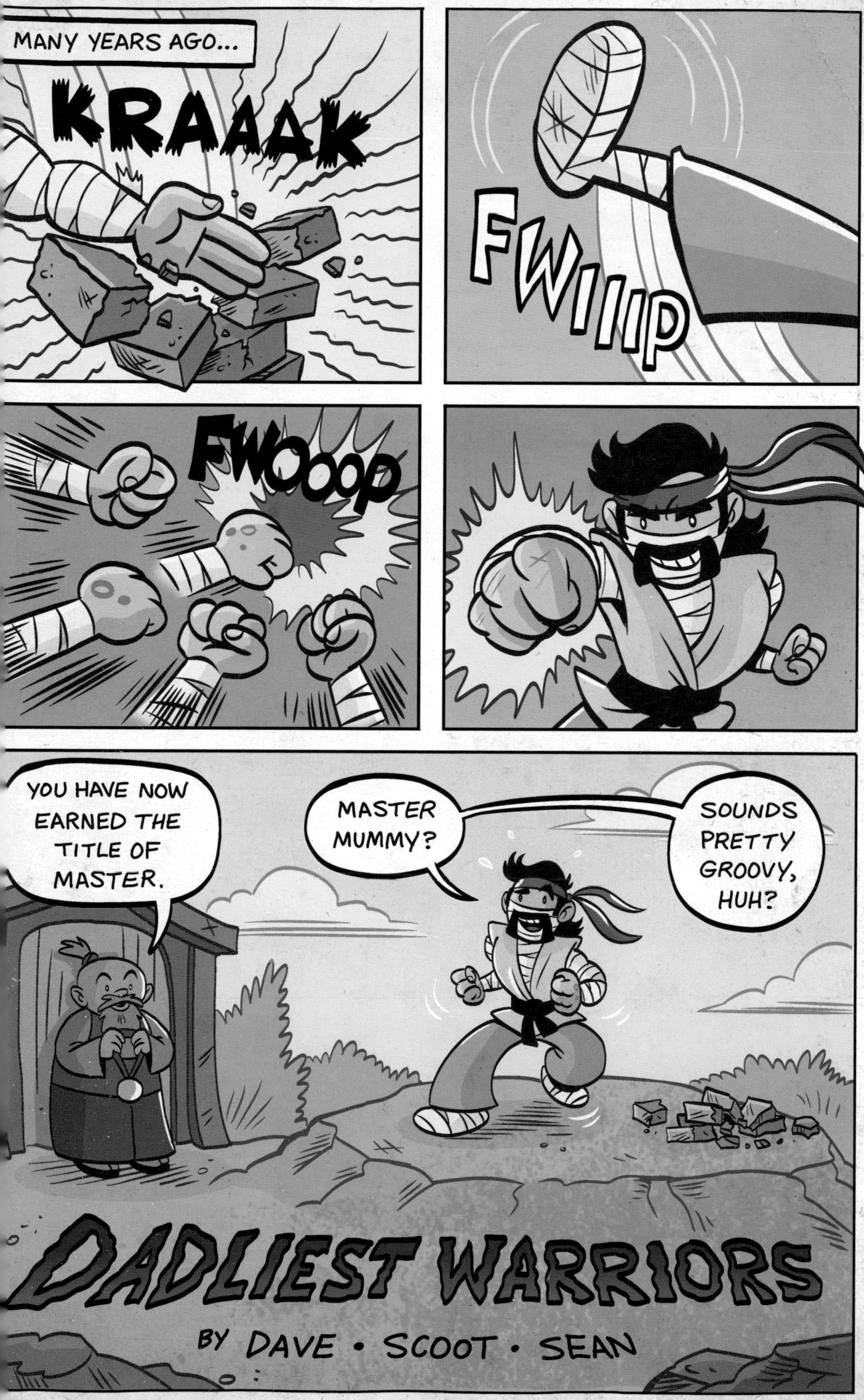
MANY YEARS AGO...
KRAAAK
FWIIIP
FWOOOP
YOU HAVE NOW EARNED THE TITLE OF MASTER.
MASTER MUMMY?
SOUNDS PRETTY GROOVY, HUH?
DADLIEST WARRIORS
BY DAVE • SCOOT • SEAN

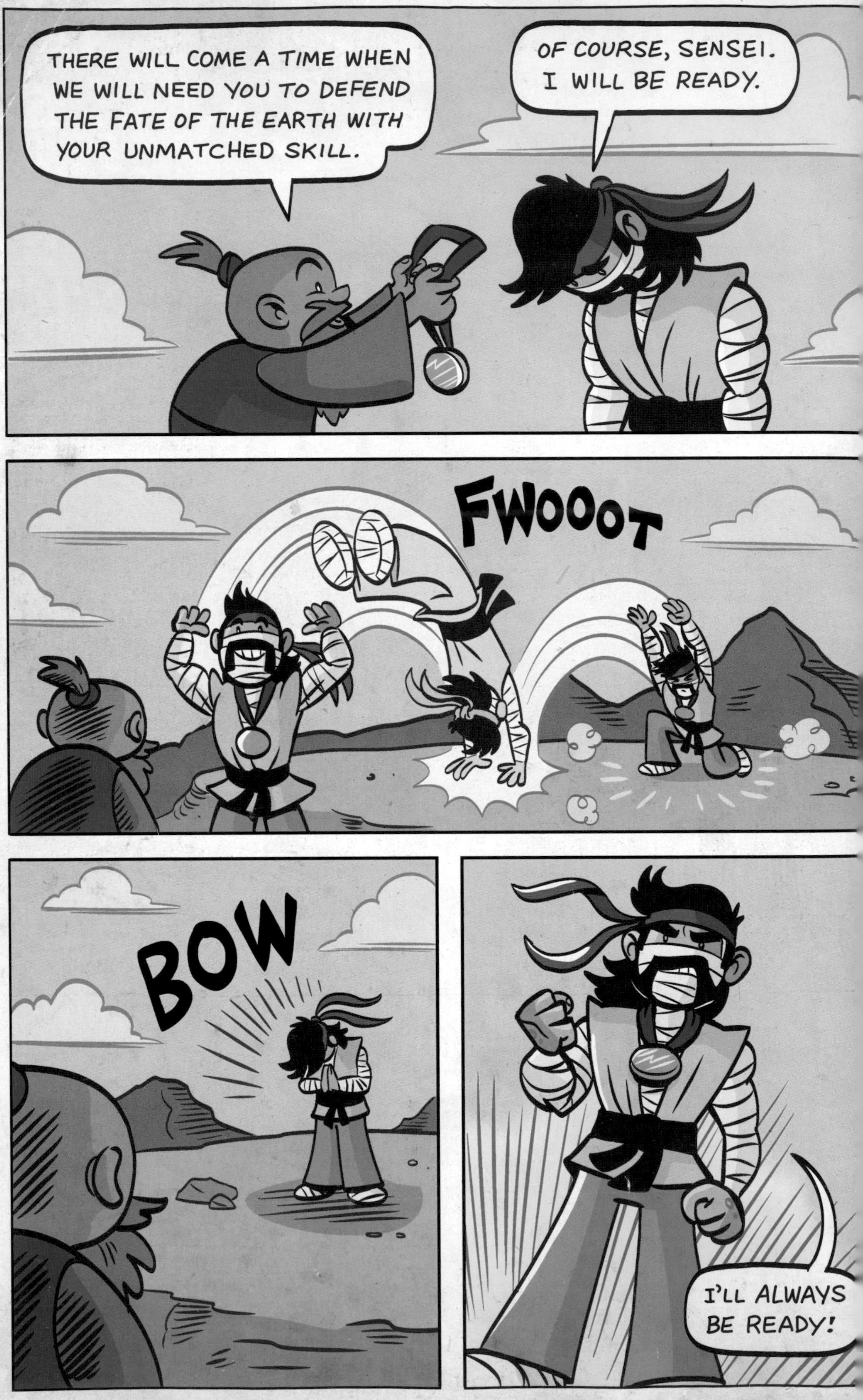
THERE WILL COME A TIME WHEN WE WILL NEED YOU TO DEFEND THE FATE OF THE EARTH WITH YOUR UNMATCHED SKILL.
OF COURSE, SENSEI. I WILL BE READY.
FWOOOT
BOW
I'LL ALWAYS BE READY!

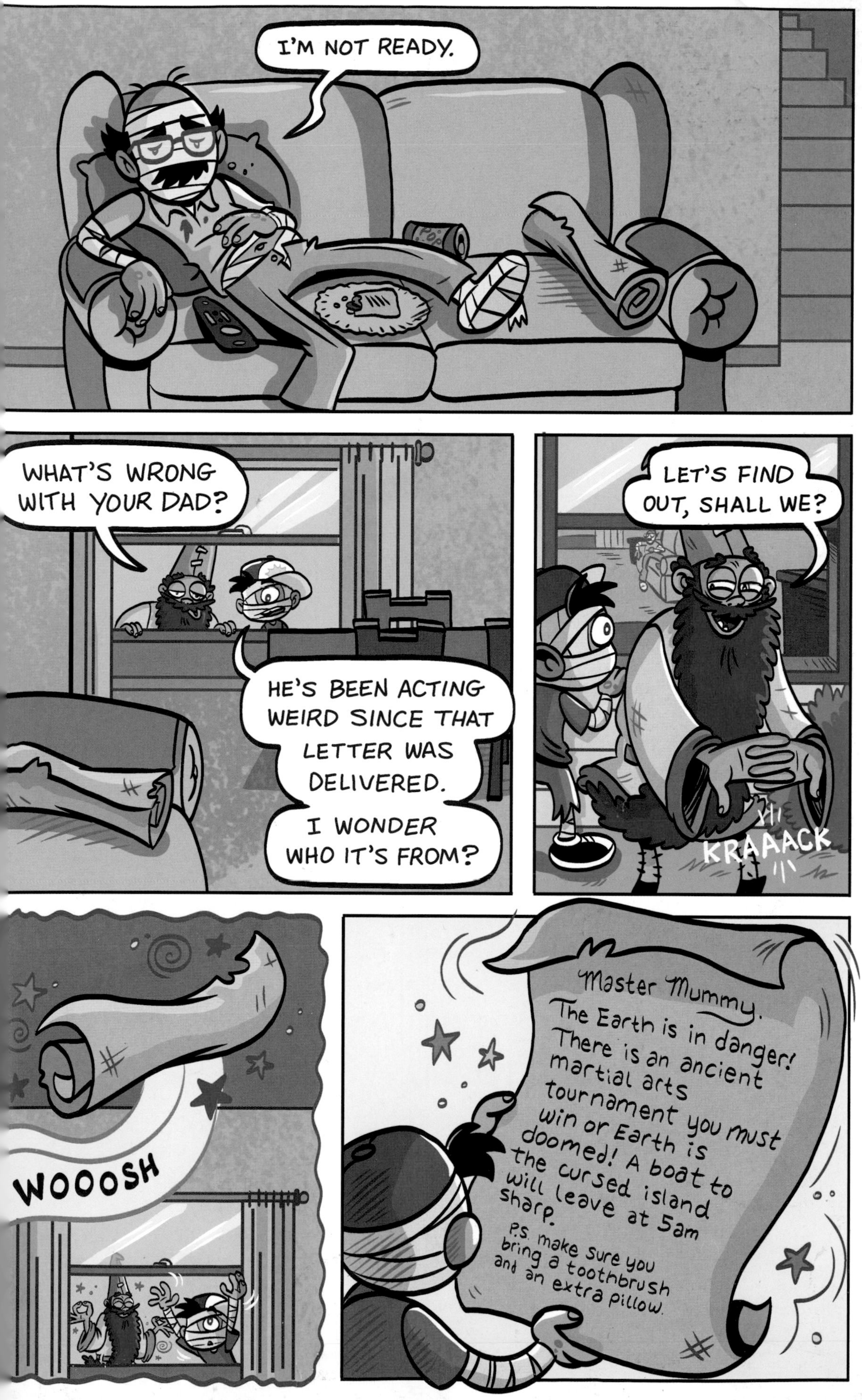
I'M NOT READY.
WHAT'S WRONG WITH YOUR DAD?
HE'S BEEN ACTING WEIRD SINCE THAT LETTER WAS DELIVERED.
I WONDER WHO IT'S FROM?
LET'S FIND OUT, SHALL WE?
KRAAACK
WOOOSH
Master Mummy.
The Earth is in danger! There is an ancient martial arts tournament you must win or Earth is doomed! A boat to the cursed island will leave at 5am sharp.
P.S. make sure you bring a toothbrush and an extra pillow.

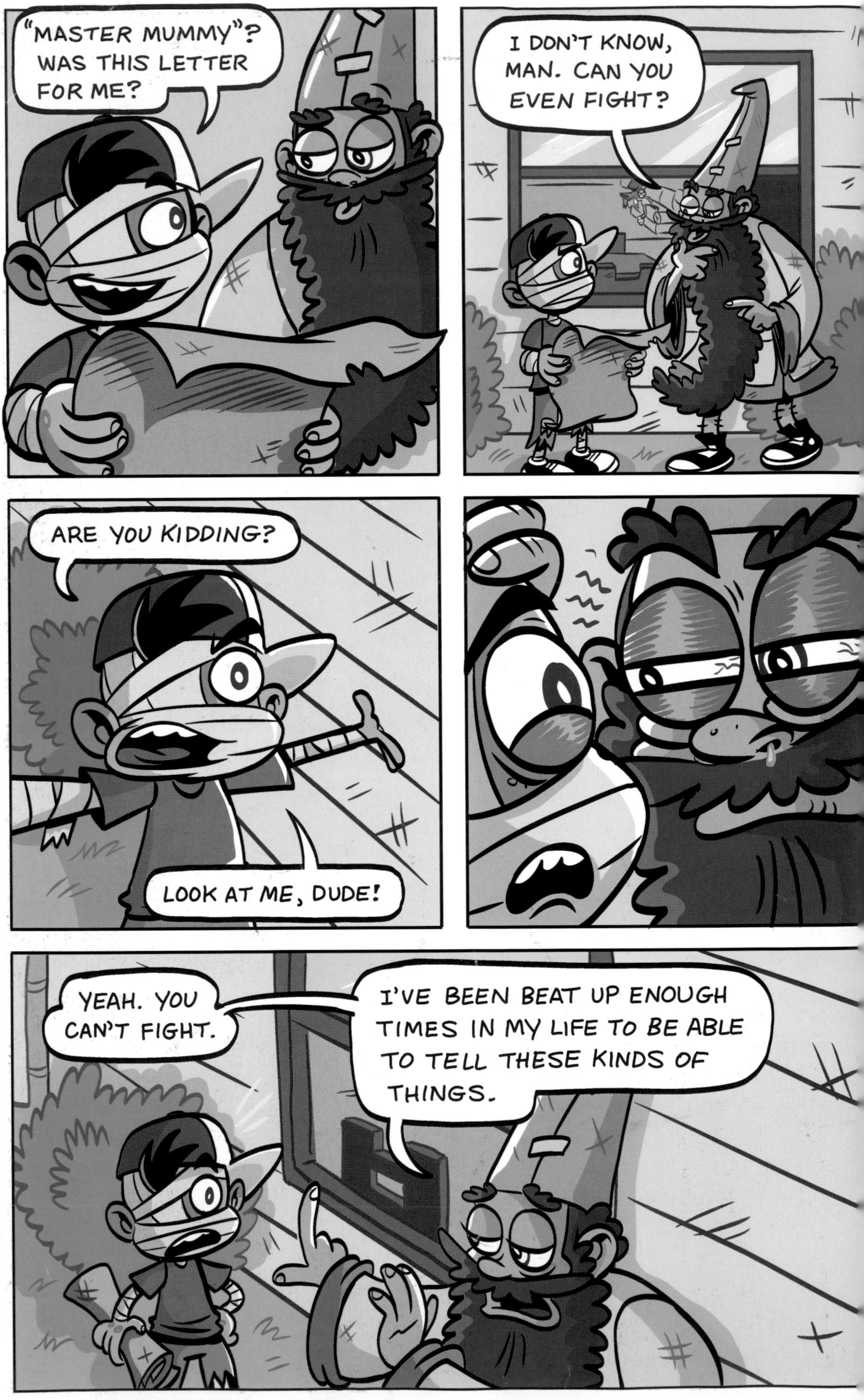
"MASTER MUMMY"? WAS THIS LETTER FOR ME?
I DON'T KNOW, MAN. CAN YOU EVEN FIGHT?
ARE YOU KIDDING?
LOOK AT ME, DUDE!
YEAH. YOU CAN'T FIGHT.
I'VE BEEN BEAT UP ENOUGH TIMES IN MY LIFE TO BE ABLE TO TELL THESE KINDS OF THINGS.

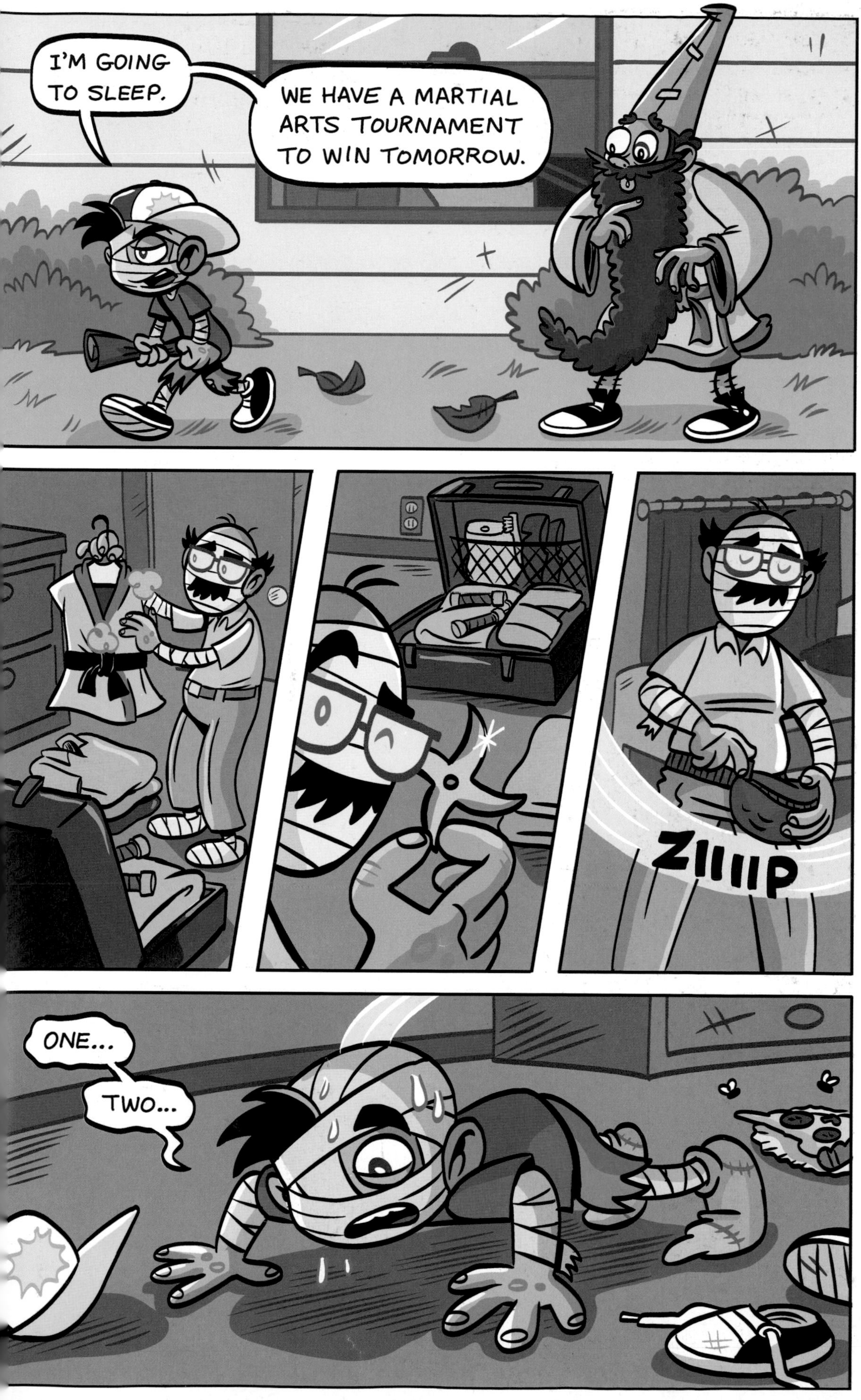
I'M GOING TO SLEEP.
WE HAVE A MARTIAL ARTS TOURNAMENT TO WIN TOMORROW.
ZIIIIP
ONE...
TWO...

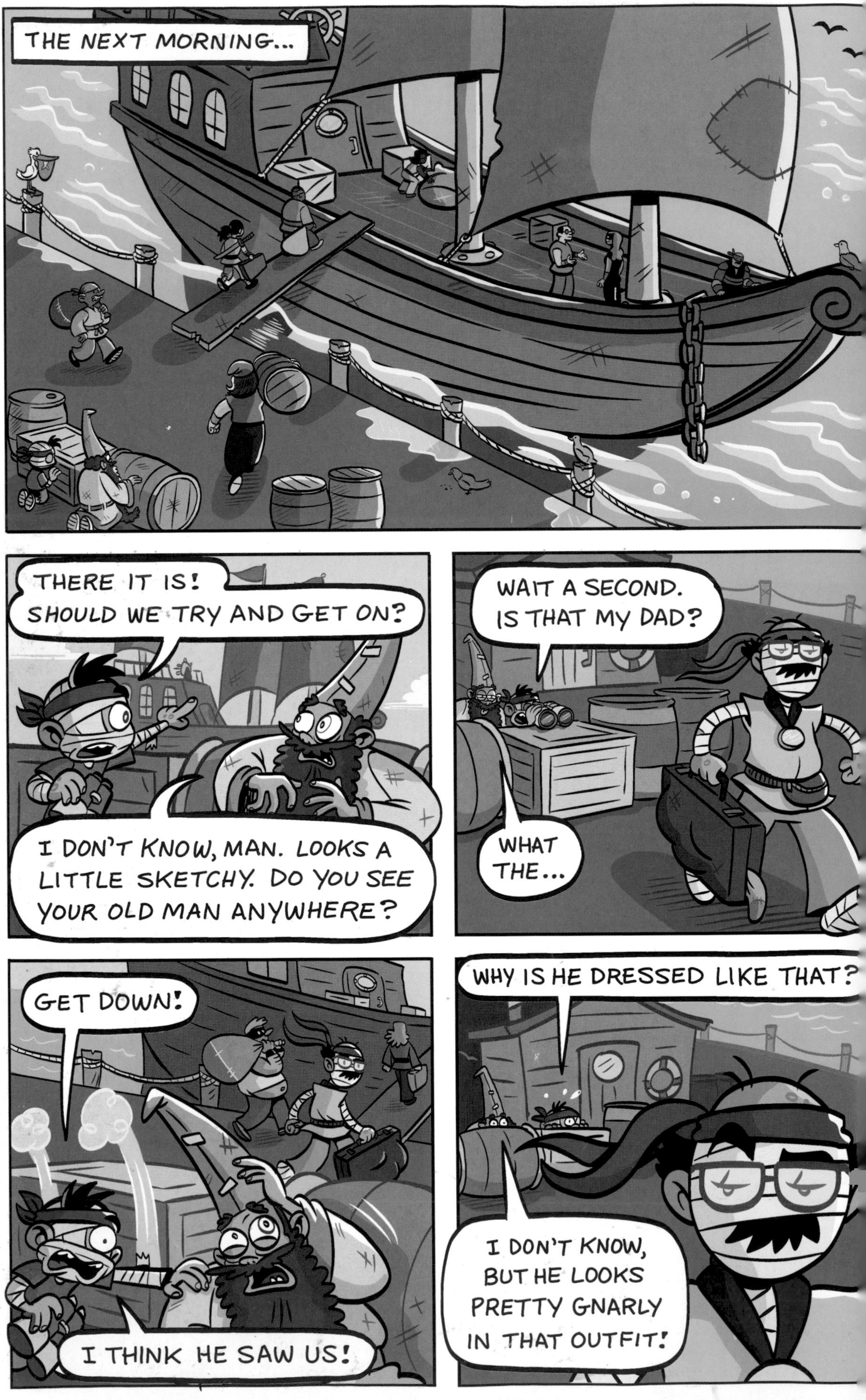
THE NEXT MORNING...
THERE IT IS! SHOULD WE TRY AND GET ON?
I DON'T KNOW, MAN. LOOKS A LITTLE SKETCHY. DO YOU SEE YOUR OLD MAN ANYWHERE?
WAIT A SECOND. IS THAT MY DAD?
WHAT THE...
GET DOWN!
I THINK HE SAW US!
WHY IS HE DRESSED LIKE THAT?
I DON'T KNOW, BUT HE LOOKS PRETTY GNARLY IN THAT OUTFIT!

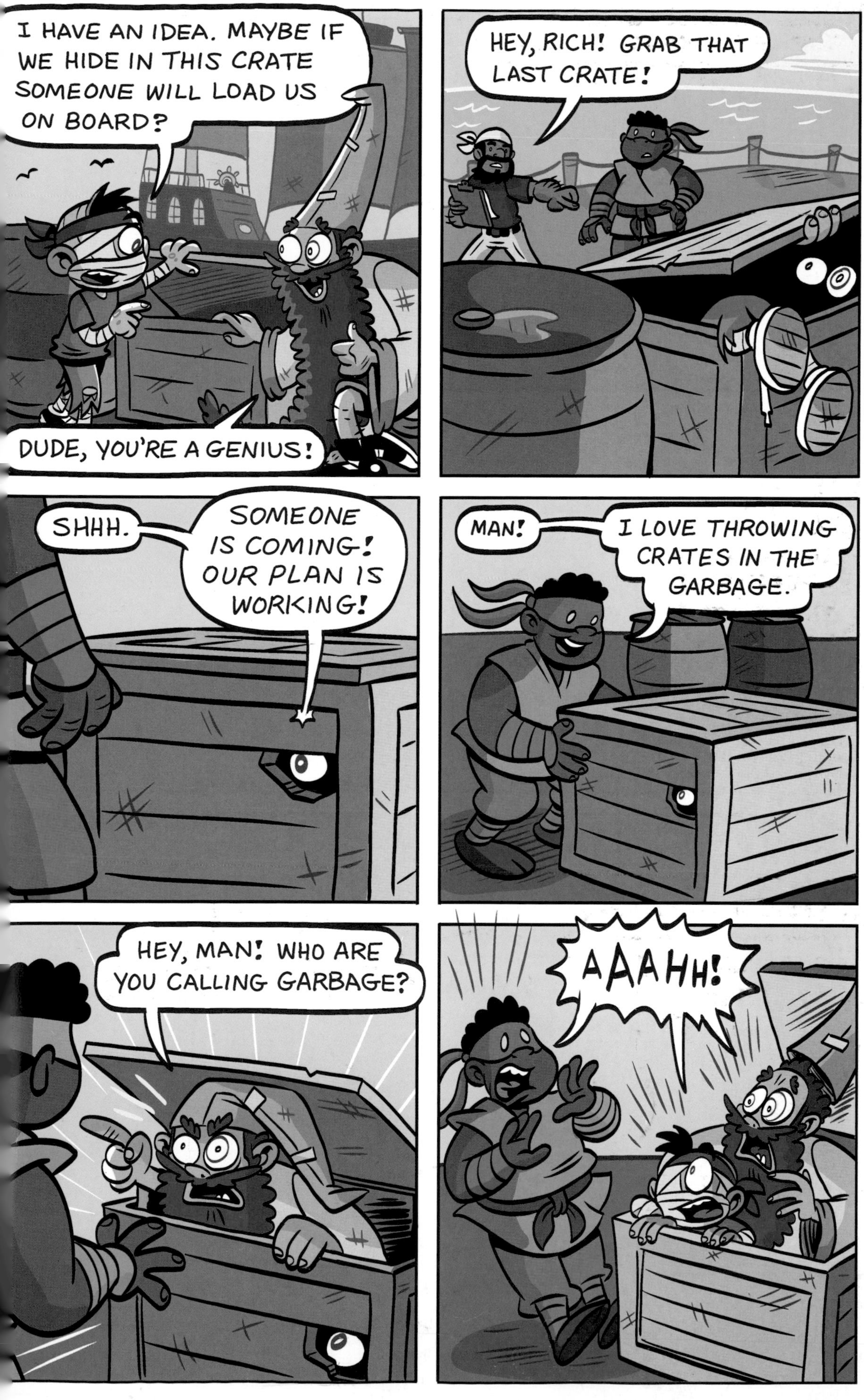
I HAVE AN IDEA. MAYBE IF WE HIDE IN THIS CRATE SOMEONE WILL LOAD US ON BOARD?
DUDE, YOU'RE A GENIUS!
HEY, RICH! GRAB THAT LAST CRATE!
SHHH.
SOMEONE IS COMING! OUR PLAN IS WORKING!
MAN!
I LOVE THROWING CRATES IN THE GARBAGE.
HEY, MAN! WHO ARE YOU CALLING GARBAGE?
AAAHH!

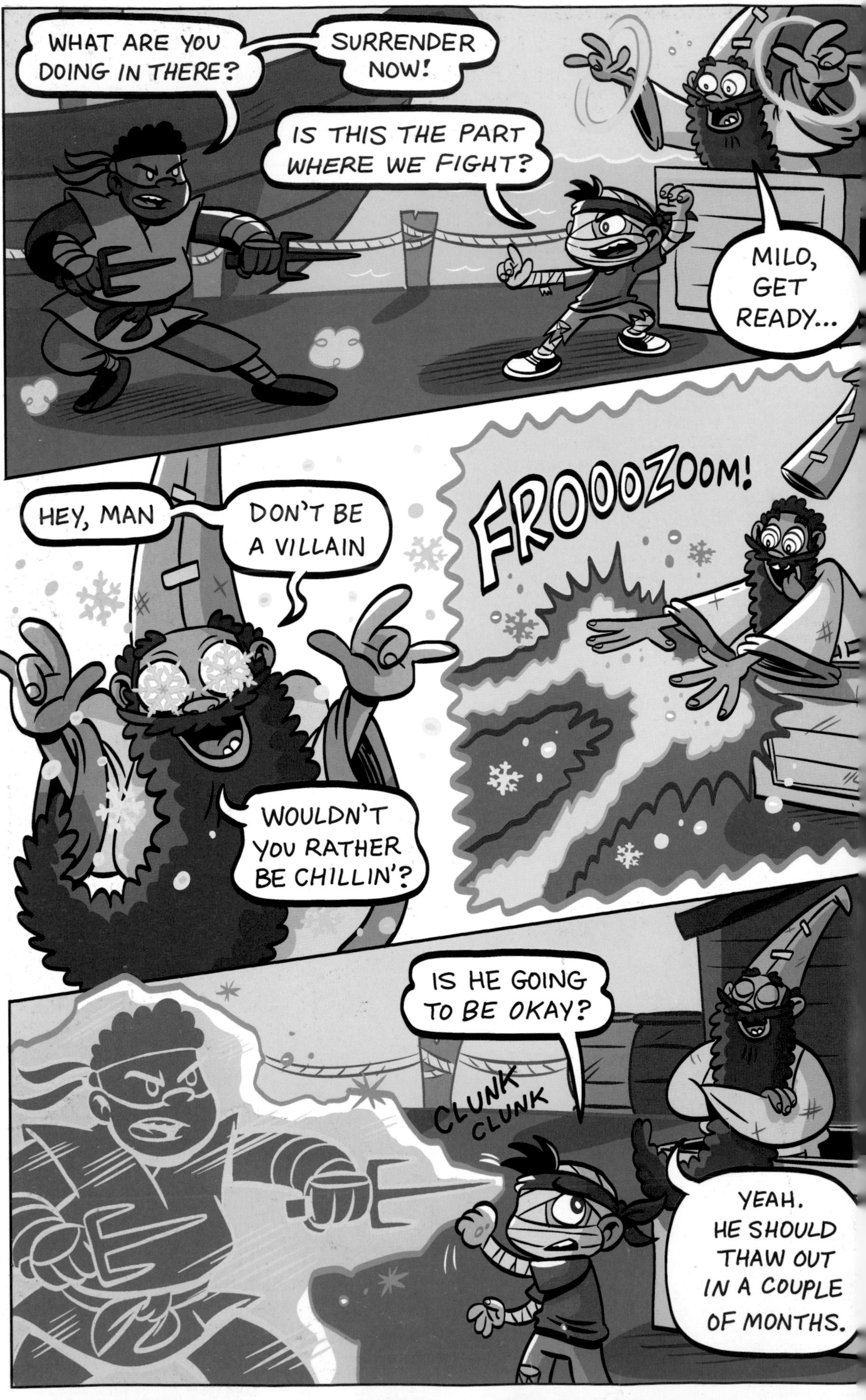
WHAT ARE YOU DOING IN THERE?
SURRENDER NOW!
IS THIS THE PART WHERE WE FIGHT?
MILO, GET READY...
HEY, MAN
DON'T BE A VILLAIN
WOULDN'T YOU RATHER BE CHILLIN'?
FROOOZOOM!
IS HE GOING TO BE OKAY?
CLUNK CLUNK
YEAH. HE SHOULD THAW OUT IN A COUPLE OF MONTHS.

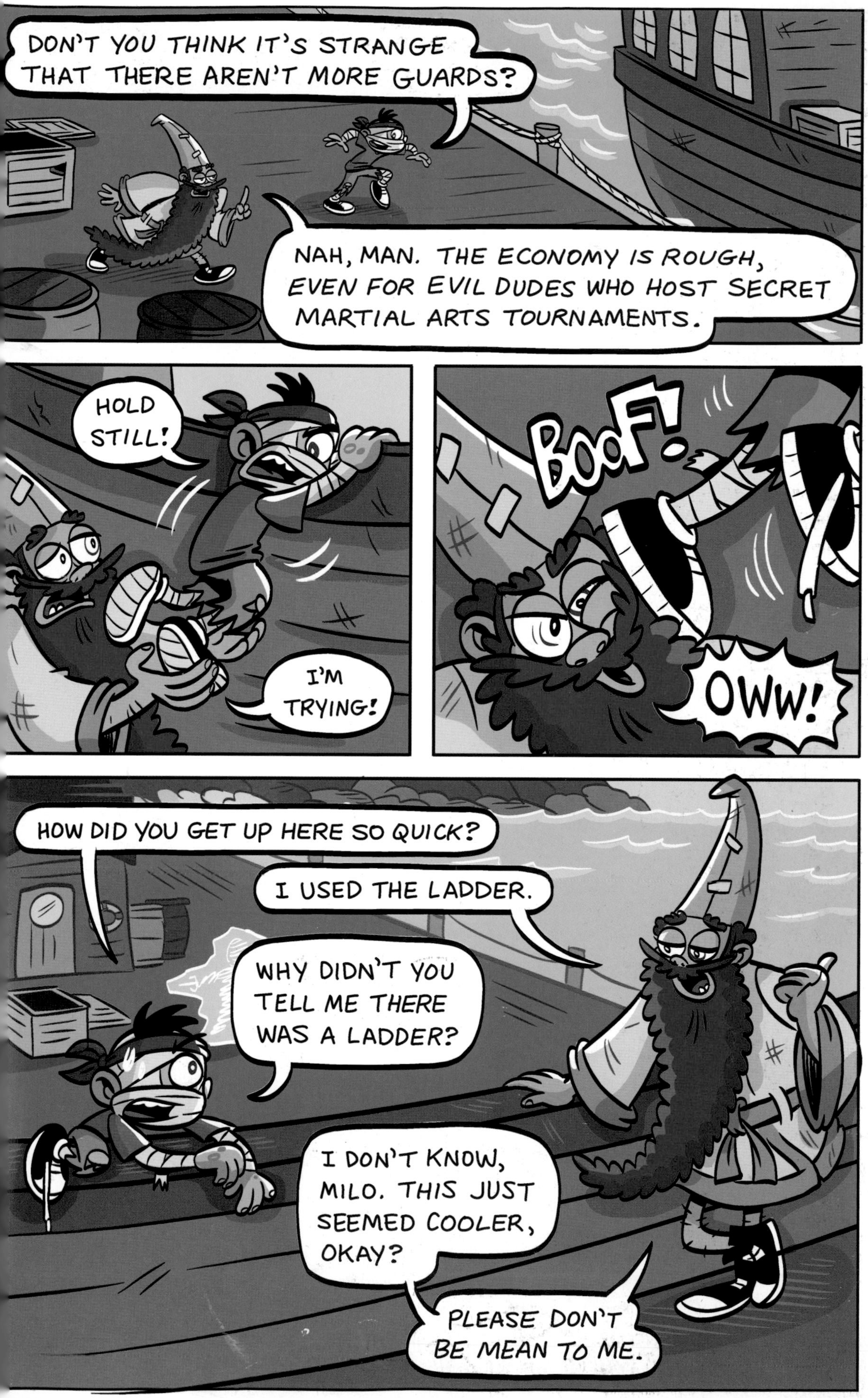
DON'T YOU THINK IT'S STRANGE THAT THERE AREN'T MORE GUARDS?
NAH, MAN. THE ECONOMY IS ROUGH, EVEN FOR EVIL DUDES WHO HOST SECRET MARTIAL ARTS TOURNAMENTS.
HOLD STILL!
I'M TRYING!
BOOF!
OWW!
HOW DID YOU GET UP HERE SO QUICK?
I USED THE LADDER.
WHY DIDN'T YOU TELL ME THERE WAS A LADDER?
I DON'T KNOW, MILO. THIS JUST SEEMED COOLER, OKAY?
PLEASE DON'T BE MEAN TO ME.

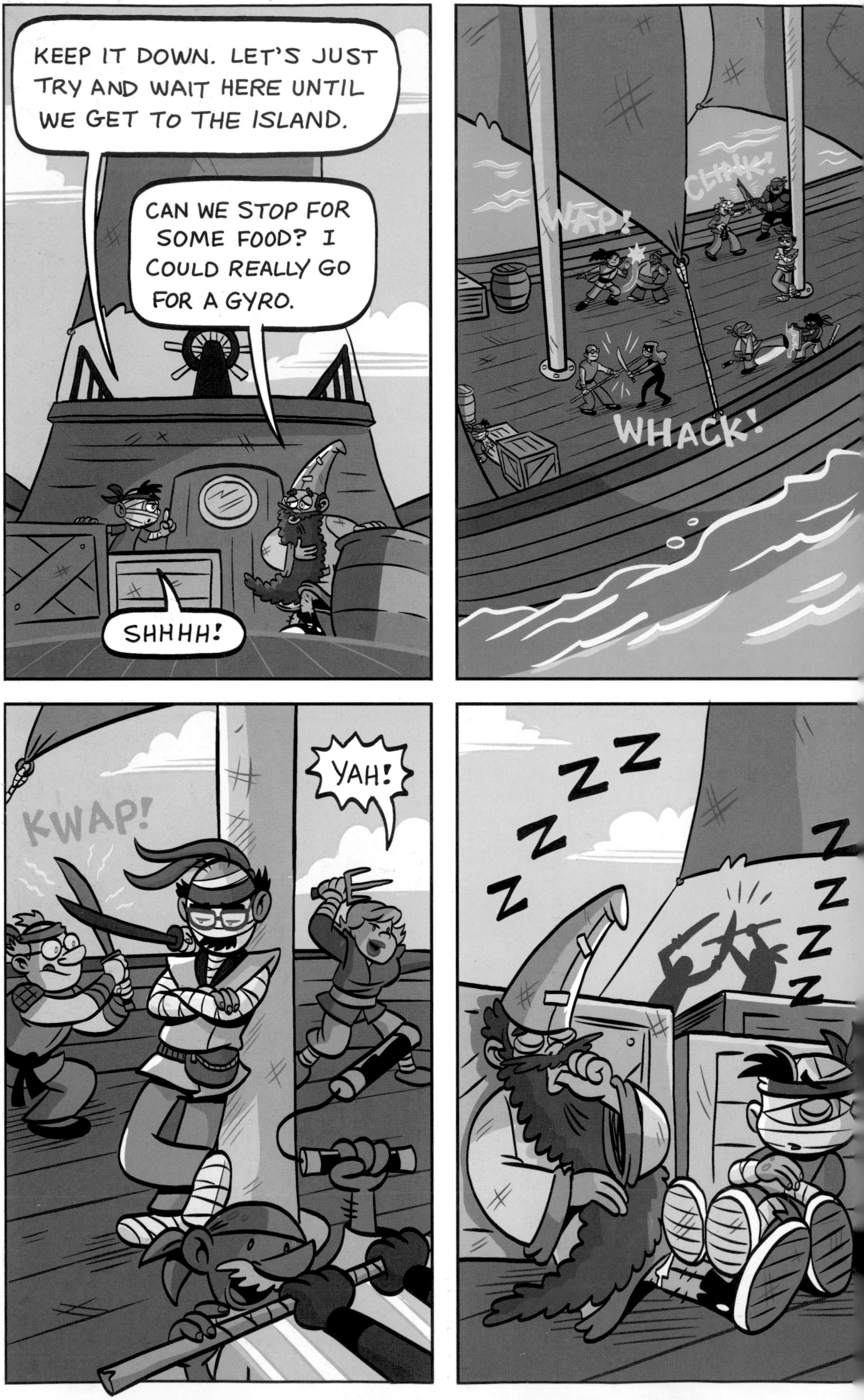
KEEP IT DOWN. LET'S JUST TRY AND WAIT HERE UNTIL WE GET TO THE ISLAND.
CAN WE STOP FOR SOME FOOD? I COULD REALLY GO FOR A GYRO.
SHHHH!
CLINK!
WAP!
WHACK!
KWAP!
YAH!
Z Z Z Z Z
Z Z Z Z Z

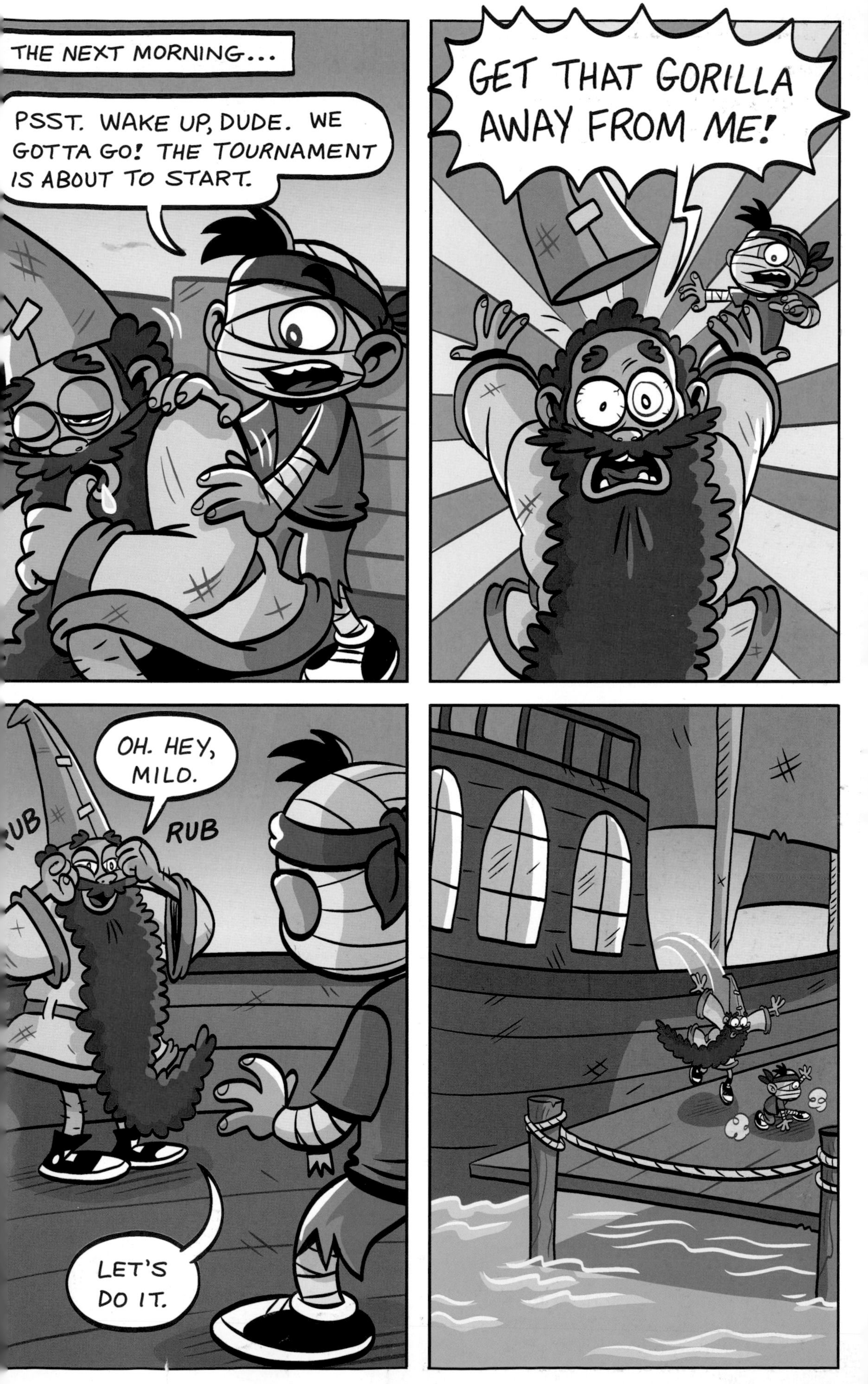
THE NEXT MORNING...
PSST. WAKE UP, DUDE. WE GOTTA GO! THE TOURNAMENT IS ABOUT TO START.
GET THAT GORILLA AWAY FROM ME!
OH. HEY, MILO.
RUB
RUB
LET'S DO IT.

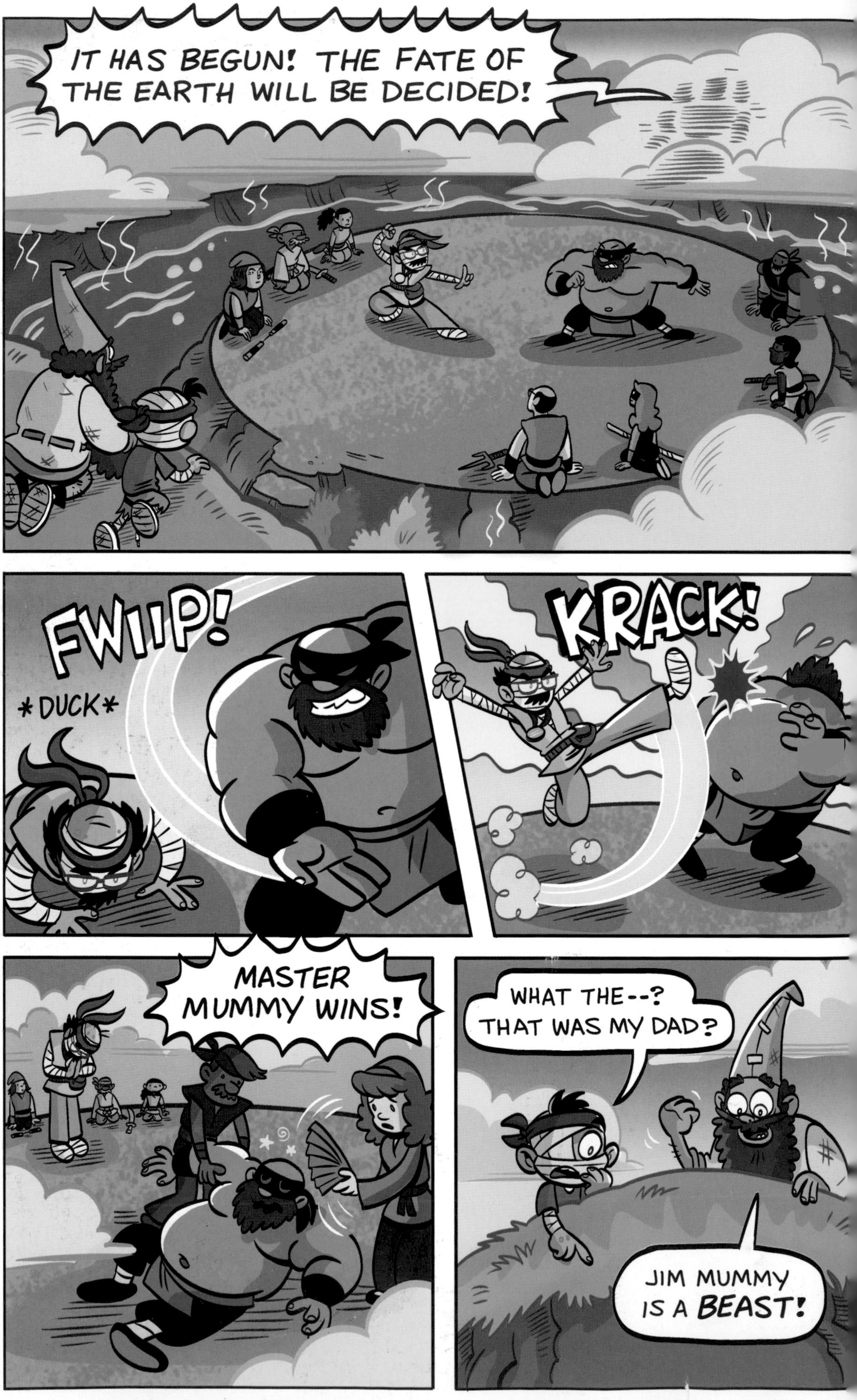
IT HAS BEGUN! THE FATE OF THE EARTH WILL BE DECIDED!
FWIIP!
DUCK
KRACK!
MASTER MUMMY WINS!
WHAT THE--? THAT WAS MY DAD?
JIM MUMMY IS A BEAST!

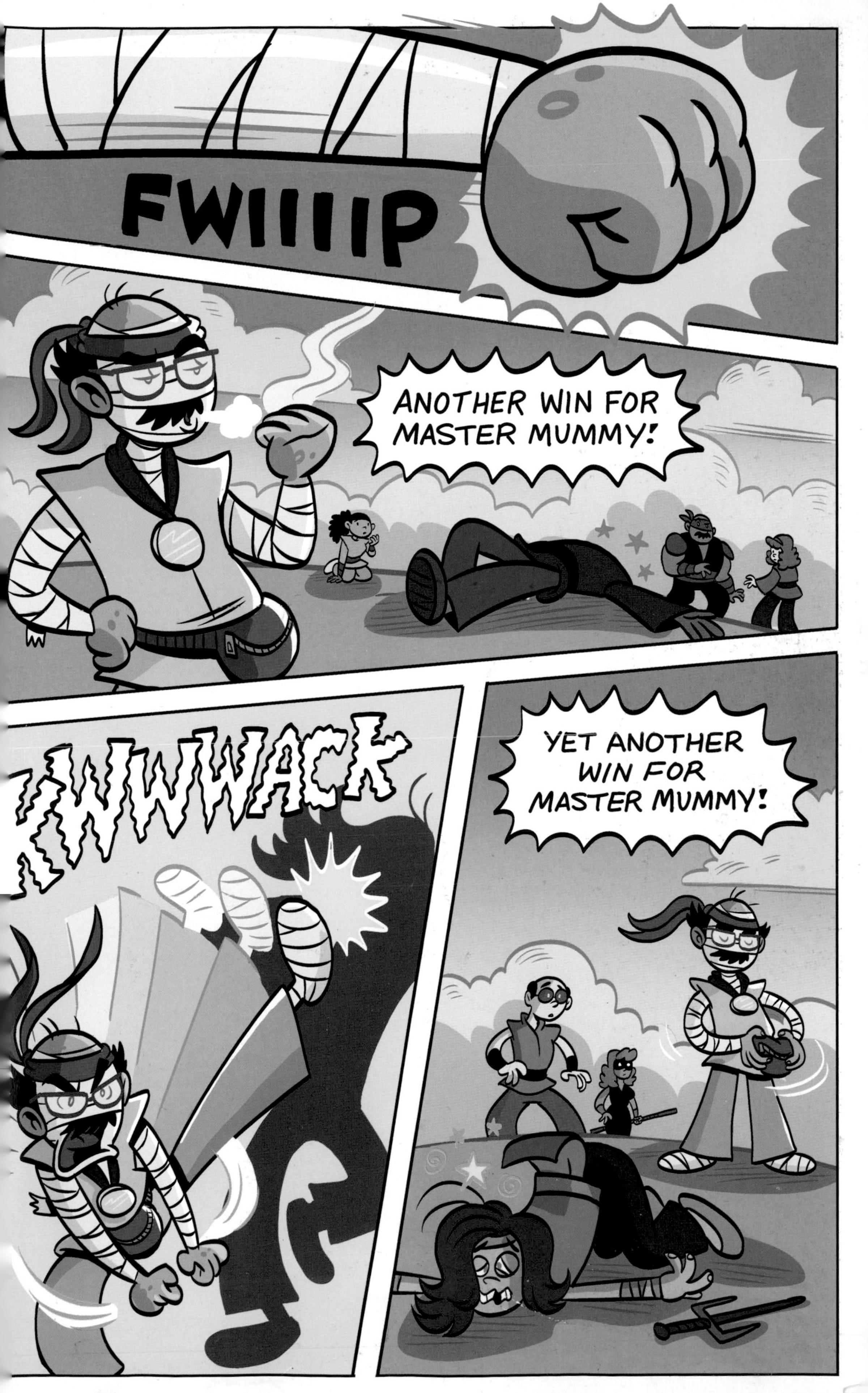
FWIIIIP
ANOTHER WIN FOR MASTER MUMMY!
KWWWACK
YET ANOTHER WIN FOR MASTER MUMMY!

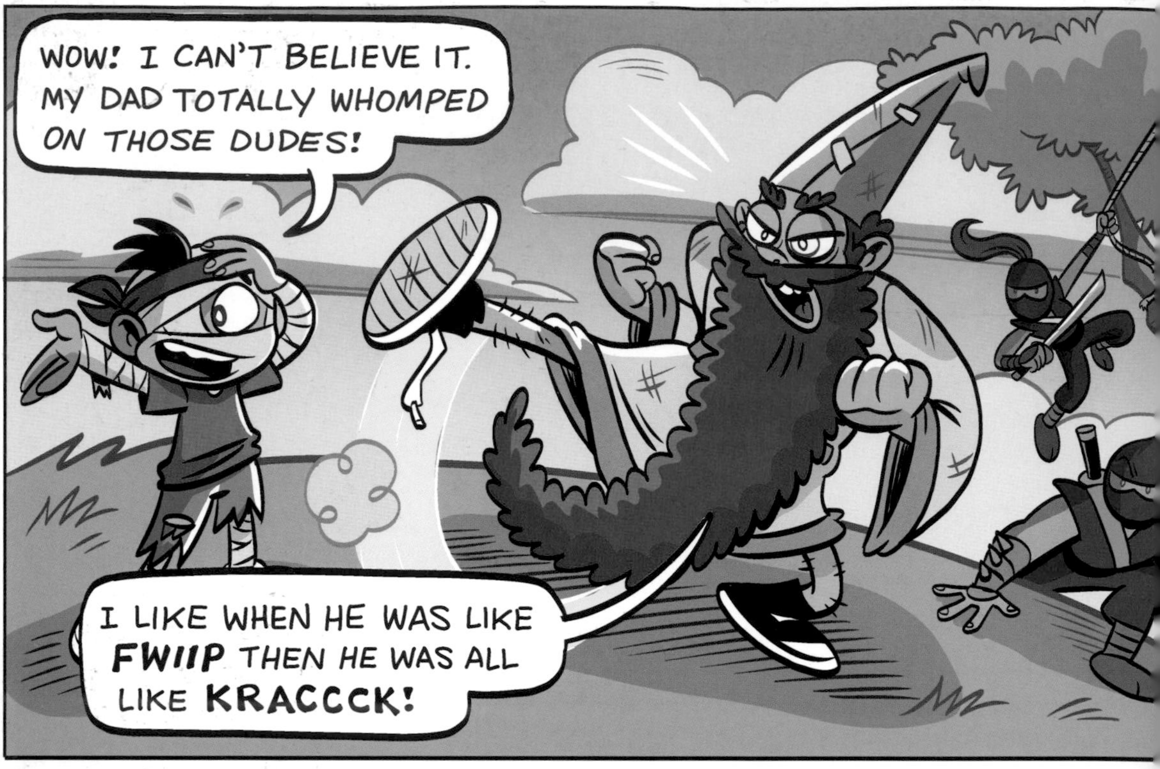
WOW! I CAN'T BELIEVE IT. MY DAD TOTALLY WHOMPED ON THOSE DUDES!
I LIKE WHEN HE WAS LIKE FWIIP THEN HE WAS ALL LIKE KRACCCK!

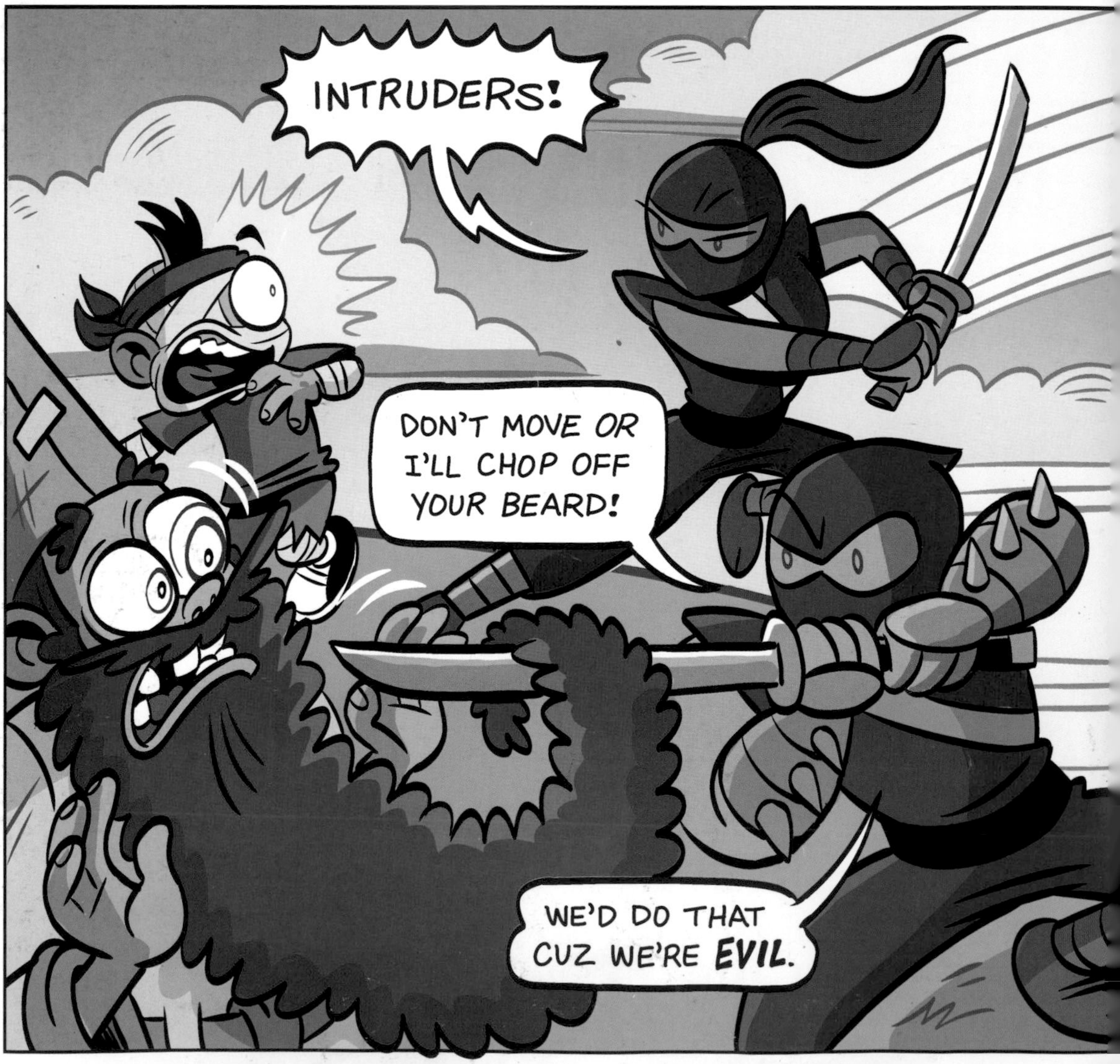
INTRUDERS!
DON'T MOVE OR I'LL CHOP OFF YOUR BEARD!
WE'D DO THAT CUZ WE'RE EVIL.

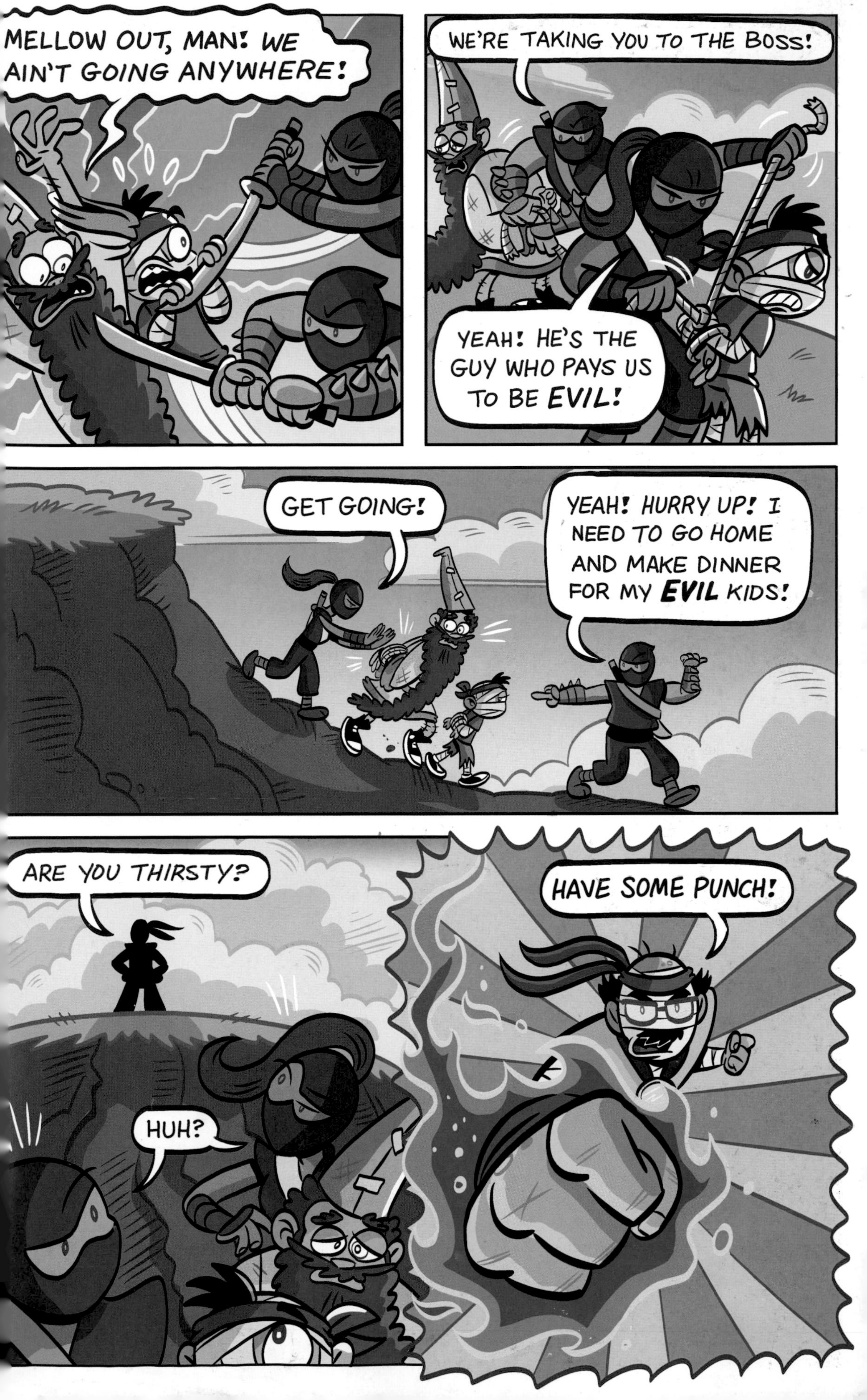
MELLOW OUT, MAN! WE AIN'T GOING ANYWHERE!
WE'RE TAKING YOU TO THE BOSS!
YEAH! HE'S THE GUY WHO PAYS US TO BE EVIL!
GET GOING!
YEAH! HURRY UP! I NEED TO GO HOME AND MAKE DINNER FOR MY EVIL KIDS!
ARE YOU THIRSTY?
HUH?
HAVE SOME PUNCH!

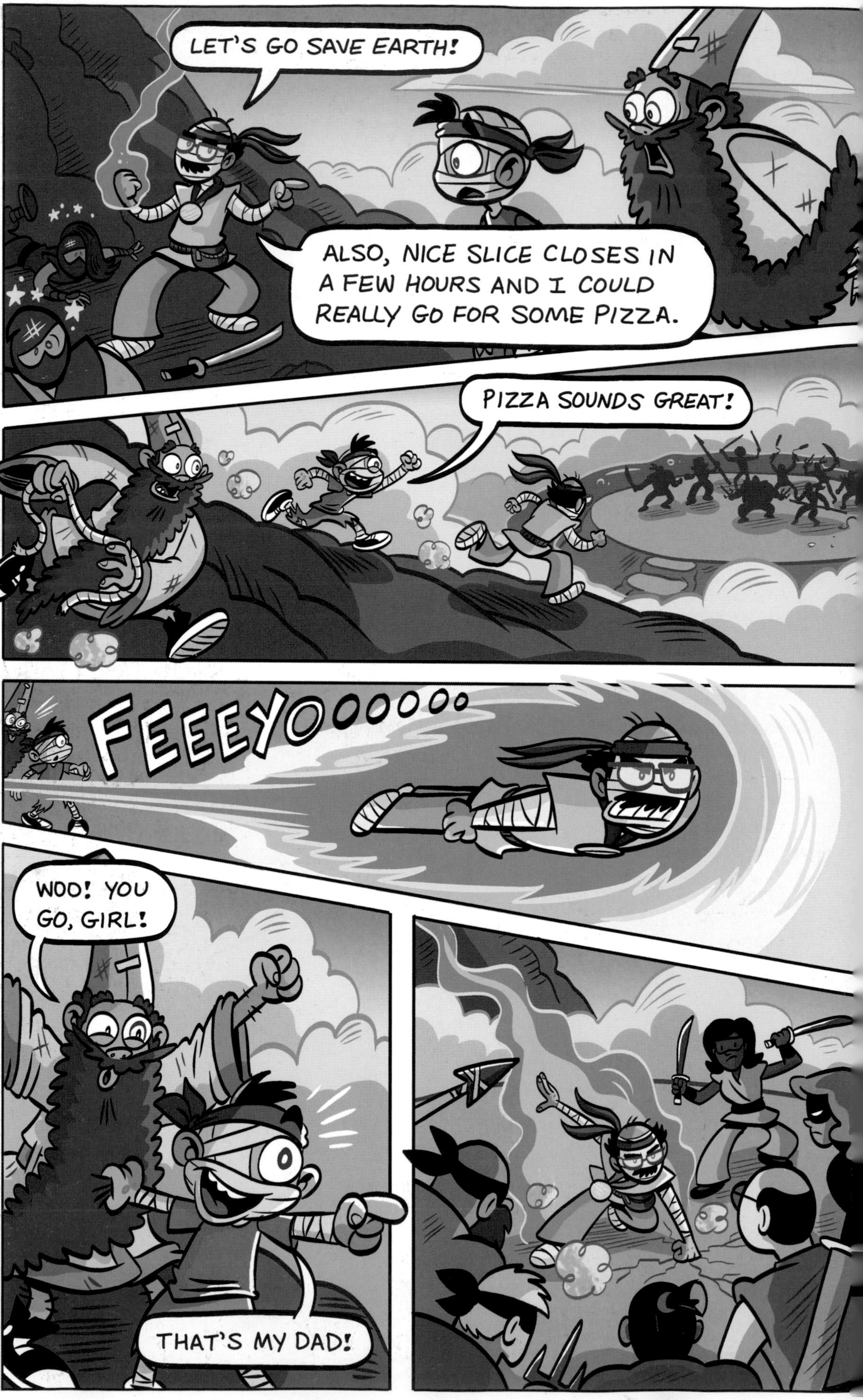
LET'S GO SAVE EARTH!
ALSO, NICE SLICE CLOSES IN A FEW HOURS AND I COULD REALLY GO FOR SOME PIZZA.
PIZZA SOUNDS GREAT!
FEEEYOOOOOO
WOO! YOU GO, GIRL!
THAT'S MY DAD!

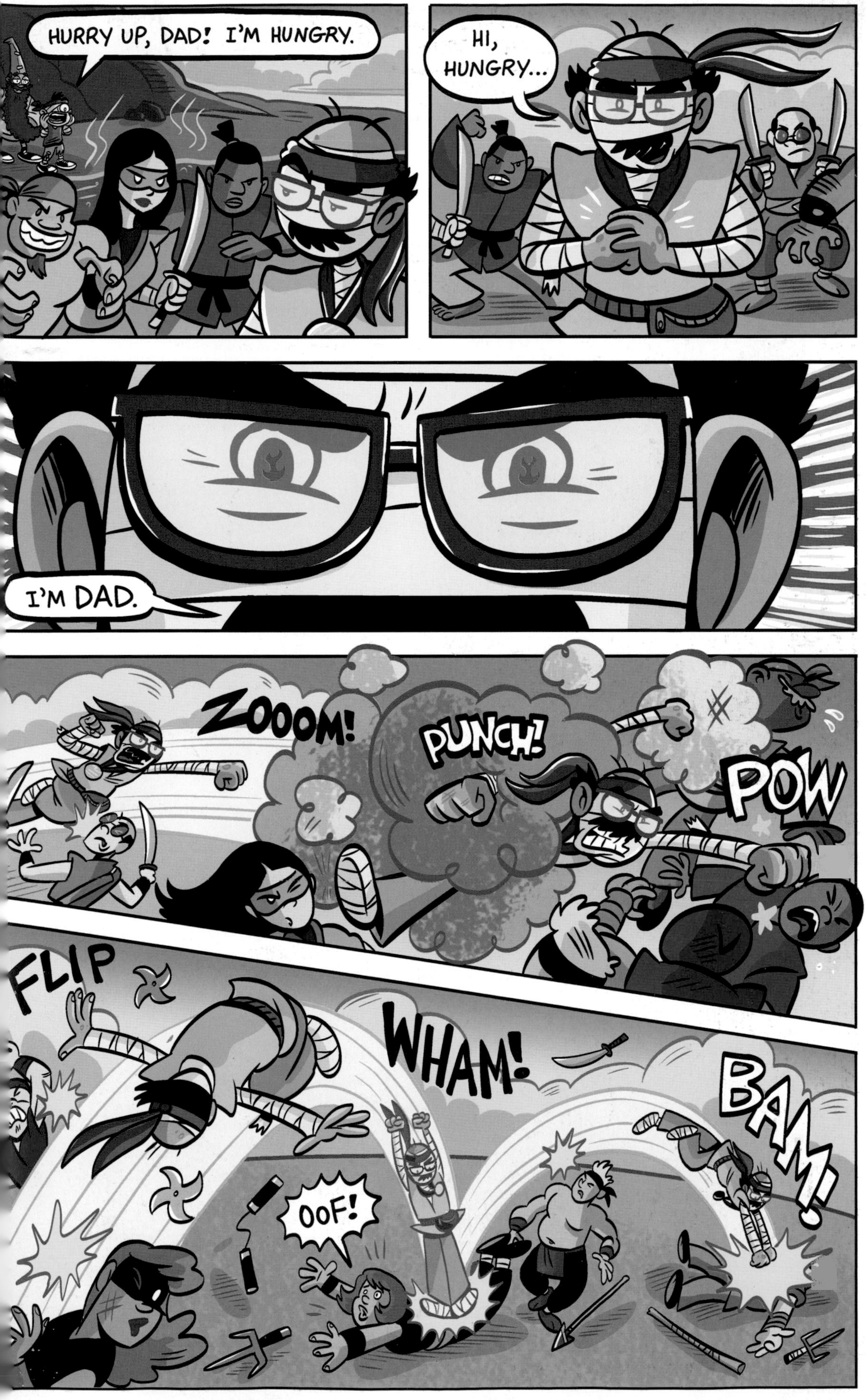
HURRY UP, DAD! I'M HUNGRY.
HI, HUNGRY...
I'M DAD.
ZOOOM!
PUNCH!
POW
FLIP
WHAM!
BAM!
OOF!

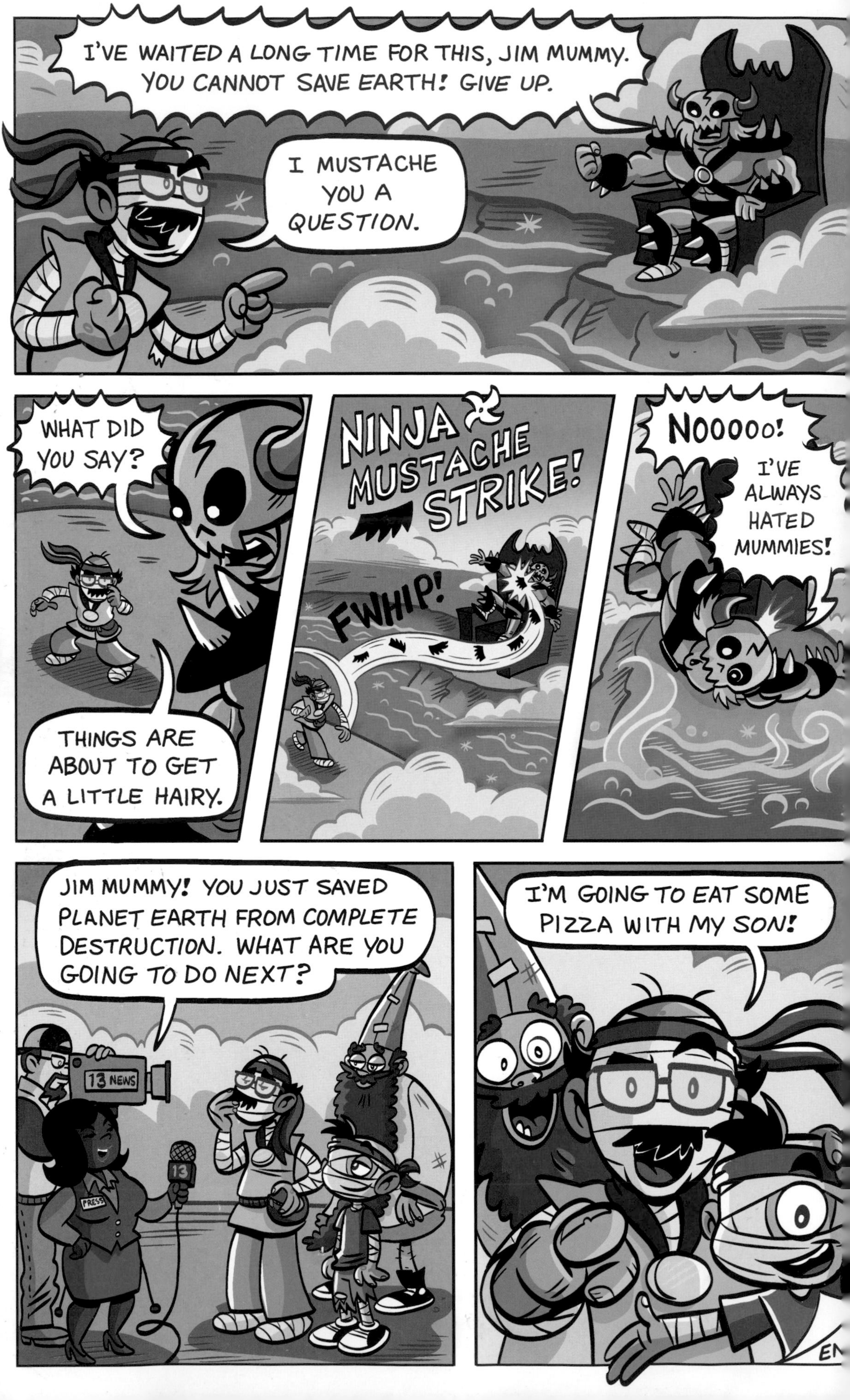
I'VE WAITED A LONG TIME FOR THIS, JIM MUMMY. YOU CANNOT SAVE EARTH! GIVE UP.
I MUSTACHE YOU A QUESTION.
WHAT DID YOU SAY?
THINGS ARE ABOUT TO GET A LITTLE HAIRY.
NINJA MUSTACHE STRIKE!
FWHIP!
NOOOOO!
I'VE ALWAYS HATED MUMMIES!
JIM MUMMY! YOU JUST SAVED PLANET EARTH FROM COMPLETE DESTRUCTION. WHAT ARE YOU GOING TO DO NEXT?
13 NEWS
13
PRESS
I'M GOING TO EAT SOME PIZZA WITH MY SON!

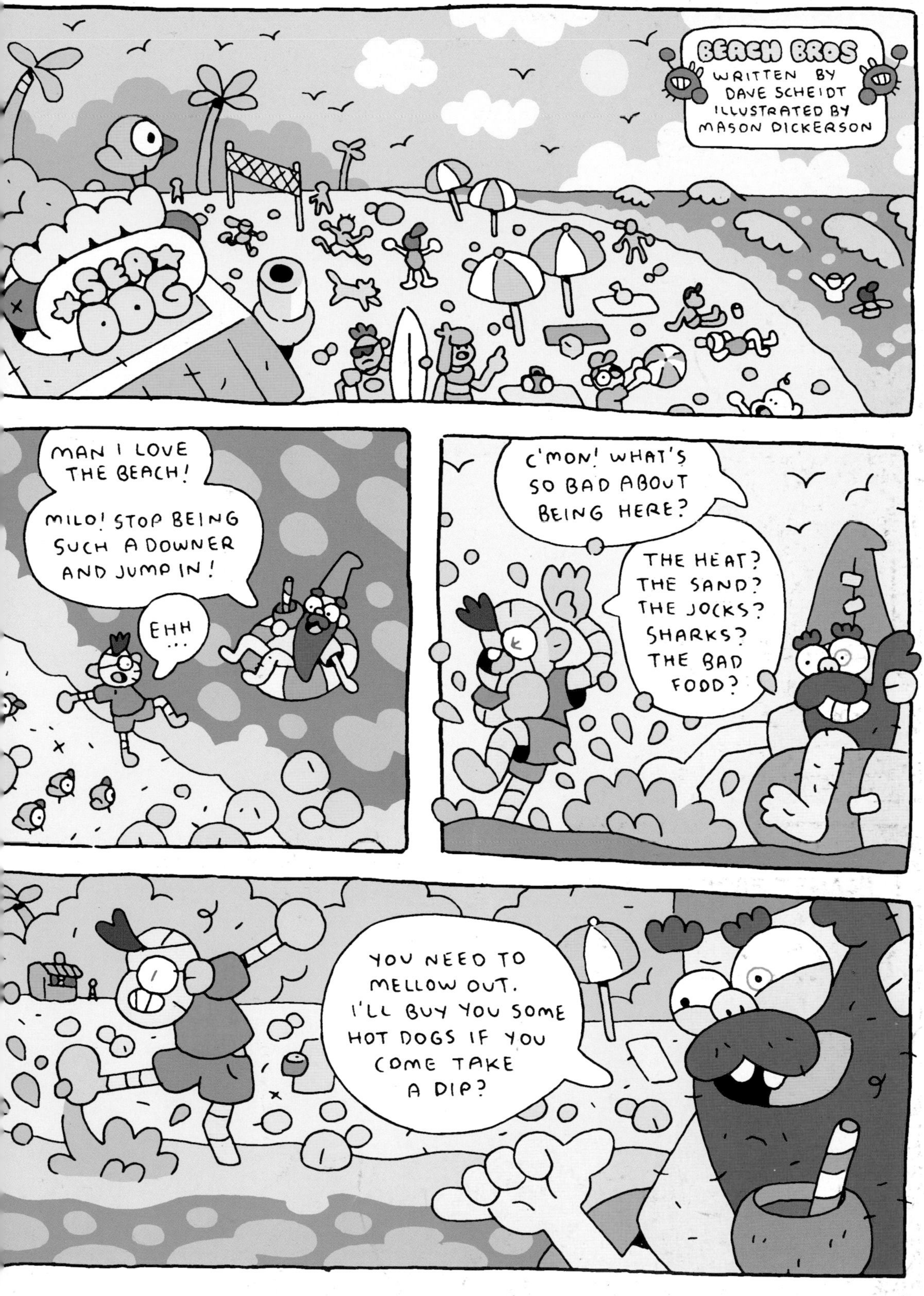
BEACH BROS
WRITTEN BY DAVE SCHEIDT
ILLUSTRATED BY MASON DICKERSON
SEA DOG
MAN I LOVE THE BEACH!
MILO! STOP BEING SUCH A DOWNER AND JUMP IN!
EHH ...
C'MON! WHAT'S SO BAD ABOUT BEING HERE?
THE HEAT? THE SAND? THE JOCKS? SHARKS? THE BAD FOOD?
YOU NEED TO MELLOW OUT. I'LL BUY YOU SOME HOT DOGS IF YOU COME TAKE A DIP?

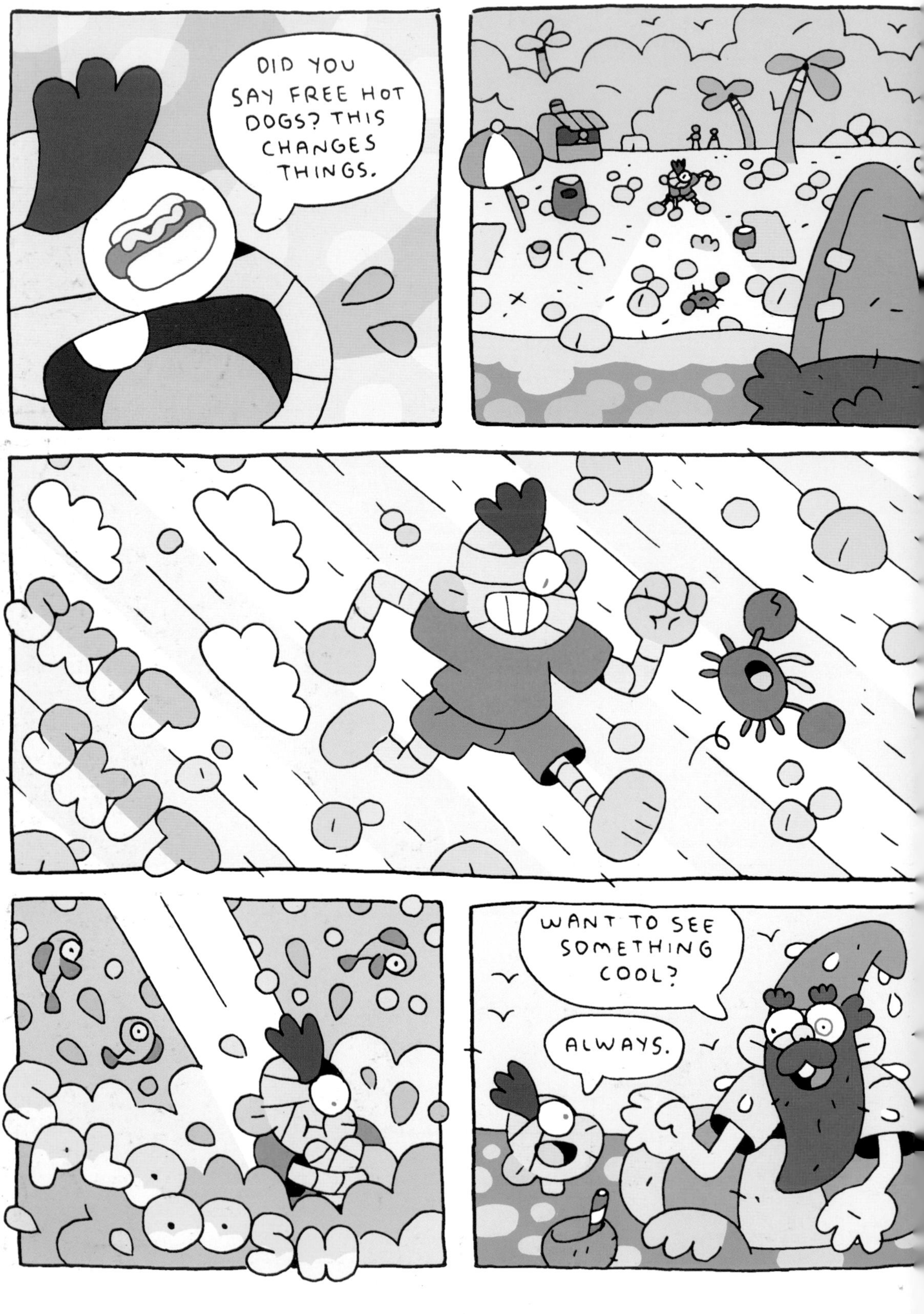
DID YOU SAY FREE HOT DOGS? THIS CHANGES THINGS.
SWOT
SWOT
SPLOOOSH
WANT TO SEE SOMETHING COOL?
ALWAYS.

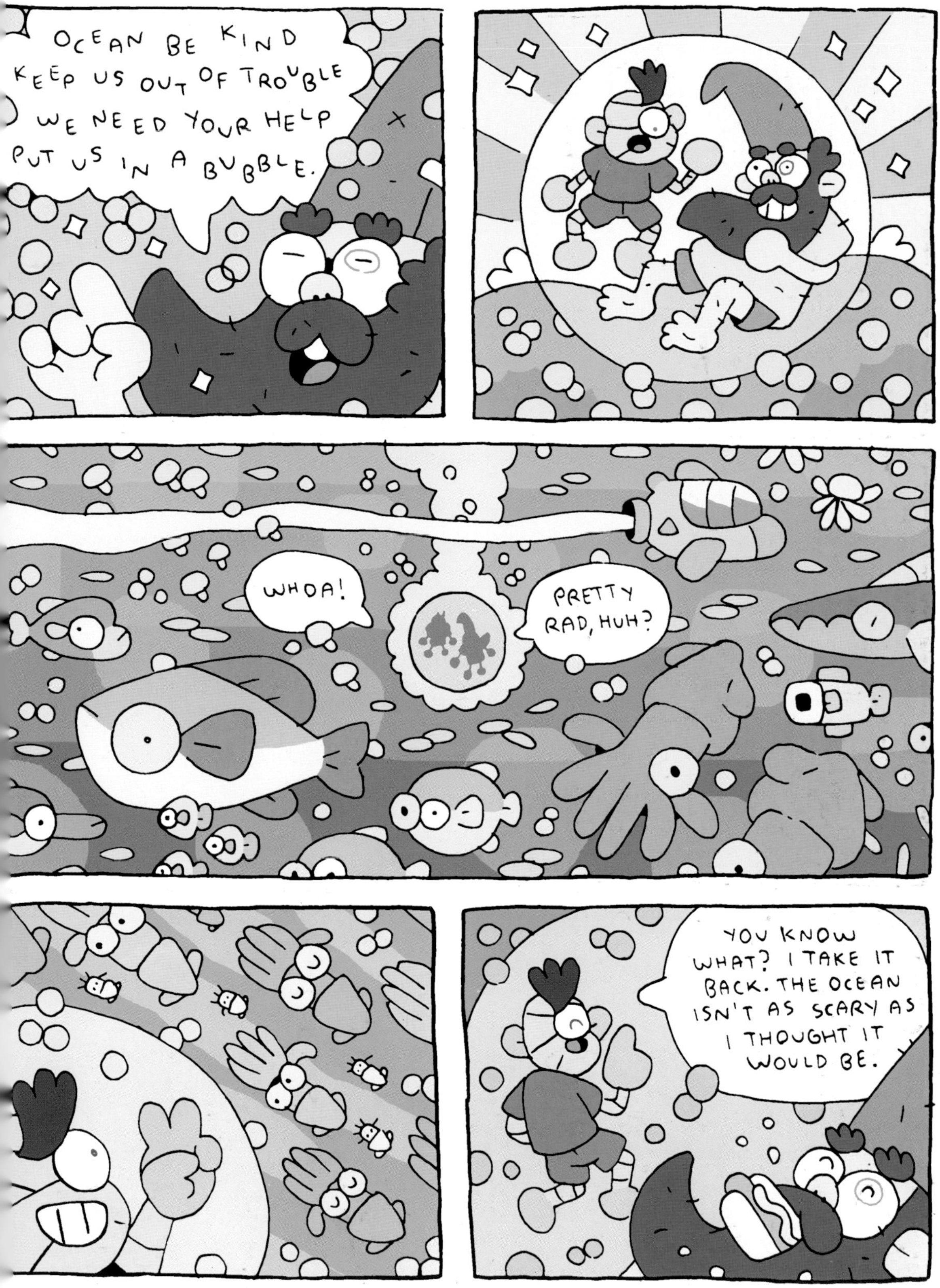
OCEAN BE KIND
KEEP US OUT OF TROUBLE
WE NEED YOUR HELP
PUT US IN A BUBBLE.
WHOA!
PRETTY RAD, HUH?
YOU KNOW WHAT? I TAKE IT BACK. THE OCEAN ISN'T AS SCARY AS I THOUGHT IT WOULD BE.

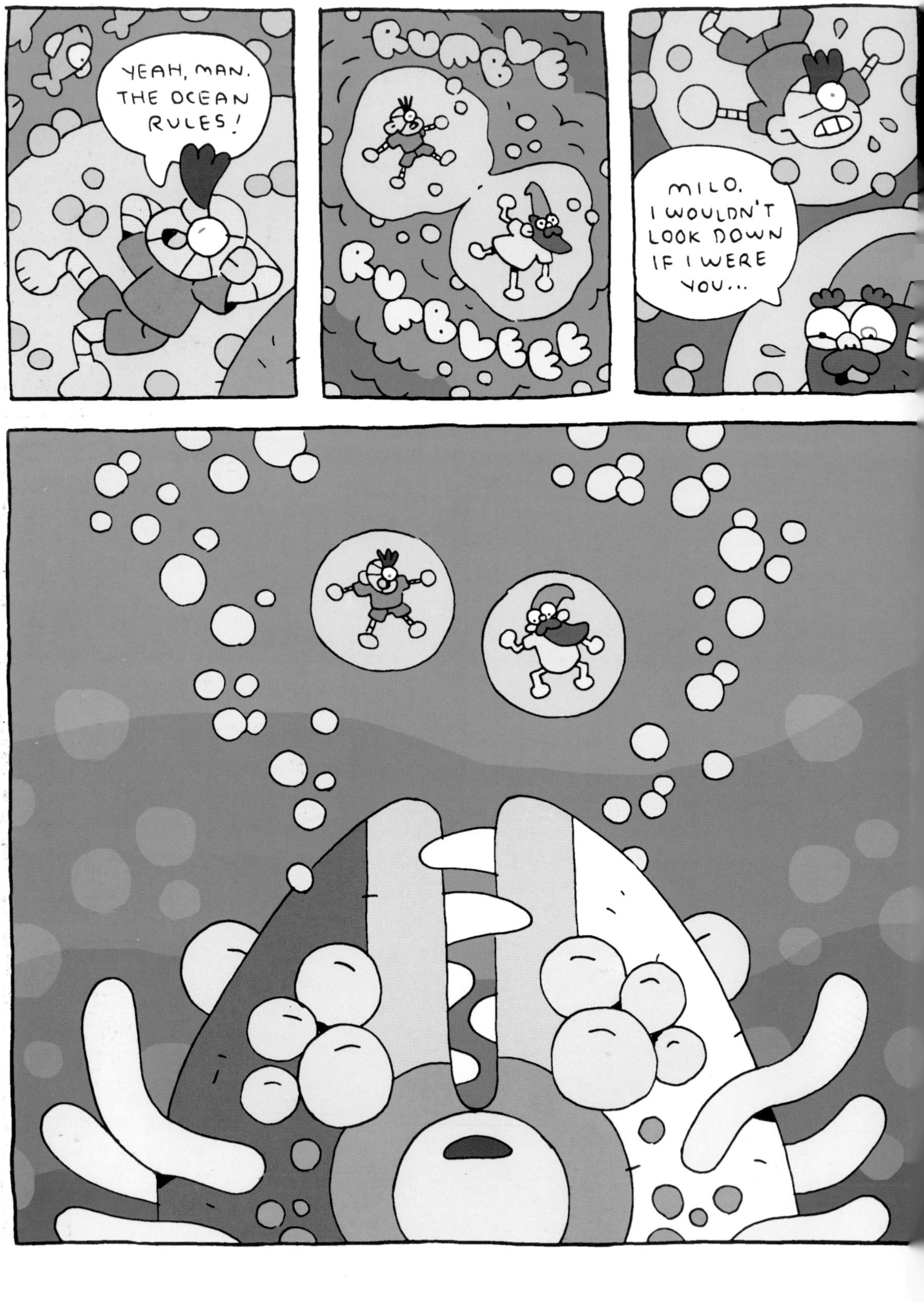
YEAH, MAN. THE OCEAN RULES!
RUMBLE
RUMBLEEE
MILO. I WOULDN'T LOOK DOWN IF I WERE YOU...

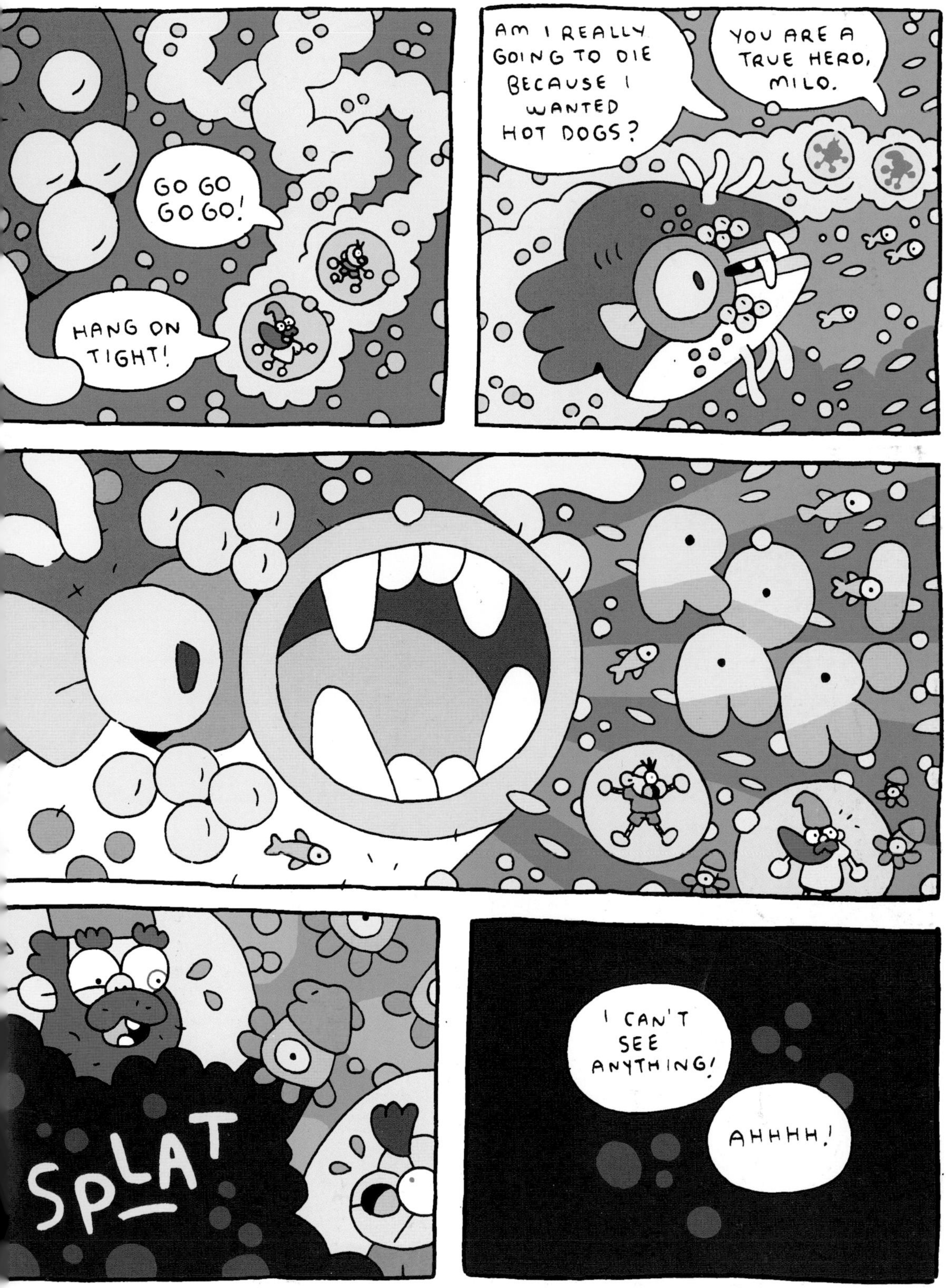
GO GO GO GO!
HANG ON TIGHT!
AM I REALLY GOING TO DIE BECAUSE I WANTED HOT DOGS?
YOU ARE A TRUE HERO, MILO.
ROAR
SPLAT
I CAN'T SEE ANYTHING!
AHHHH!

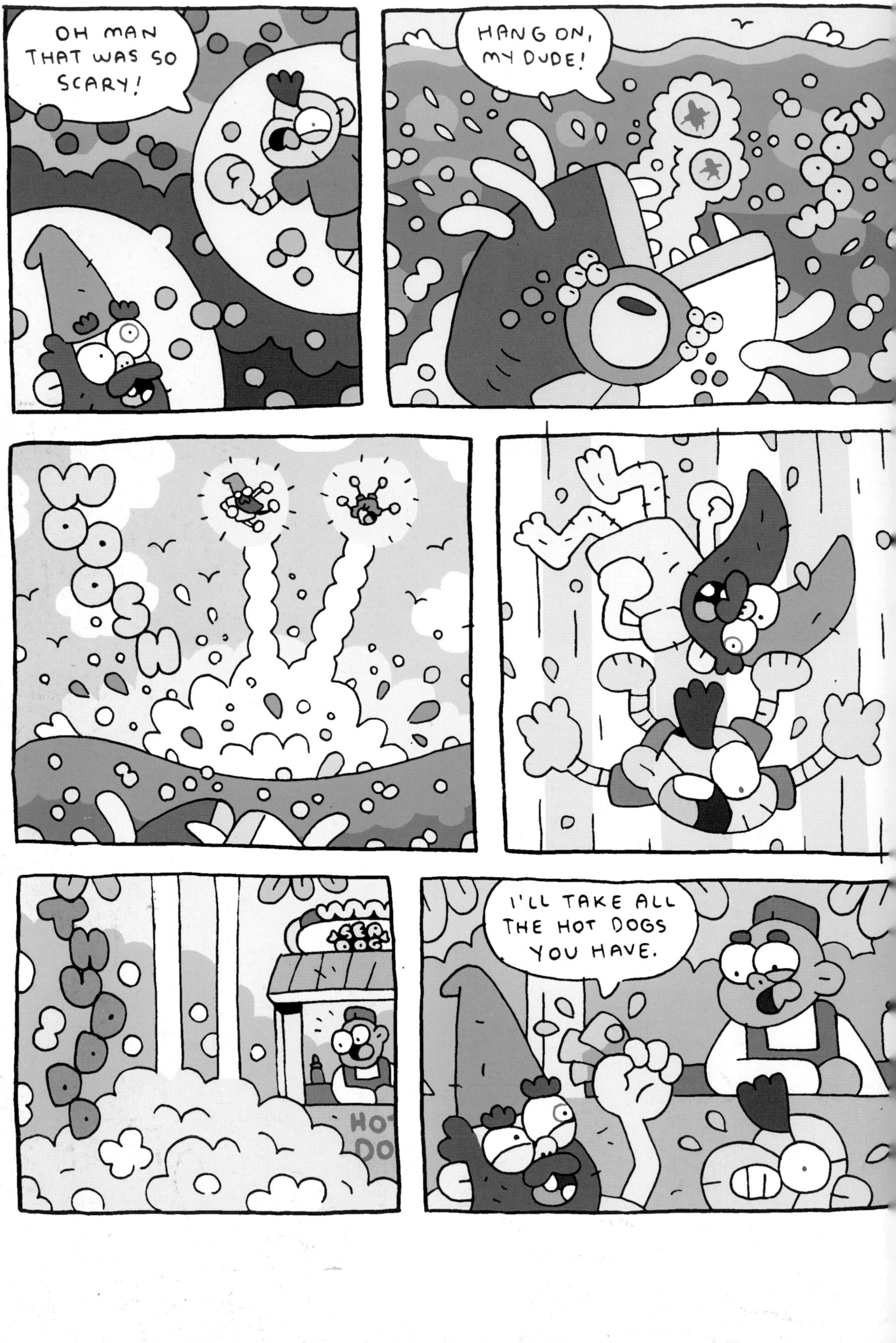
OH MAN THAT WAS SO SCARY!
HANG ON, MY DUDE!
WOOSH
WOOOSH
THUDDD
SEA DOG
I'LL TAKE ALL THE HOT DOGS YOU HAVE.

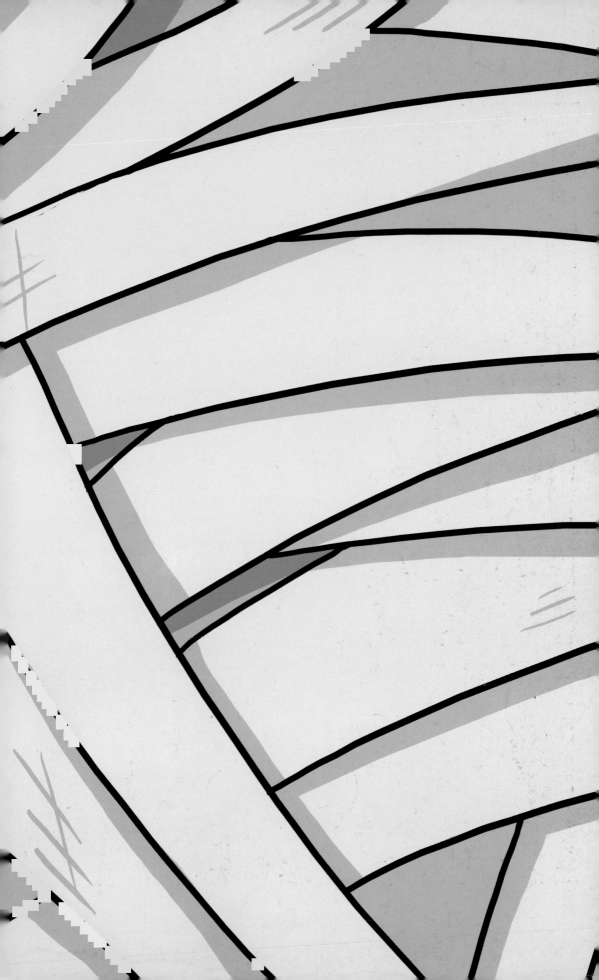

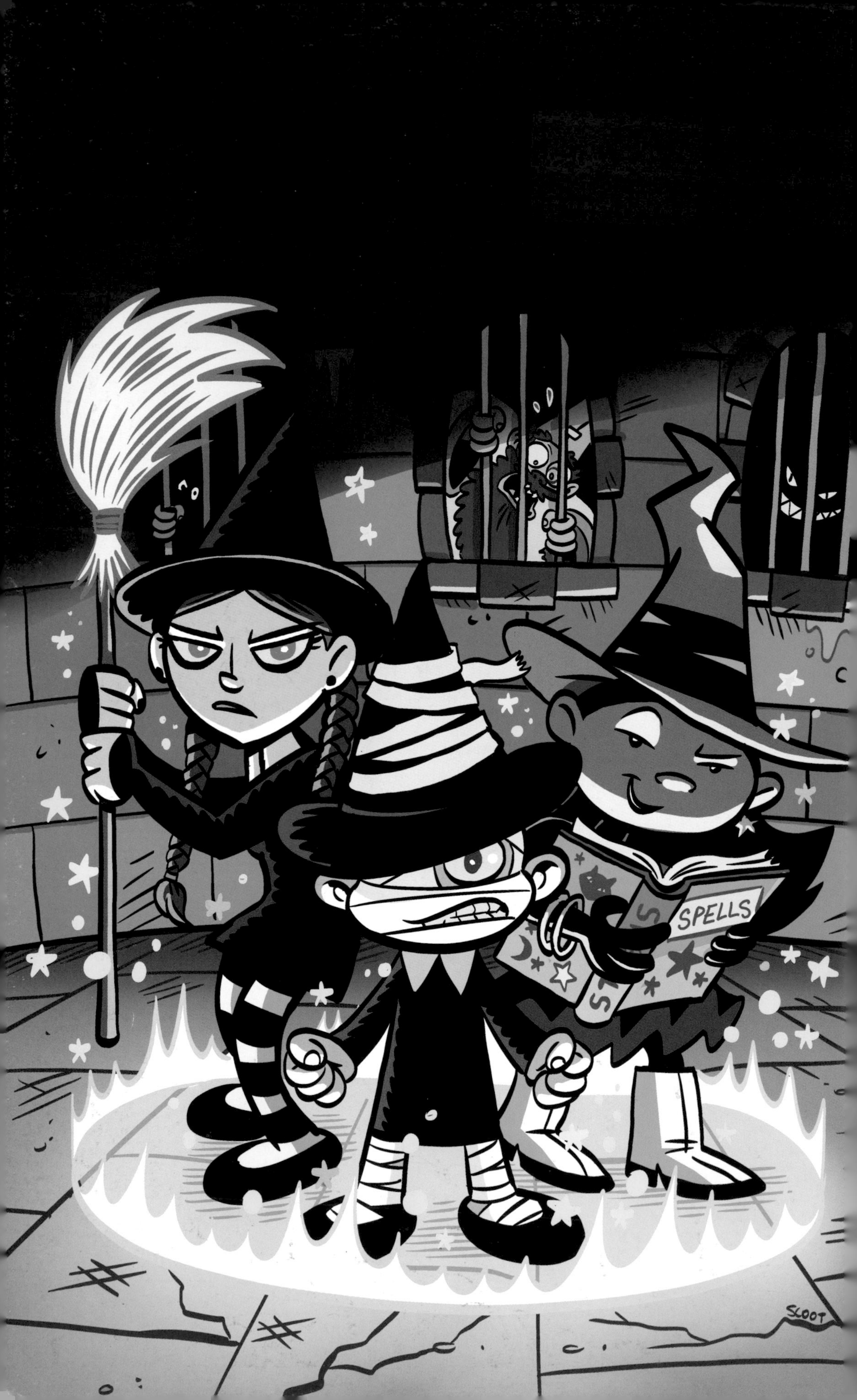
SPELLS
SCOOT

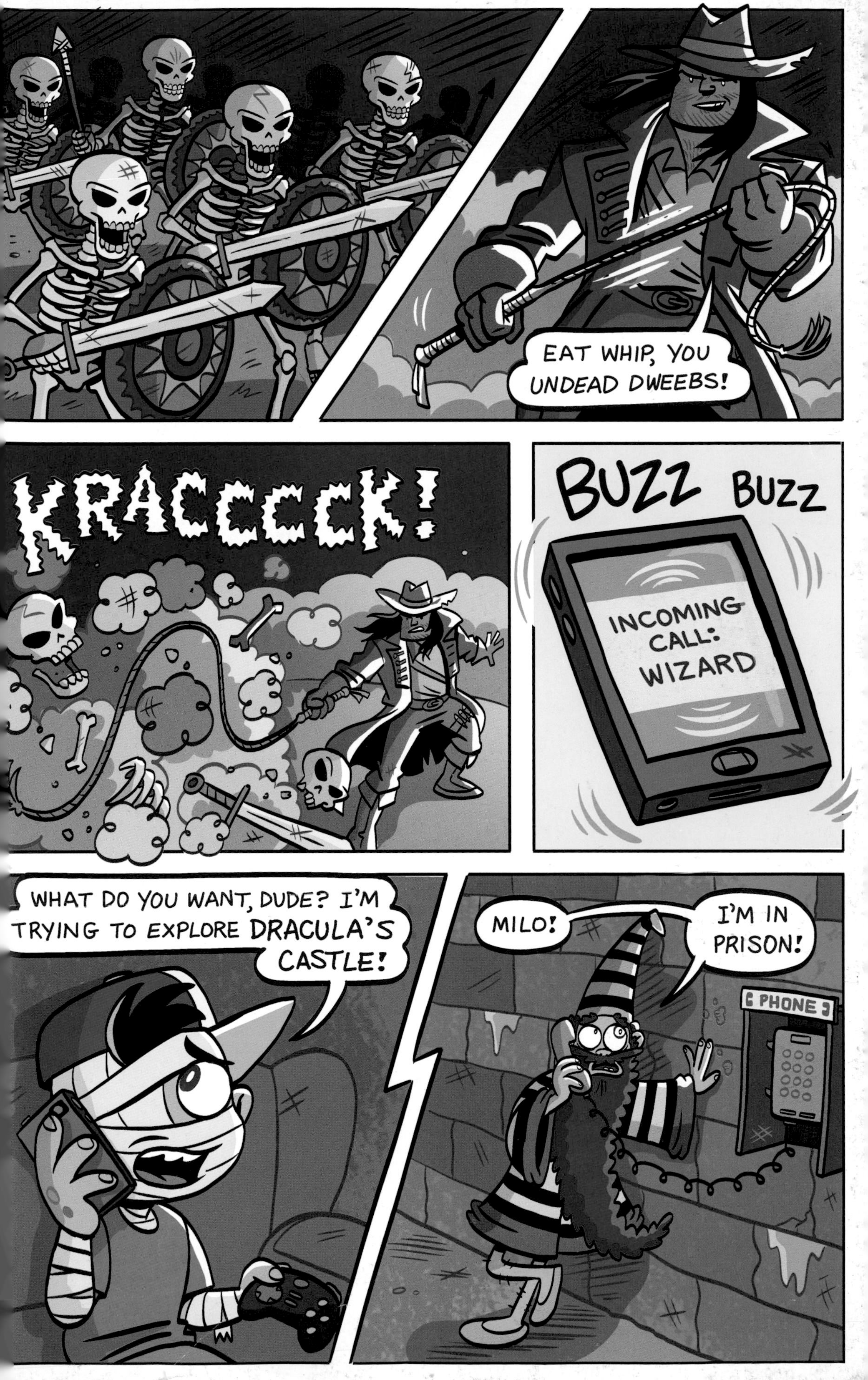
EAT WHIP, YOU UNDEAD DWEEBS!
KRACCCCK!
BUZZ BUZZ
INCOMING CALL: WIZARD
WHAT DO YOU WANT, DUDE? I'M TRYING TO EXPLORE DRACULA'S CASTLE!
MILO!
I'M IN PRISON!
PHONE

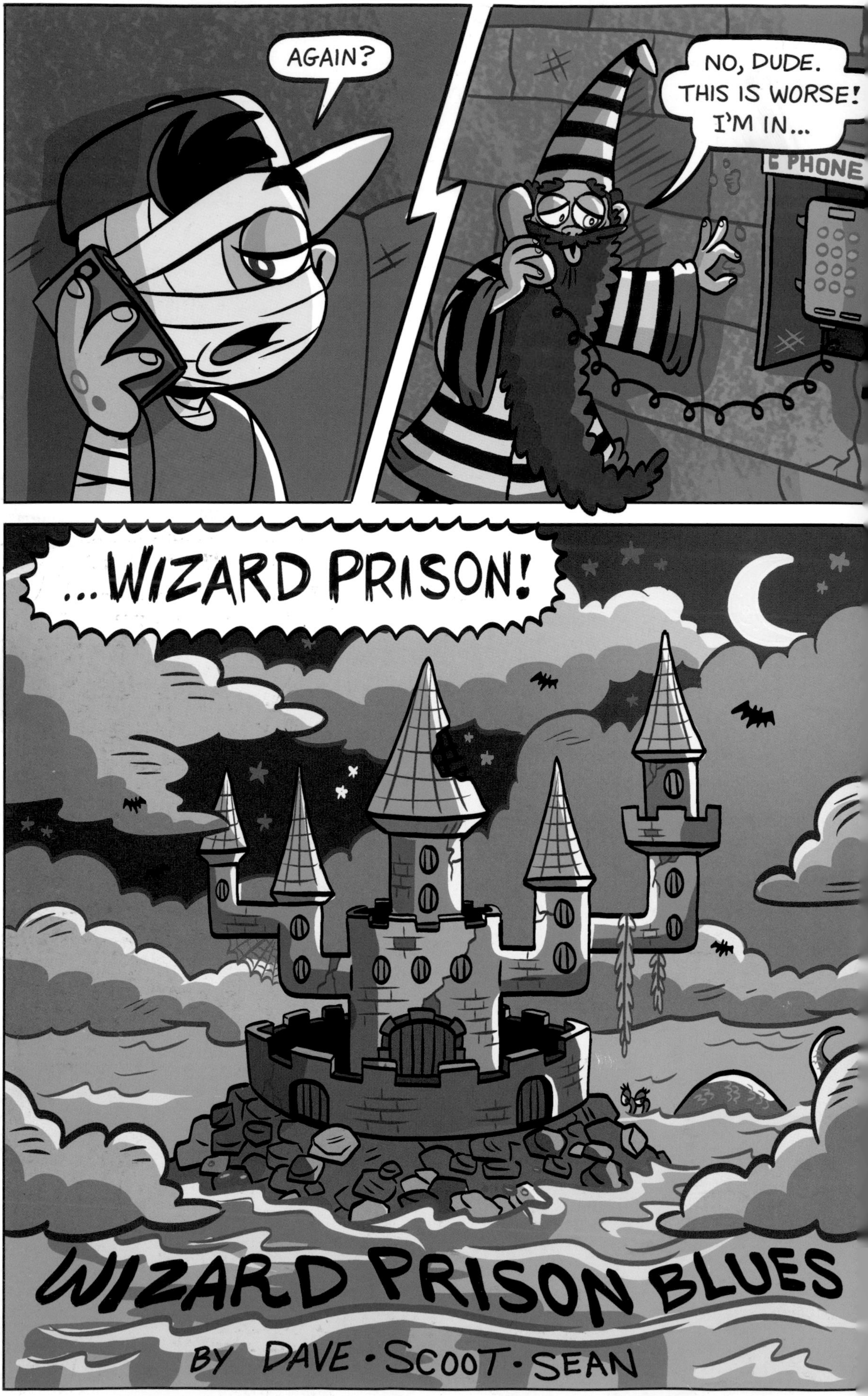
AGAIN?
NO, DUDE. THIS IS WORSE! I'M IN...
PHONE
...WIZARD PRISON!
WIZARD PRISON BLUES
BY DAVE · SCOOT · SEAN

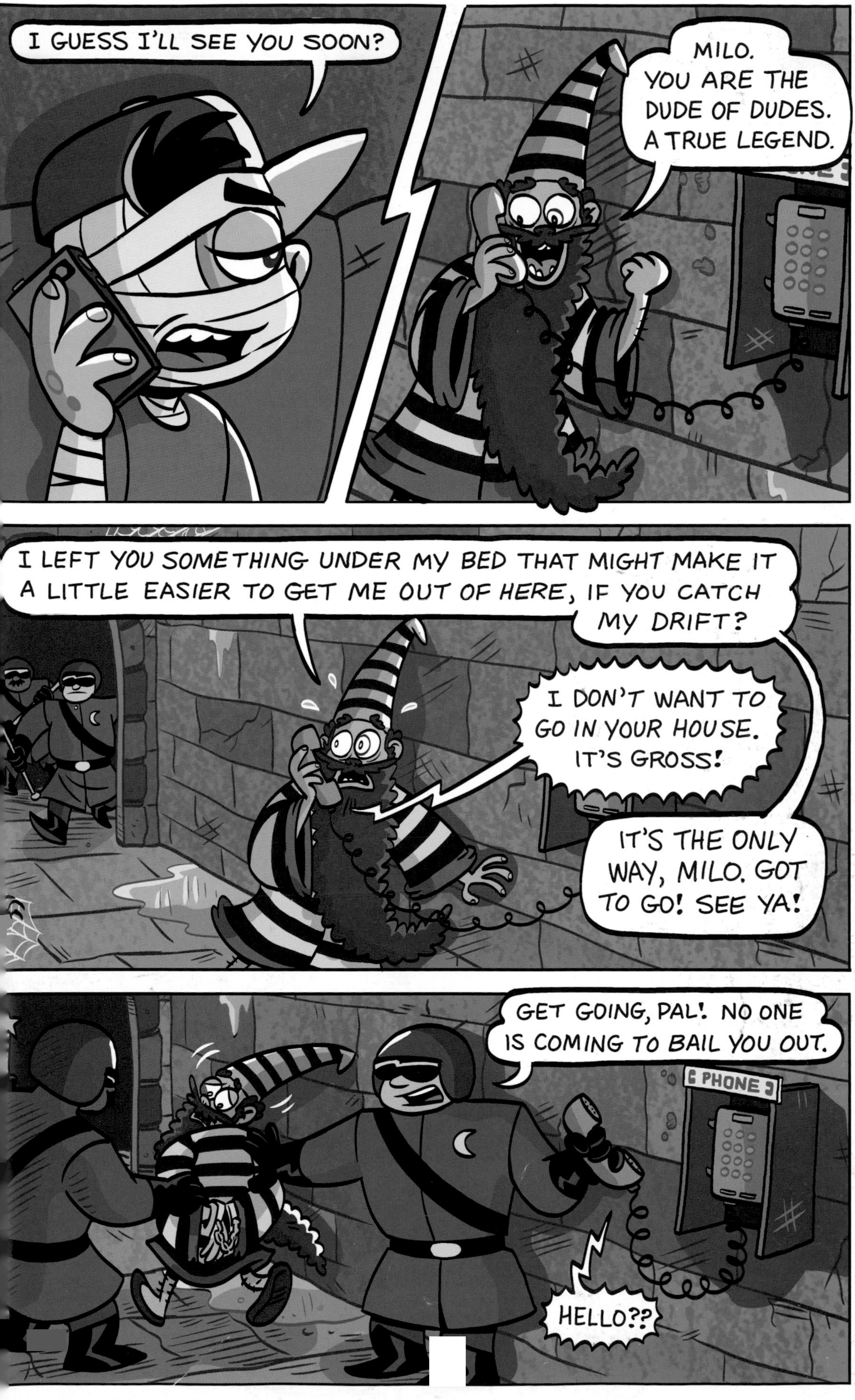
I GUESS I'LL SEE YOU SOON?
MILO. YOU ARE THE DUDE OF DUDES. A TRUE LEGEND.
I LEFT YOU SOMETHING UNDER MY BED THAT MIGHT MAKE IT A LITTLE EASIER TO GET ME OUT OF HERE, IF YOU CATCH MY DRIFT?
I DON'T WANT TO GO IN YOUR HOUSE. IT'S GROSS!
IT'S THE ONLY WAY, MILO. GOT TO GO! SEE YA!
GET GOING, PAL! NO ONE IS COMING TO BAIL YOU OUT.
PHONE
HELLO??

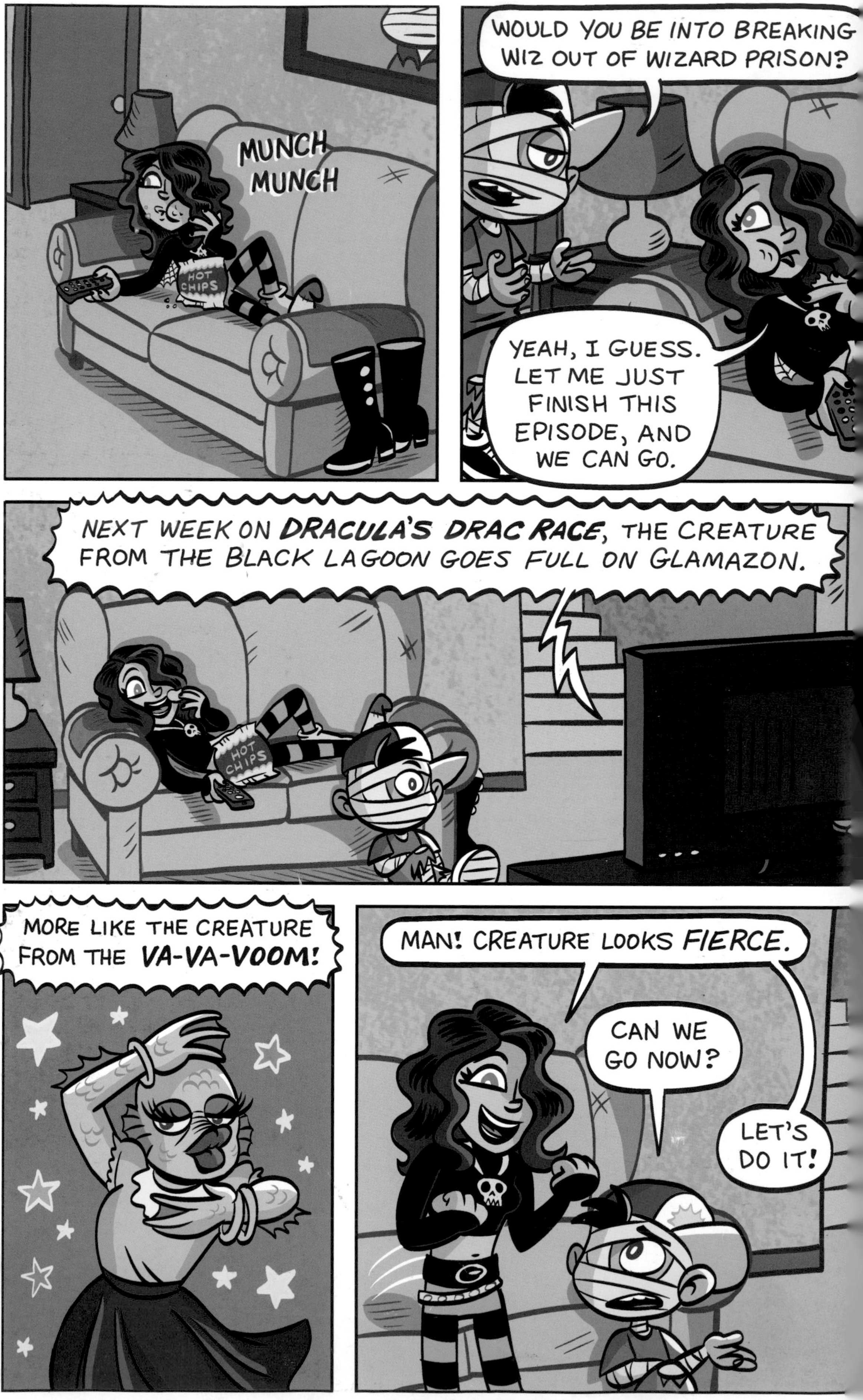
MUNCH
MUNCH
HOT CHIPS
WOULD YOU BE INTO BREAKING WIZ OUT OF WIZARD PRISON?
YEAH, I GUESS. LET ME JUST FINISH THIS EPISODE, AND WE CAN GO.
NEXT WEEK ON DRACULA'S DRAC RACE, THE CREATURE FROM THE BLACK LAGOON GOES FULL ON GLAMAZON.
HOT CHIPS
MORE LIKE THE CREATURE FROM THE VA-VA-VOOM!
MAN! CREATURE LOOKS FIERCE.
CAN WE GO NOW?
LET'S DO IT!

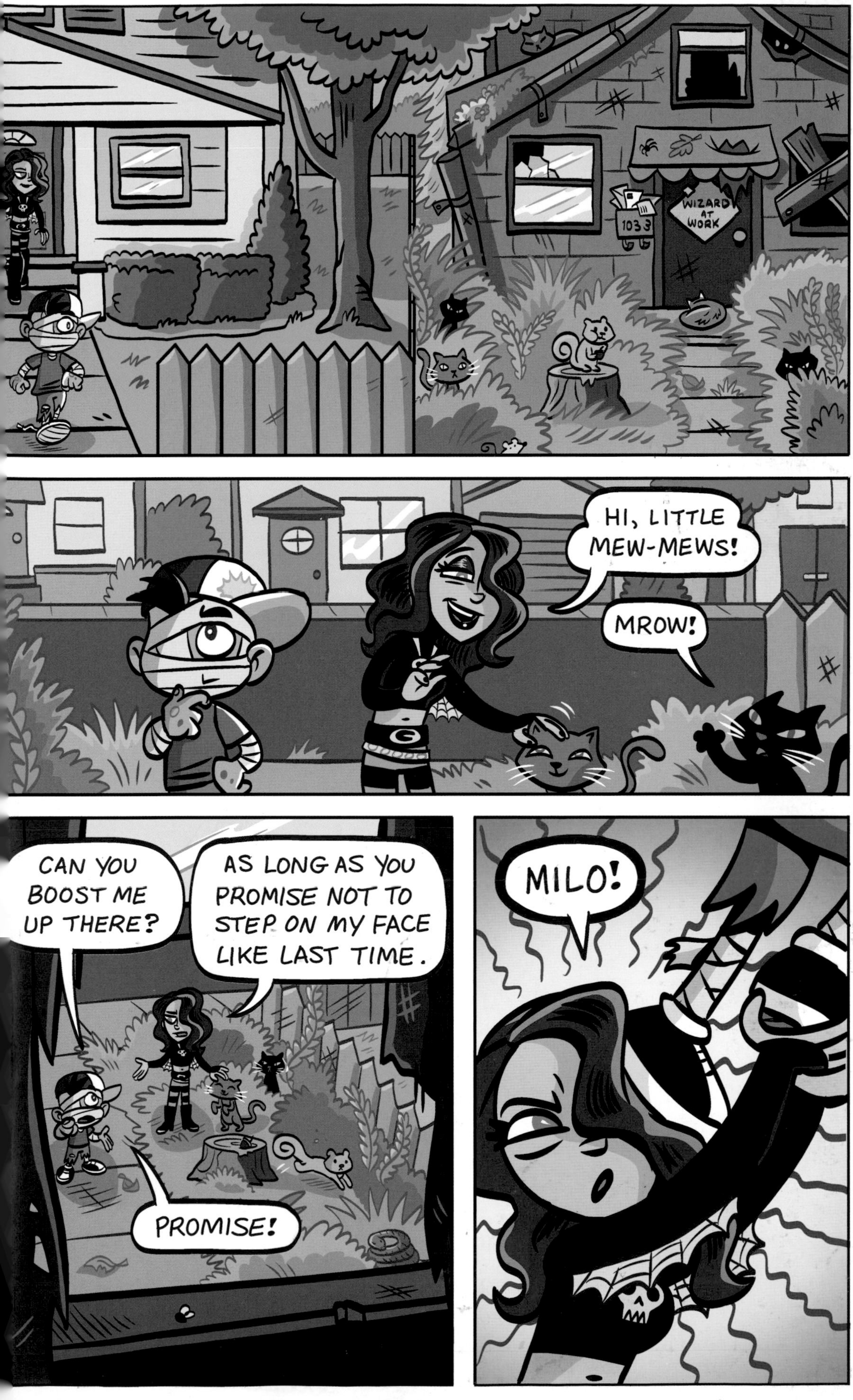
1033
WIZARD AT WORK
HI, LITTLE MEW-MEWS!
MROW!
CAN YOU BOOST ME UP THERE?
AS LONG AS YOU PROMISE NOT TO STEP ON MY FACE LIKE LAST TIME.
PROMISE!
MILO!

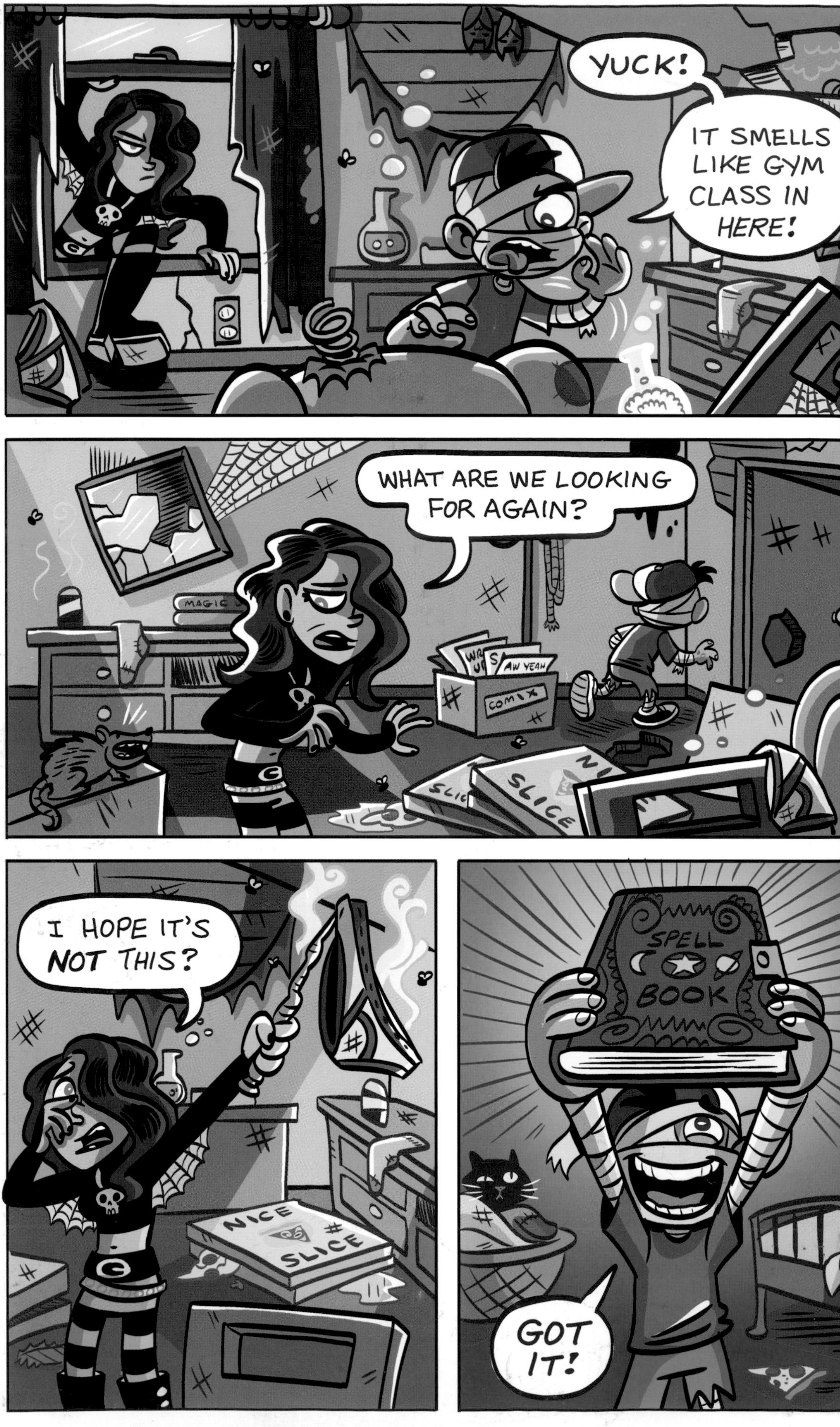
YUCK!
IT SMELLS LIKE GYM CLASS IN HERE!
WHAT ARE WE LOOKING FOR AGAIN?
AW YEAH
COMIX
SLICE
I HOPE IT'S **NOT** THIS?
NICE SLICE
SPELL BOOK
GOT IT!

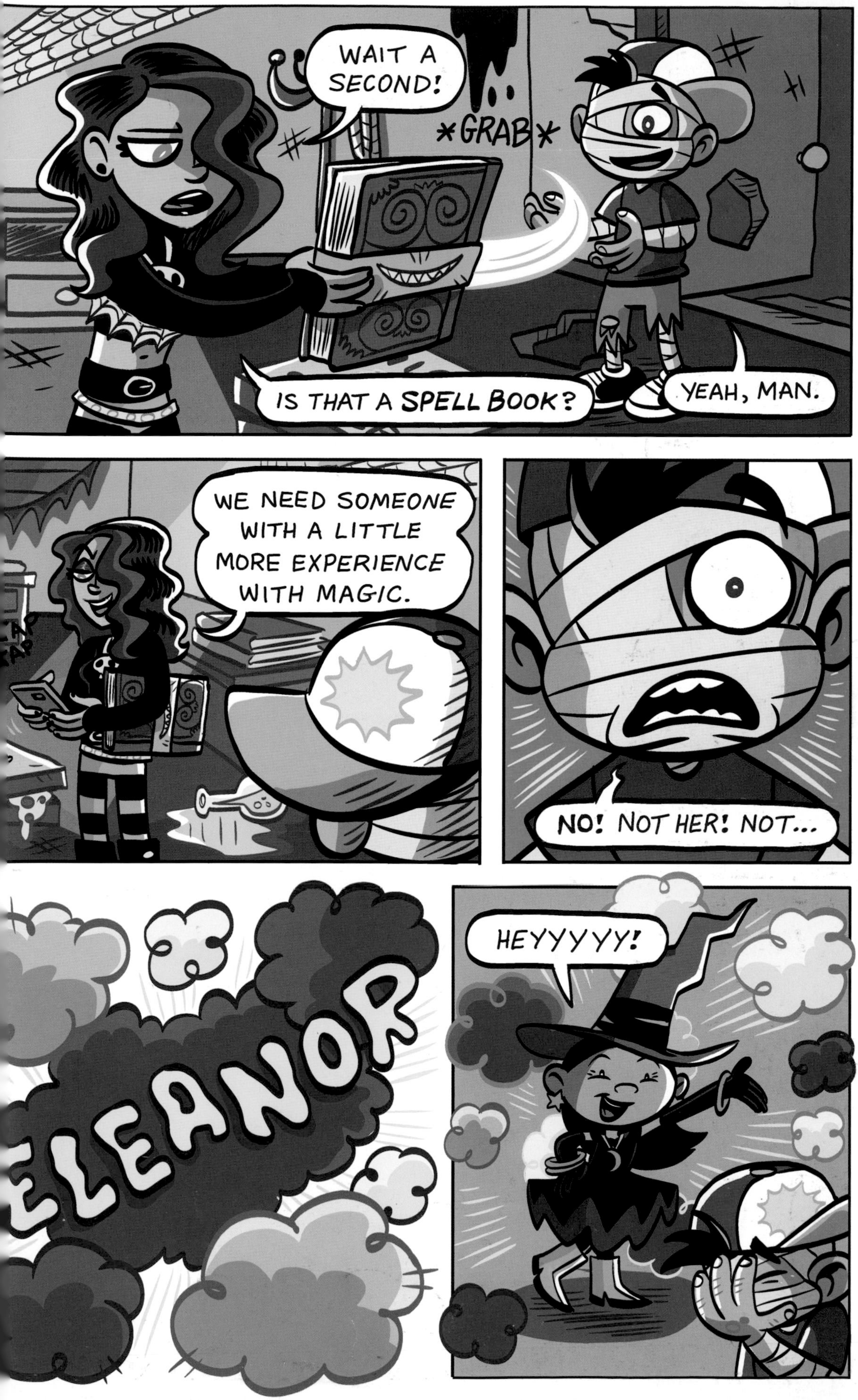
WAIT A SECOND!
GRAB
IS THAT A SPELL BOOK?
YEAH, MAN.
WE NEED SOMEONE WITH A LITTLE MORE EXPERIENCE WITH MAGIC.
NO! NOT HER! NOT...
ELEANOR
HEYYYYY!

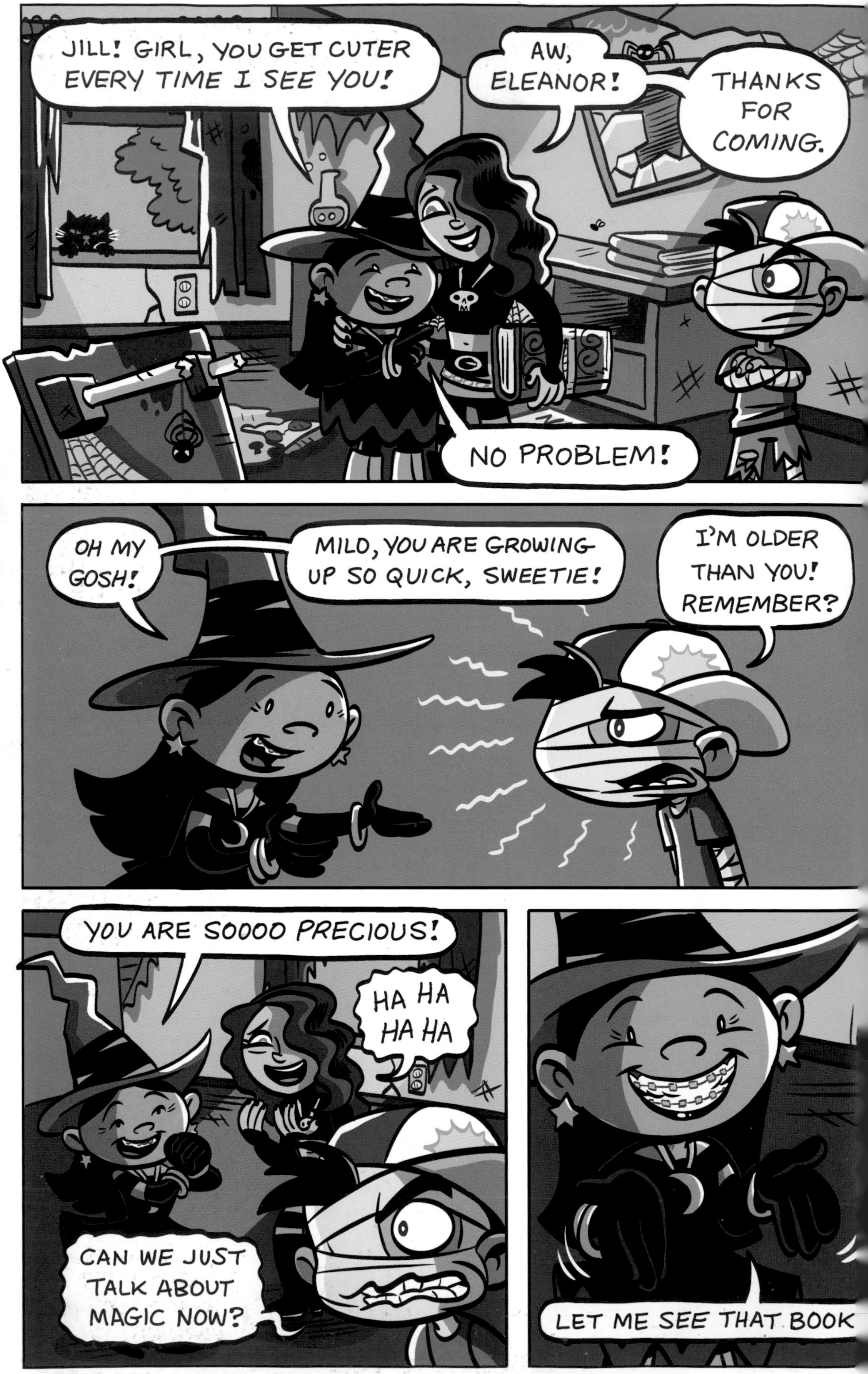
JILL! GIRL, YOU GET CUTER EVERY TIME I SEE YOU!
AW, ELEANOR!
THANKS FOR COMING.
NO PROBLEM!
OH MY GOSH!
MILO, YOU ARE GROWING UP SO QUICK, SWEETIE!
I'M OLDER THAN YOU! REMEMBER?
YOU ARE SOOOO PRECIOUS!
HA HA HA HA
CAN WE JUST TALK ABOUT MAGIC NOW?
LET ME SEE THAT BOOK

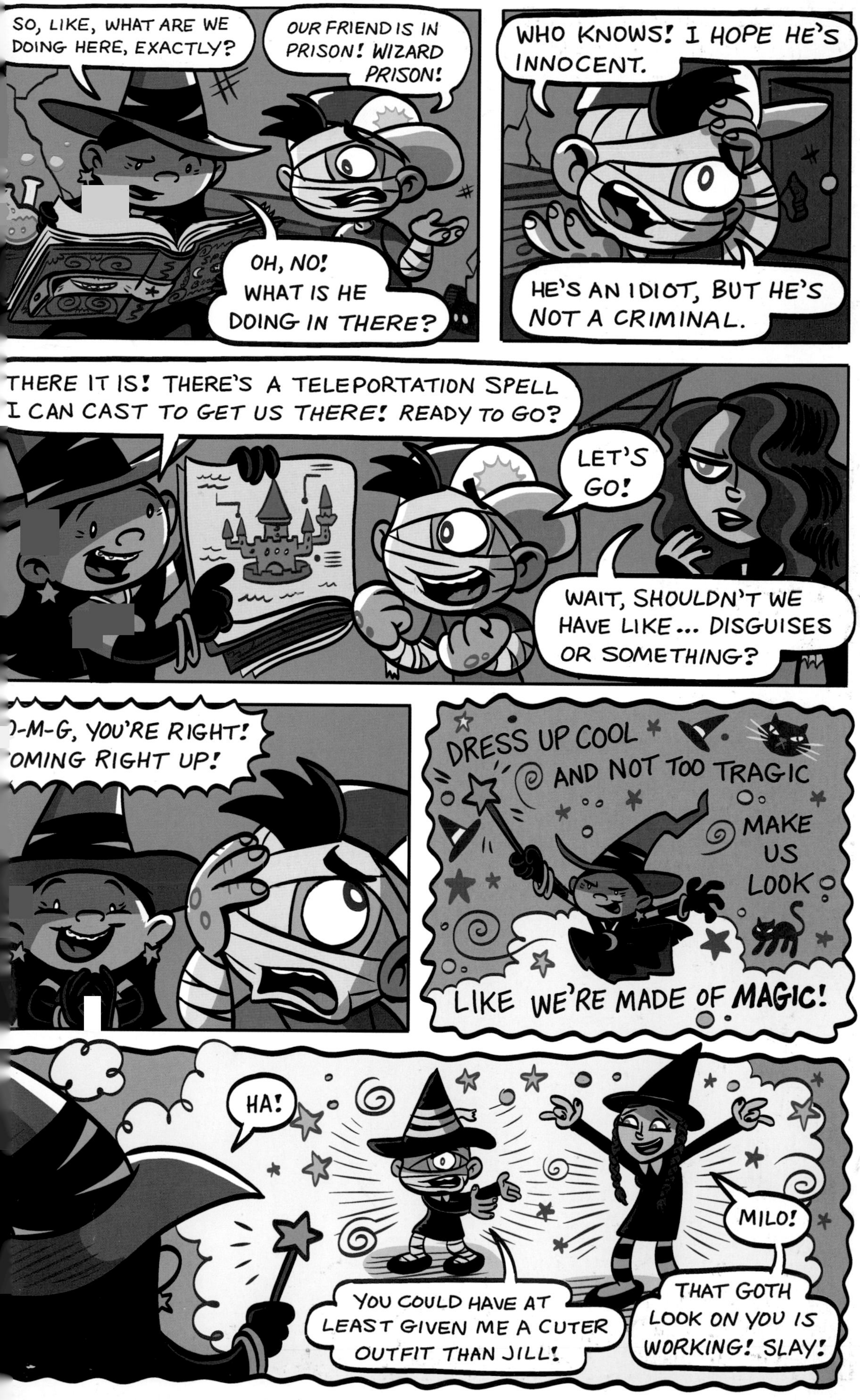

SO, LIKE, WHAT ARE WE DOING HERE, EXACTLY?
OUR FRIEND IS IN PRISON! WIZARD PRISON!
OH, NO! WHAT IS HE DOING IN THERE?
WHO KNOWS! I HOPE HE'S INNOCENT.
HE'S AN IDIOT, BUT HE'S NOT A CRIMINAL.
THERE IT IS! THERE'S A TELEPORTATION SPELL I CAN CAST TO GET US THERE! READY TO GO?
LET'S GO!
WAIT, SHOULDN'T WE HAVE LIKE... DISGUISES OR SOMETHING?
-M-G, YOU'RE RIGHT!
OMING RIGHT UP!
DRESS UP COOL AND NOT TOO TRAGIC MAKE US LOOK LIKE WE'RE MADE OF **MAGIC!**
HA!
YOU COULD HAVE AT LEAST GIVEN ME A CUTER OUTFIT THAN JILL!
MILO!
THAT GOTH LOOK ON YOU IS WORKING! SLAY!

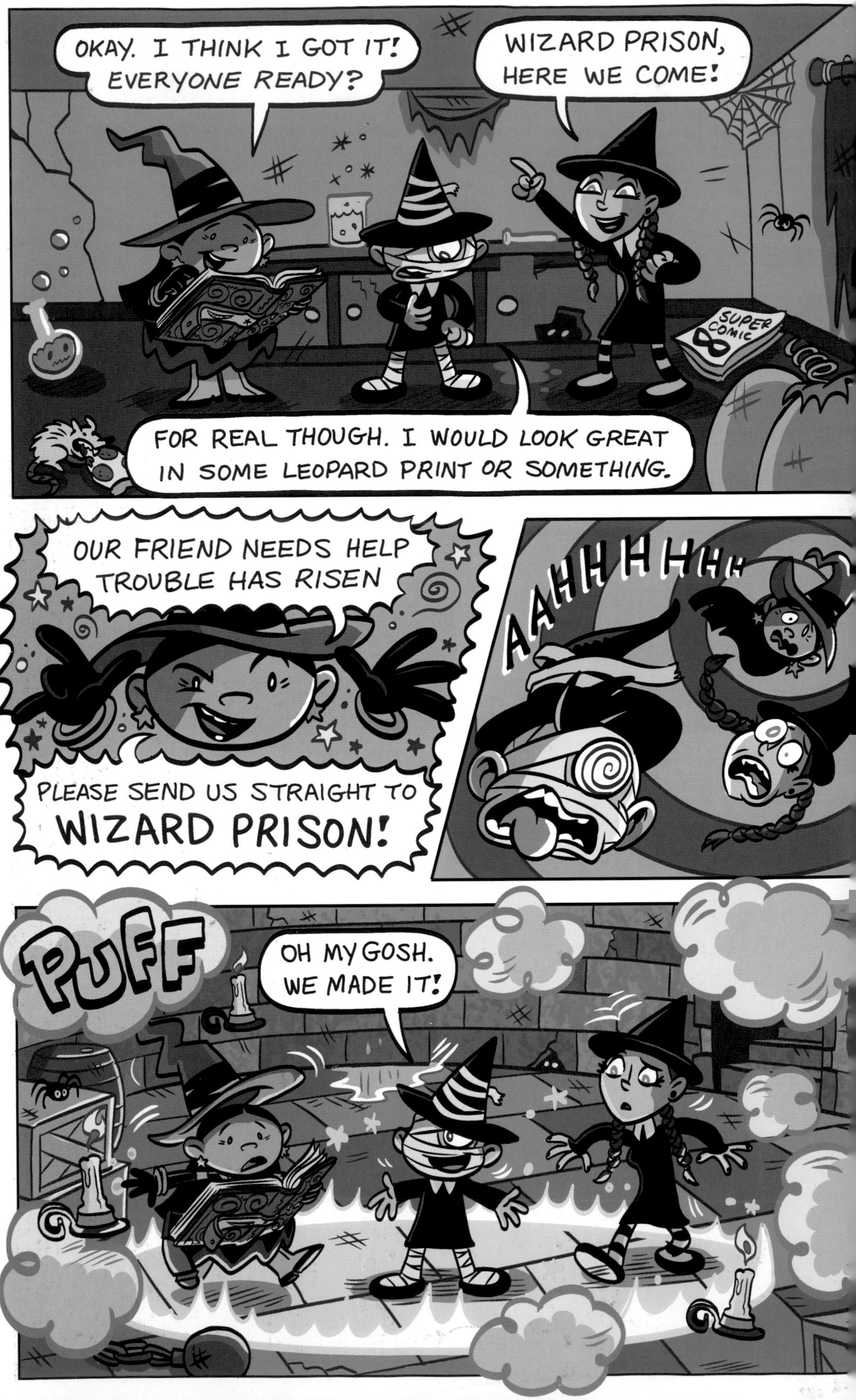
OKAY. I THINK I GOT IT! EVERYONE READY?
WIZARD PRISON, HERE WE COME!
FOR REAL THOUGH. I WOULD LOOK GREAT IN SOME LEOPARD PRINT OR SOMETHING.
SUPER COMIC
OUR FRIEND NEEDS HELP TROUBLE HAS RISEN
PLEASE SEND US STRAIGHT TO WIZARD PRISON!
AAHHHHHHH
PUFF
OH MY GOSH. WE MADE IT!

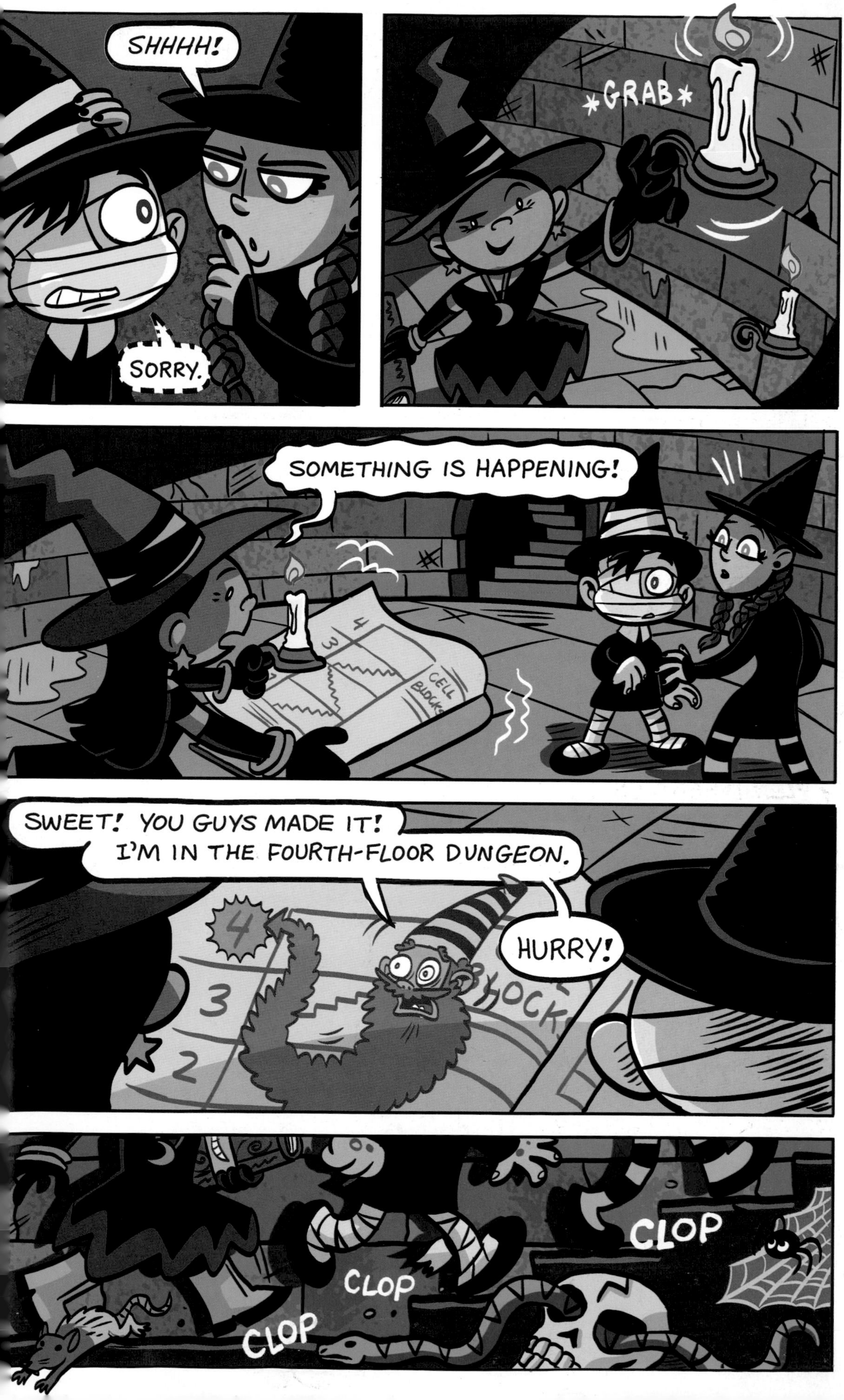
SHHHH!
SORRY.
GRAB
SOMETHING IS HAPPENING!
4
3
CELL BLOCKS
SWEET! YOU GUYS MADE IT!
I'M IN THE FOURTH-FLOOR DUNGEON.
HURRY!
4
3
2
CLOP
CLOP
CLOP

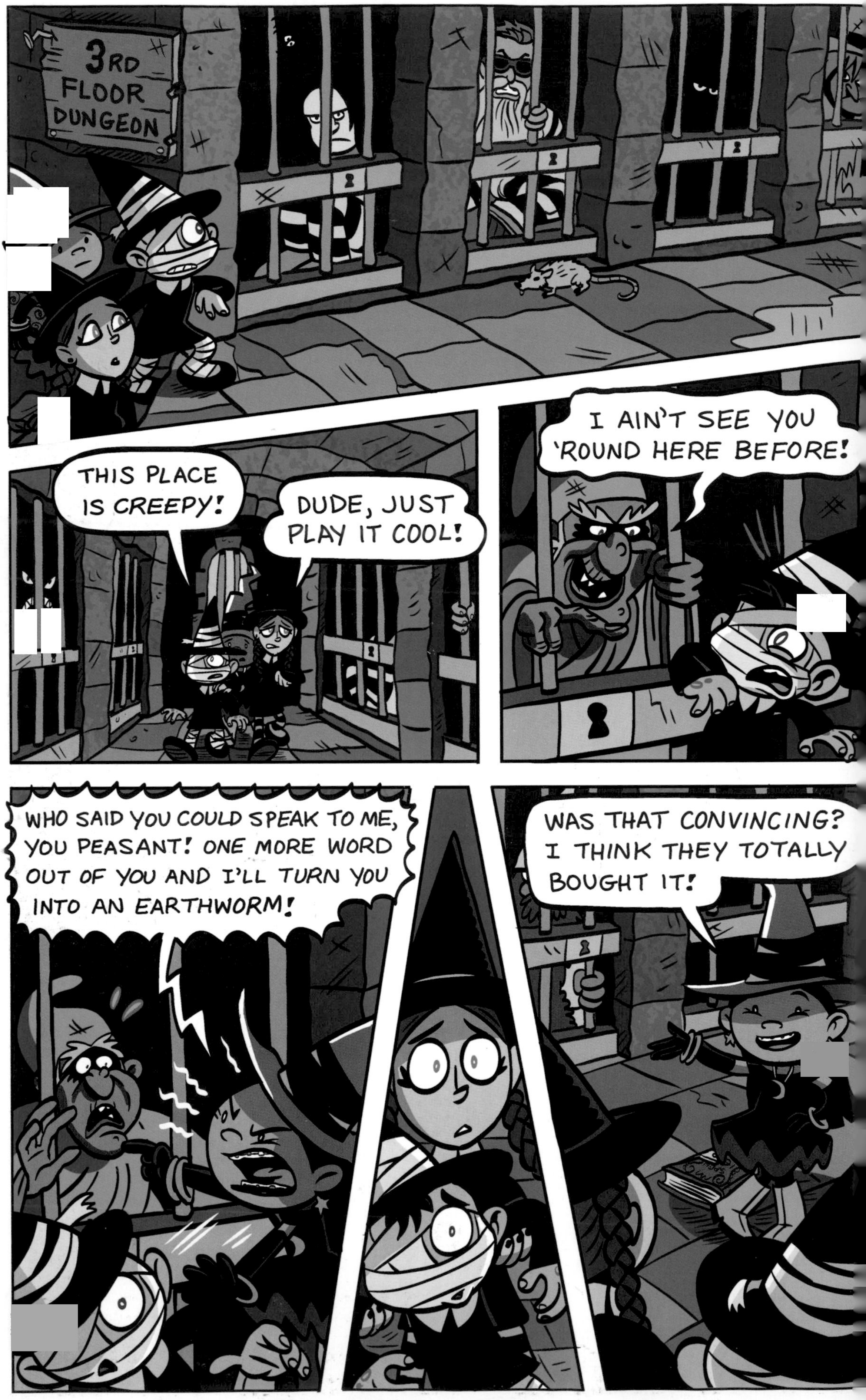
3RD FLOOR DUNGEON
THIS PLACE IS CREEPY!
DUDE, JUST PLAY IT COOL!
I AIN'T SEE YOU 'ROUND HERE BEFORE!
WHO SAID YOU COULD SPEAK TO ME, YOU PEASANT! ONE MORE WORD OUT OF YOU AND I'LL TURN YOU INTO AN EARTHWORM!
WAS THAT CONVINCING? I THINK THEY TOTALLY BOUGHT IT!

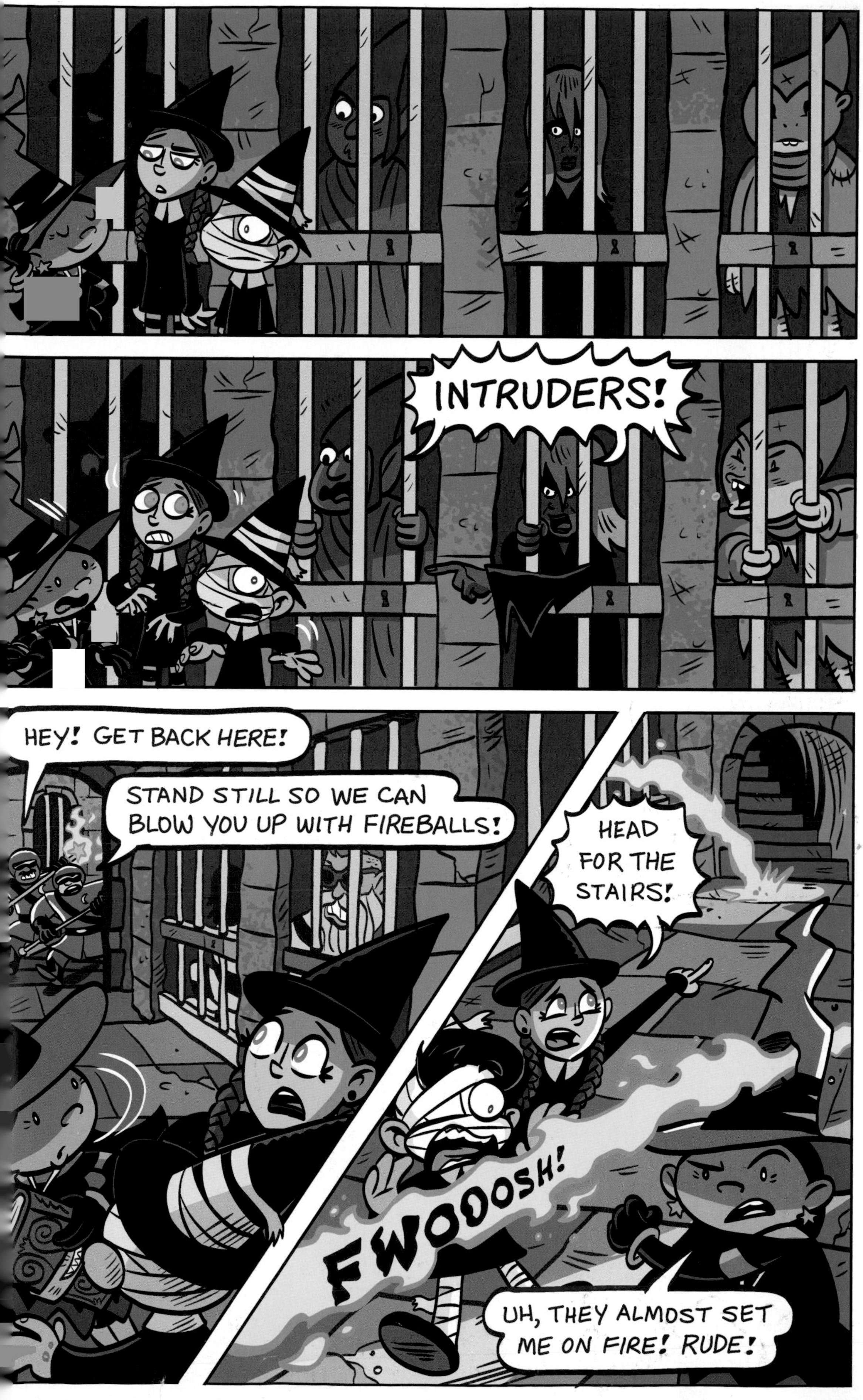
INTRUDERS!
HEY! GET BACK HERE!
STAND STILL SO WE CAN BLOW YOU UP WITH FIREBALLS!
HEAD FOR THE STAIRS!
FWOOOSH!
UH, THEY ALMOST SET ME ON FIRE! RUDE!

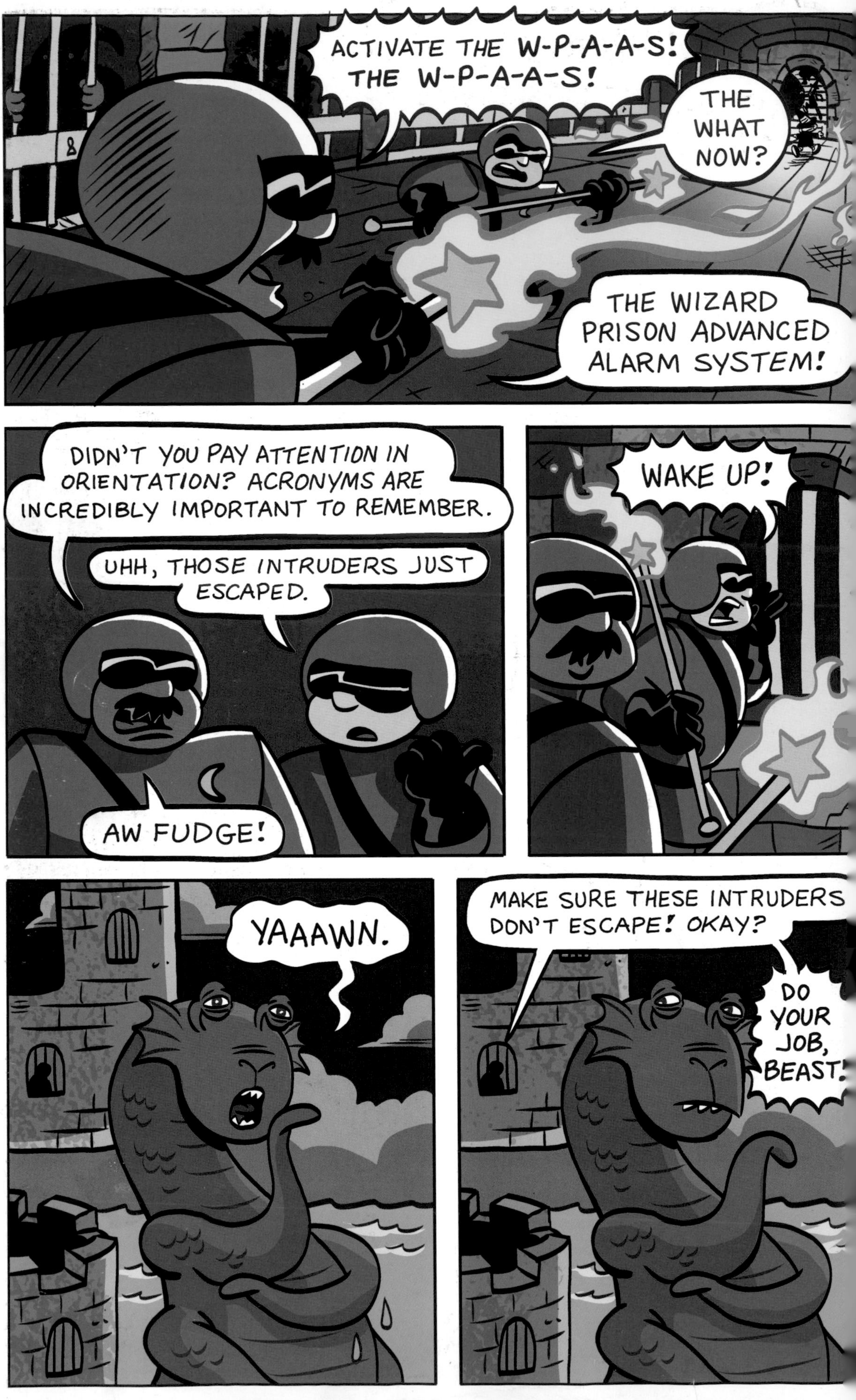
ACTIVATE THE W-P-A-A-S! THE W-P-A-A-S!
THE WHAT NOW?
THE WIZARD PRISON ADVANCED ALARM SYSTEM!
DIDN'T YOU PAY ATTENTION IN ORIENTATION? ACRONYMS ARE INCREDIBLY IMPORTANT TO REMEMBER.
UHH, THOSE INTRUDERS JUST ESCAPED.
AW FUDGE!
WAKE UP!
YAAAWN.
MAKE SURE THESE INTRUDERS DON'T ESCAPE! OKAY?
DO YOUR JOB, BEAST!

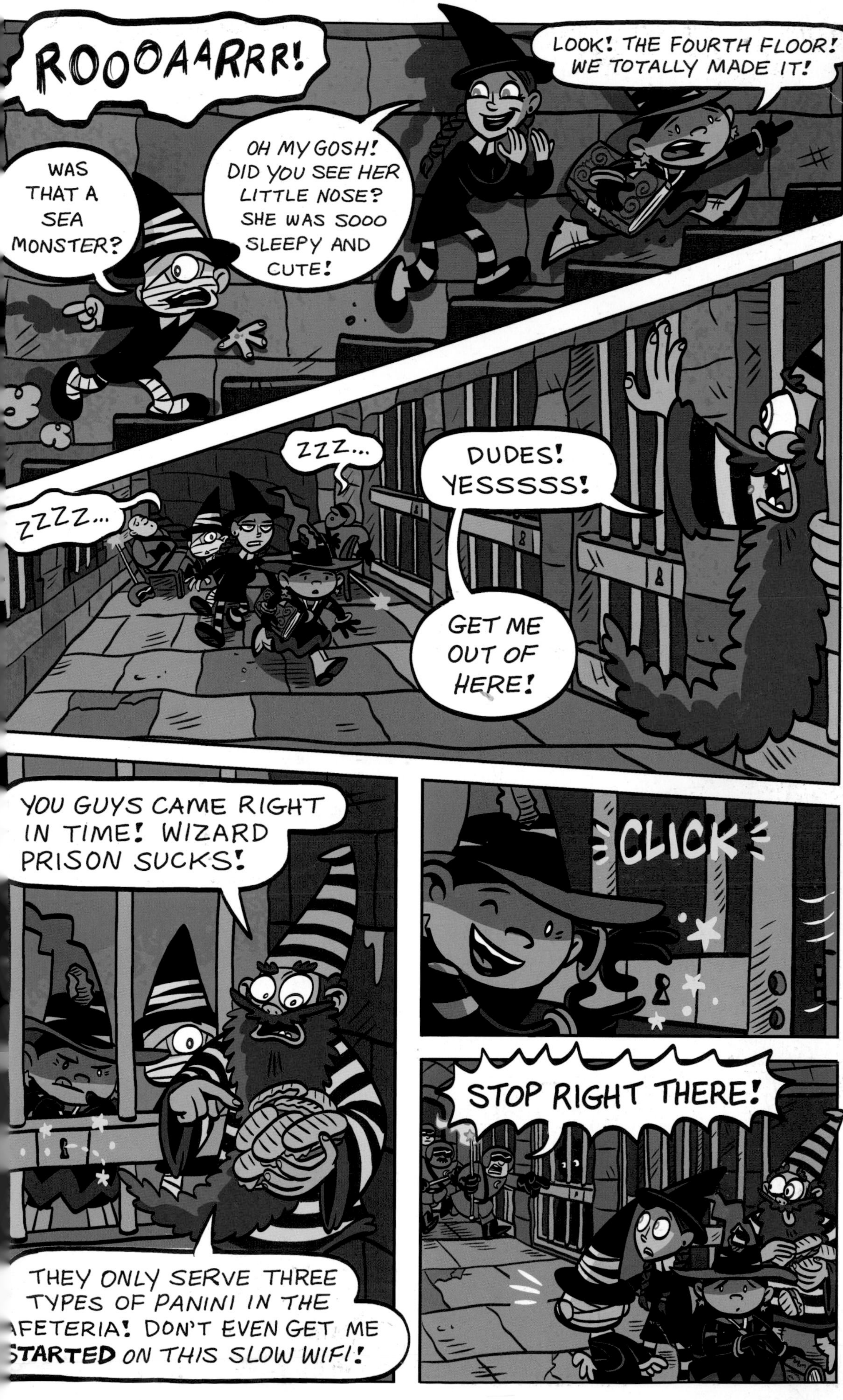
ROOOAARRR!
LOOK! THE FOURTH FLOOR! WE TOTALLY MADE IT!
WAS THAT A SEA MONSTER?
OH MY GOSH! DID YOU SEE HER LITTLE NOSE? SHE WAS SOOO SLEEPY AND CUTE!
ZZZZ...
ZZZ...
DUDES! YESSSSS!
GET ME OUT OF HERE!
YOU GUYS CAME RIGHT IN TIME! WIZARD PRISON SUCKS!
THEY ONLY SERVE THREE TYPES OF PANINI IN THE AFETERIA! DON'T EVEN GET ME STARTED ON THIS SLOW WIFI!
CLICK
STOP RIGHT THERE!

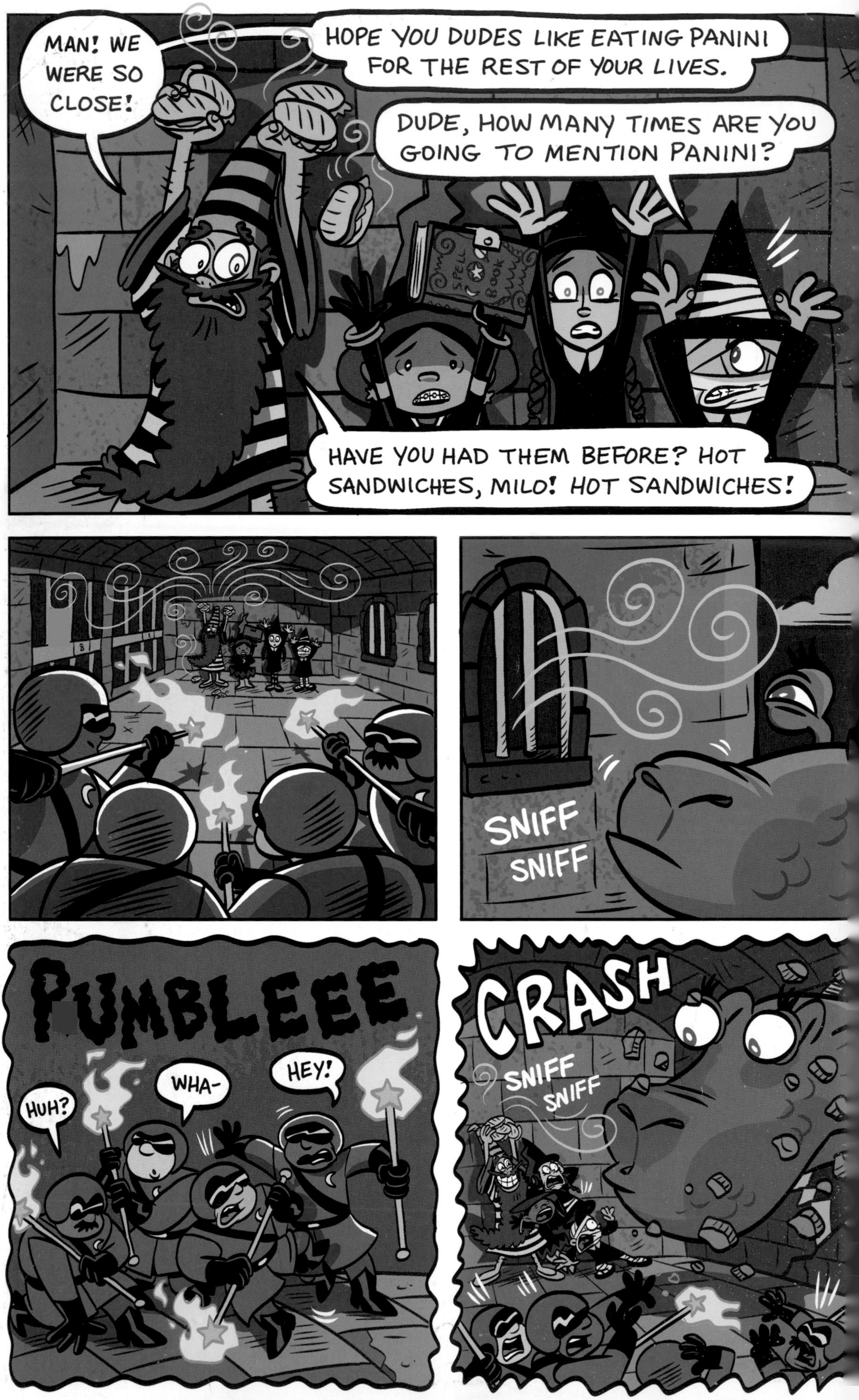
MAN! WE WERE SO CLOSE!
HOPE YOU DUDES LIKE EATING PANINI FOR THE REST OF YOUR LIVES.
DUDE, HOW MANY TIMES ARE YOU GOING TO MENTION PANINI?
HAVE YOU HAD THEM BEFORE? HOT SANDWICHES, MILO! HOT SANDWICHES!
SNIFF
SNIFF
PUMBLEEE
HUH?
WHA-
HEY!
CRASH
SNIFF
SNIFF

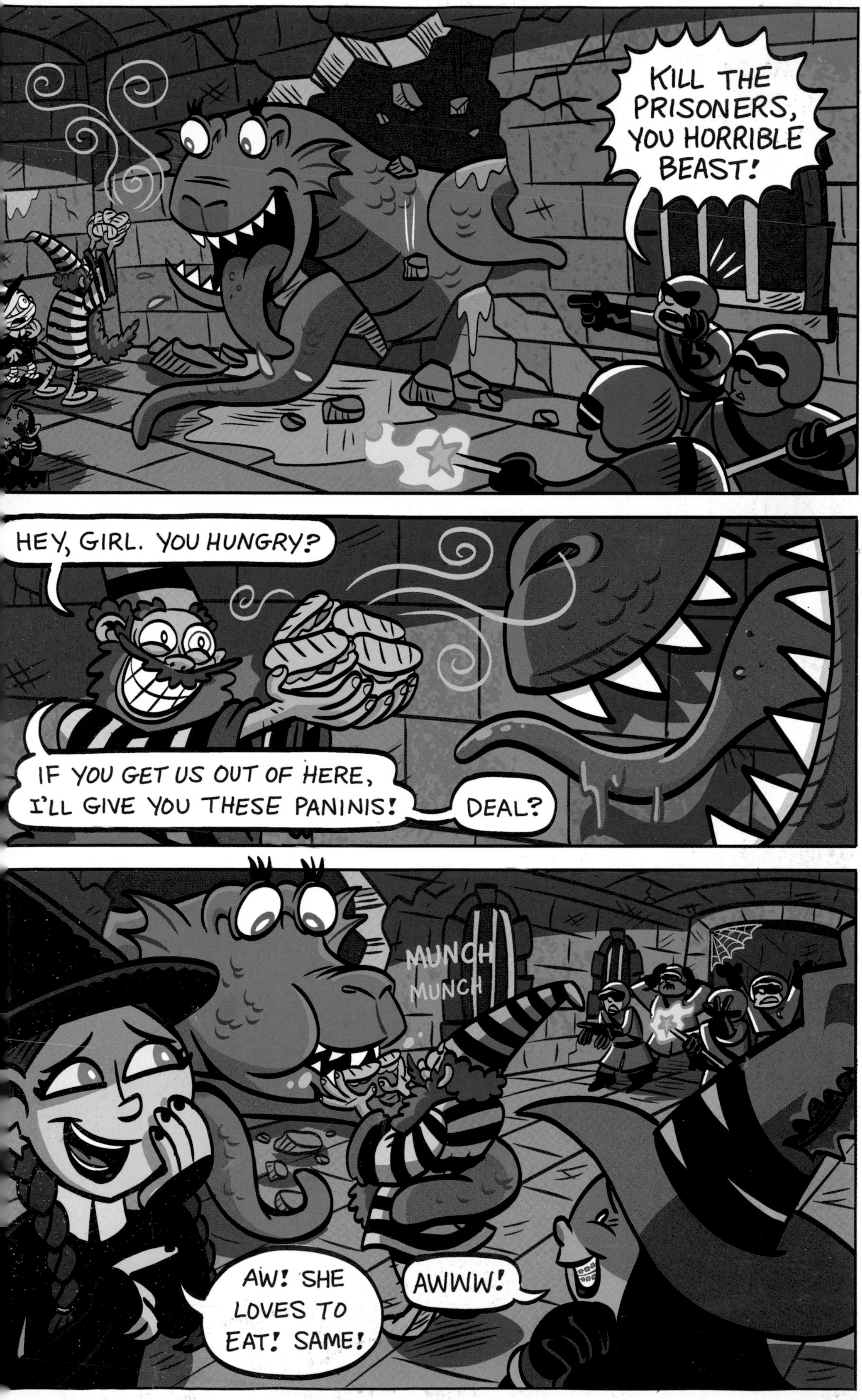
KILL THE PRISONERS, YOU HORRIBLE BEAST!
HEY, GIRL. YOU HUNGRY?
IF YOU GET US OUT OF HERE, I'LL GIVE YOU THESE PANINIS!
DEAL?
MUNCH MUNCH
AW! SHE LOVES TO EAT! SAME!
AWWW!

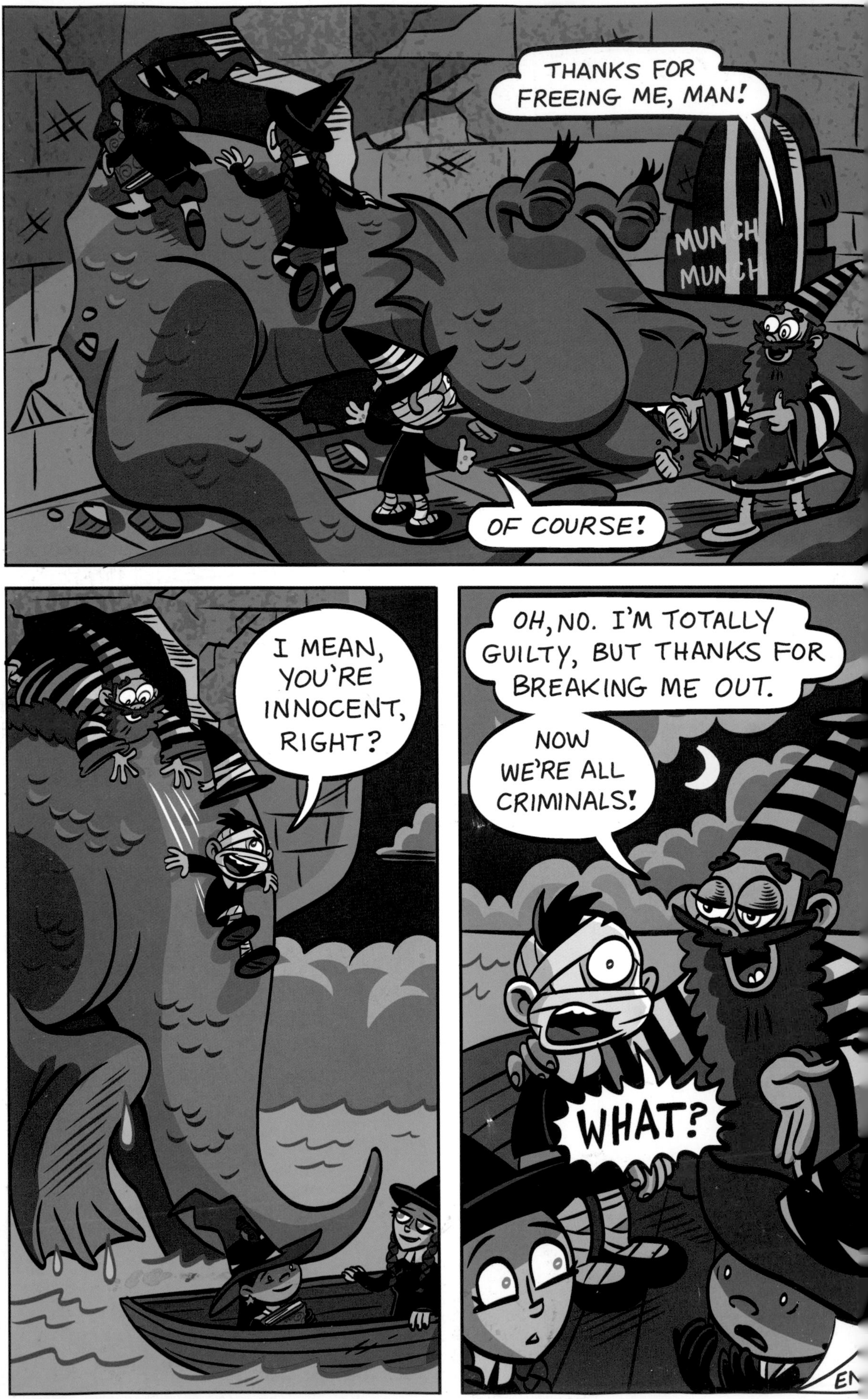

THANKS FOR FREEING ME, MAN!
MUNCH
MUNCH
OF COURSE!
I MEAN, YOU'RE INNOCENT, RIGHT?
OH, NO. I'M TOTALLY GUILTY, BUT THANKS FOR BREAKING ME OUT.
NOW WE'RE ALL CRIMINALS!
WHAT?

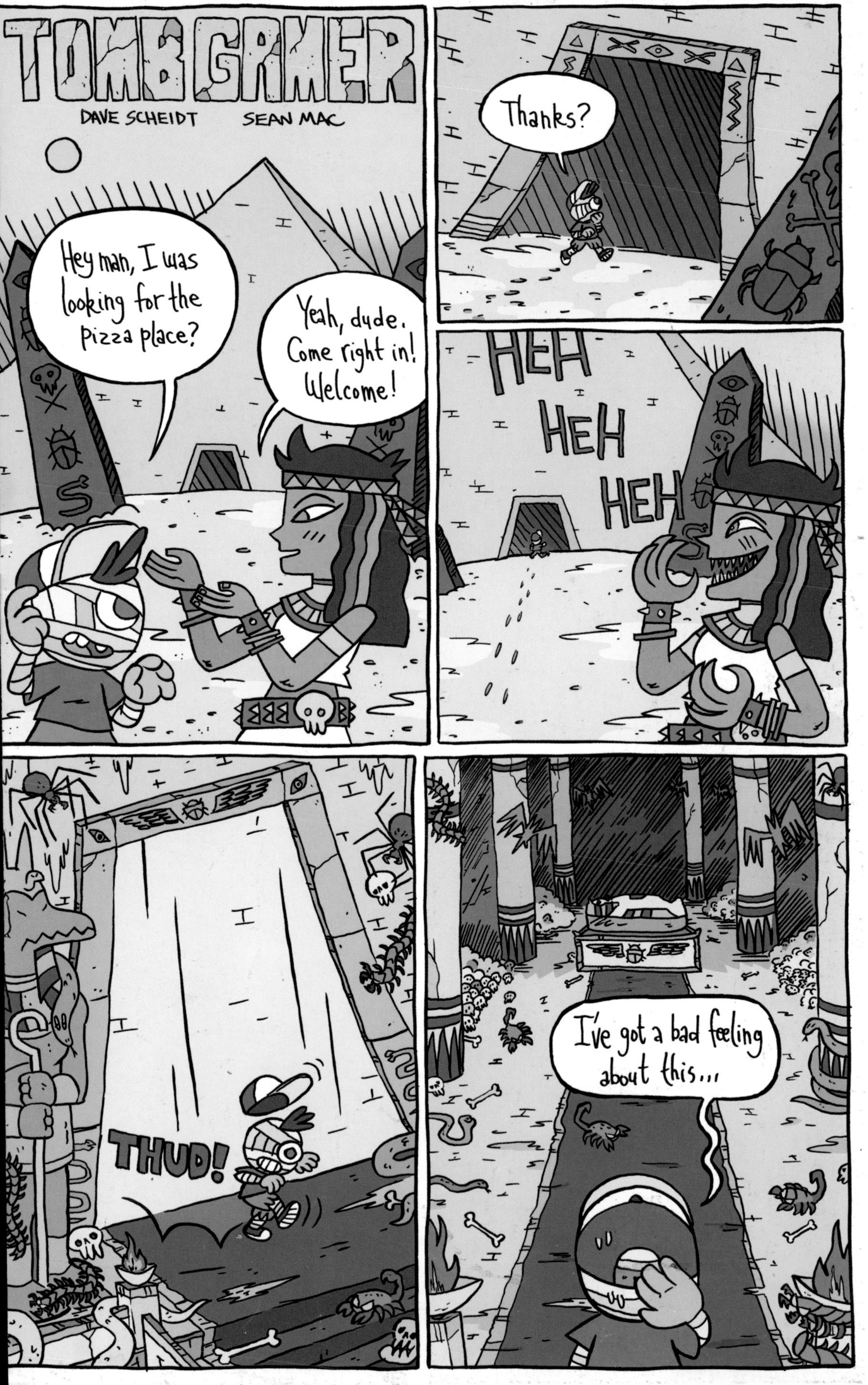
TOMB GAMER
DAVE SCHEIDT
SEAN MAC
Hey man, I was looking for the pizza place?
Yeah, dude. Come right in! Welcome!
Thanks?
HEH HEH HEH
THUD!
I've got a bad feeling about this...

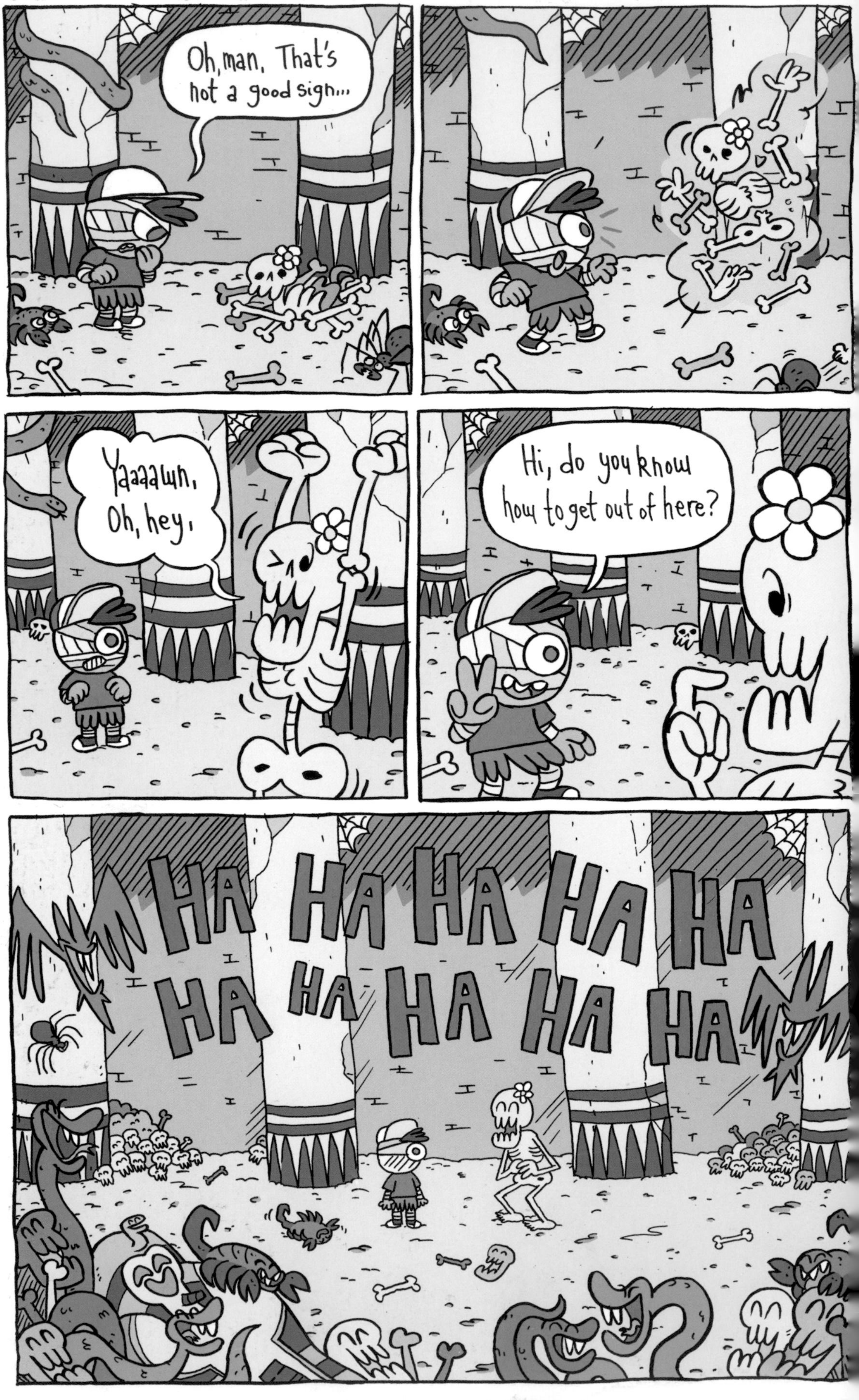
Oh, man. That's not a good sign...
Yaaaawn. Oh, hey.
Hi, do you know how to get out of here?
HA HA HA HA HA HA HA HA HA HA HA

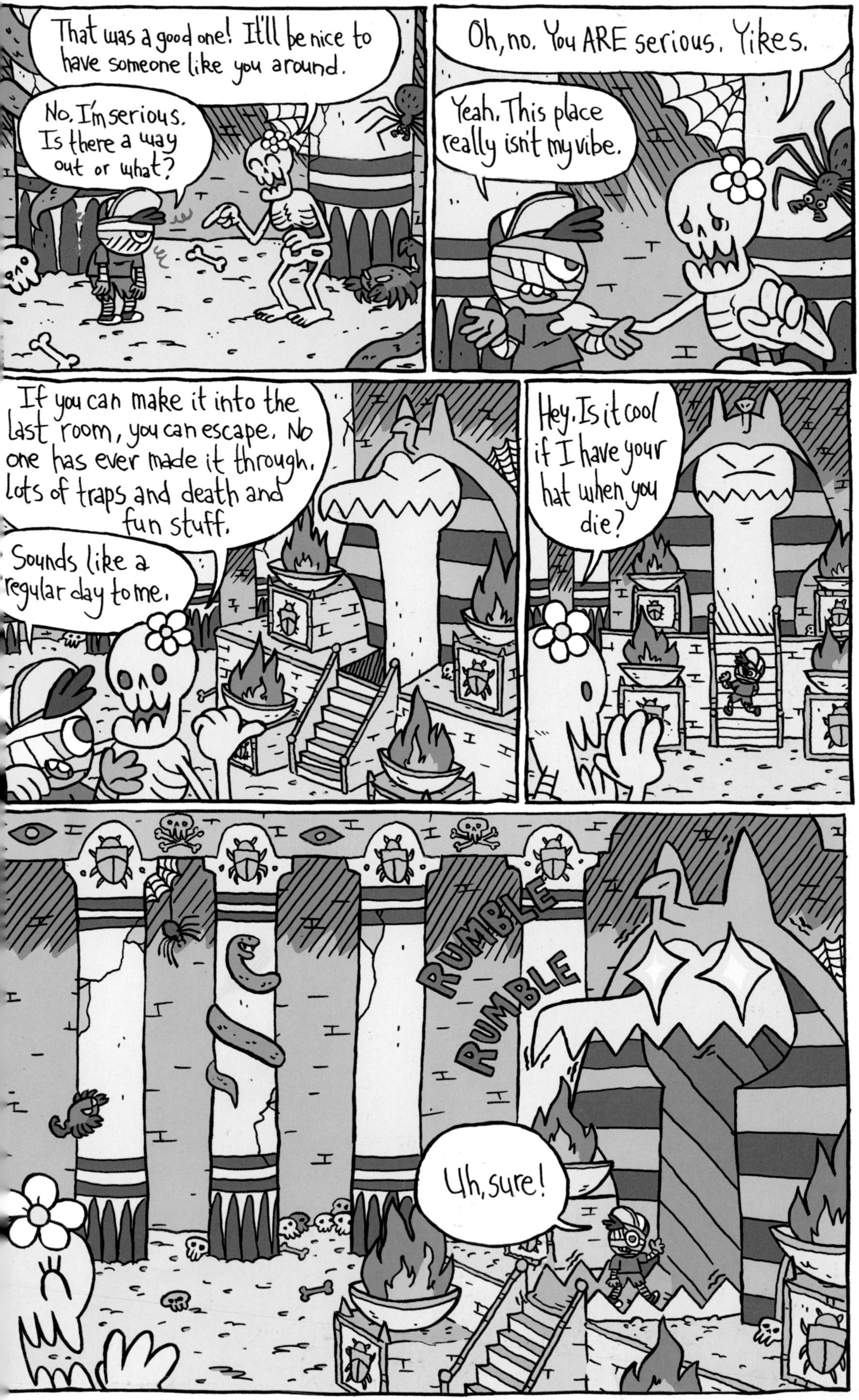
That was a good one! It'll be nice to have someone like you around.
No, I'm serious. Is there a way out or what?
Oh, no. You ARE serious. Yikes.
Yeah. This place really isn't my vibe.
If you can make it into the last room, you can escape. No one has ever made it through. Lots of traps and death and fun stuff.
Sounds like a regular day to me.
Hey. Is it cool if I have your hat when you die?
RUMBLE
RUMBLE
Uh, sure!

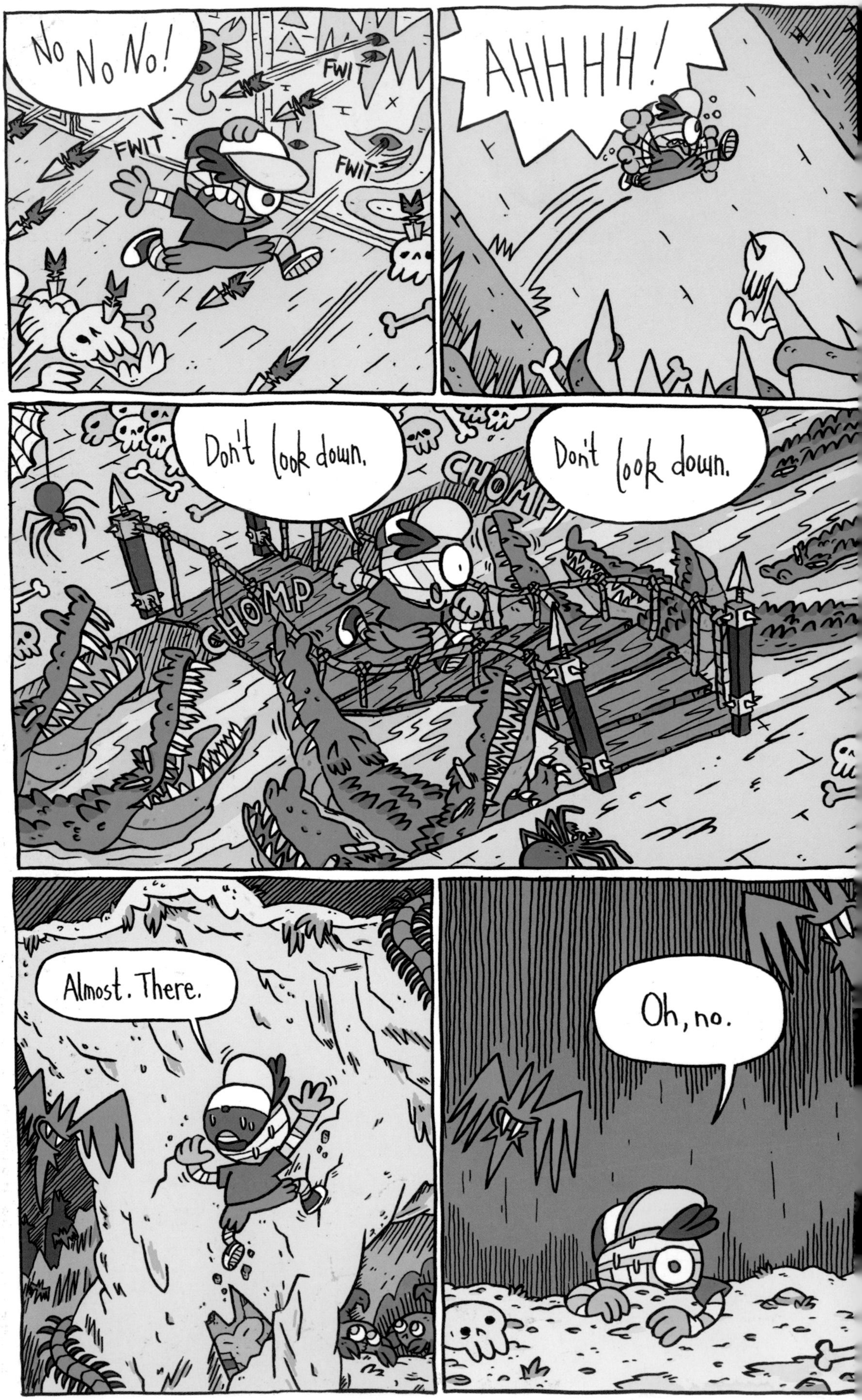
No No No!
FWIT
FWIT
FWIT
AHHHH!
Don't look down.
CHOMP
CHOMP
Don't look down.
Almost. There.
Oh, no.

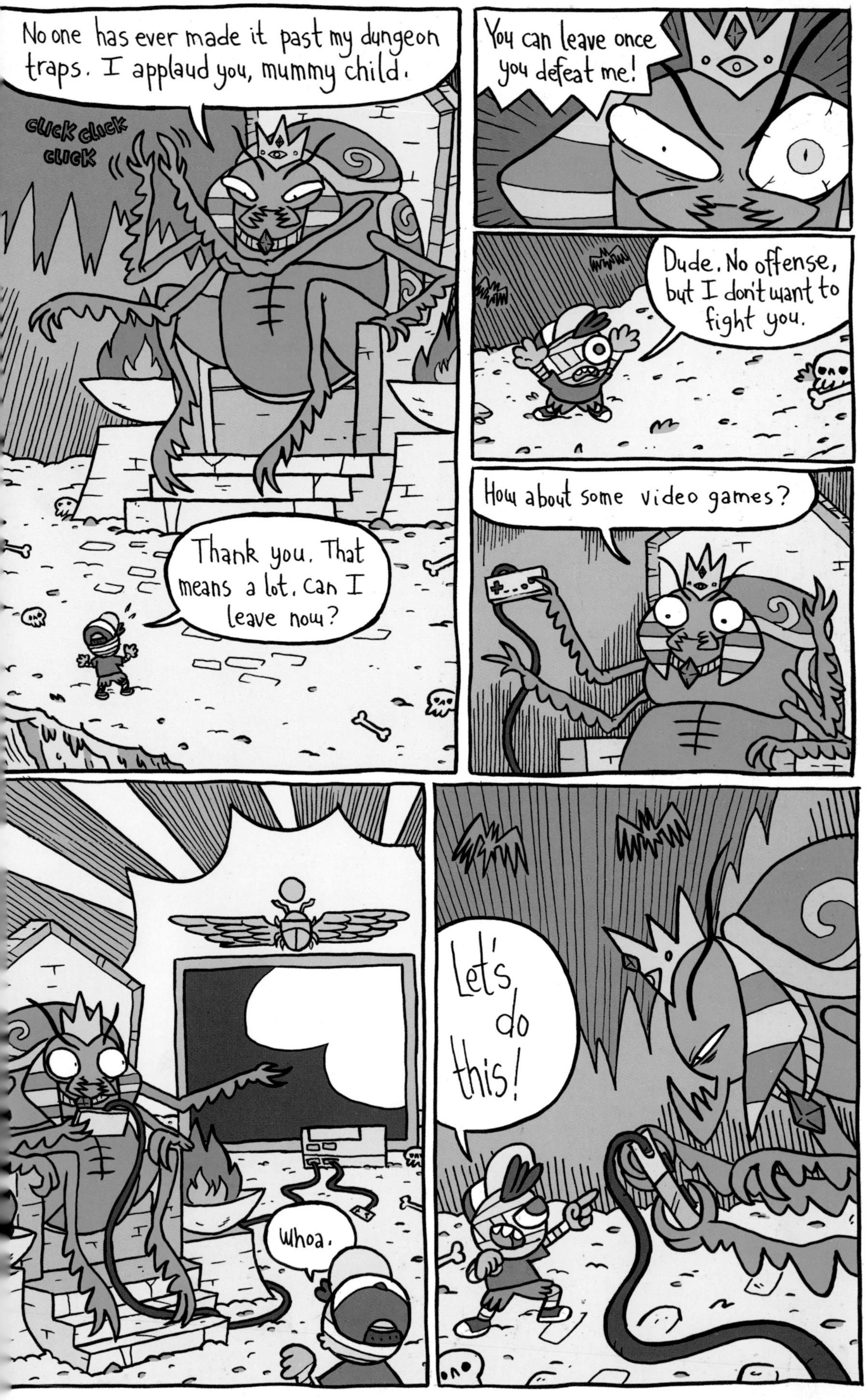
No one has ever made it past my dungeon traps. I applaud you, mummy child.
CLICK CLICK CLICK
You can leave once you defeat me!
Thank you. That means a lot. Can I leave now?
Dude. No offense, but I don't want to fight you.
How about some video games?
Whoa.
Let's do this!

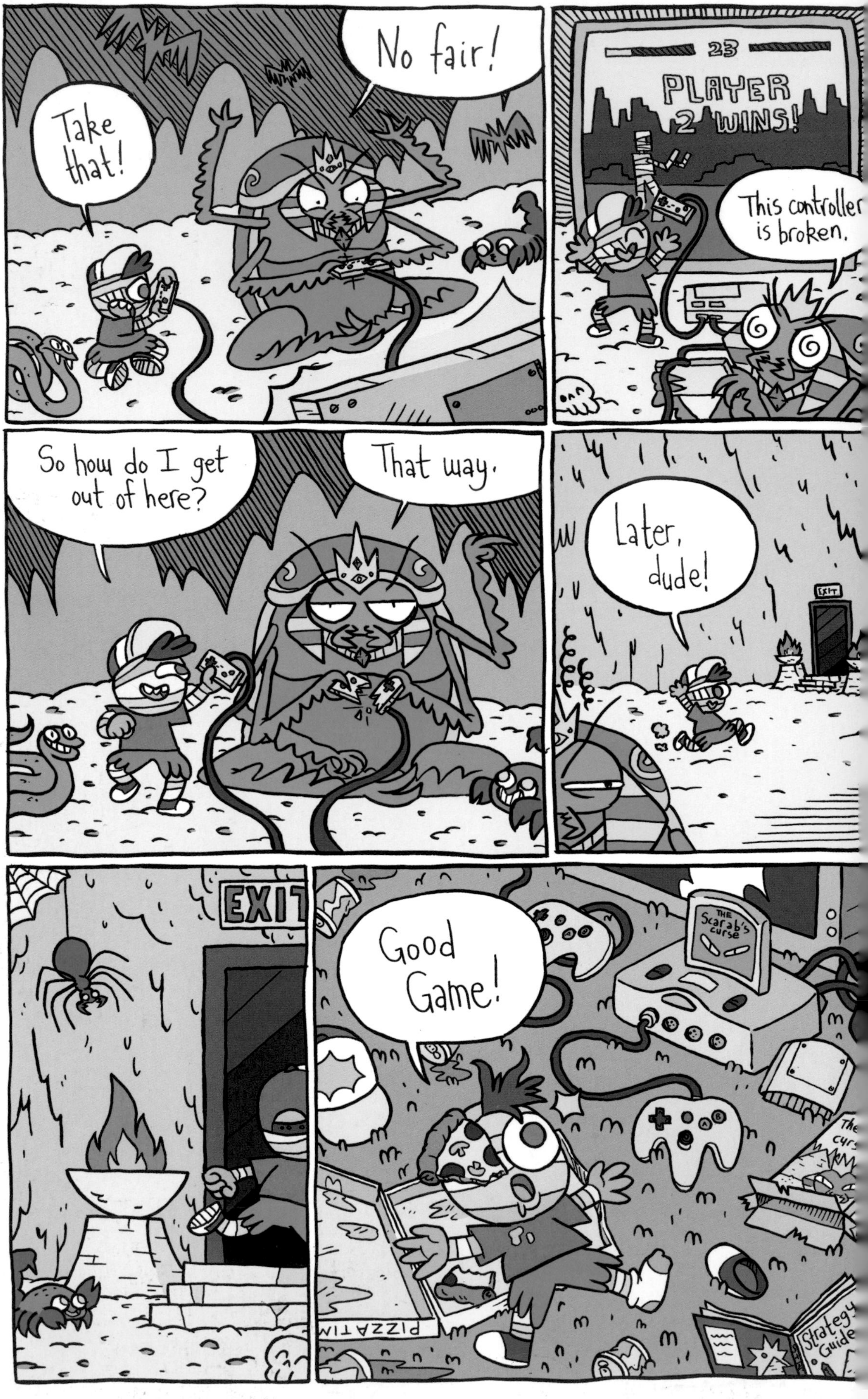
Take that!
No fair!
23
PLAYER 2 WINS!
This controller is broken.
So how do I get out of here?
That way.
Later, dude!
EXIT
EXIT
Good Game!
THE Scarab's curse
Strategy Guide

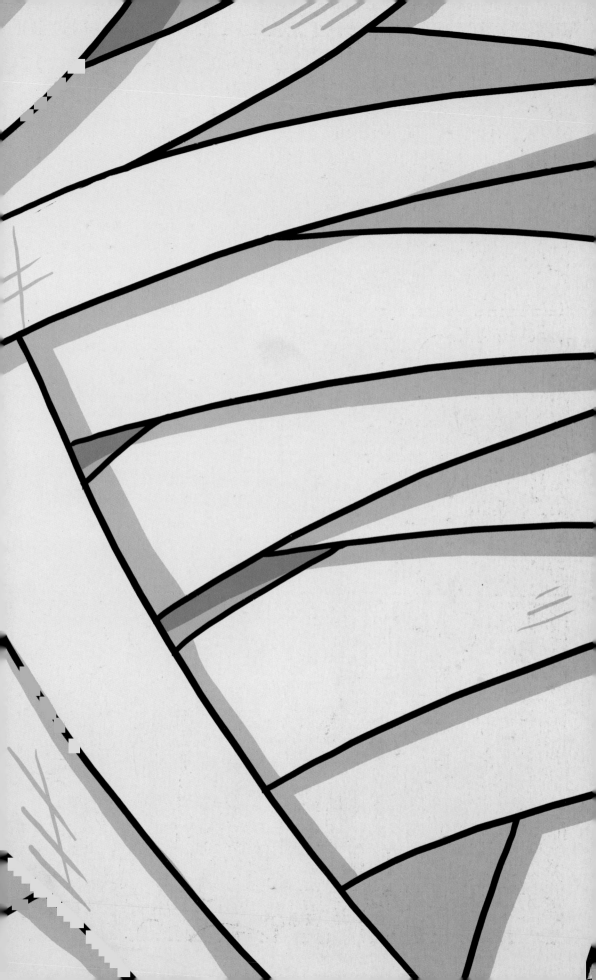

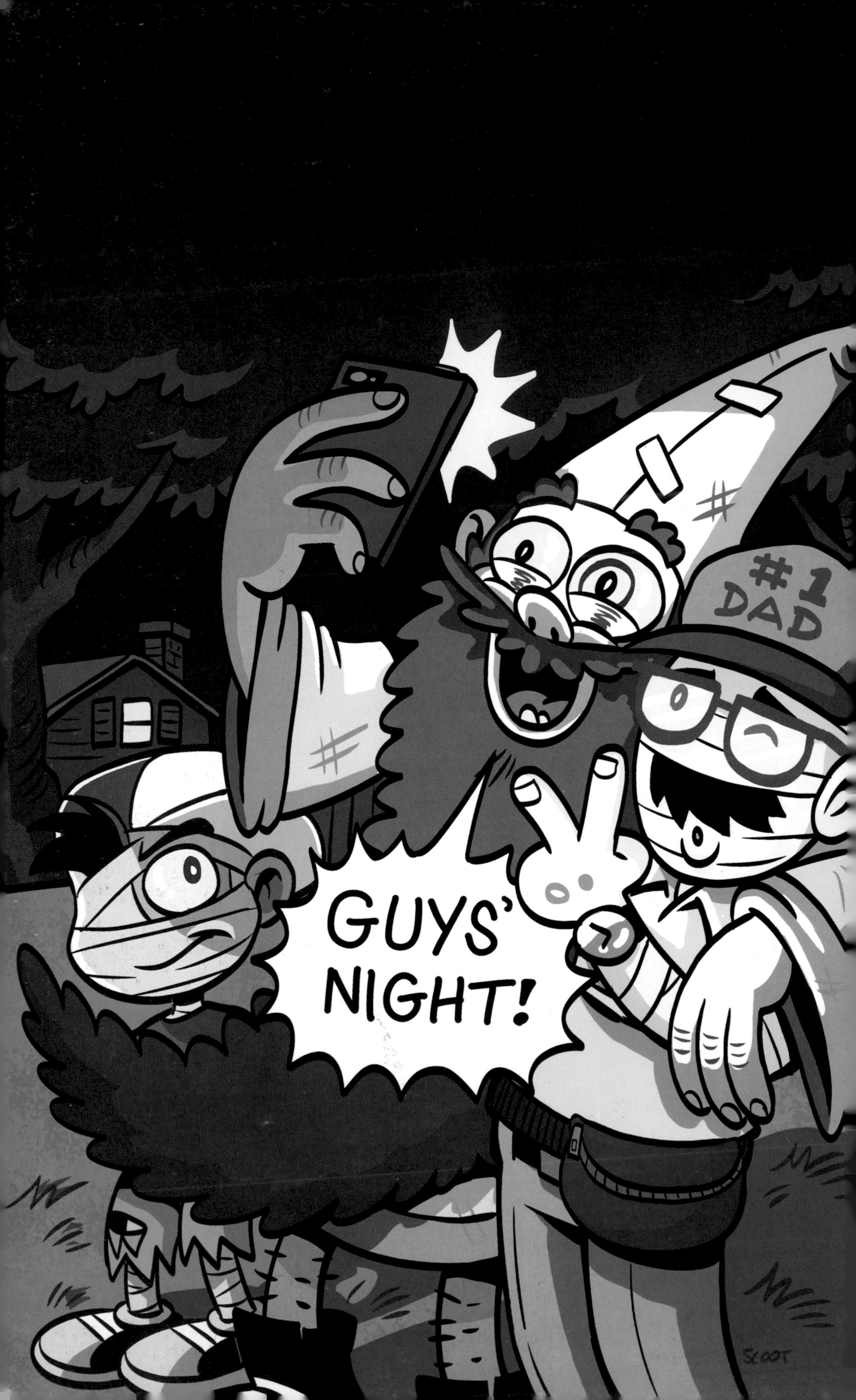
#1 DAD
GUYS' NIGHT!
SCOOT

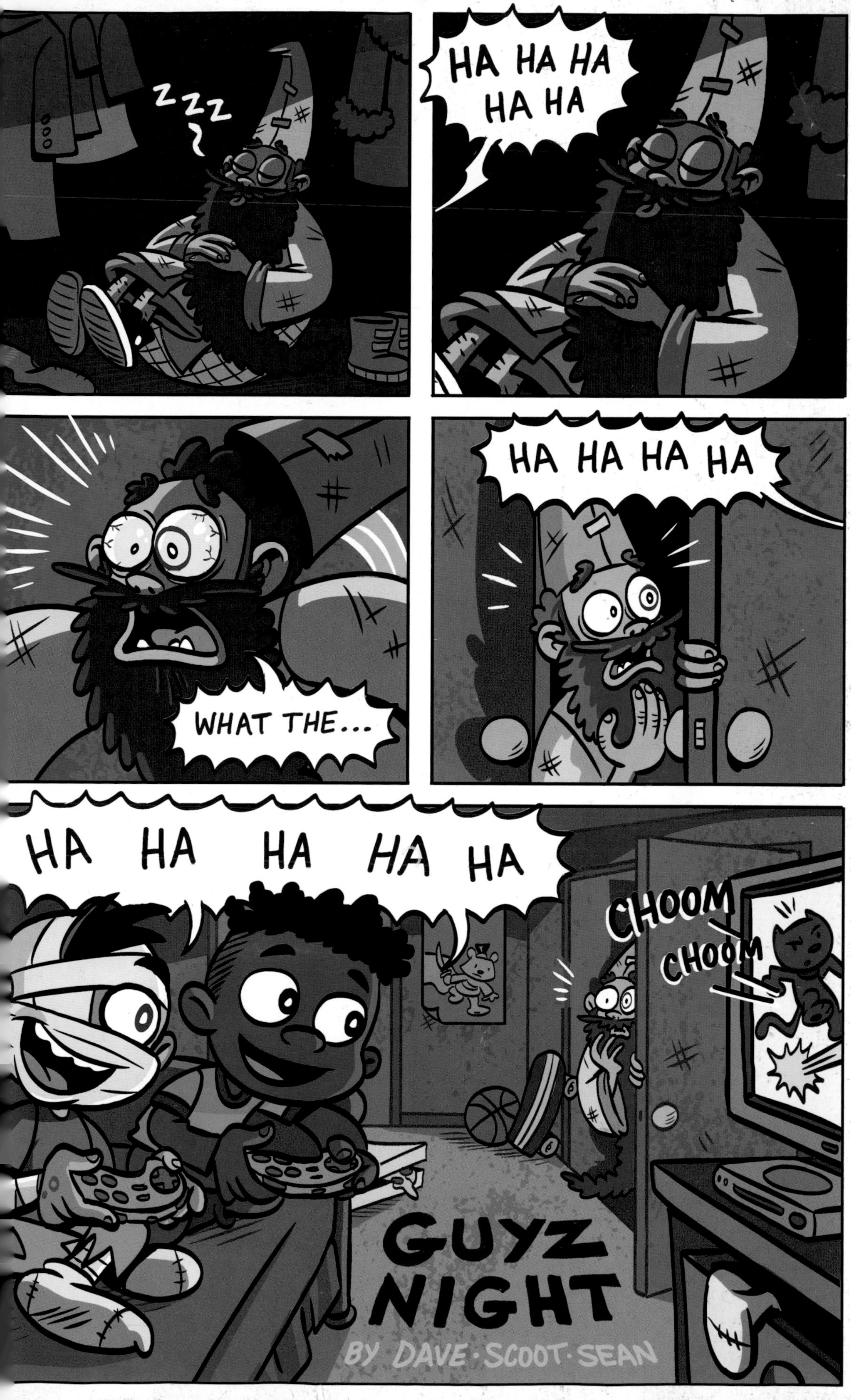
ZZZ
HA HA HA HA HA
WHAT THE...
HA HA HA HA
HA HA HA HA HA
CHOOM
CHOOM
GUYZ NIGHT
BY DAVE · SCOOT · SEAN

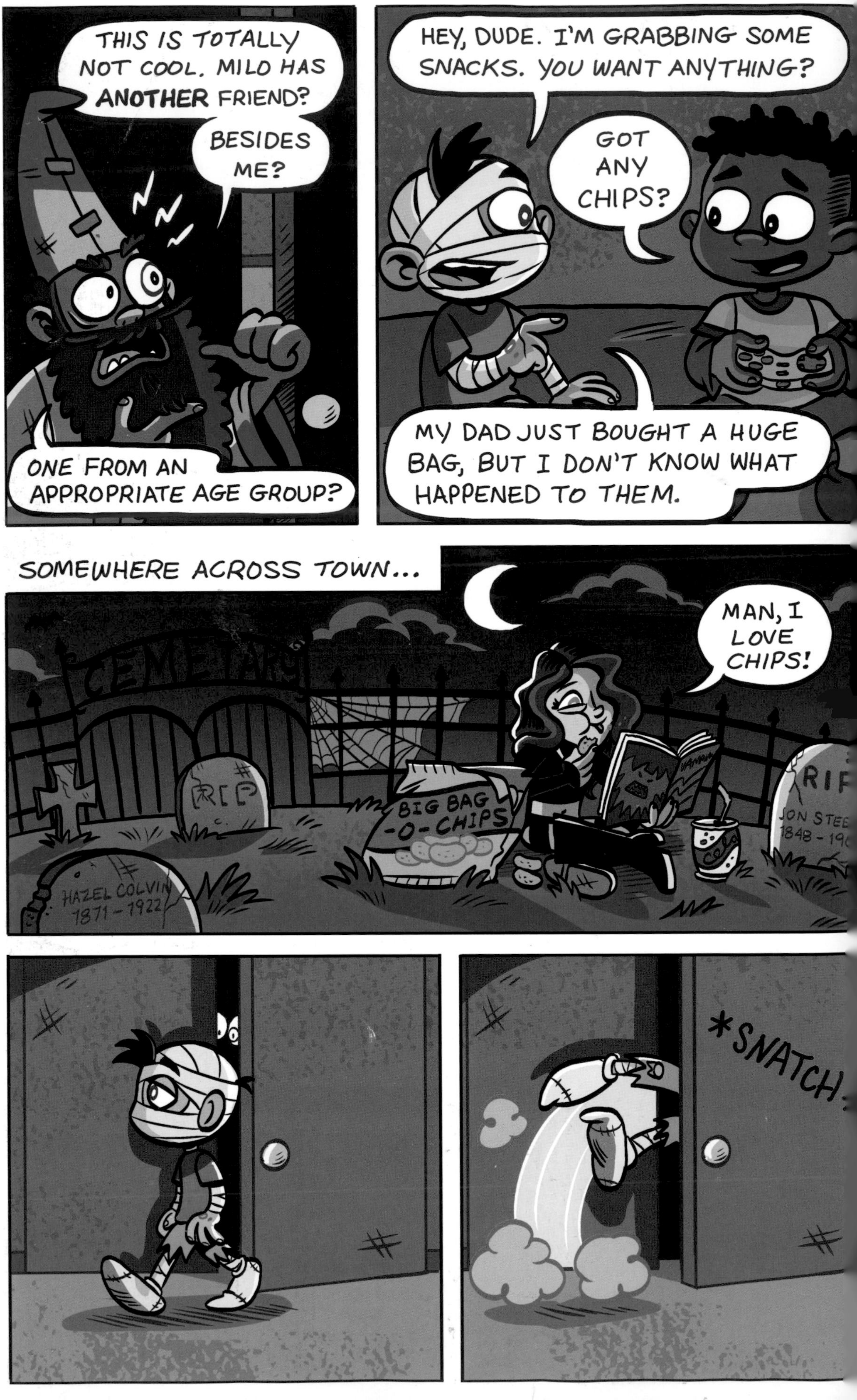
THIS IS TOTALLY NOT COOL. MILO HAS ANOTHER FRIEND?
BESIDES ME?
ONE FROM AN APPROPRIATE AGE GROUP?
HEY, DUDE. I'M GRABBING SOME SNACKS. YOU WANT ANYTHING?
GOT ANY CHIPS?
MY DAD JUST BOUGHT A HUGE BAG, BUT I DON'T KNOW WHAT HAPPENED TO THEM.
SOMEWHERE ACROSS TOWN...
CEMETARY
MAN, I LOVE CHIPS!
BIG BAG -O- CHIPS
RIP
HAZEL COLVIN 1871 - 1922
SNATCH

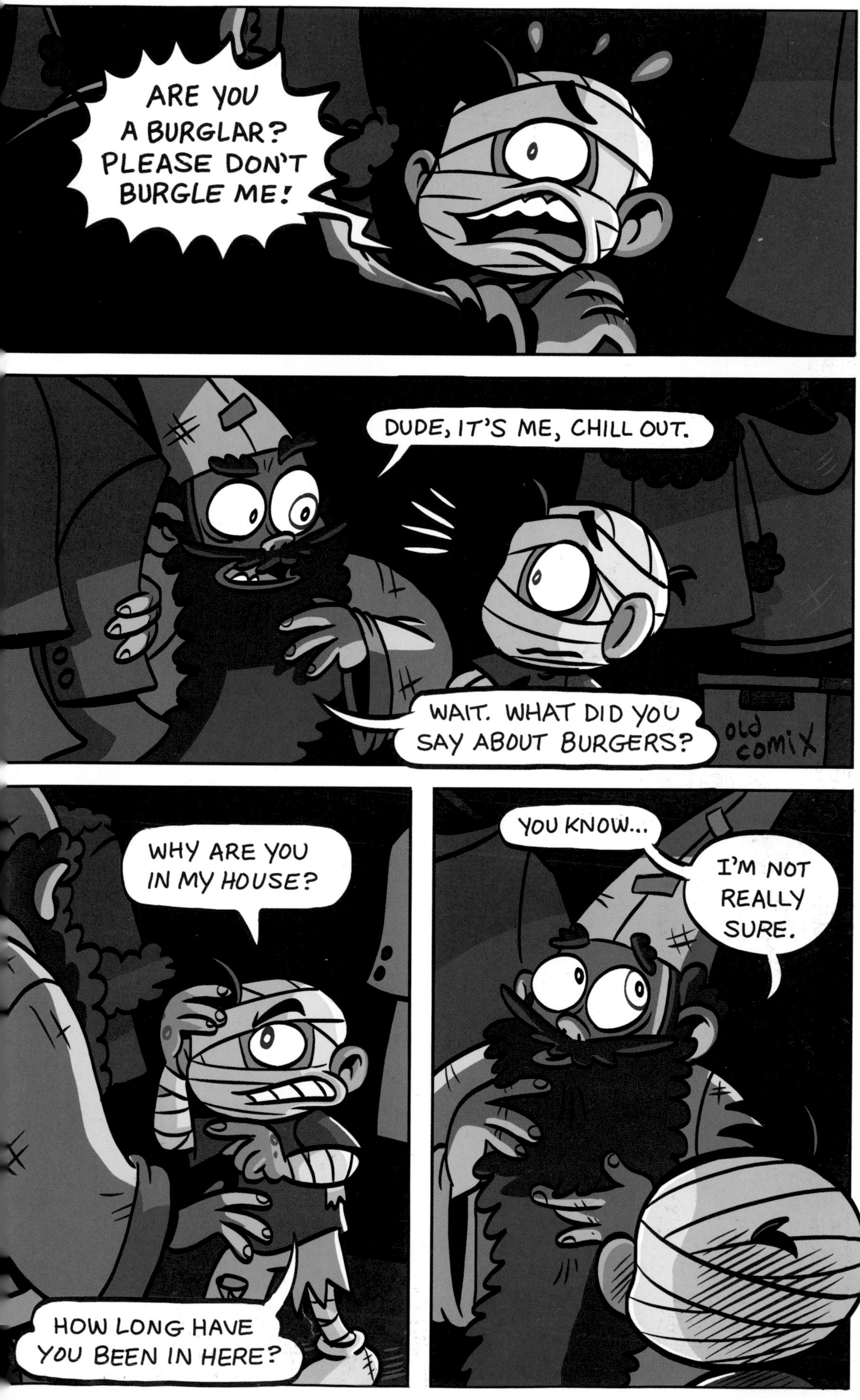
ARE YOU A BURGLAR? PLEASE DON'T BURGLE ME!
DUDE, IT'S ME, CHILL OUT.
WAIT. WHAT DID YOU SAY ABOUT BURGERS?
old comix
WHY ARE YOU IN MY HOUSE?
HOW LONG HAVE YOU BEEN IN HERE?
YOU KNOW...
I'M NOT REALLY SURE.

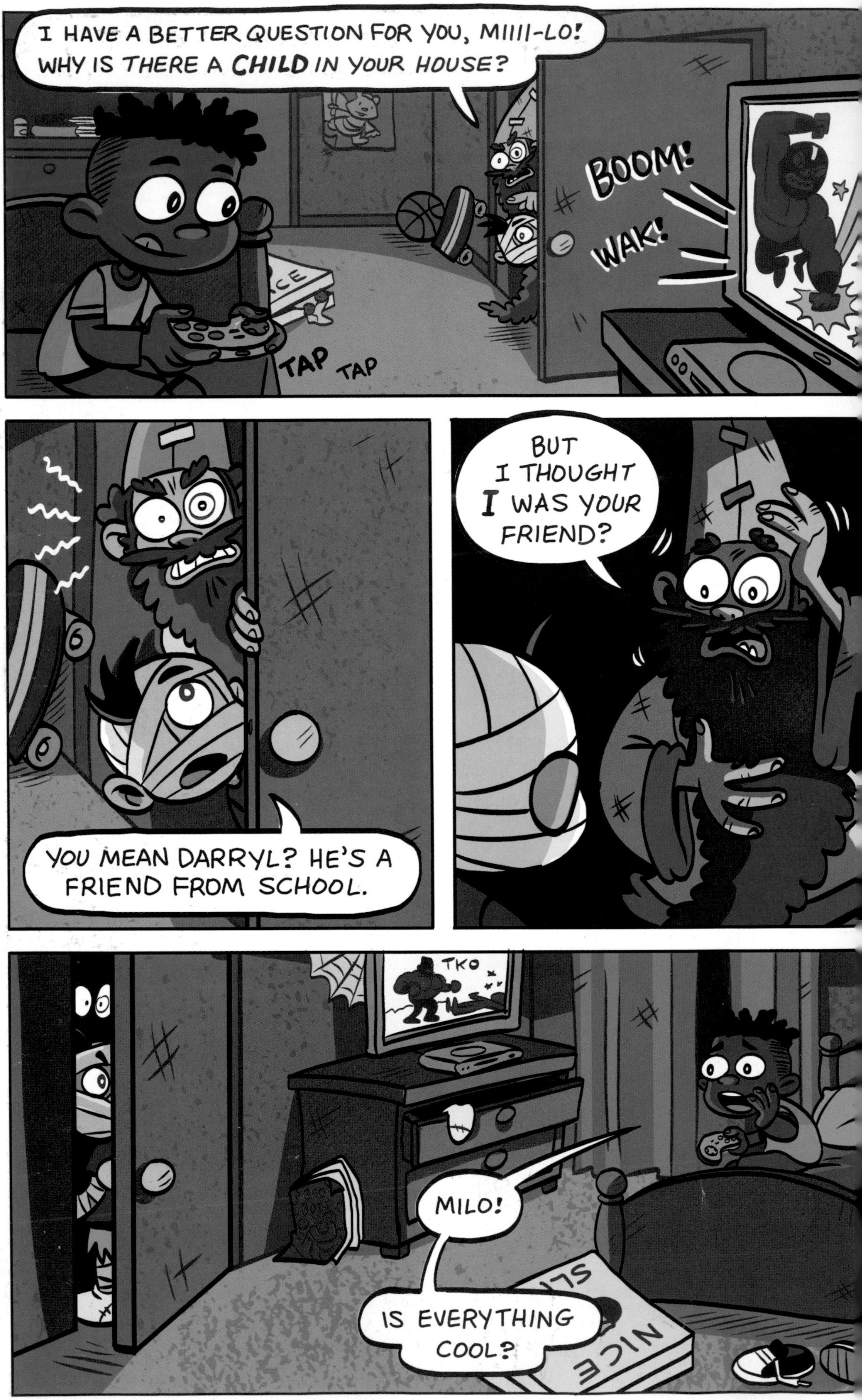
I HAVE A BETTER QUESTION FOR YOU, MIIII-LO! WHY IS THERE A CHILD IN YOUR HOUSE?
BOOM!
WAK!
TAP TAP
YOU MEAN DARRYL? HE'S A FRIEND FROM SCHOOL.
BUT I THOUGHT I WAS YOUR FRIEND?
TKO
MILO!
IS EVERYTHING COOL?
NICE

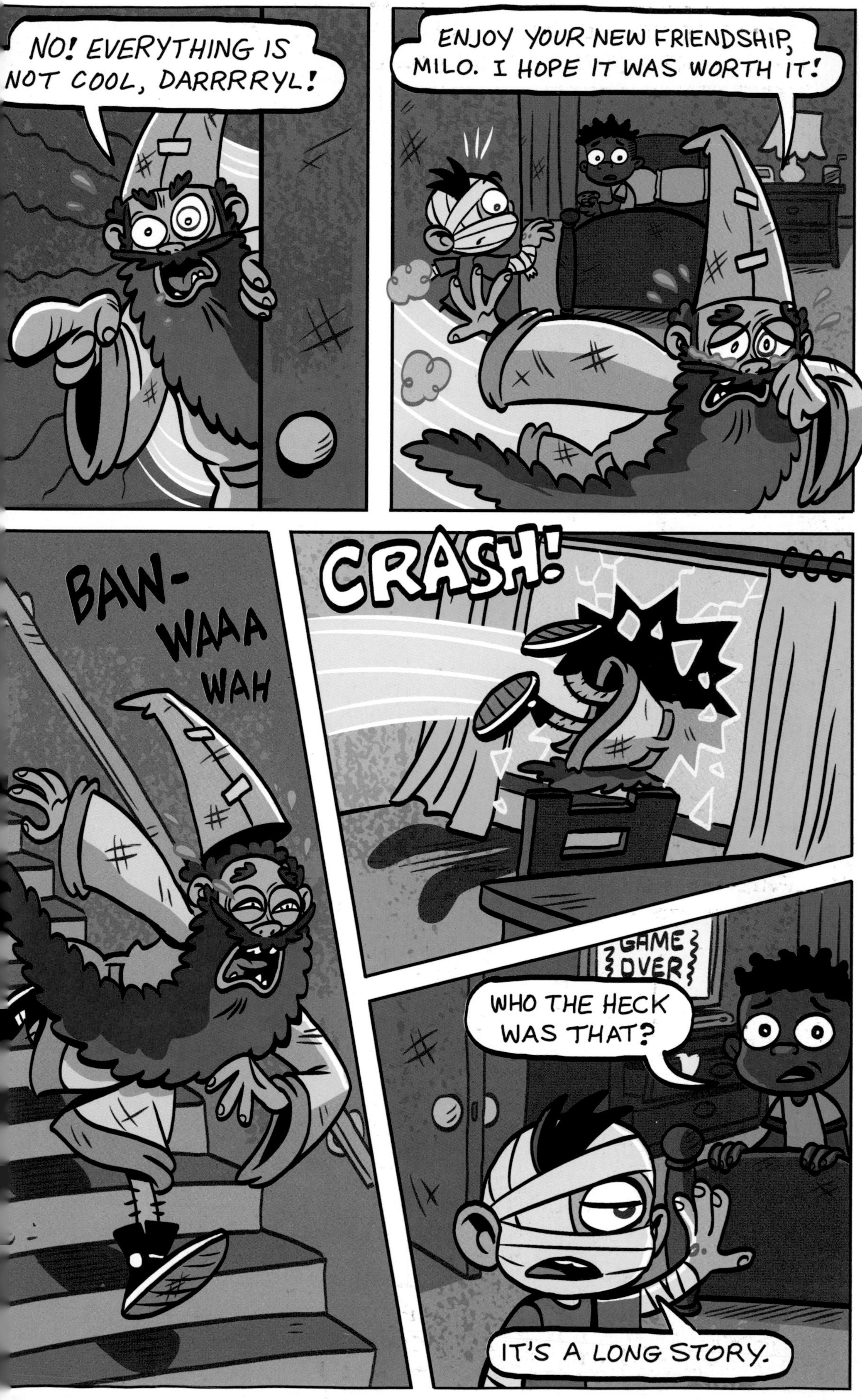
NO! EVERYTHING IS NOT COOL, DARRRRYL!
ENJOY YOUR NEW FRIENDSHIP, MILO. I HOPE IT WAS WORTH IT!
BAW-WAAA WAH
CRASH!
GAME OVER
WHO THE HECK WAS THAT?
IT'S A LONG STORY.

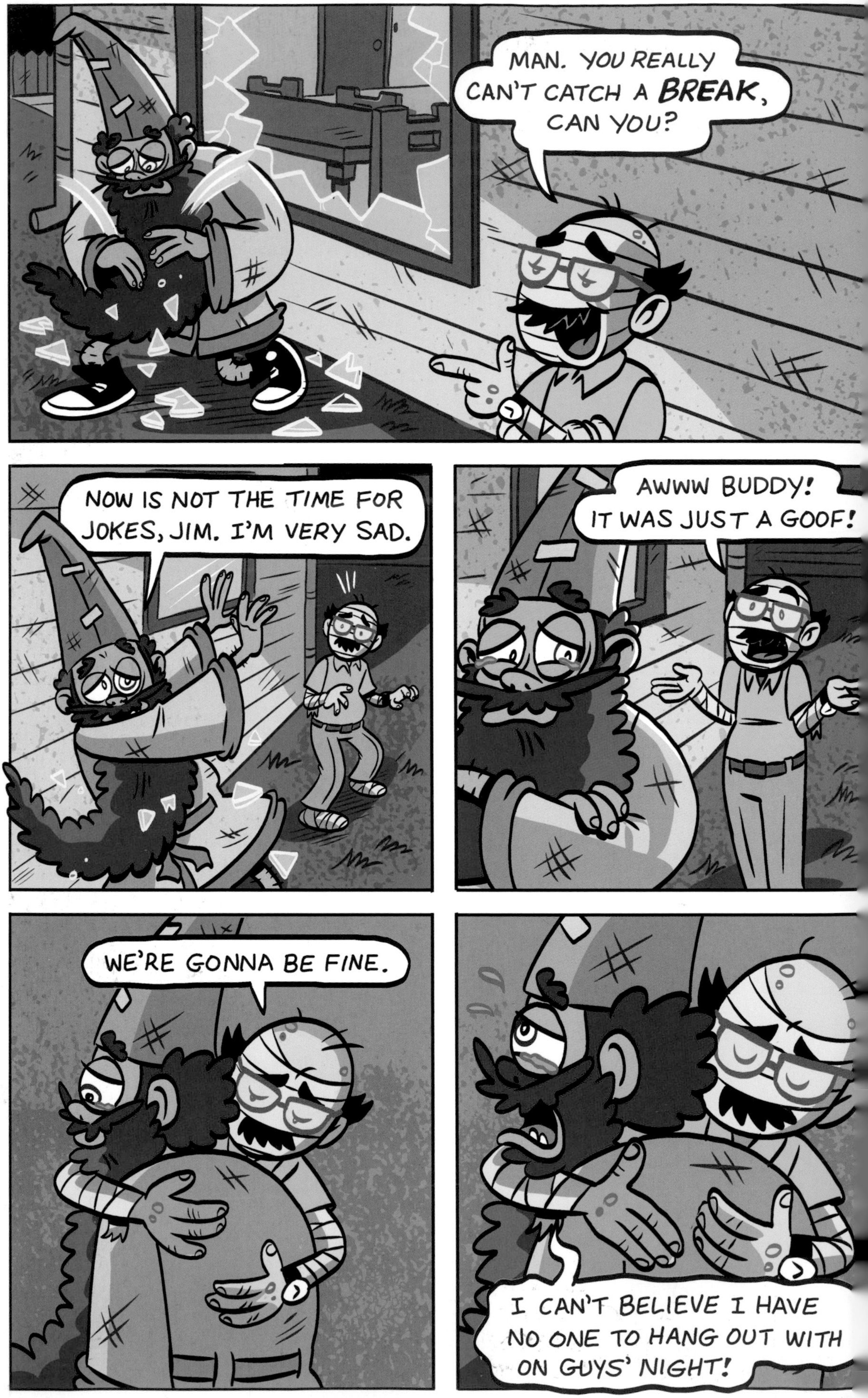
MAN. YOU REALLY CAN'T CATCH A BREAK, CAN YOU?
NOW IS NOT THE TIME FOR JOKES, JIM. I'M VERY SAD.
AWWW BUDDY! IT WAS JUST A GOOF!
WE'RE GONNA BE FINE.
I CAN'T BELIEVE I HAVE NO ONE TO HANG OUT WITH ON GUYS' NIGHT!

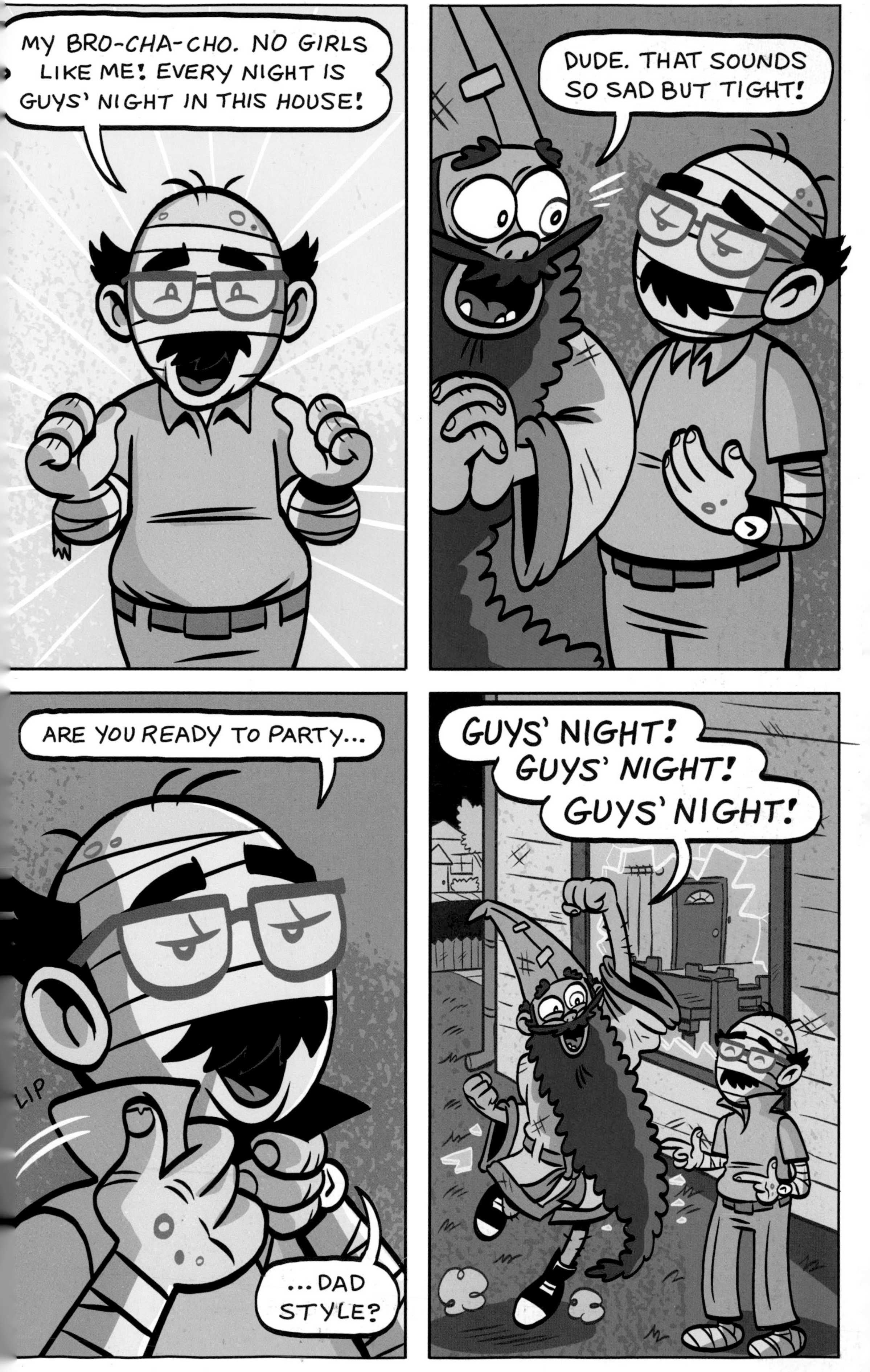
MY BRO-CHA-CHO. NO GIRLS LIKE ME! EVERY NIGHT IS GUYS' NIGHT IN THIS HOUSE!
DUDE. THAT SOUNDS SO SAD BUT TIGHT!
ARE YOU READY TO PARTY...
LIP
...DAD STYLE?
GUYS' NIGHT! GUYS' NIGHT! GUYS' NIGHT!

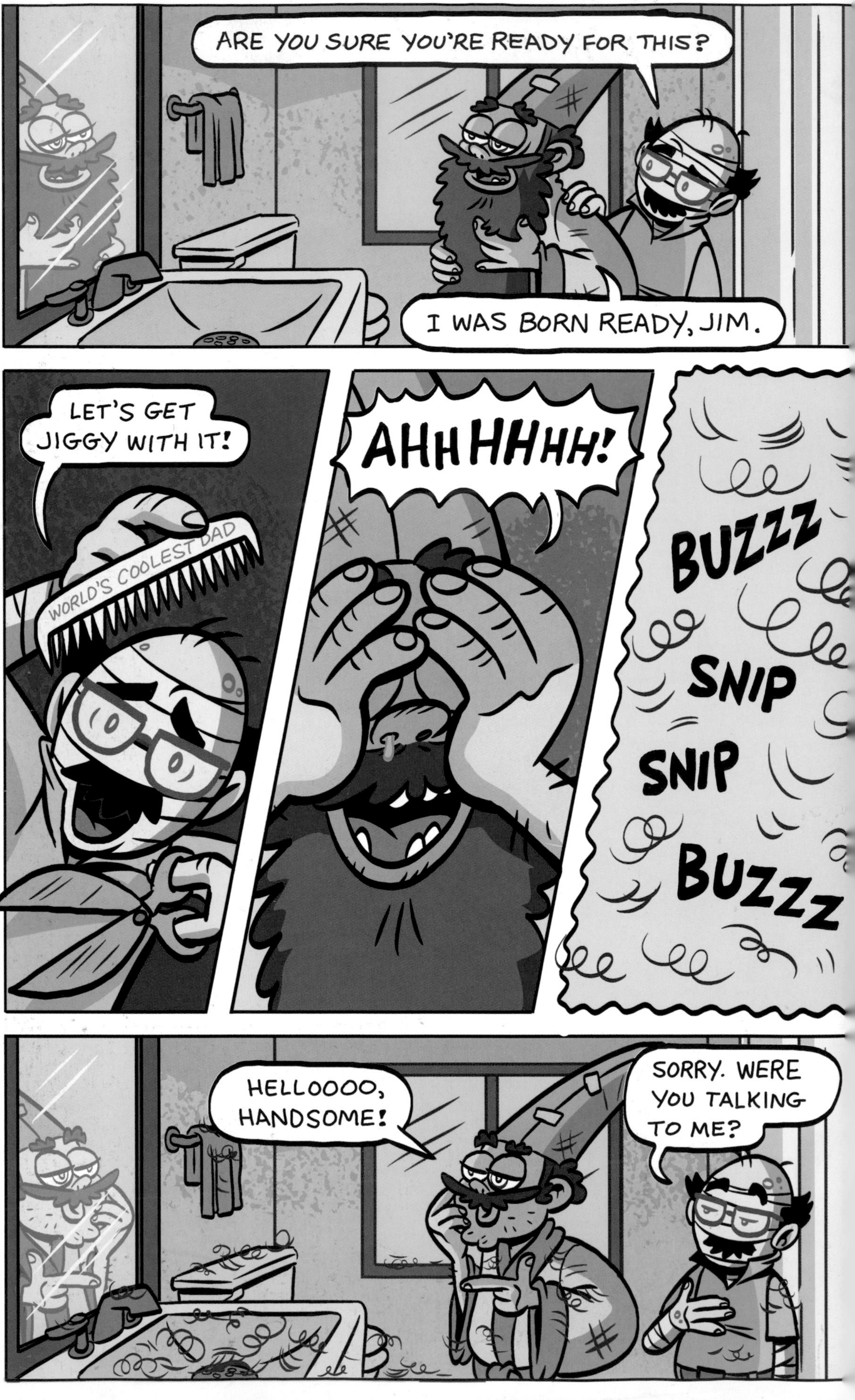
ARE YOU SURE YOU'RE READY FOR THIS?
I WAS BORN READY, JIM.
LET'S GET JIGGY WITH IT!
WORLD'S COOLEST DAD
AHHHHHH!
BUZZZ
SNIP
SNIP
BUZZZZ
HELLOOOO, HANDSOME!
SORRY. WERE YOU TALKING TO ME?

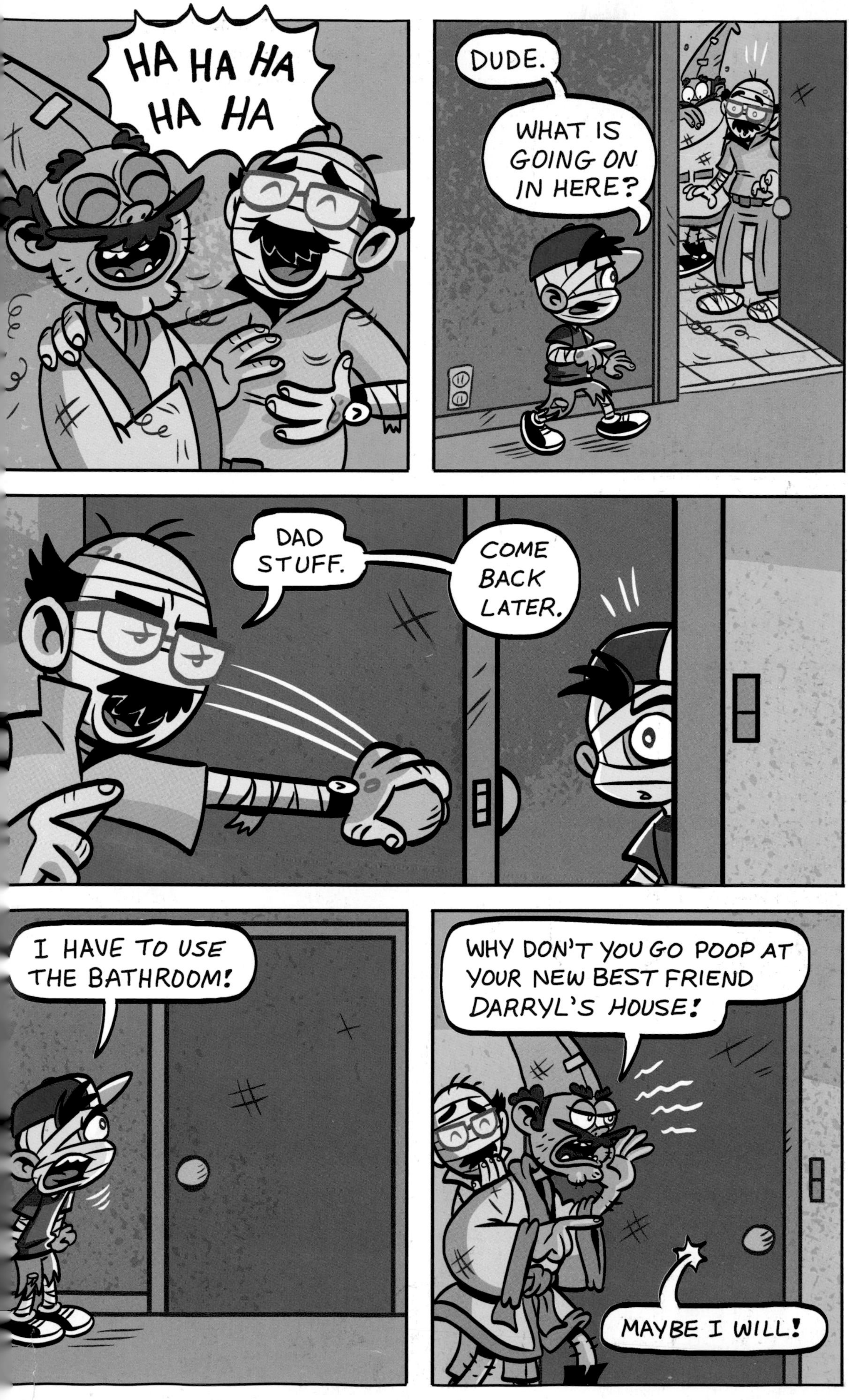
HA HA HA HA HA
DUDE.
WHAT IS GOING ON IN HERE?
DAD STUFF.
COME BACK LATER.
I HAVE TO USE THE BATHROOM!
WHY DON'T YOU GO POOP AT YOUR NEW BEST FRIEND DARRYL'S HOUSE!
MAYBE I WILL!

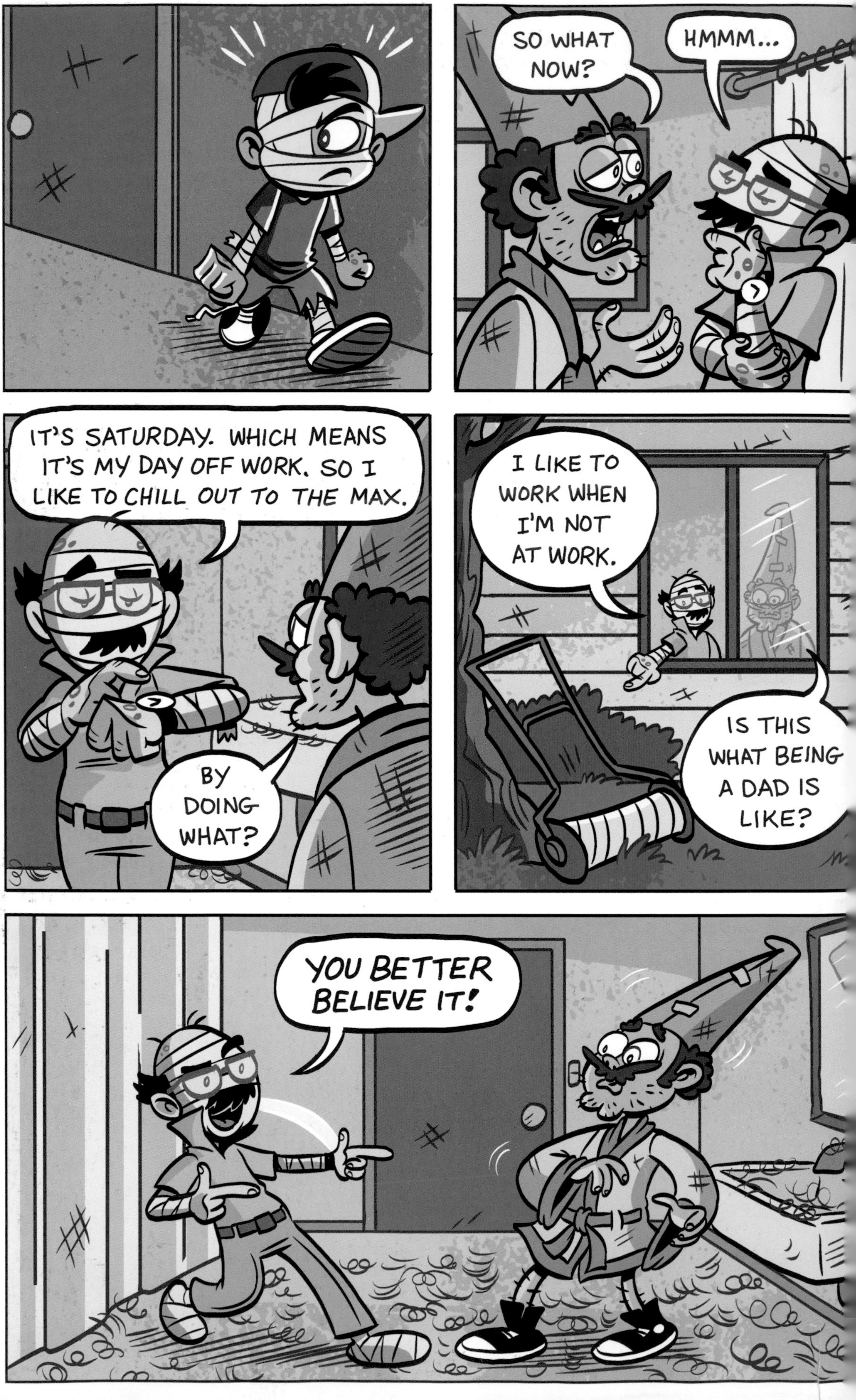
SO WHAT NOW?
HMMM...
IT'S SATURDAY. WHICH MEANS IT'S MY DAY OFF WORK. SO I LIKE TO CHILL OUT TO THE MAX.
BY DOING WHAT?
I LIKE TO WORK WHEN I'M NOT AT WORK.
IS THIS WHAT BEING A DAD IS LIKE?
YOU BETTER BELIEVE IT!

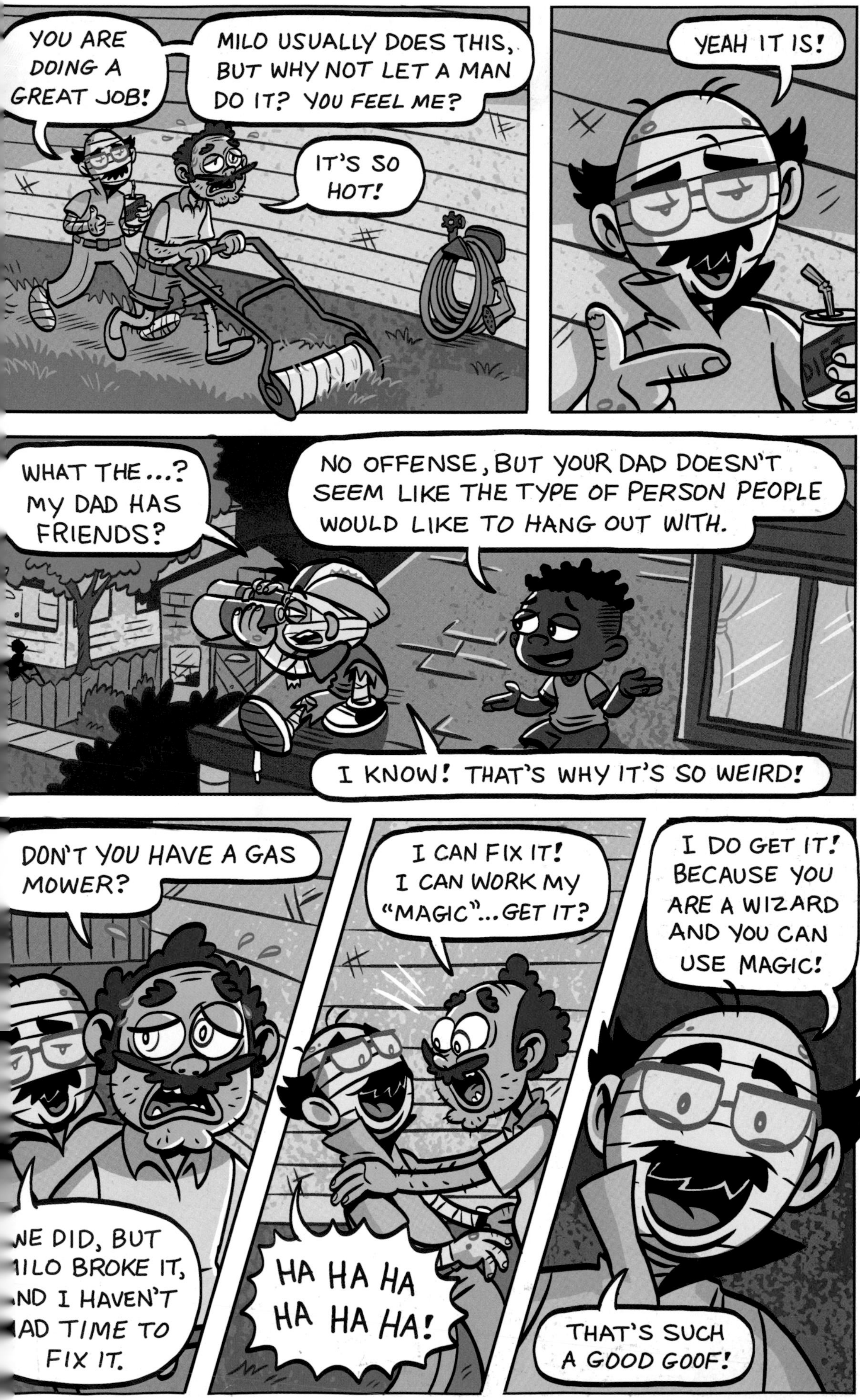
YOU ARE DOING A GREAT JOB!
MILO USUALLY DOES THIS, BUT WHY NOT LET A MAN DO IT? YOU FEEL ME?
IT'S SO HOT!
YEAH IT IS!
WHAT THE...? MY DAD HAS FRIENDS?
NO OFFENSE, BUT YOUR DAD DOESN'T SEEM LIKE THE TYPE OF PERSON PEOPLE WOULD LIKE TO HANG OUT WITH.
I KNOW! THAT'S WHY IT'S SO WEIRD!
DON'T YOU HAVE A GAS MOWER?
WE DID, BUT MILO BROKE IT, AND I HAVEN'T HAD TIME TO FIX IT.
I CAN FIX IT! I CAN WORK MY "MAGIC"... GET IT?
HA HA HA HA HA HA!
I DO GET IT! BECAUSE YOU ARE A WIZARD AND YOU CAN USE MAGIC!
THAT'S SUCH A GOOD GOOF!

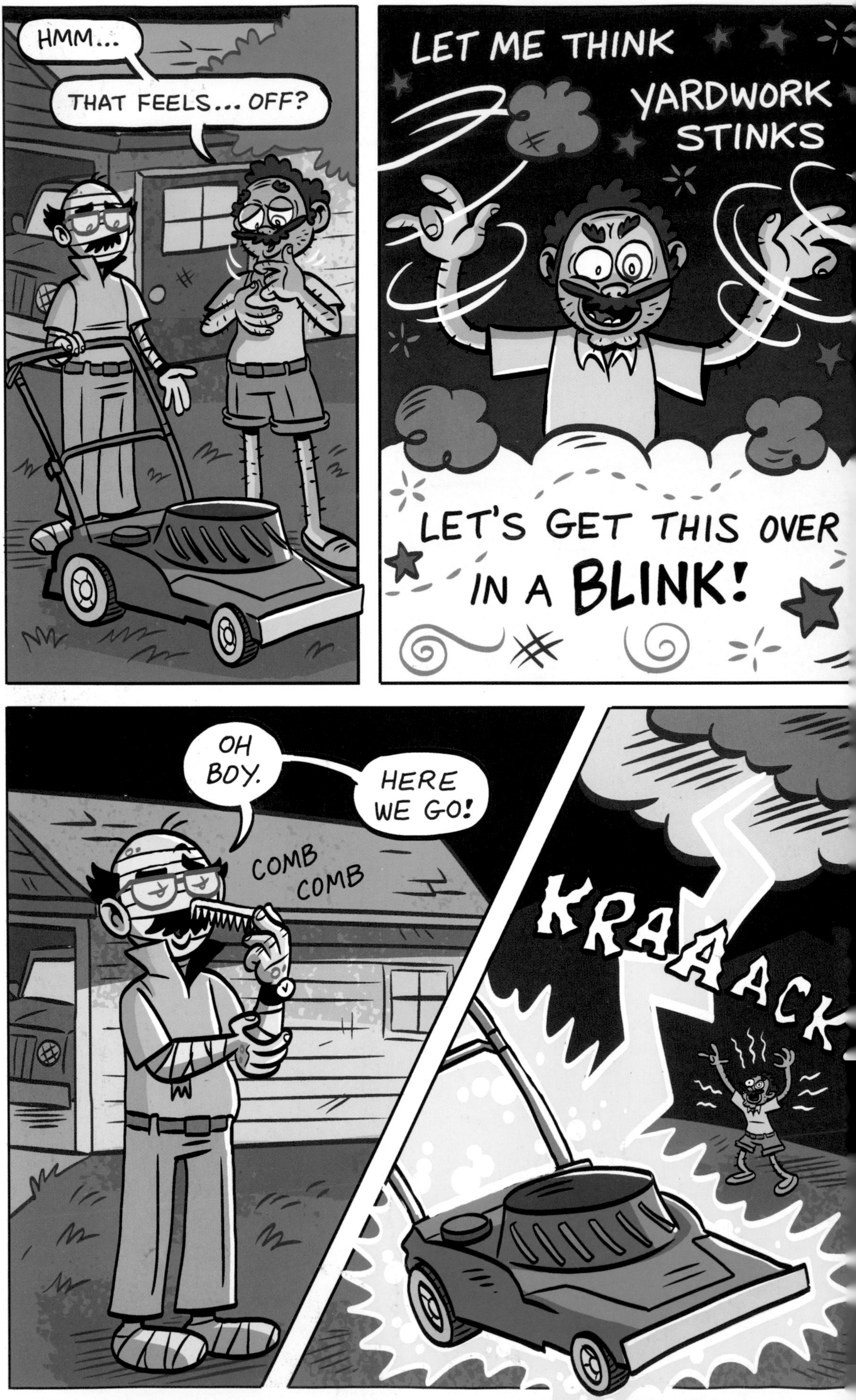
HMM...
THAT FEELS... OFF?
LET ME THINK
YARDWORK STINKS
LET'S GET THIS OVER IN A BLINK!
OH BOY.
HERE WE GO!
COMB COMB
KRAAAACK

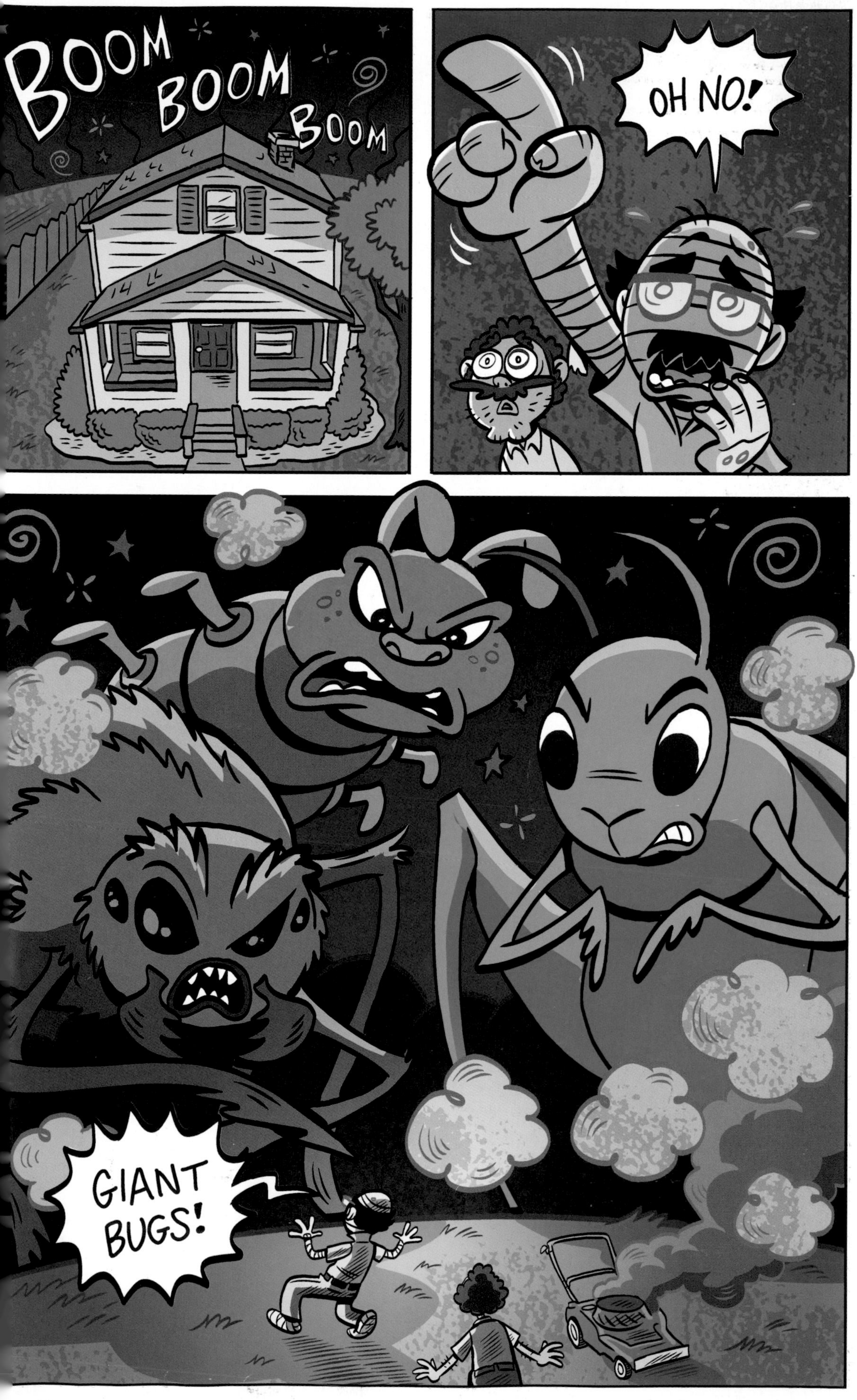
BOOM BOOM BOOM
OH NO!
GIANT BUGS!

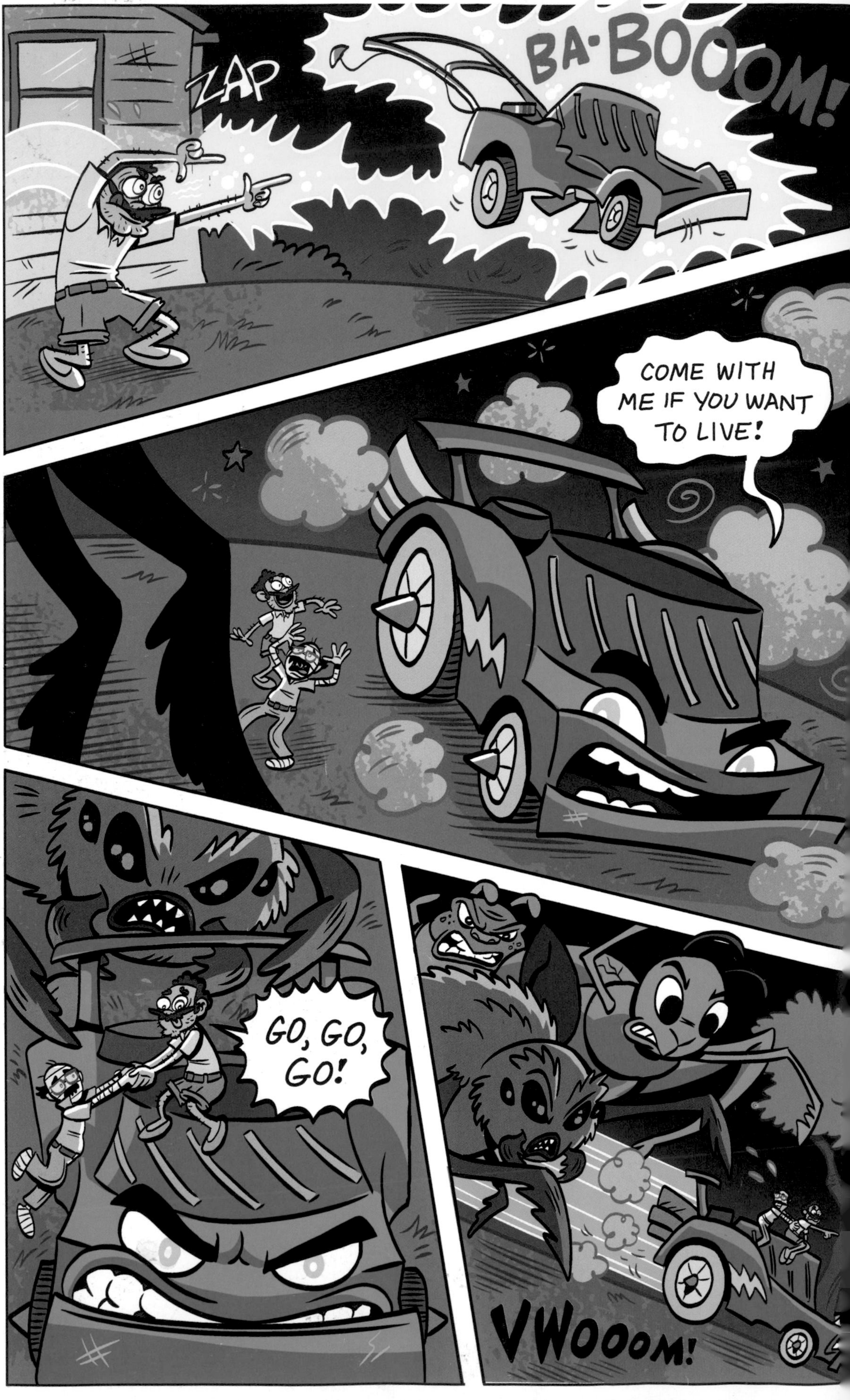
ZAP
BA-BOOOOM!
COME WITH ME IF YOU WANT TO LIVE!
GO, GO, GO!
VWOOOOM!

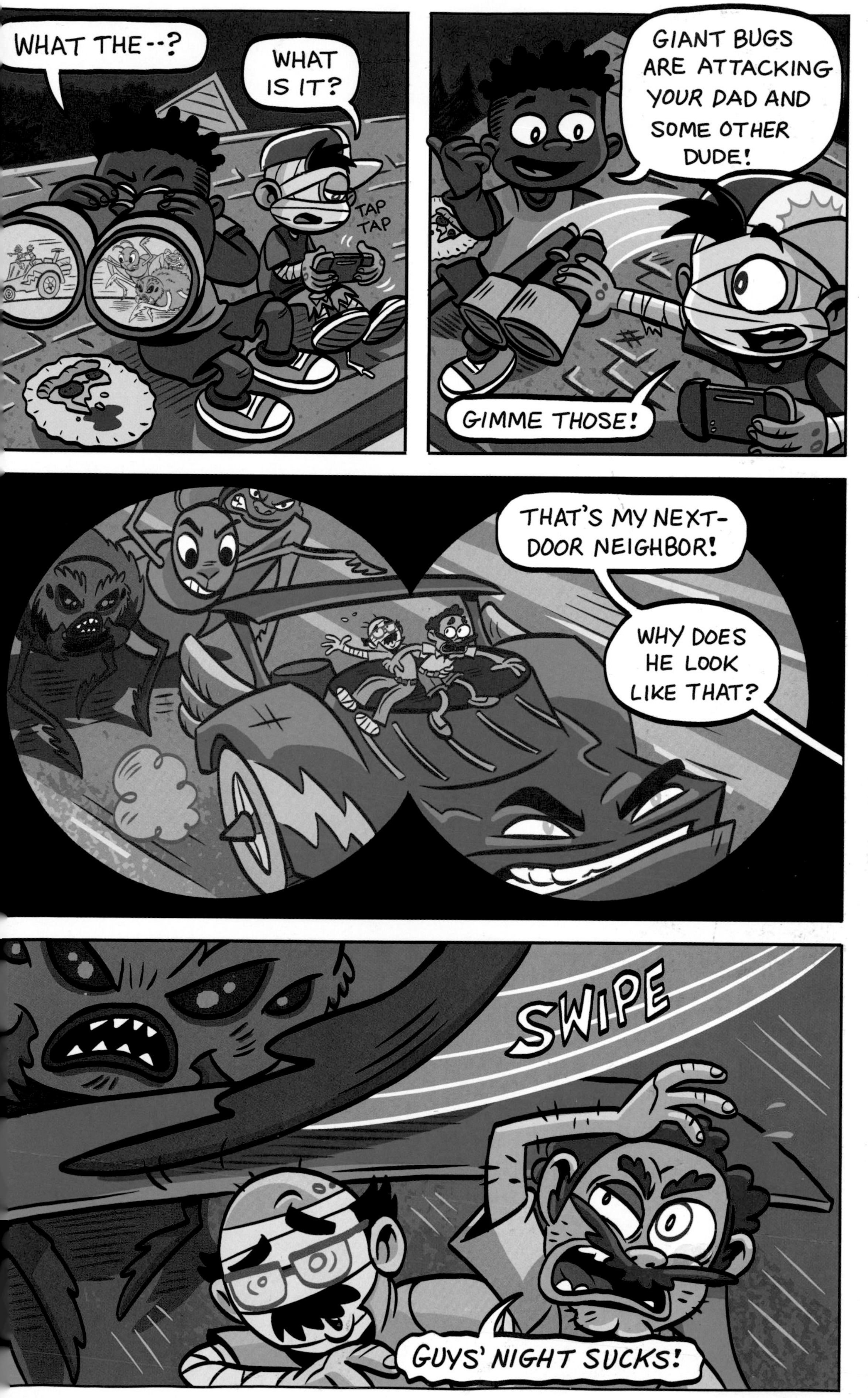
WHAT THE--?
WHAT IS IT?
TAP TAP
GIANT BUGS ARE ATTACKING YOUR DAD AND SOME OTHER DUDE!
GIMME THOSE!
THAT'S MY NEXT-DOOR NEIGHBOR!
WHY DOES HE LOOK LIKE THAT?
SWIPE
GUYS' NIGHT SUCKS!

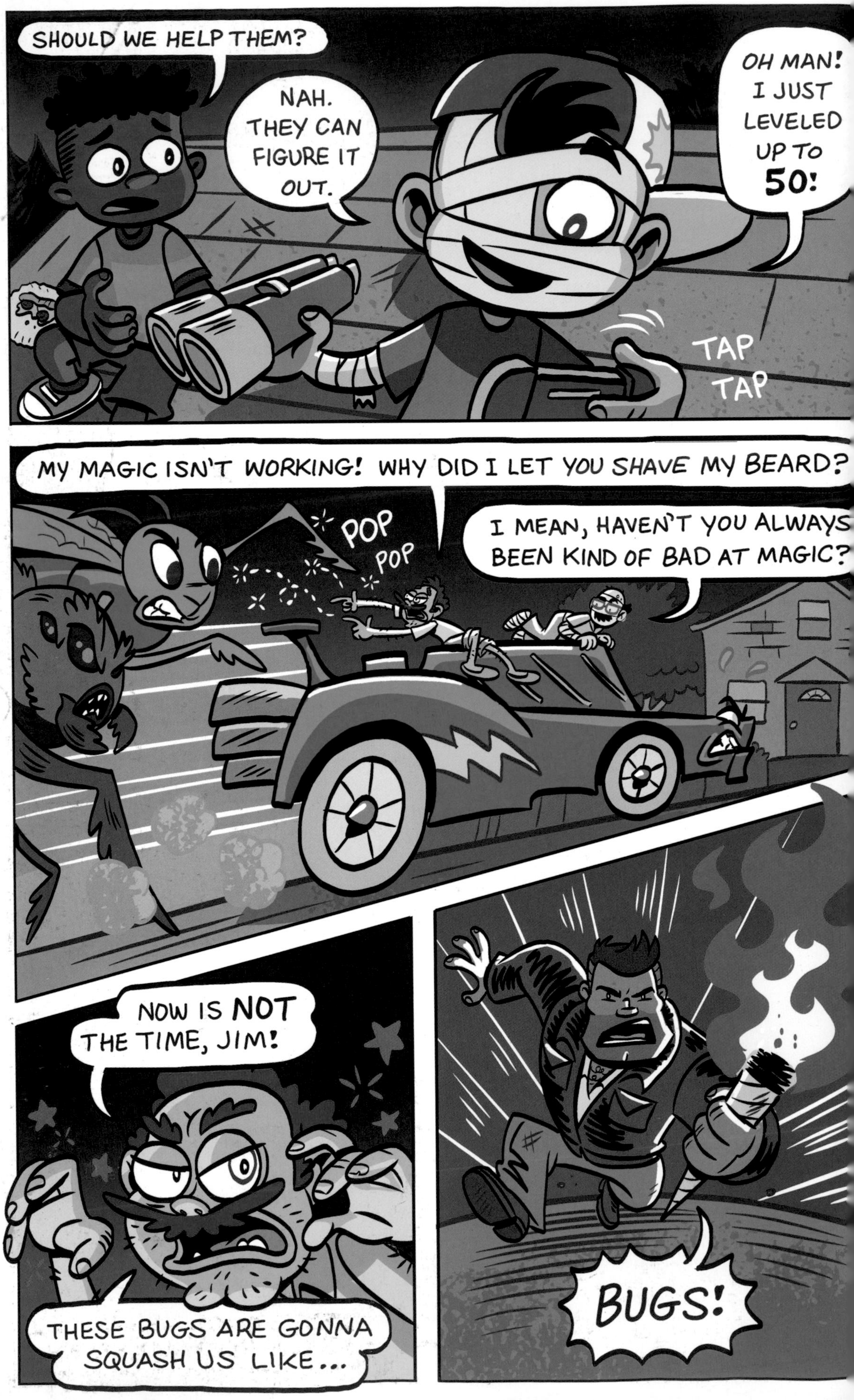
SHOULD WE HELP THEM?
NAH. THEY CAN FIGURE IT OUT.
OH MAN! I JUST LEVELED UP TO 50!
TAP TAP
MY MAGIC ISN'T WORKING! WHY DID I LET YOU SHAVE MY BEARD?
POP POP
I MEAN, HAVEN'T YOU ALWAYS BEEN KIND OF BAD AT MAGIC?
NOW IS NOT THE TIME, JIM!
THESE BUGS ARE GONNA SQUASH US LIKE...
BUGS!

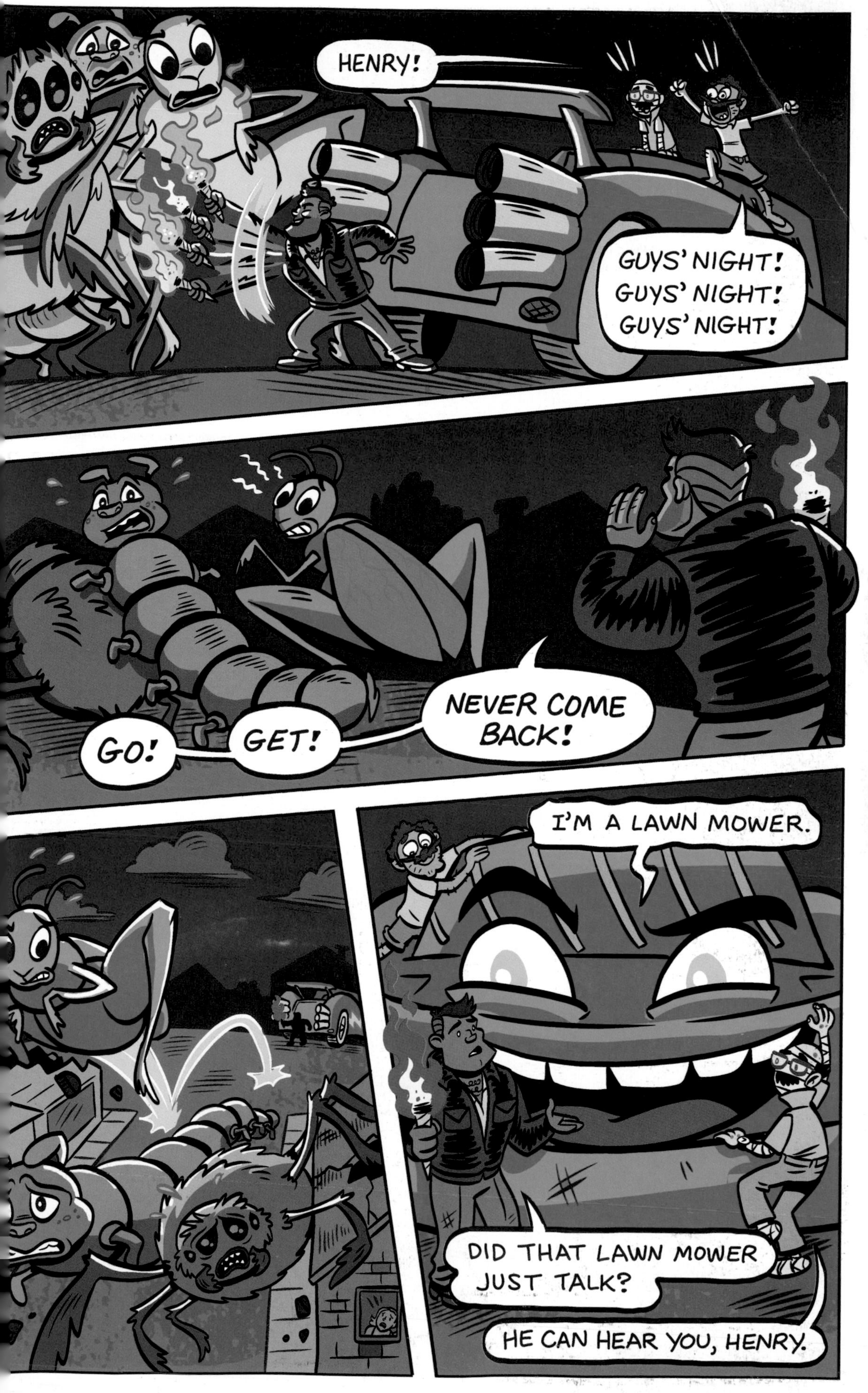
HENRY!
GUYS' NIGHT!
GUYS' NIGHT!
GUYS' NIGHT!
GO!
GET!
NEVER COME BACK!
I'M A LAWN MOWER.
DID THAT LAWN MOWER JUST TALK?
HE CAN HEAR YOU, HENRY.

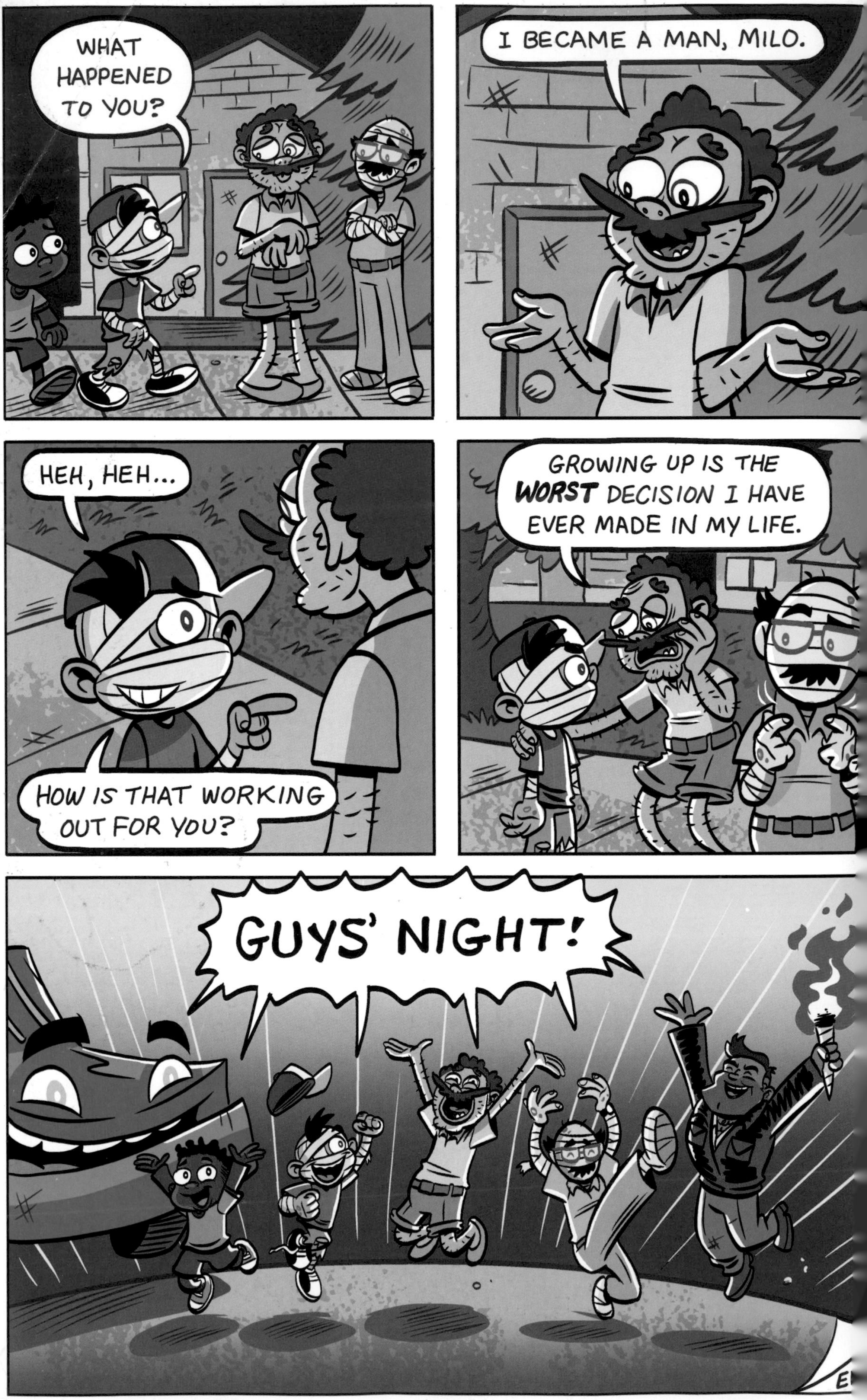
WHAT HAPPENED TO YOU?
I BECAME A MAN, MILO.
HEH, HEH...
HOW IS THAT WORKING OUT FOR YOU?
GROWING UP IS THE **WORST** DECISION I HAVE EVER MADE IN MY LIFE.
GUYS' NIGHT!

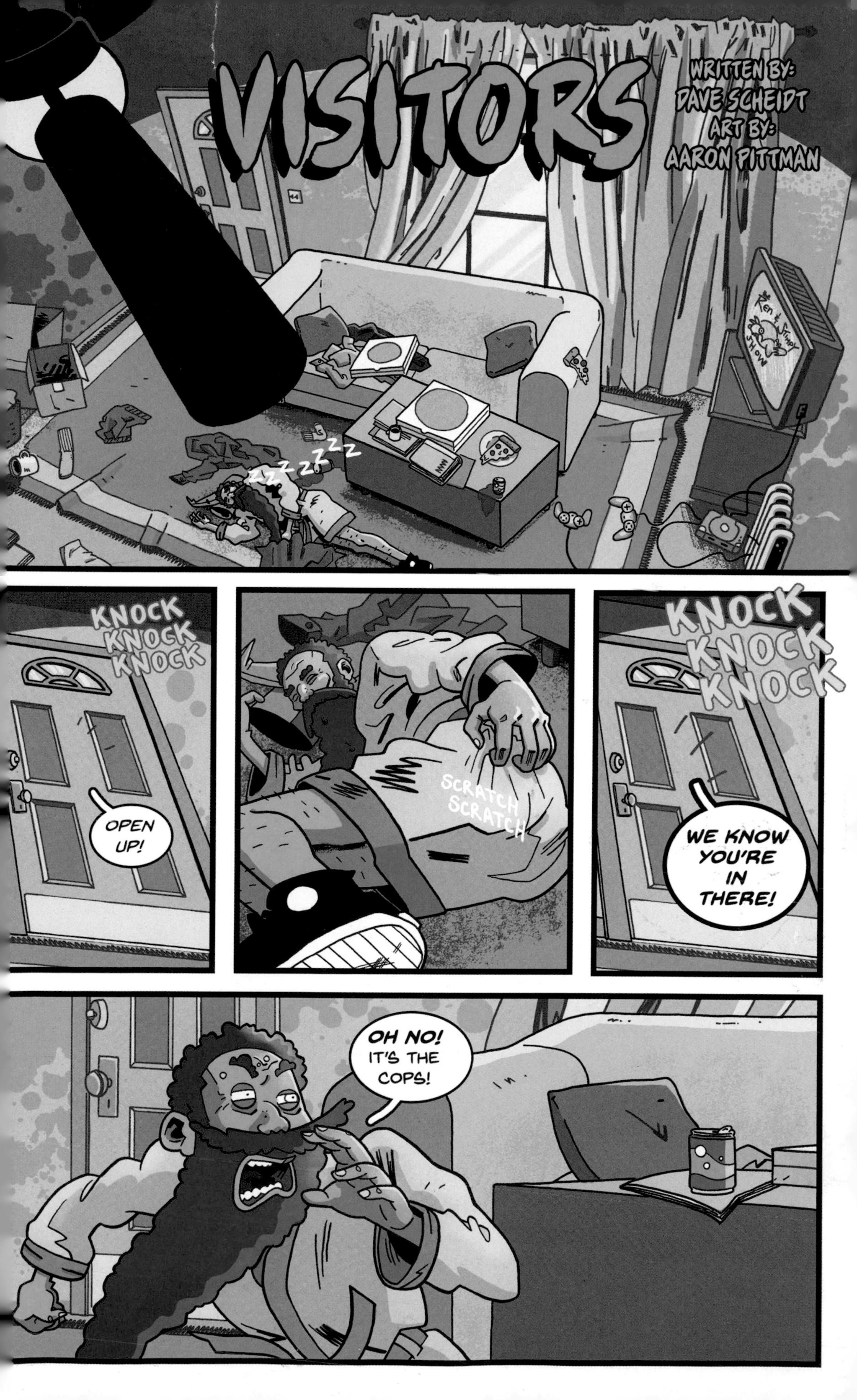
VISITORS
WRITTEN BY: DAVE SCHEIDT
ART BY: AARON PITTMAN
The Ren & Stimpy Show
ZZZZZZZ
KNOCK KNOCK KNOCK
OPEN UP!
SCRATCH SCRATCH
KNOCK KNOCK KNOCK
WE KNOW YOU'RE IN THERE!
OH NO! IT'S THE COPS!

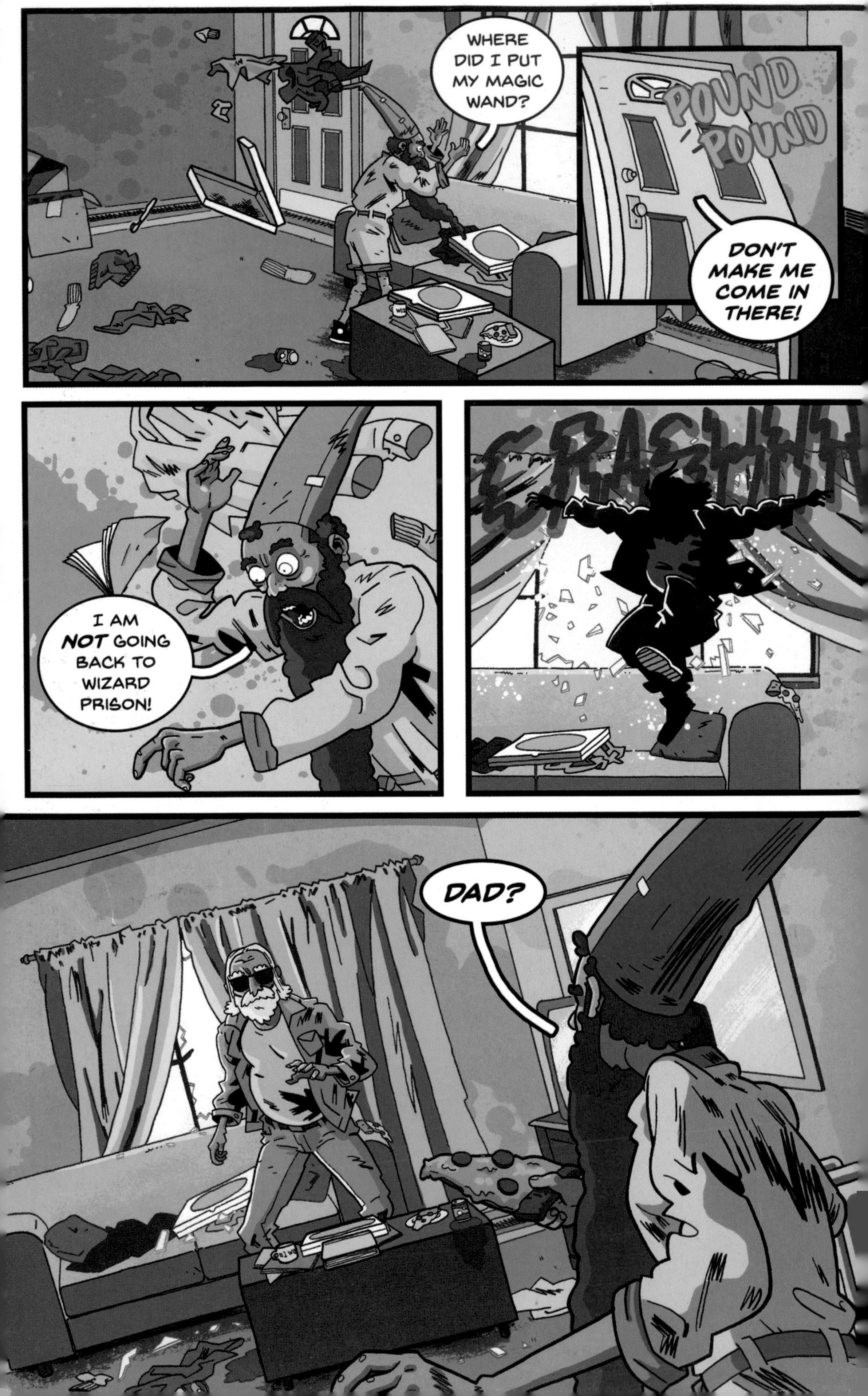
WHERE DID I PUT MY MAGIC WAND?
POUND POUND
DON'T MAKE ME COME IN THERE!
I AM NOT GOING BACK TO WIZARD PRISON!
CRASHHH
DAD?

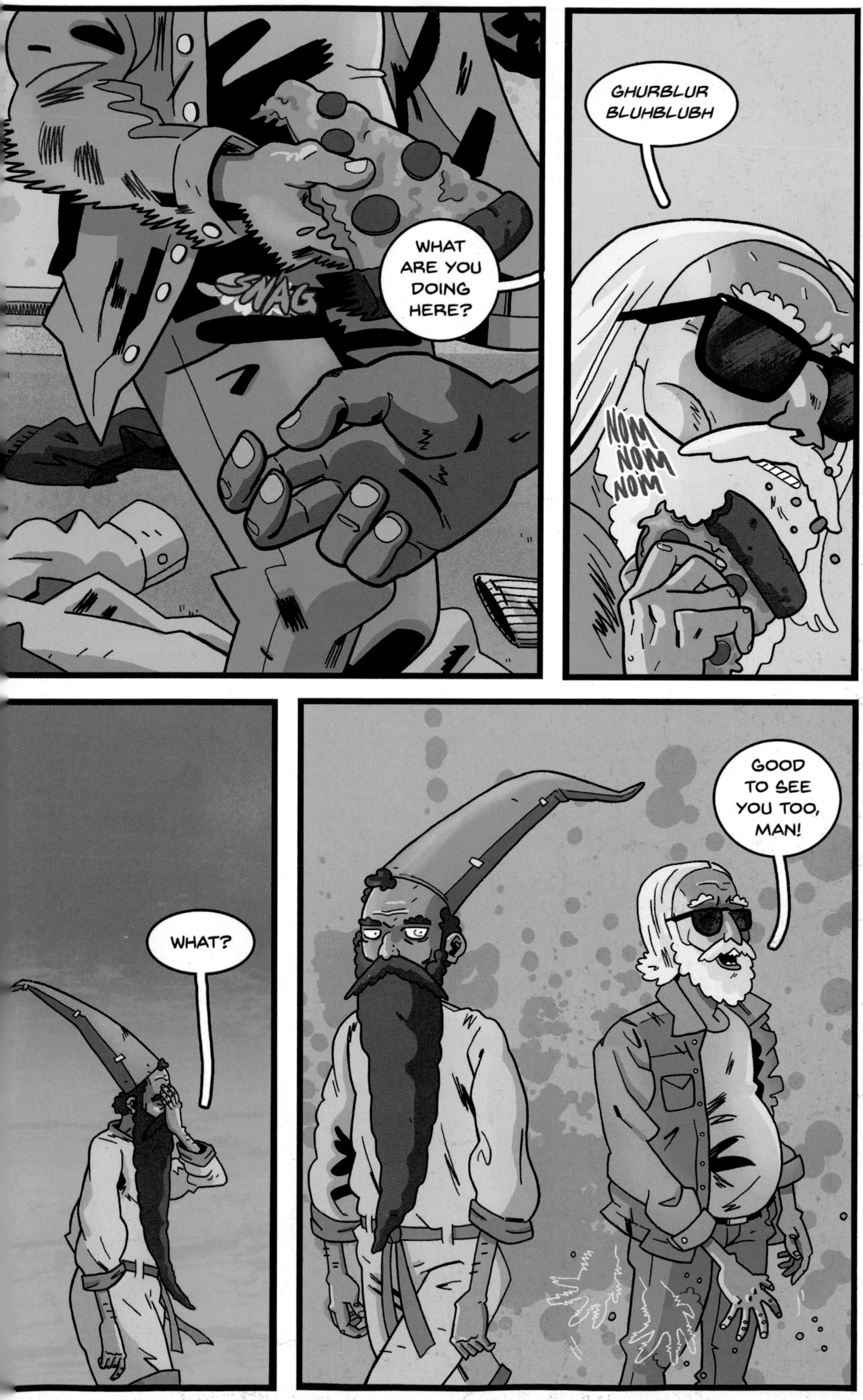
SNAG
WHAT ARE YOU DOING HERE?
GHURBLUR BLUHBLUBH
NOM NOM NOM
WHAT?
GOOD TO SEE YOU TOO, MAN!

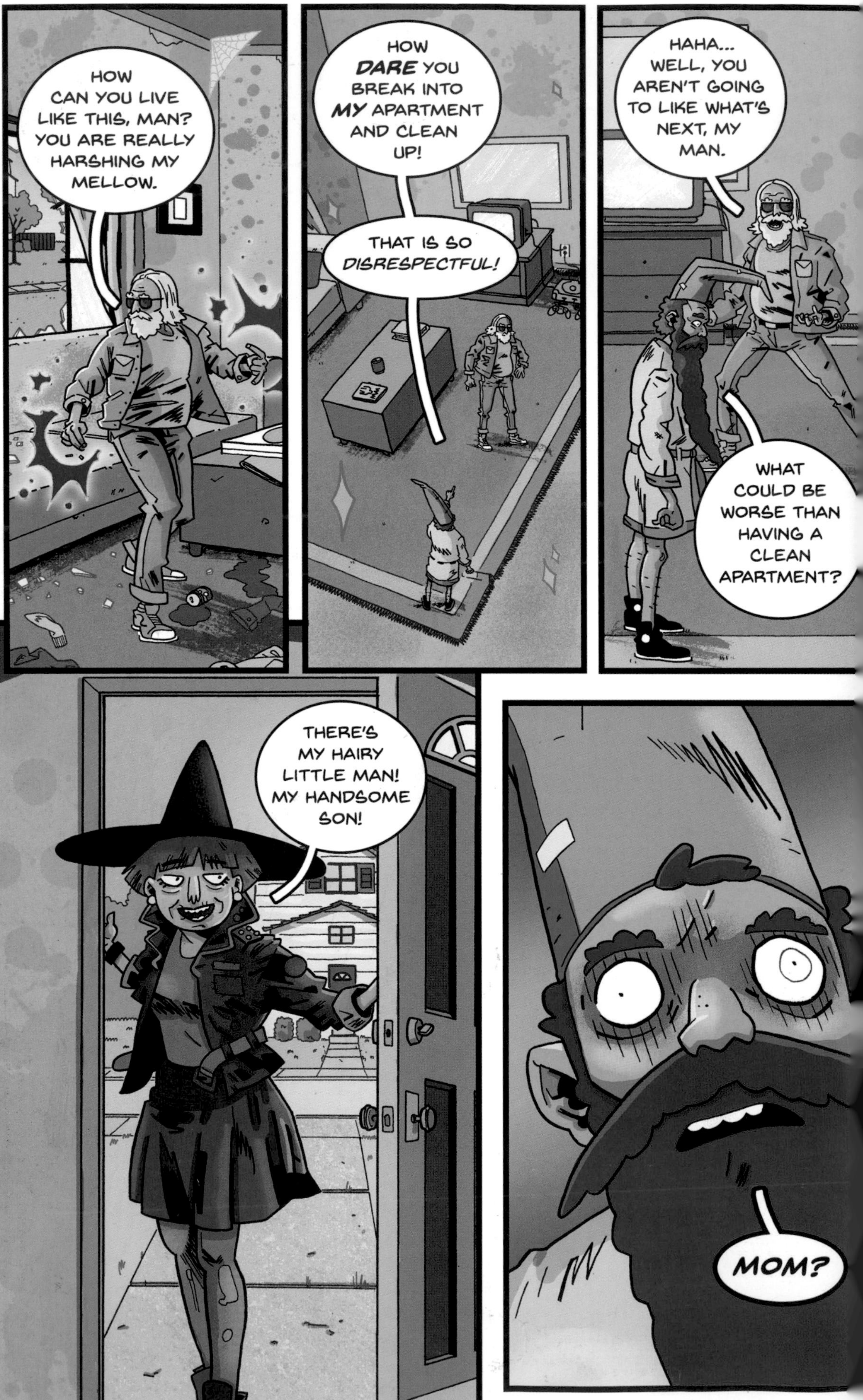
HOW CAN YOU LIVE LIKE THIS, MAN? YOU ARE REALLY HARSHING MY MELLOW.
HOW DARE YOU BREAK INTO MY APARTMENT AND CLEAN UP!
THAT IS SO DISRESPECTFUL!
HAHA... WELL, YOU AREN'T GOING TO LIKE WHAT'S NEXT, MY MAN.
WHAT COULD BE WORSE THAN HAVING A CLEAN APARTMENT?
THERE'S MY HAIRY LITTLE MAN! MY HANDSOME SON!
MOM?

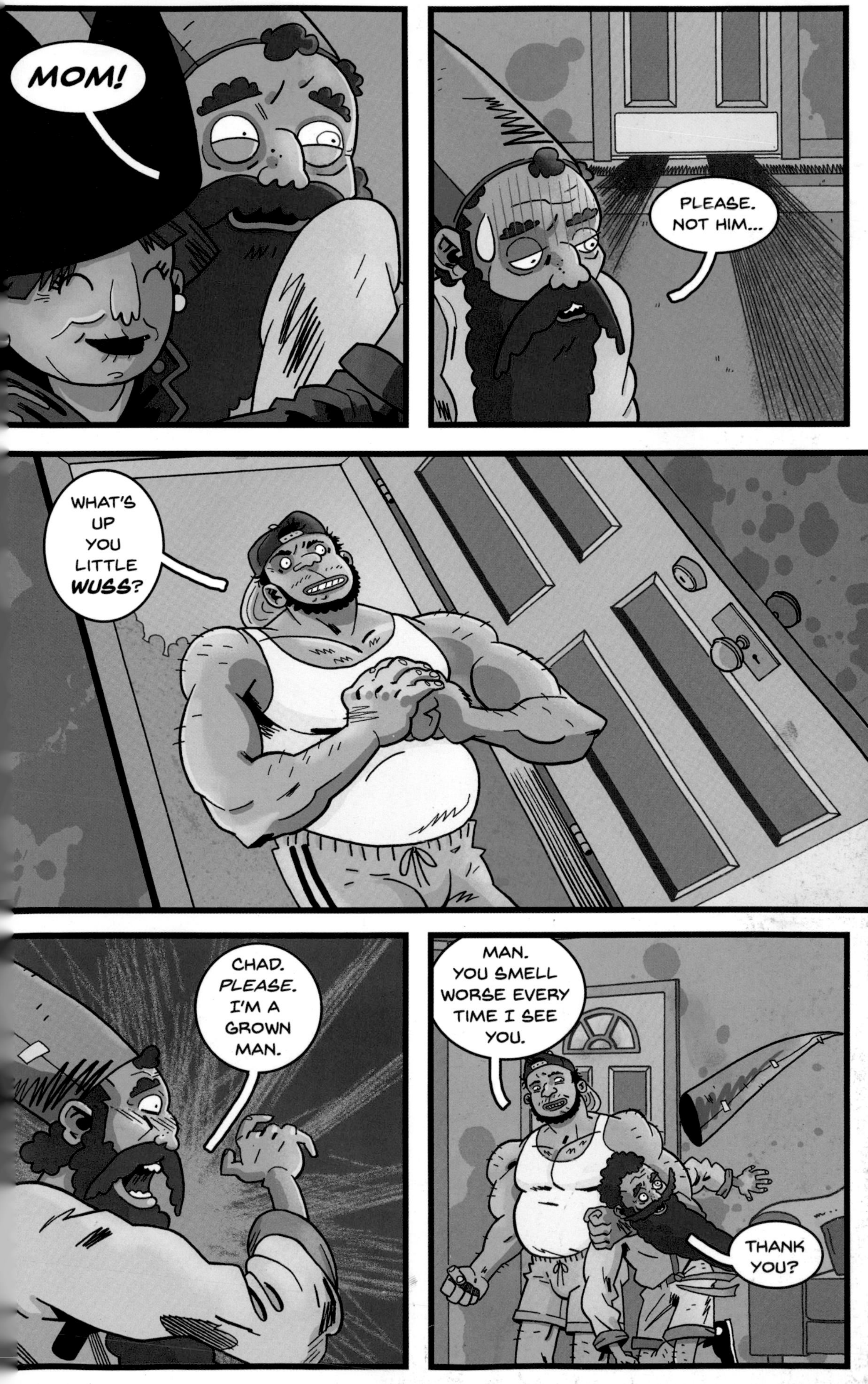
MOM!
PLEASE. NOT HIM...
WHAT'S UP YOU LITTLE WUSS?
CHAD. PLEASE. I'M A GROWN MAN.
MAN. YOU SMELL WORSE EVERY TIME I SEE YOU.
THANK YOU?

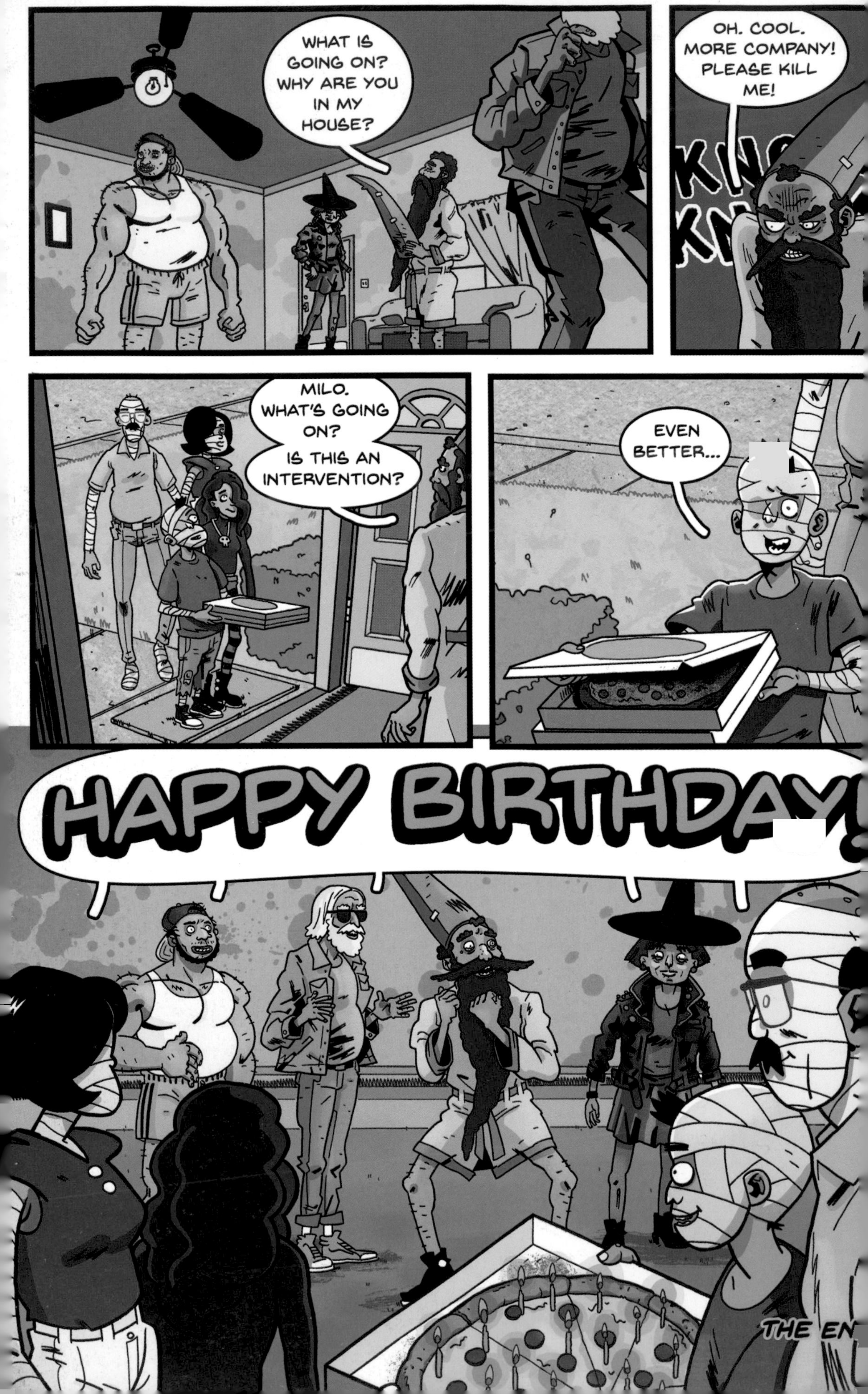
WHAT IS GOING ON? WHY ARE YOU IN MY HOUSE?
OH. COOL. MORE COMPANY! PLEASE KILL ME!
MILO. WHAT'S GOING ON?
IS THIS AN INTERVENTION?
EVEN BETTER...
HAPPY BIRTHDAY!
THE EN

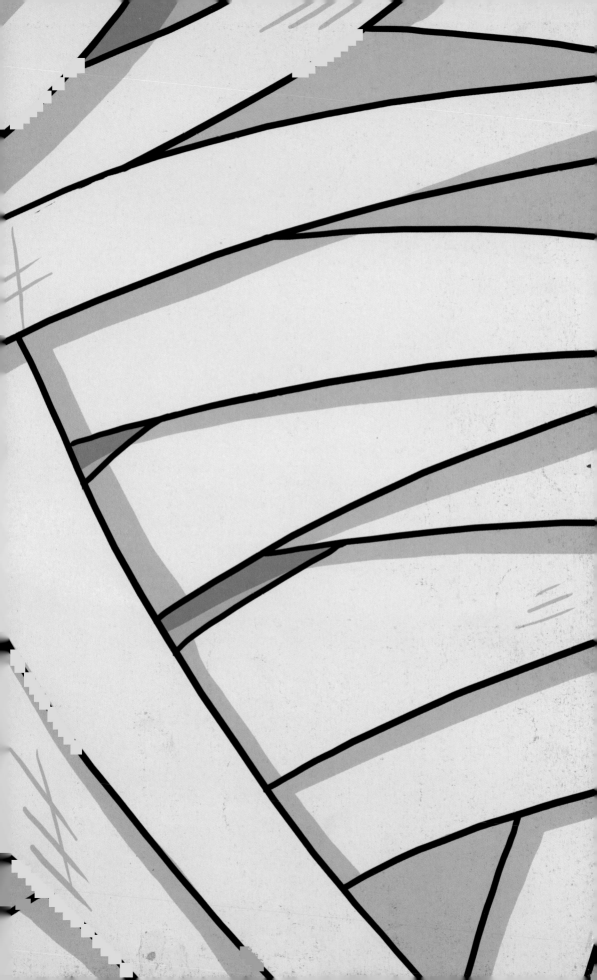

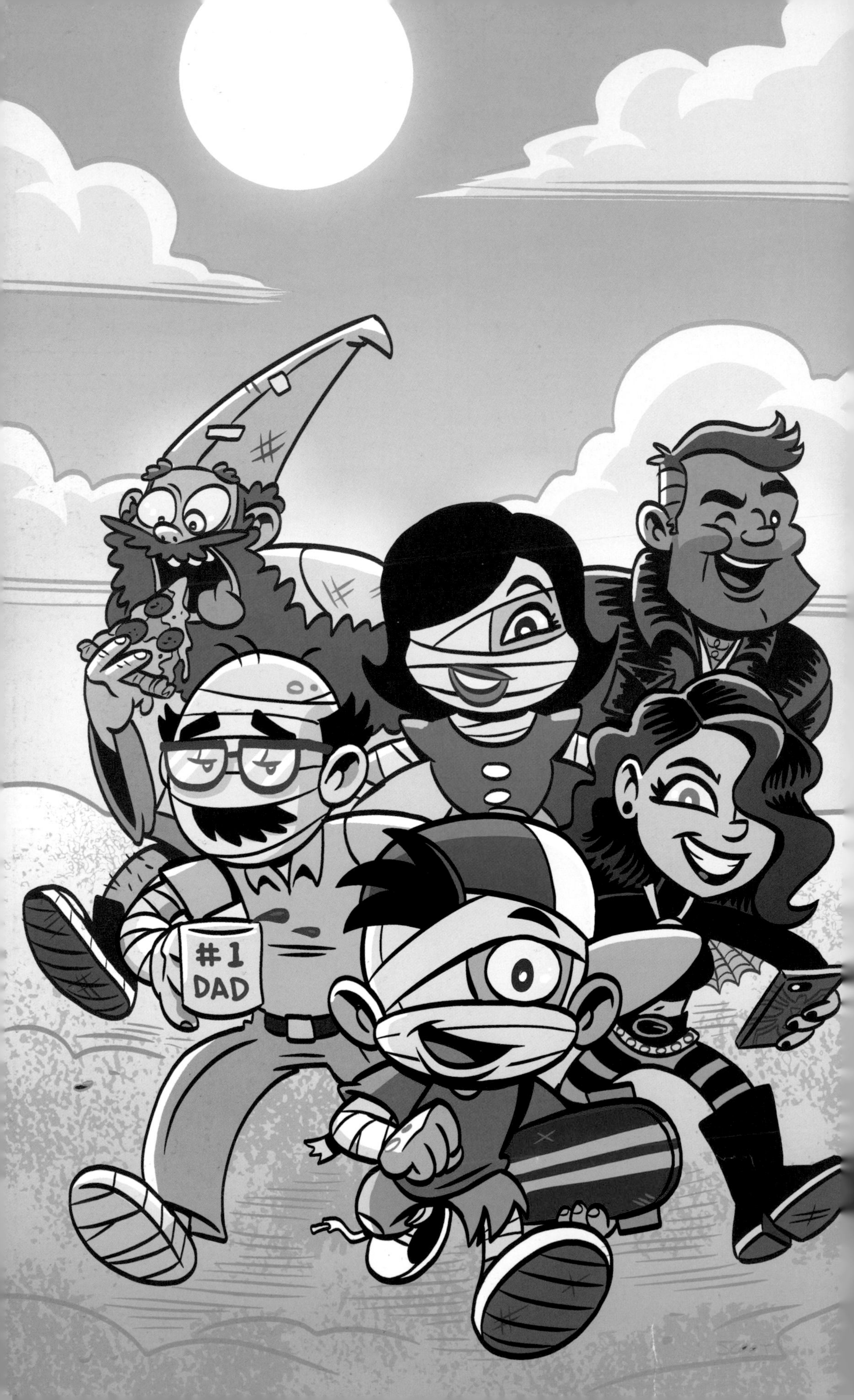
#1
DAD

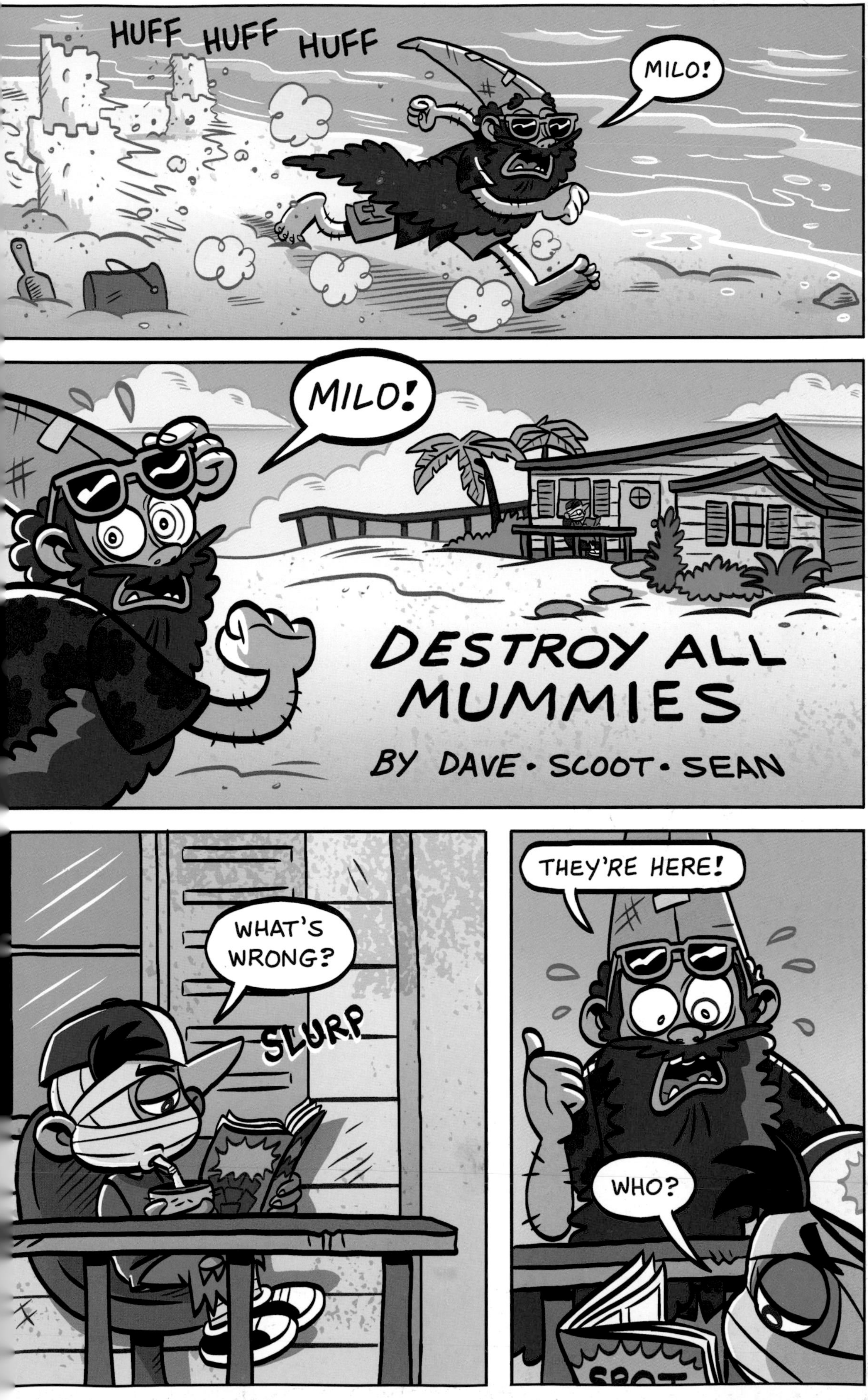
HUFF HUFF HUFF
MILO!
MILO!
DESTROY ALL MUMMIES
BY DAVE • SCOOT • SEAN
WHAT'S WRONG?
SLURP
THEY'RE HERE!
WHO?

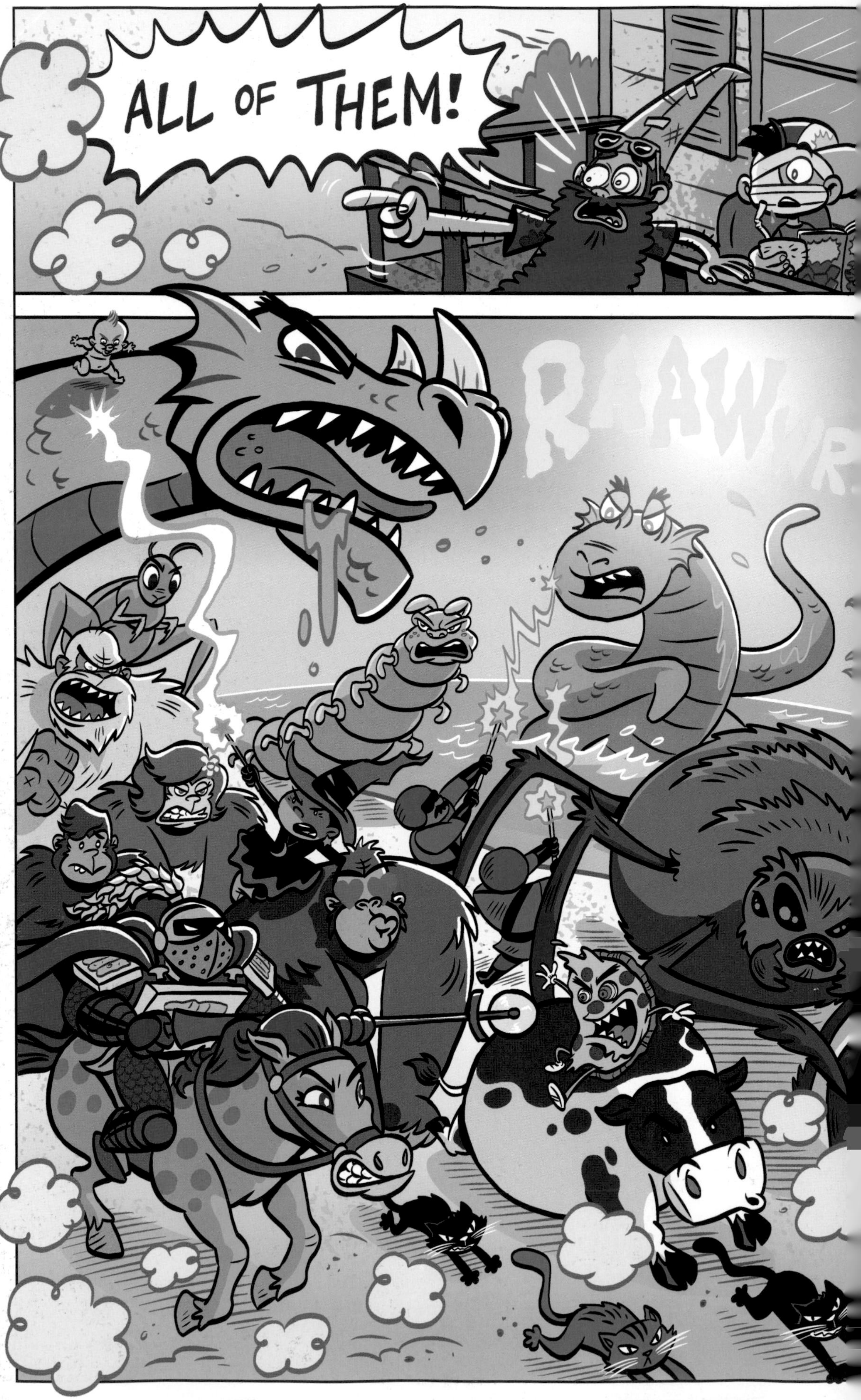
ALL OF THEM!
RAAW

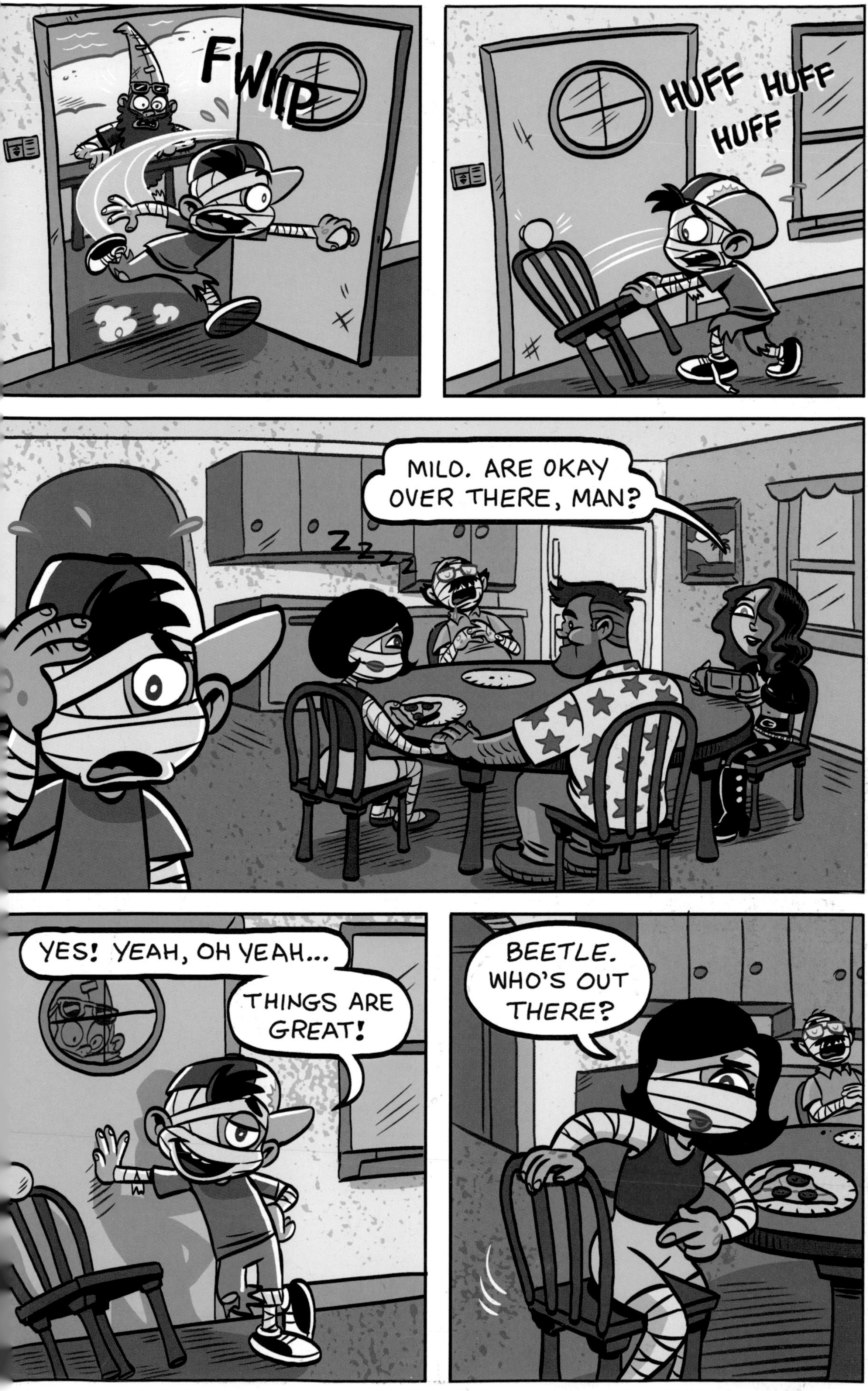
FWIIP
HUFF HUFF
HUFF
MILO. ARE OKAY OVER THERE, MAN?
ZZZZ
YES! YEAH, OH YEAH...
THINGS ARE GREAT!
BEETLE. WHO'S OUT THERE?

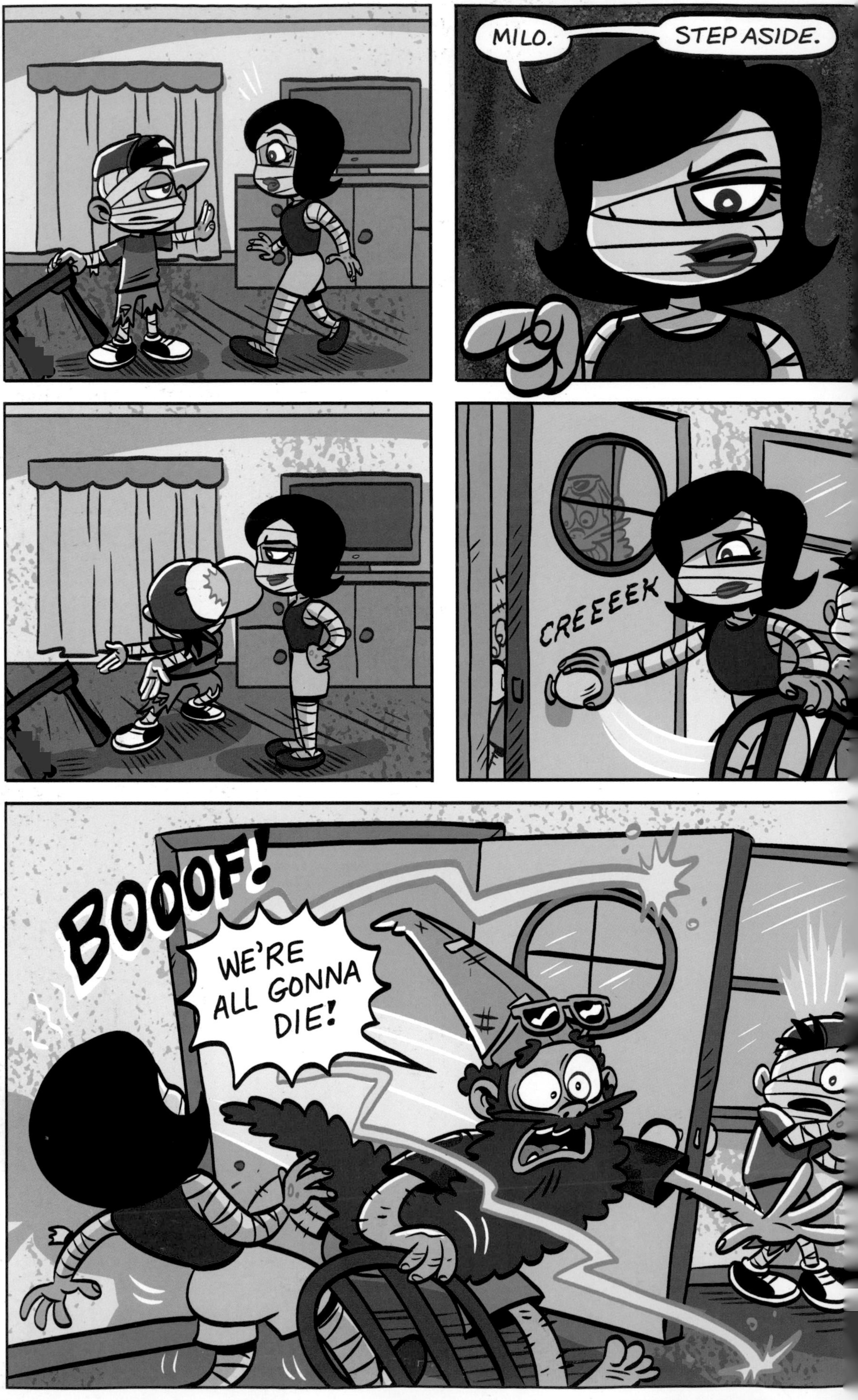
MILO.
STEP ASIDE.
CREEEEK
BOOOF!
WE'RE ALL GONNA DIE!

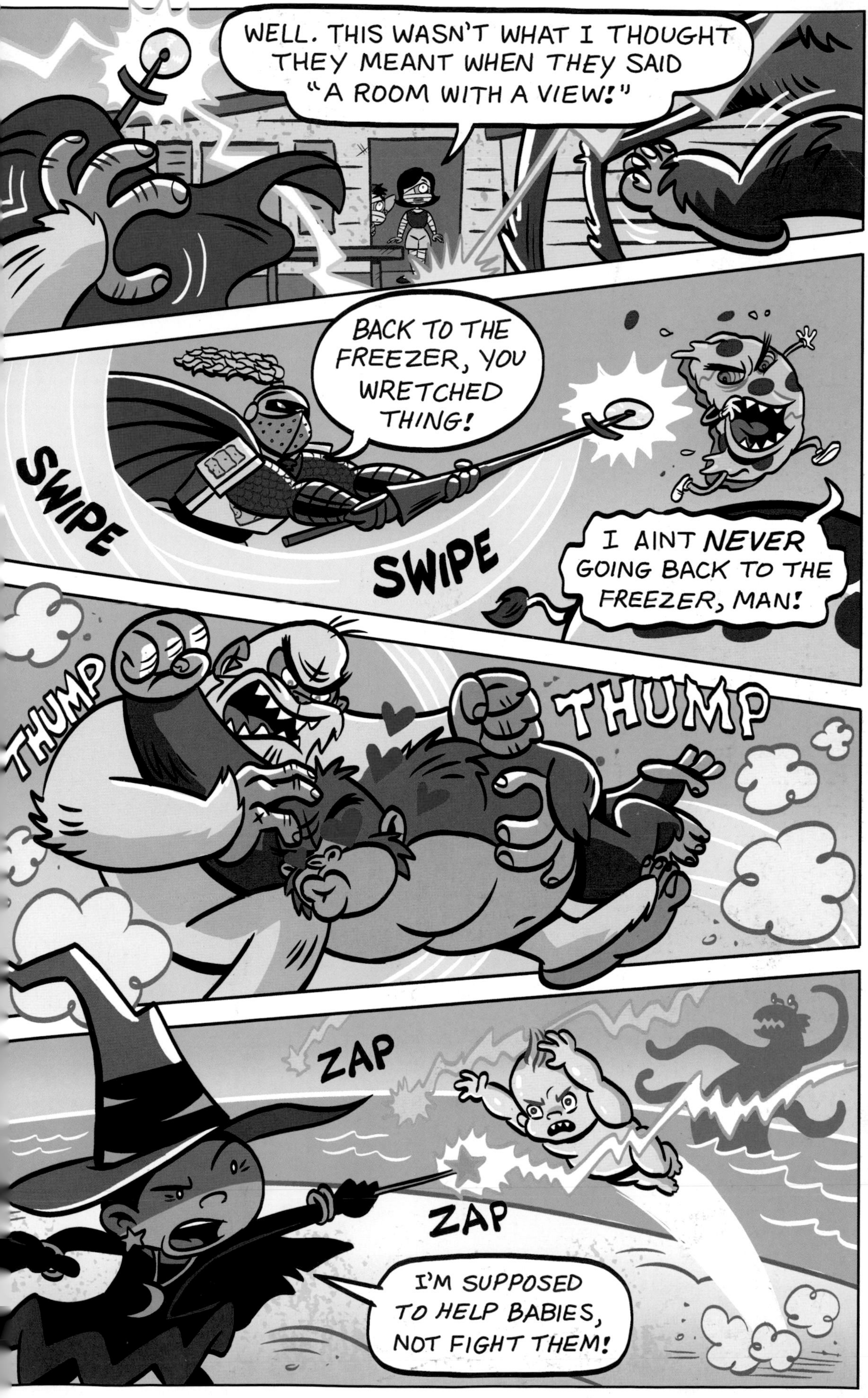
WELL. THIS WASN'T WHAT I THOUGHT THEY MEANT WHEN THEY SAID "A ROOM WITH A VIEW!"
BACK TO THE FREEZER, YOU WRETCHED THING!
SWIPE
SWIPE
I AINT NEVER GOING BACK TO THE FREEZER, MAN!
THUMP
THUMP
ZAP
ZAP
I'M SUPPOSED TO HELP BABIES, NOT FIGHT THEM!

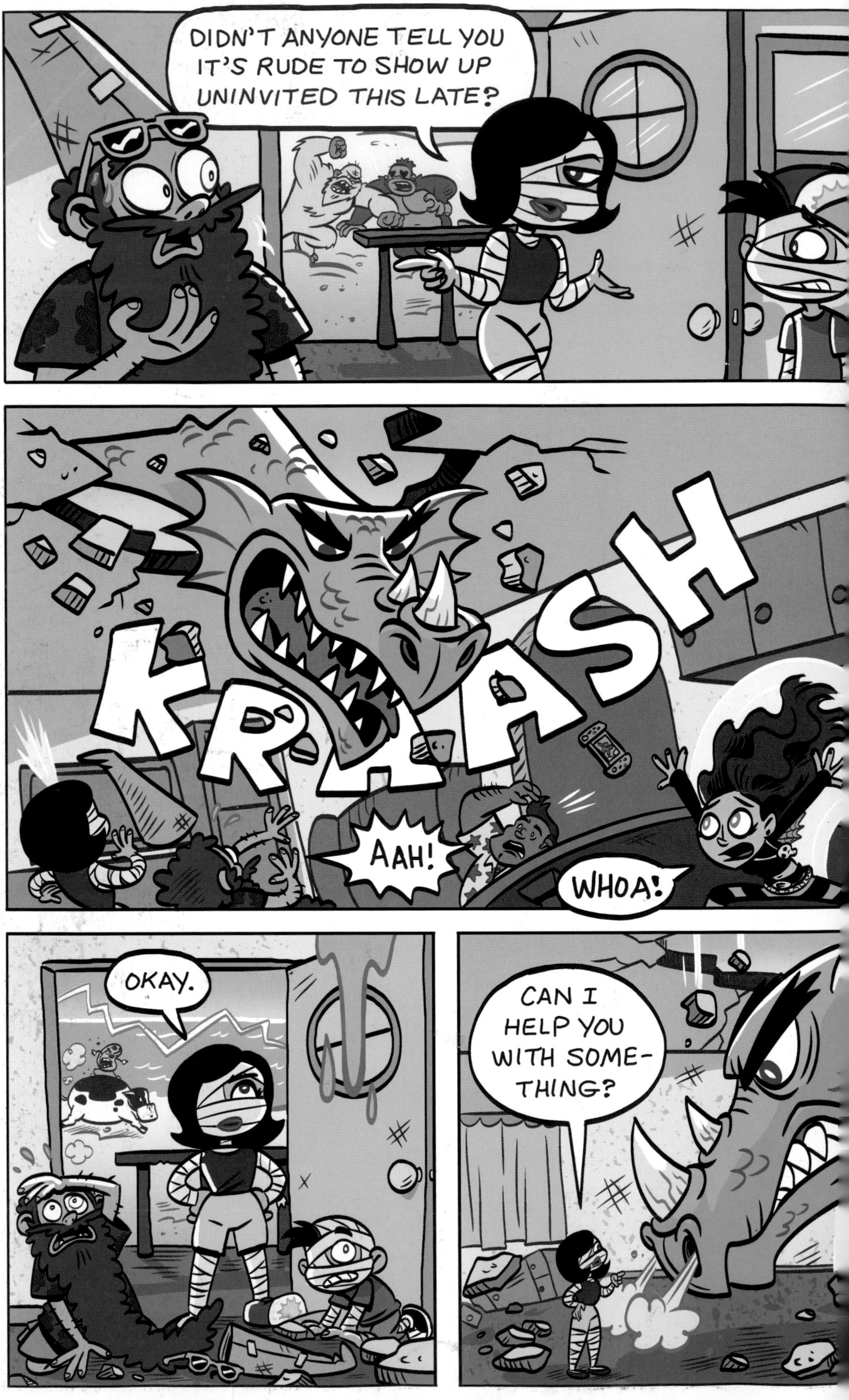
DIDN'T ANYONE TELL YOU IT'S RUDE TO SHOW UP UNINVITED THIS LATE?
KRAASH
AAH!
WHOA!
OKAY.
CAN I HELP YOU WITH SOME-THING?

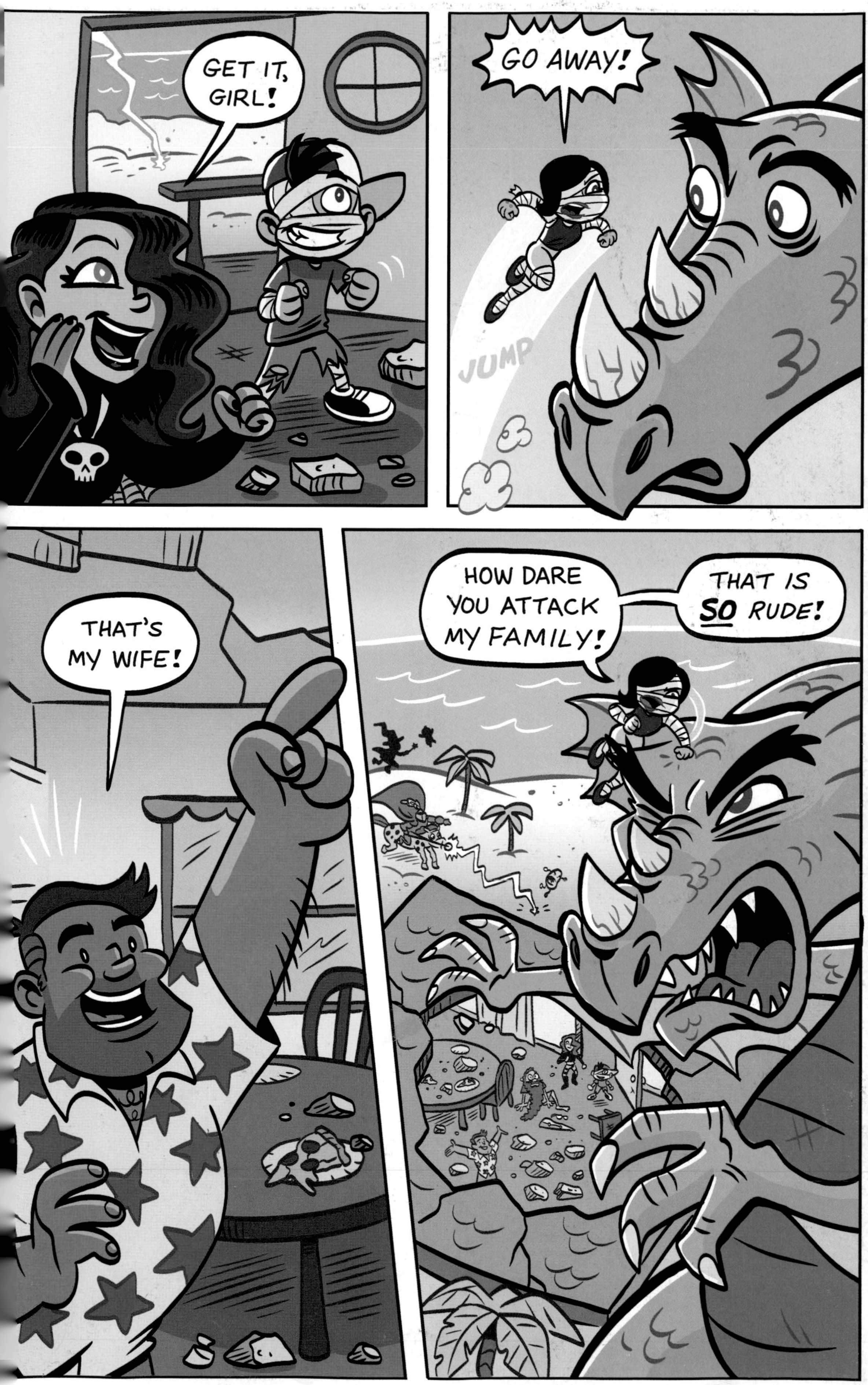
GET IT, GIRL!
GO AWAY!
JUMP
THAT'S MY WIFE!
HOW DARE YOU ATTACK MY FAMILY!
THAT IS SO RUDE!

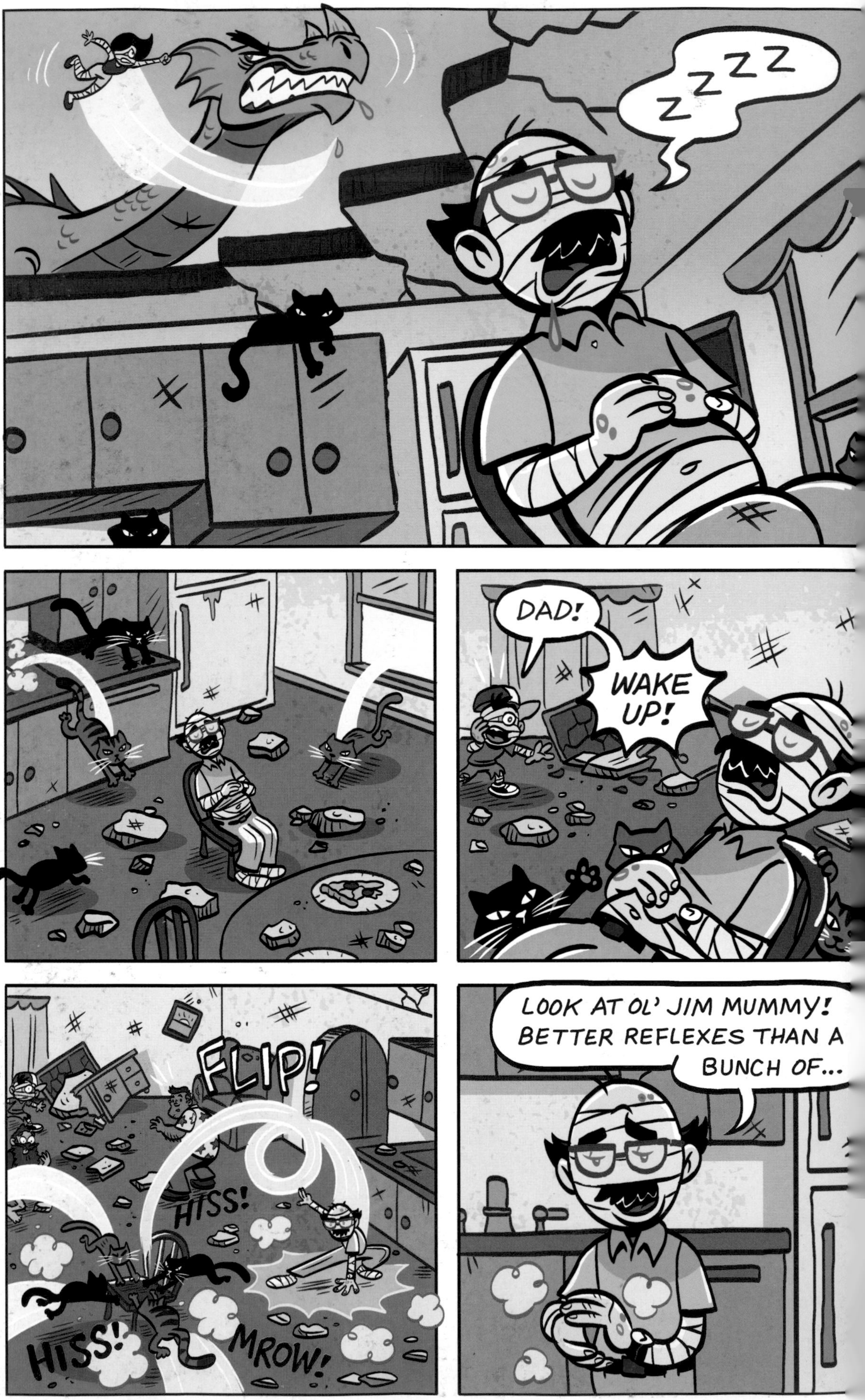
ZZZZZ
DAD!
WAKE UP!
FLIP!
HISS!
HISS!
MROW!
LOOK AT OL' JIM MUMMY! BETTER REFLEXES THAN A BUNCH OF...

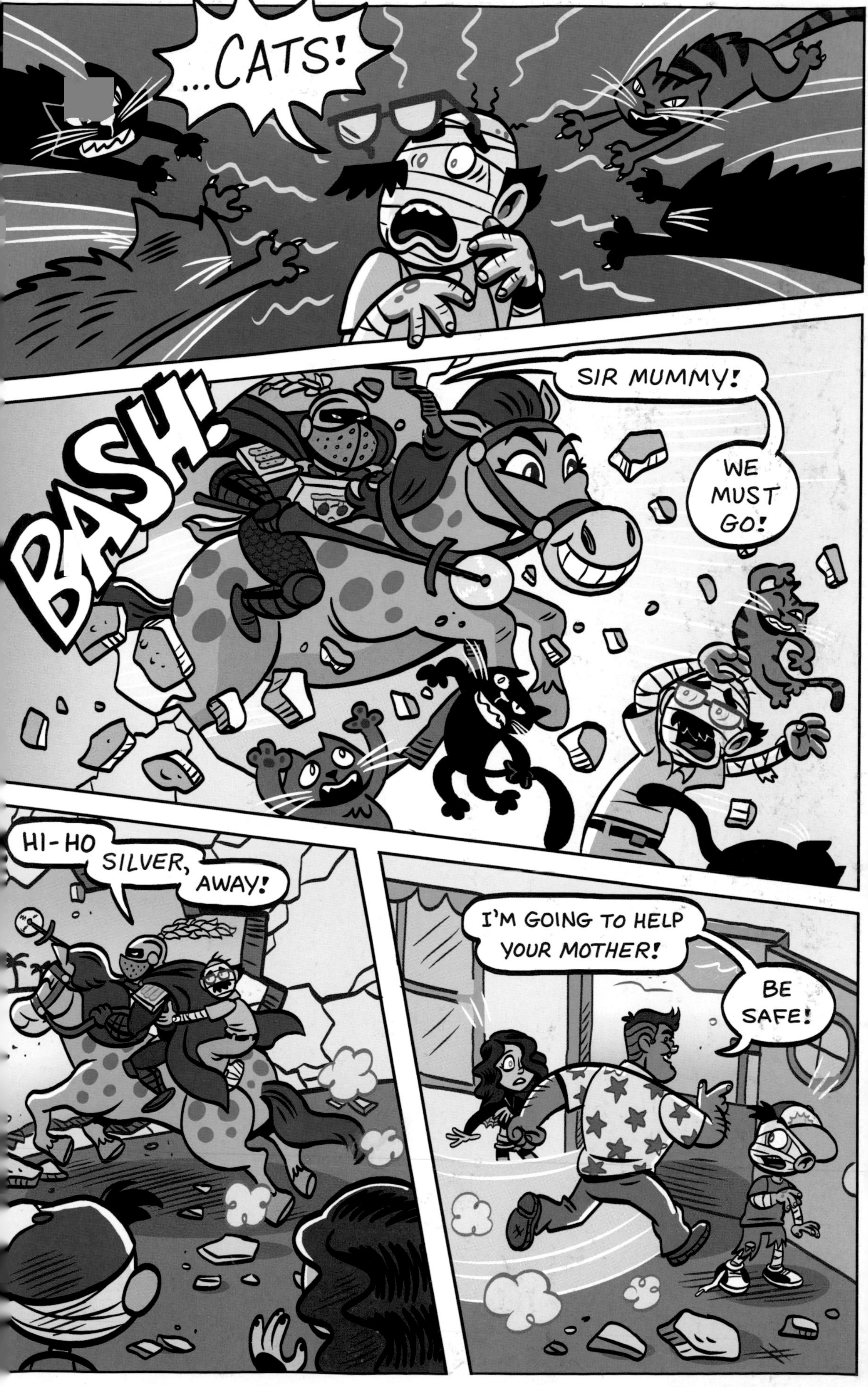
...CATS!
BASH!
SIR MUMMY!
WE MUST GO!
HI-HO
SILVER,
AWAY!
I'M GOING TO HELP YOUR MOTHER!
BE SAFE!

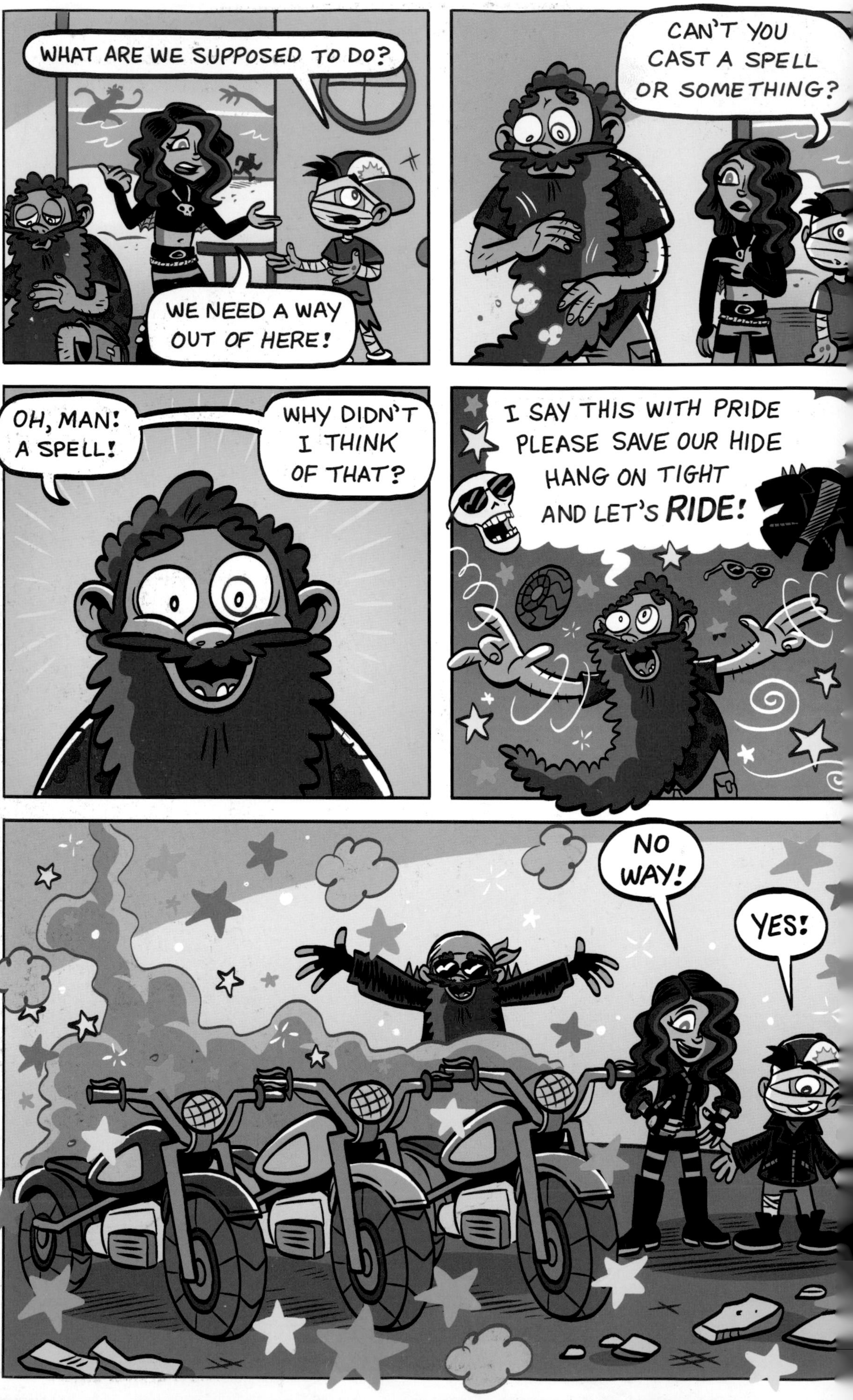
WHAT ARE WE SUPPOSED TO DO?
WE NEED A WAY OUT OF HERE!
CAN'T YOU CAST A SPELL OR SOMETHING?
OH, MAN! A SPELL!
WHY DIDN'T I THINK OF THAT?
I SAY THIS WITH PRIDE
PLEASE SAVE OUR HIDE
HANG ON TIGHT
AND LET'S RIDE!
NO WAY!
YES!

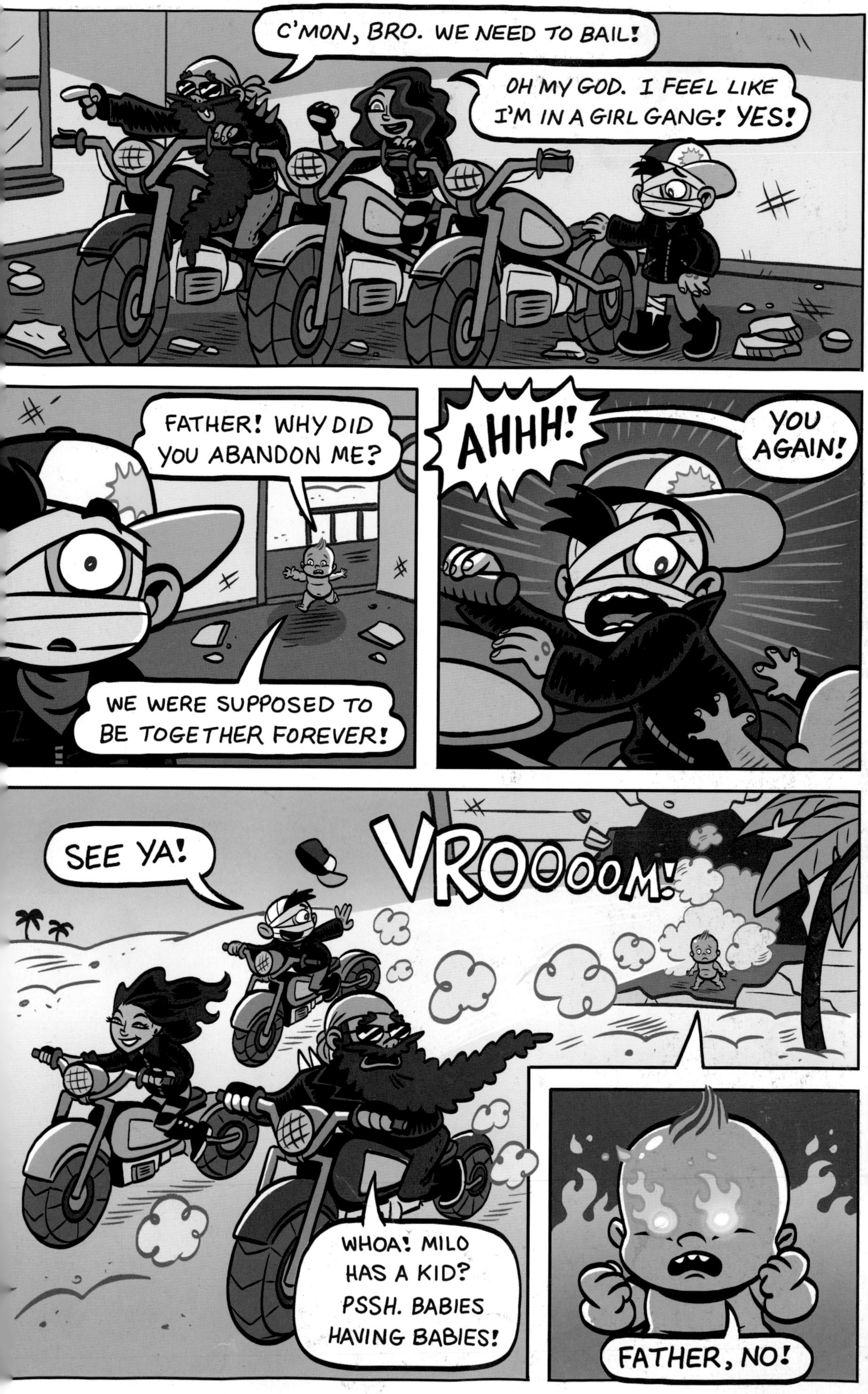
C'MON, BRO. WE NEED TO BAIL!
OH MY GOD. I FEEL LIKE I'M IN A GIRL GANG! YES!
FATHER! WHY DID YOU ABANDON ME?
WE WERE SUPPOSED TO BE TOGETHER FOREVER!
AHHH!
YOU AGAIN!
SEE YA!
VROOOOOM!
WHOA! MILO HAS A KID? PSSH. BABIES HAVING BABIES!
FATHER, NO!

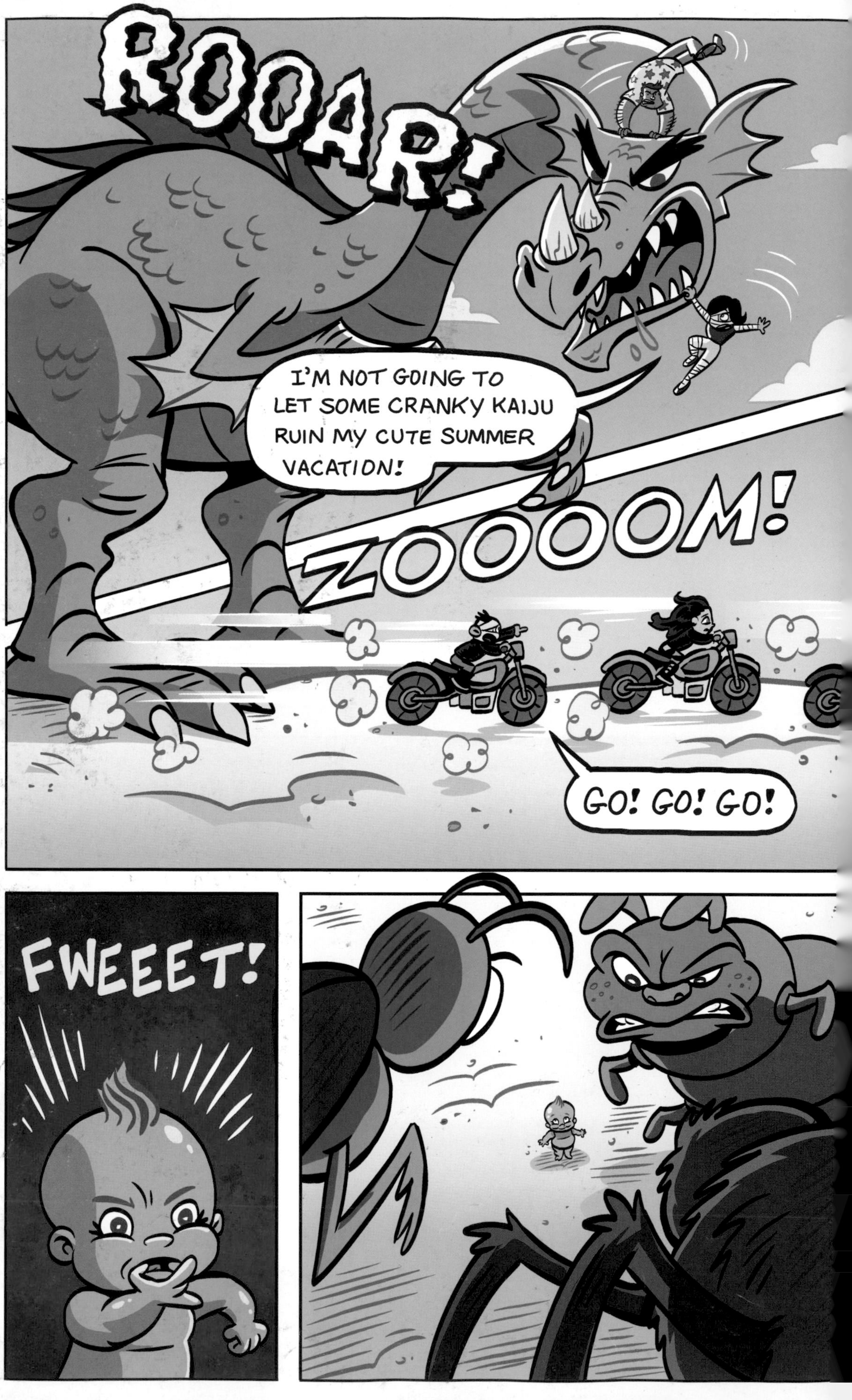
ROOAR!
I'M NOT GOING TO LET SOME CRANKY KAIJU RUIN MY CUTE SUMMER VACATION!
ZOOOOOM!
GO! GO! GO!
FWEEET!

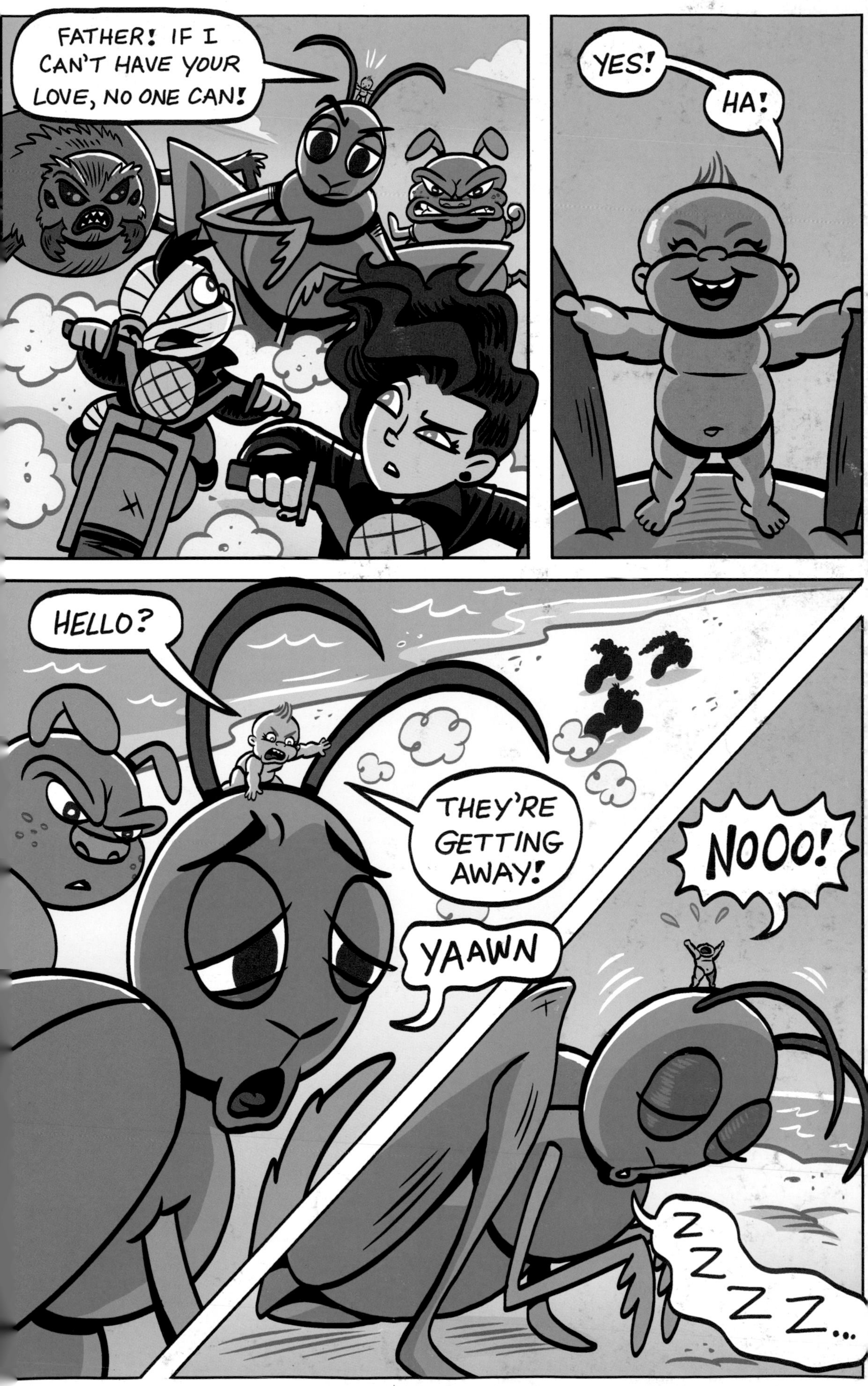
FATHER! IF I CAN'T HAVE YOUR LOVE, NO ONE CAN!
YES!
HA!
HELLO?
THEY'RE GETTING AWAY!
YAAWN
NOOO!
ZZZZ...

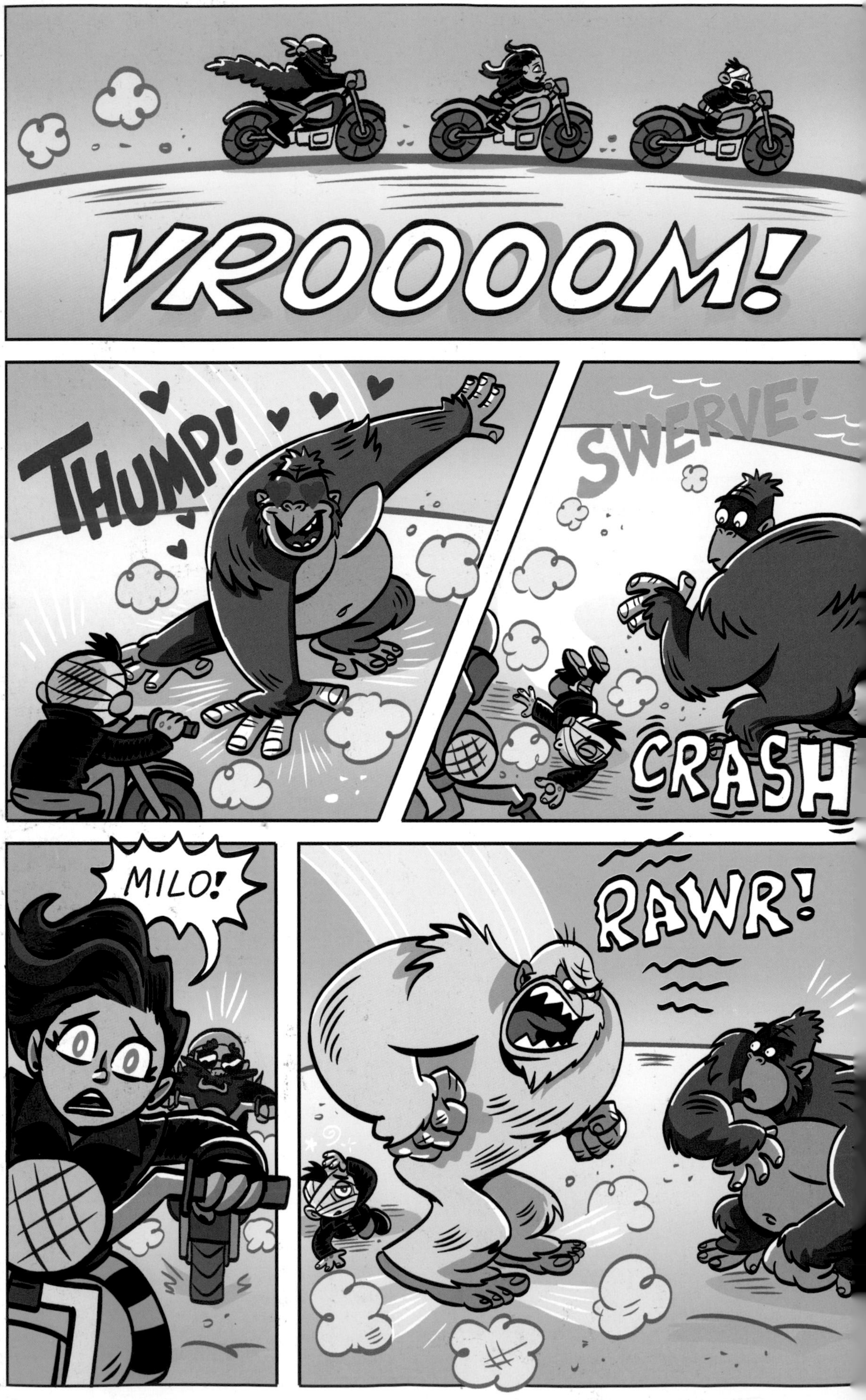
VROOOOM!
THUMP!
SWERVE!
CRASH
MILO!
RAWR!

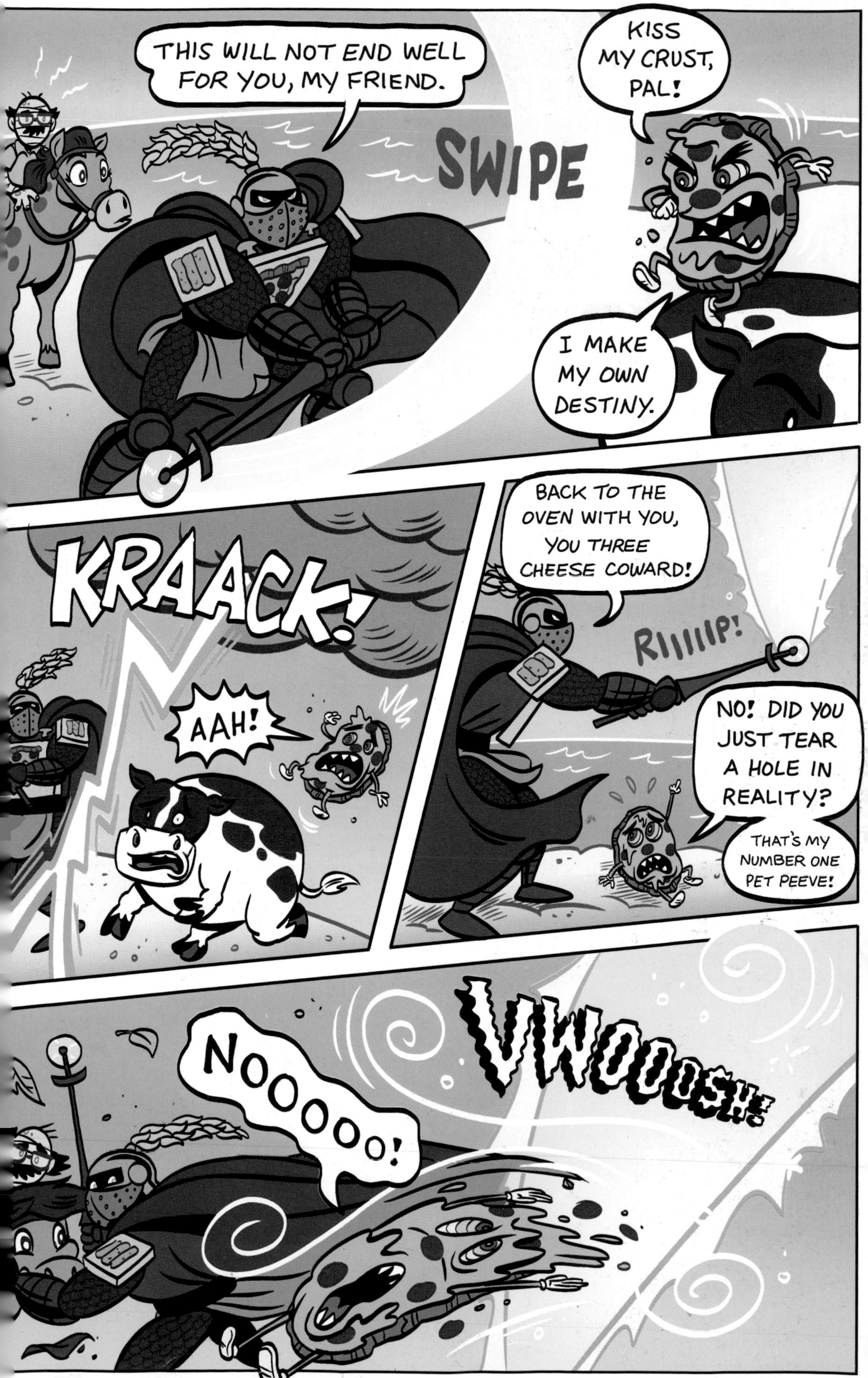
THIS WILL NOT END WELL FOR YOU, MY FRIEND.
KISS MY CRUST, PAL!
SWIPE
I MAKE MY OWN DESTINY.
KRAACK!
AAH!
BACK TO THE OVEN WITH YOU, YOU THREE CHEESE COWARD!
RIIIIIP!
NO! DID YOU JUST TEAR A HOLE IN REALITY?
THAT'S MY NUMBER ONE PET PEEVE!
NOOOOOO!
VWOOOSH!!

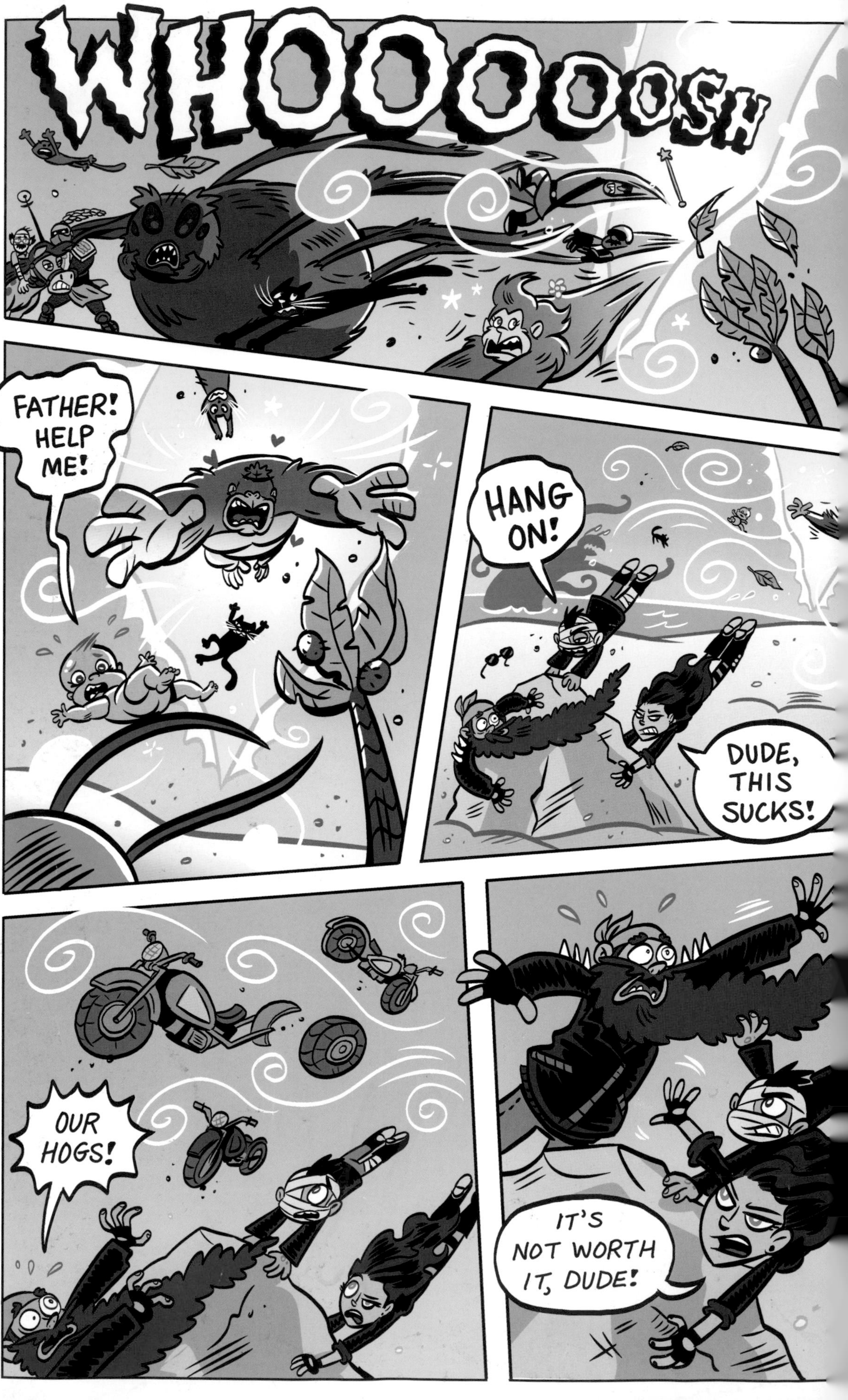
WHOOOOOOSH
FATHER! HELP ME!
HANG ON!
DUDE, THIS SUCKS!
OUR HOGS!
IT'S NOT WORTH IT, DUDE!

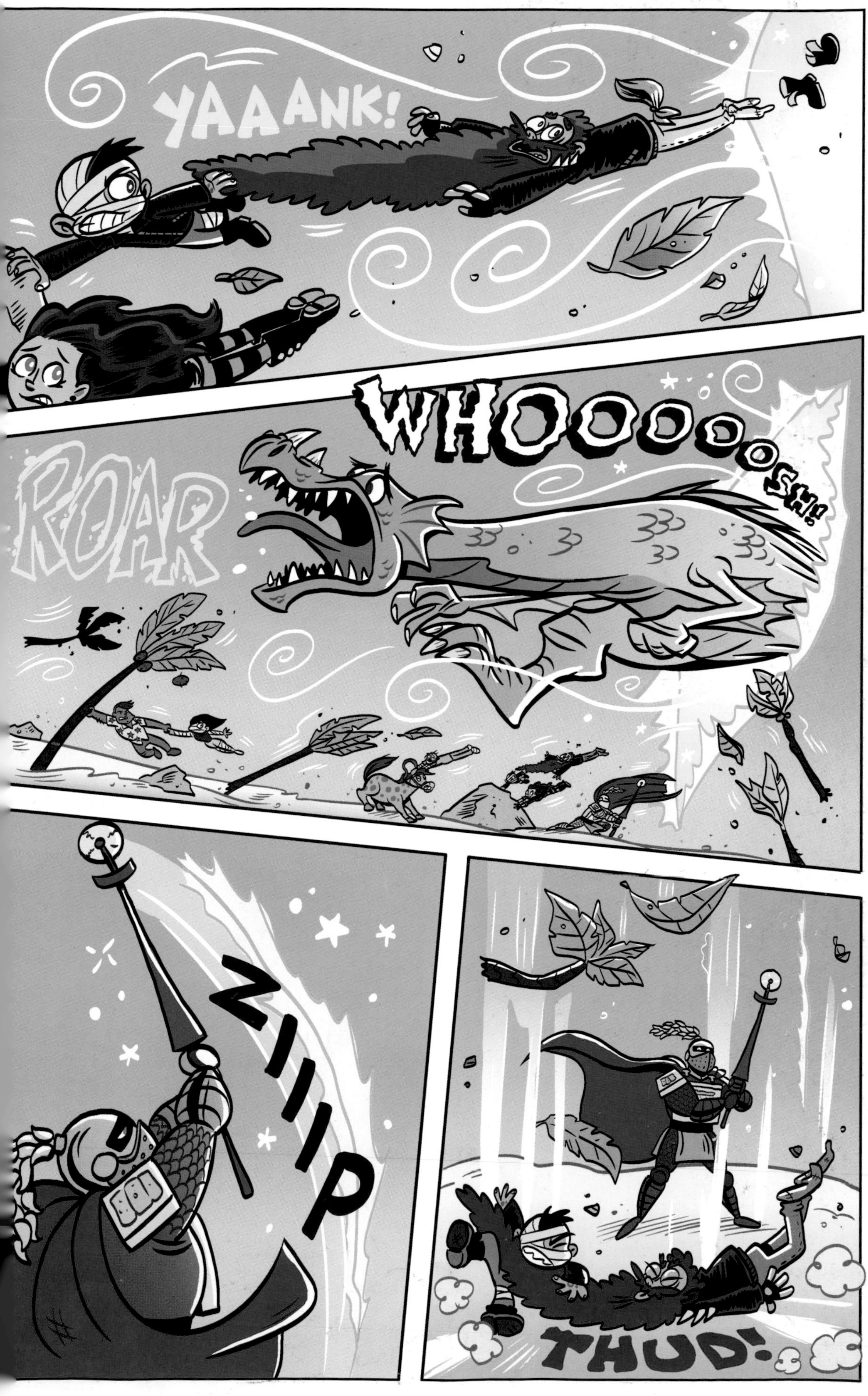
YAAANK!
WHOOOOOOSH!
ROAR
ZIIIP
THUD!

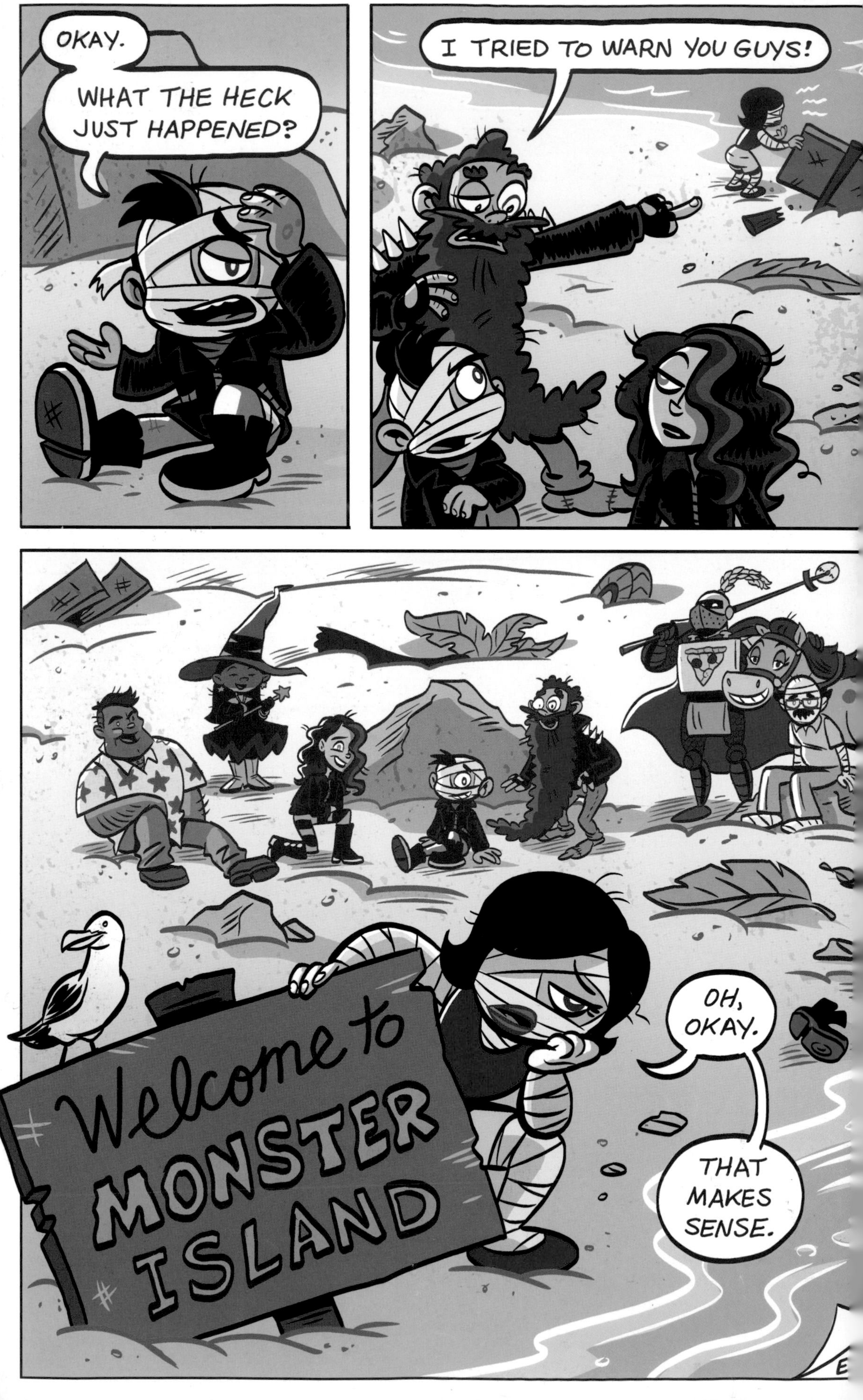
OKAY.
WHAT THE HECK JUST HAPPENED?
I TRIED TO WARN YOU GUYS!
Welcome to MONSTER ISLAND
OH, OKAY.
THAT MAKES SENSE.

HE NIGHT PATRONS!

WRITTEN BY: DAVE SCHEIDT

ART BY: SHAN MURPHY

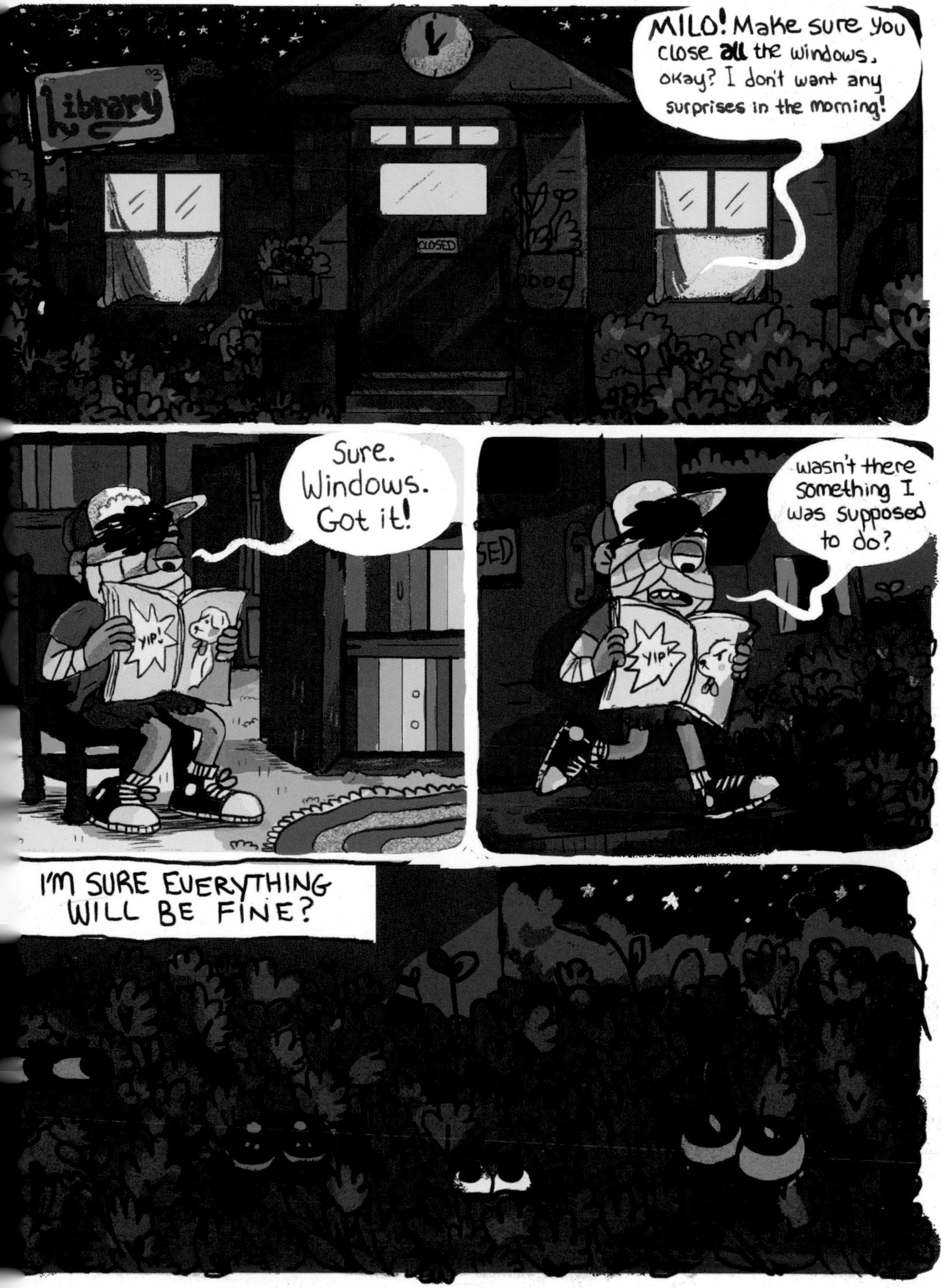

Library
MILO! Make sure you close all the windows, okay? I don't want any surprises in the morning!
CLOSED
Sure. Windows. Got it!
YIP!
wasn't there something I was supposed to do?
YIP!
I'M SURE EVERYTHING WILL BE FINE?

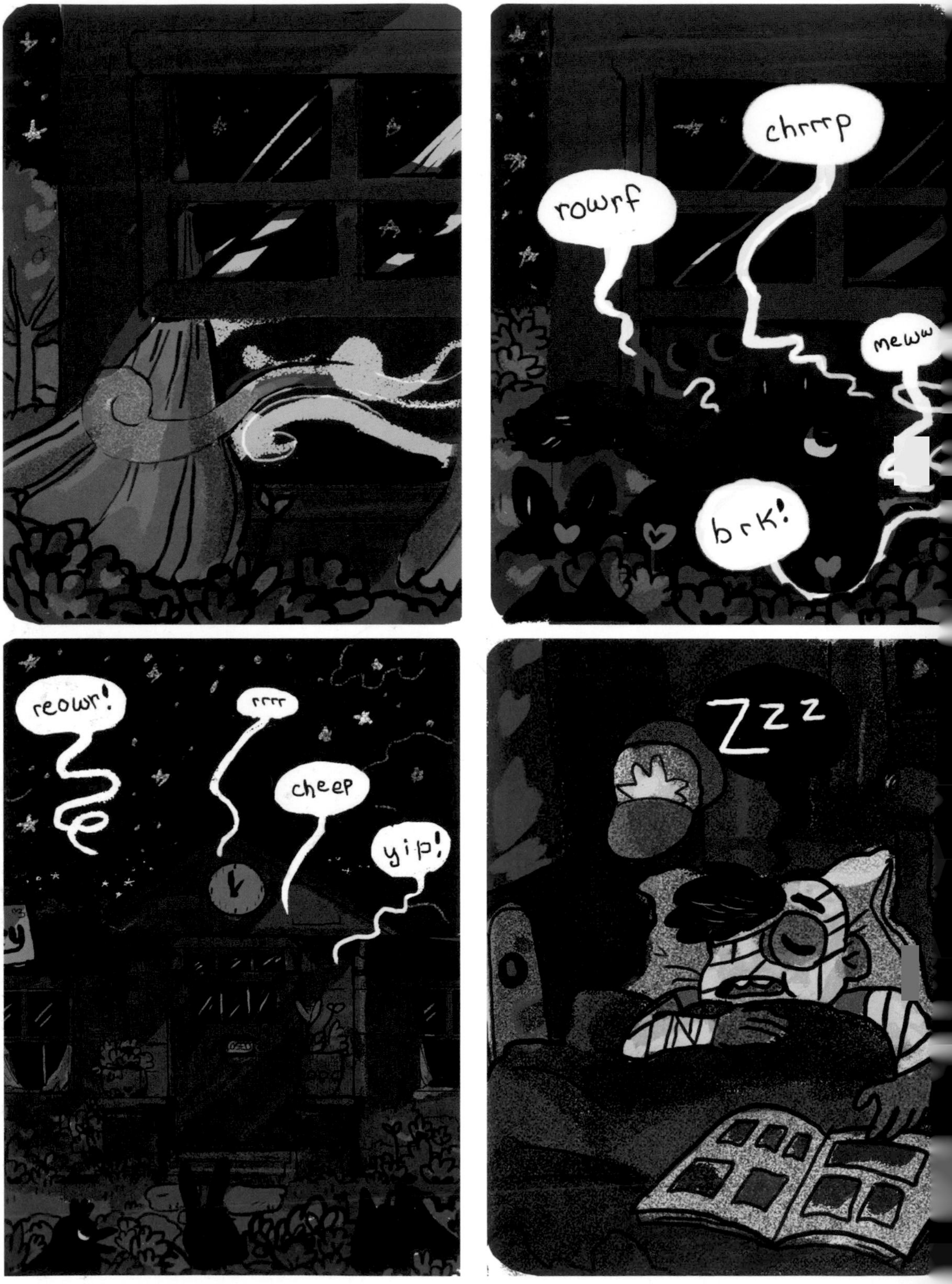
rowrf
chrrrp
meww
brk!
reowr!
rrrr
cheep
yip!
Zzz

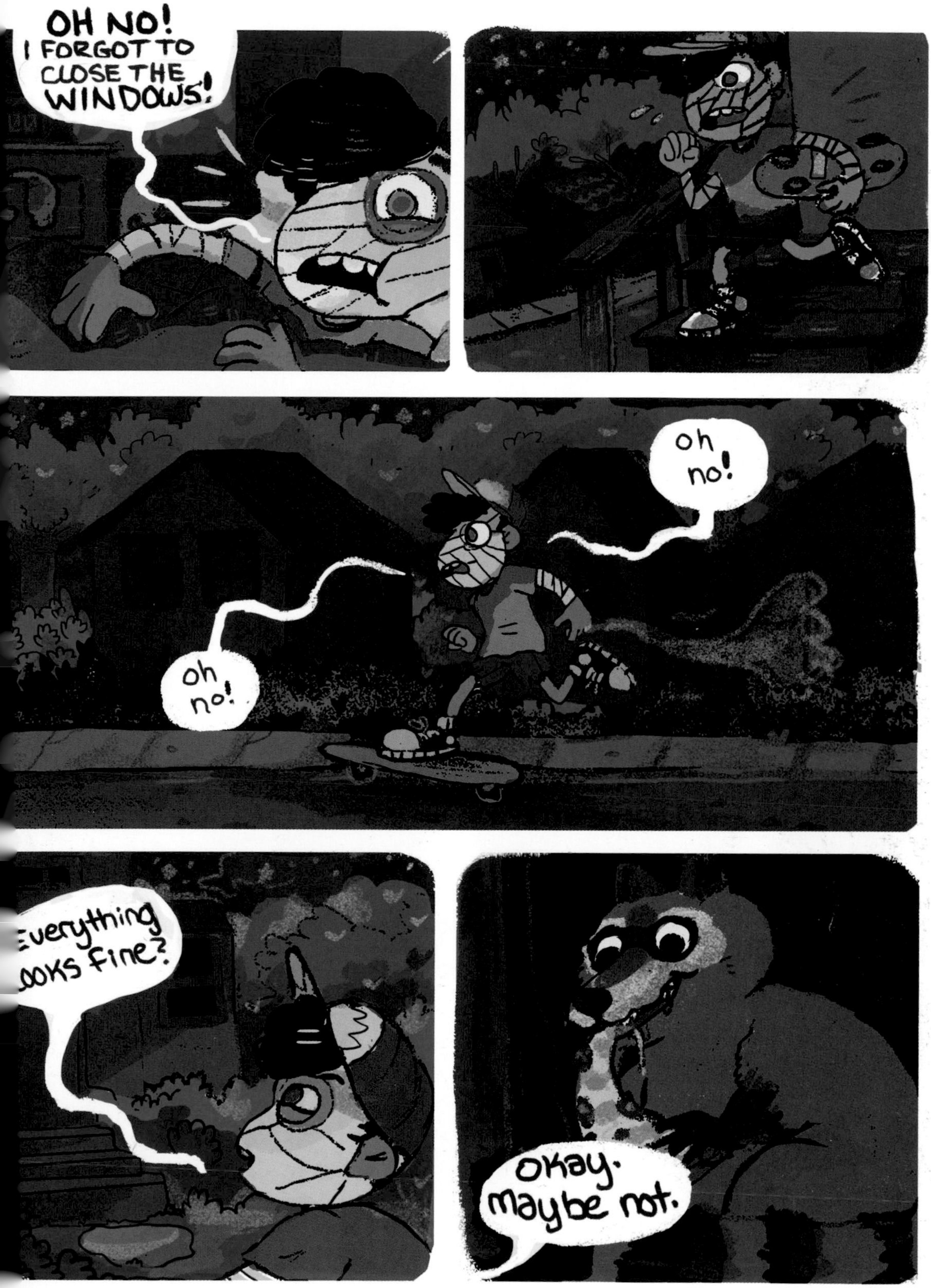
OH NO! I FORGOT TO CLOSE THE WINDOWS!
oh no!
oh no!
Everything looks fine?
okay. maybe not.

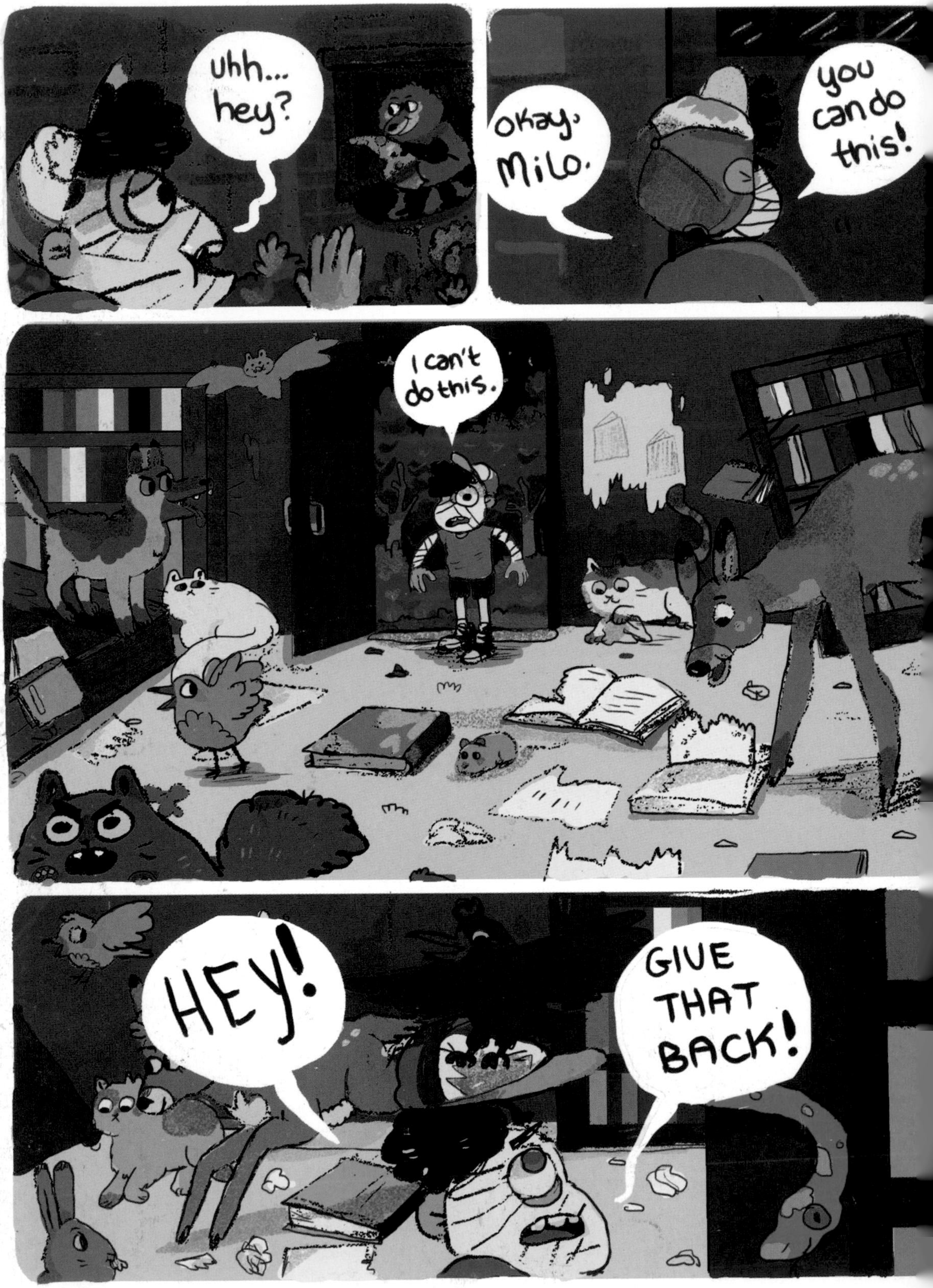
uhh... hey?
okay, Milo.
you can do this!
I can't do this.
HEY!
GIVE THAT BACK!

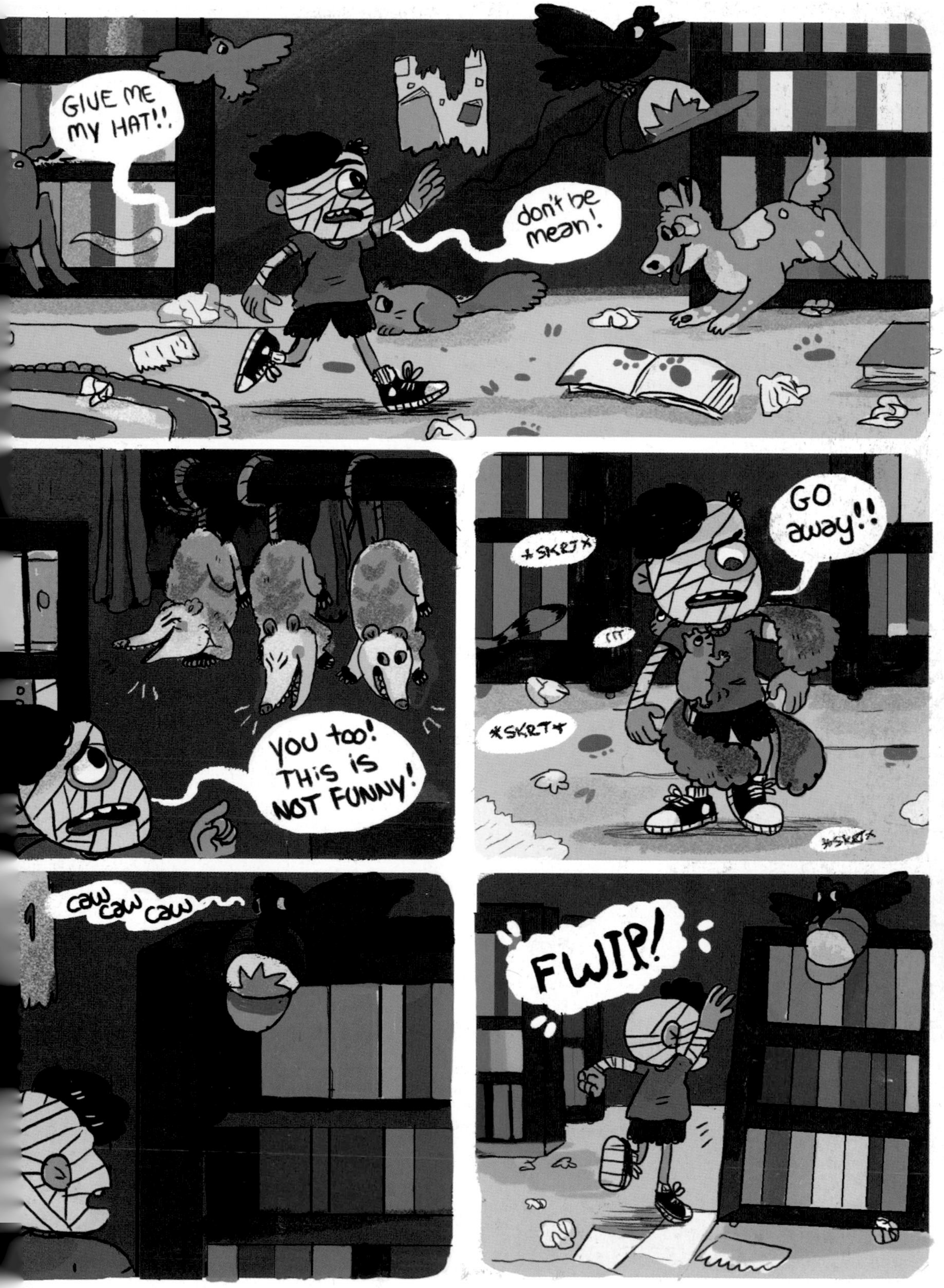
GIVE ME MY HAT!!
don't be mean!
you too! THIS is NOT FUNNY!
GO away!!
SKRT
SKRT
caw caw caw
FWIP!

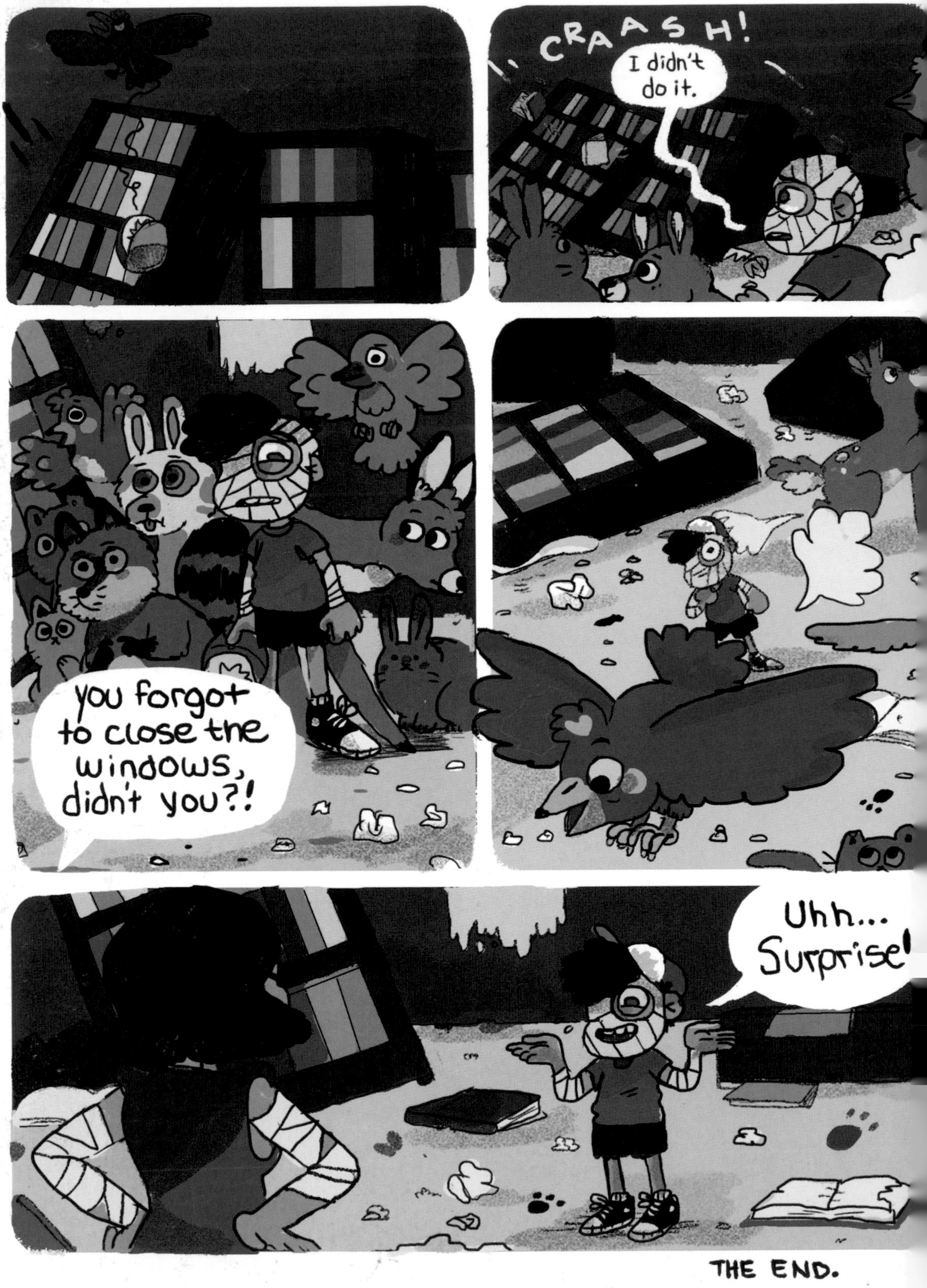
CRAASH!
I didn't do it.
you forgot to close the windows, didn't you?!
Uhh... Surprise!

THE END.

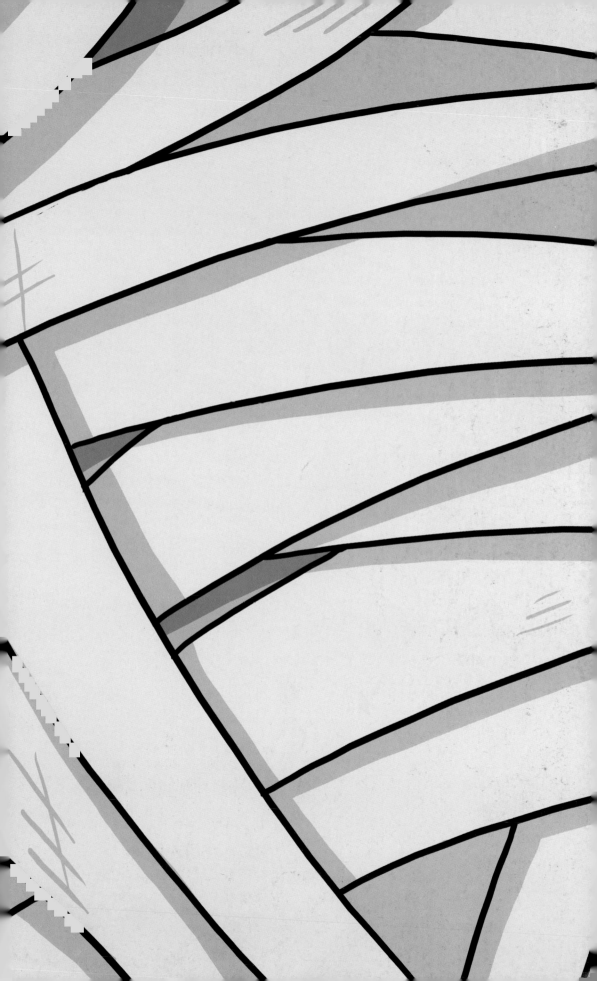

COVER ART GALLERY

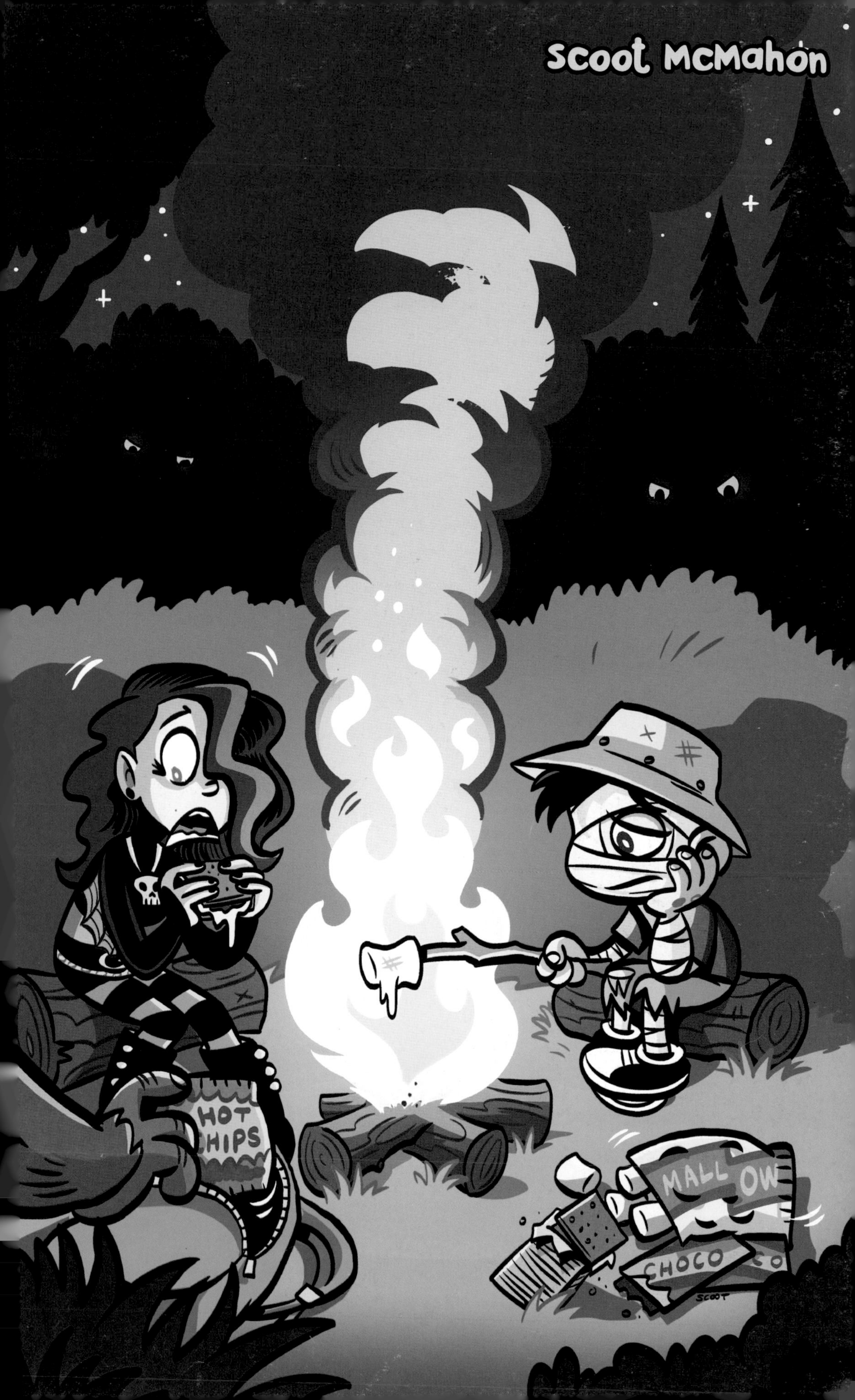
Scoot McMahon
HOT CHIPS
MALL OW
CHOCO
CO
SCOOT

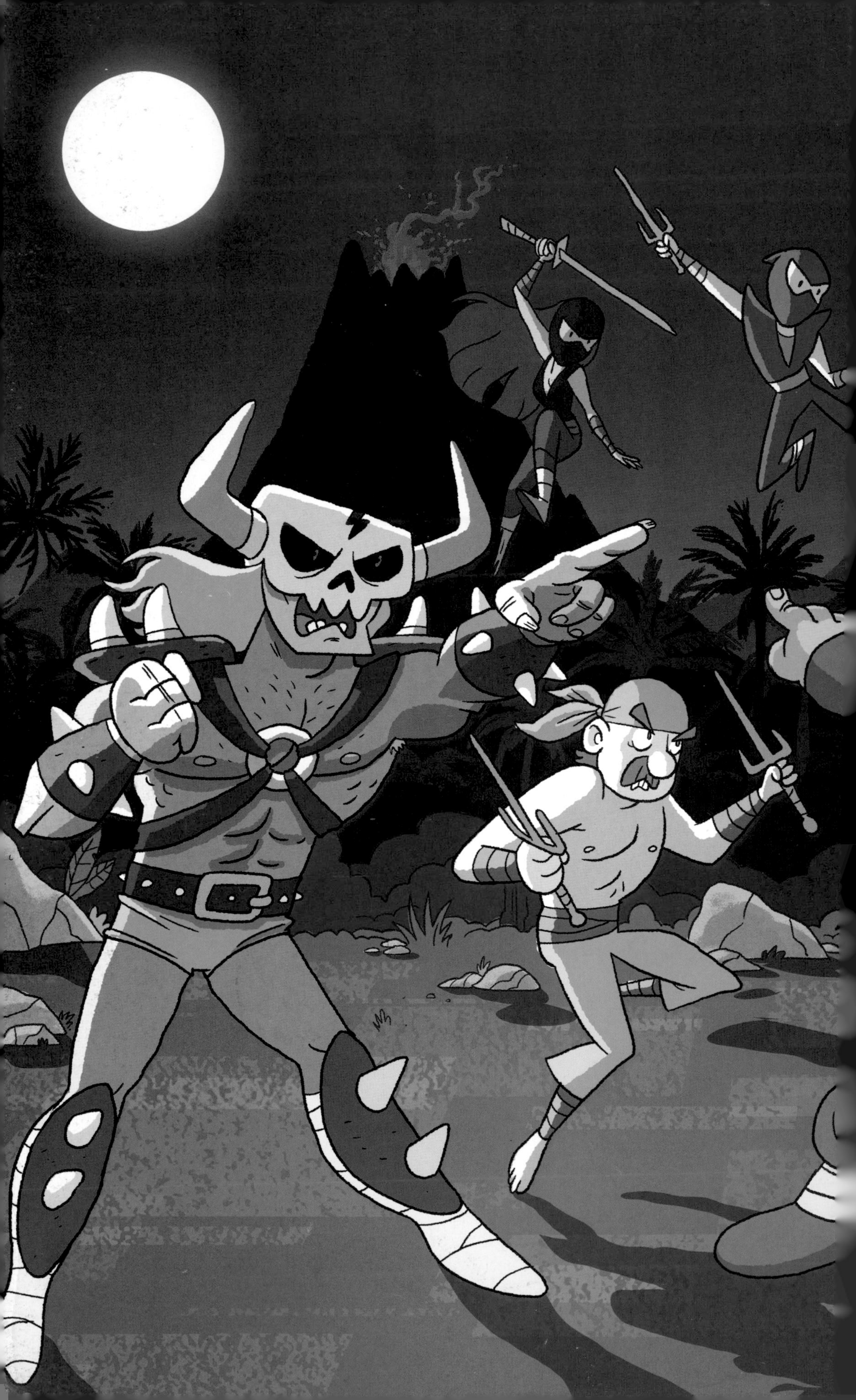

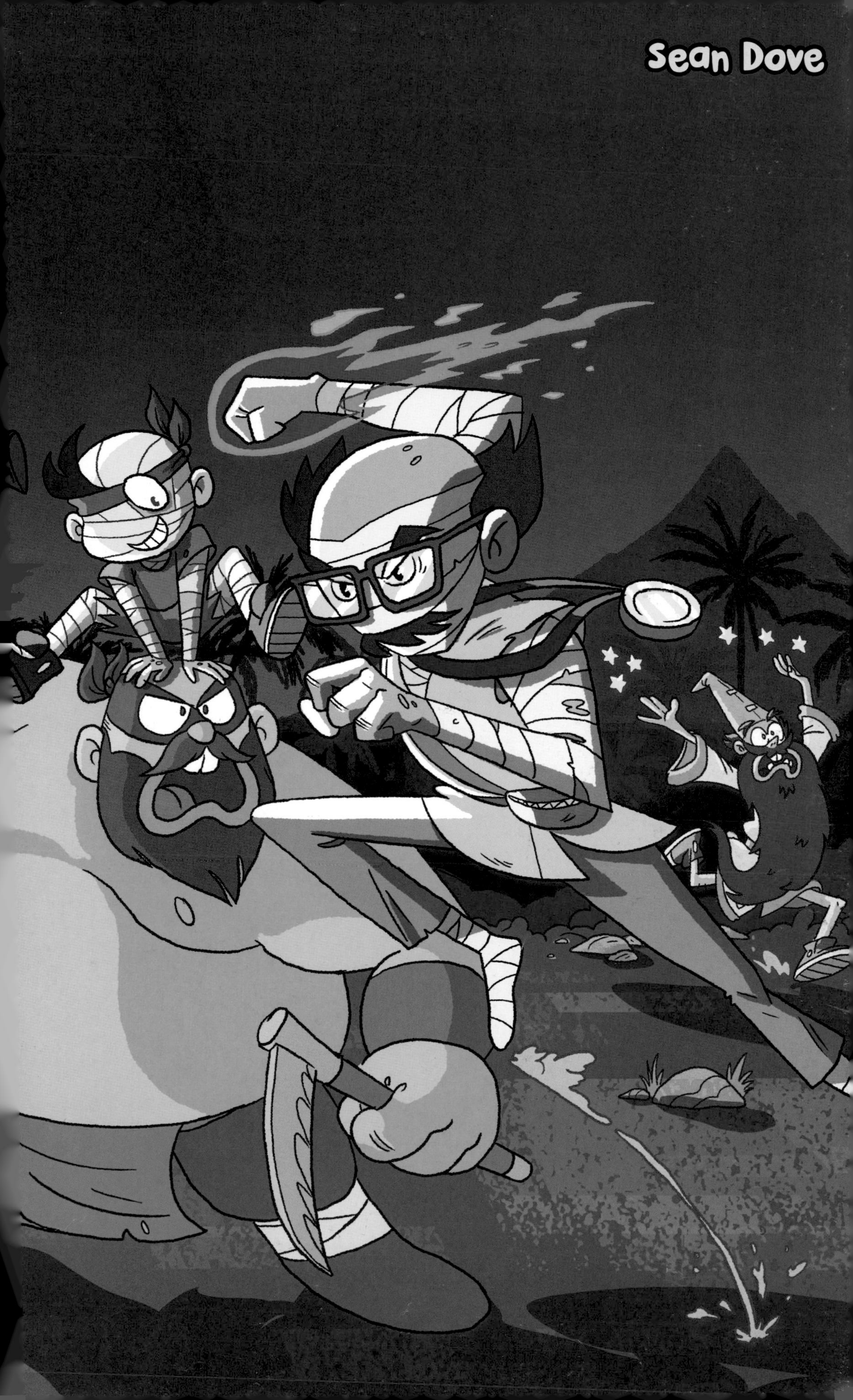
Sean Dove

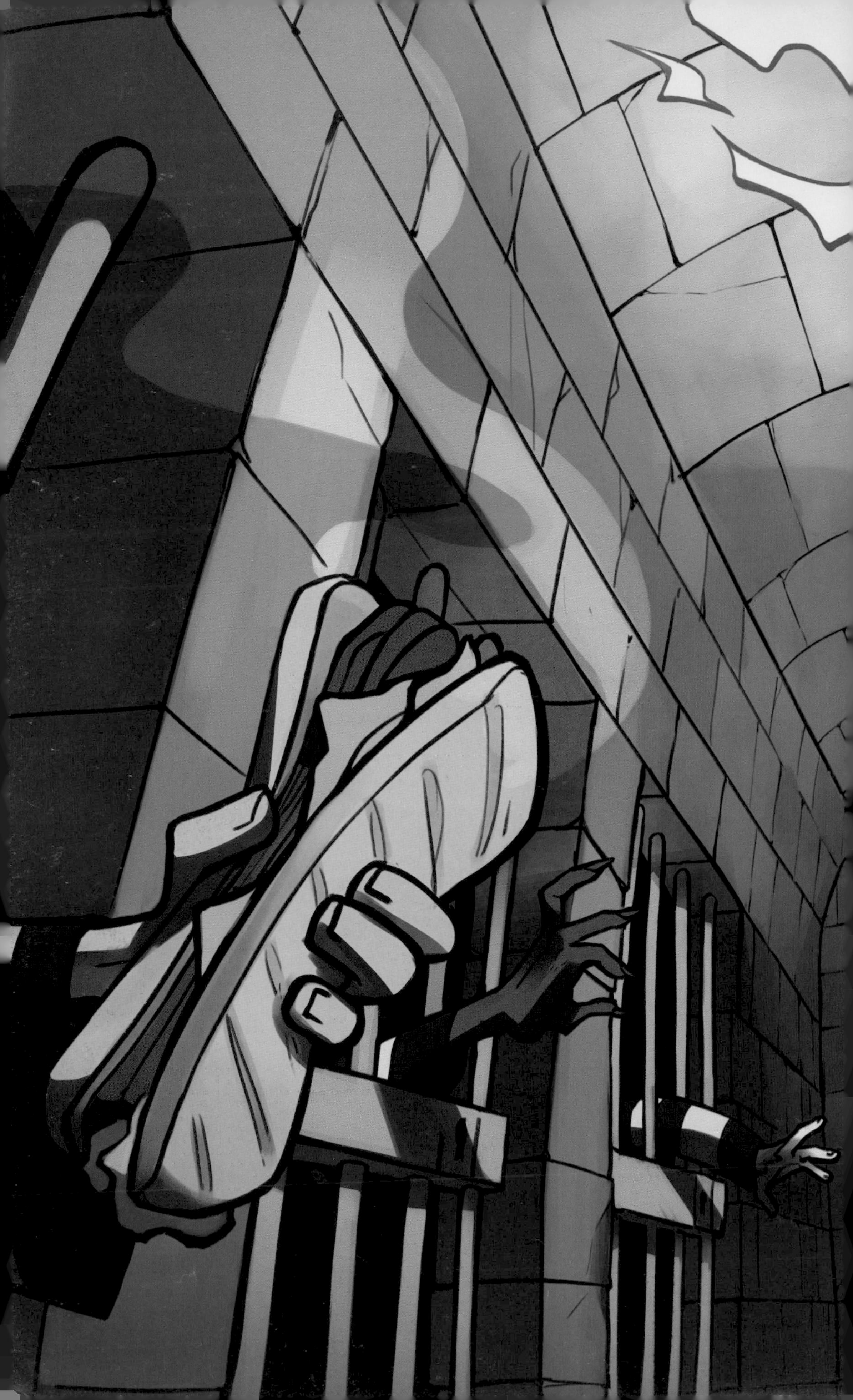

Sarah Bollinger

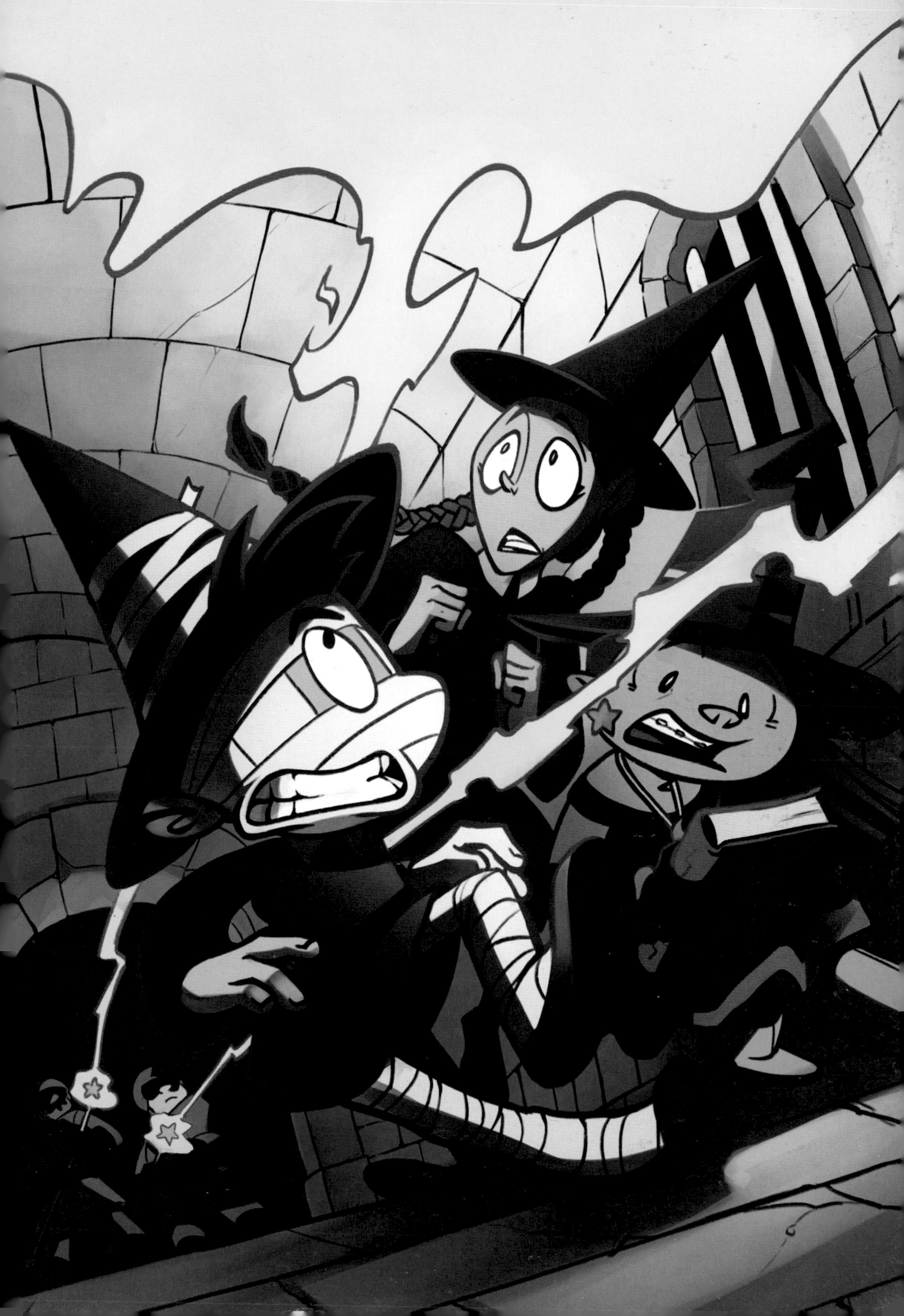

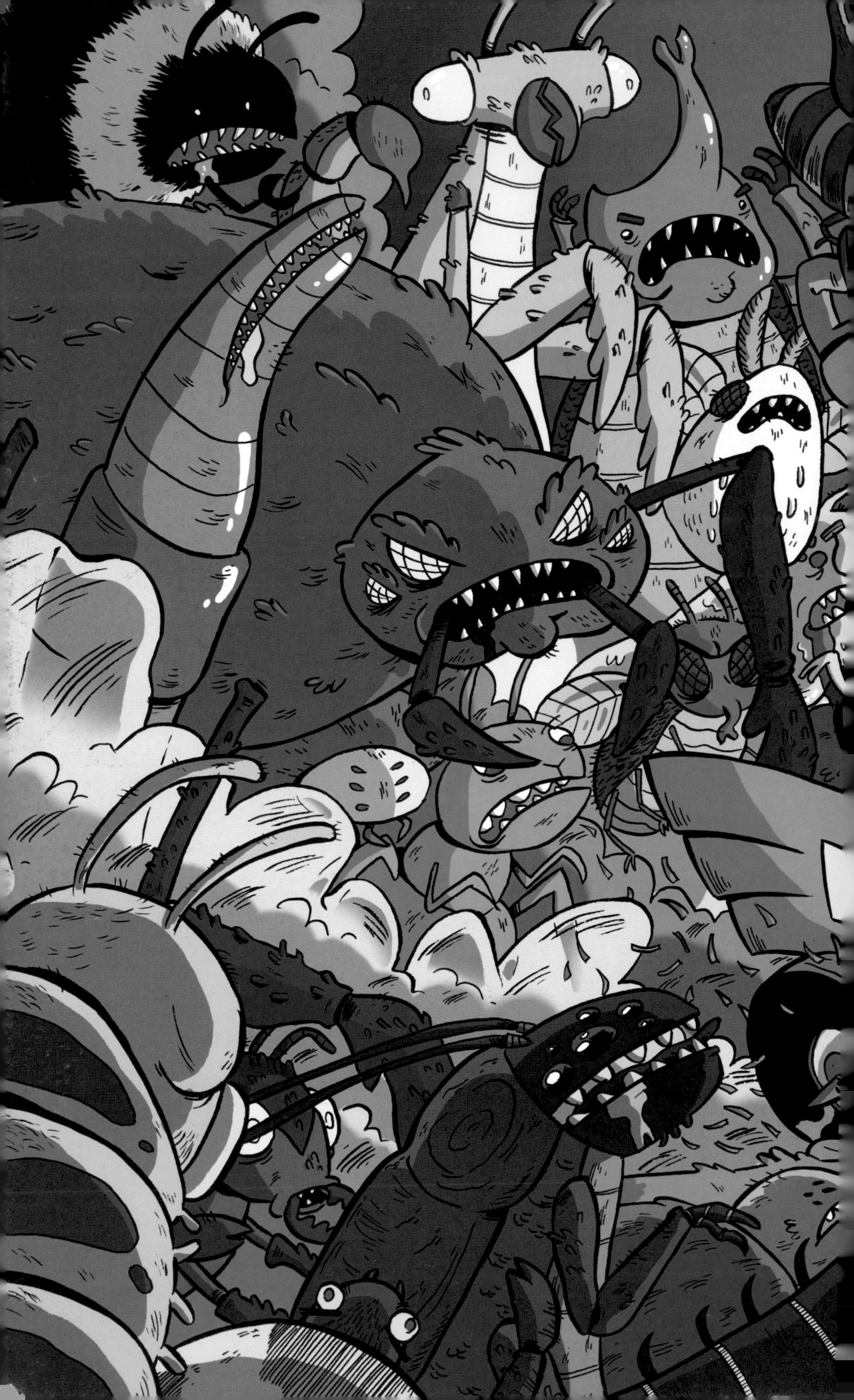

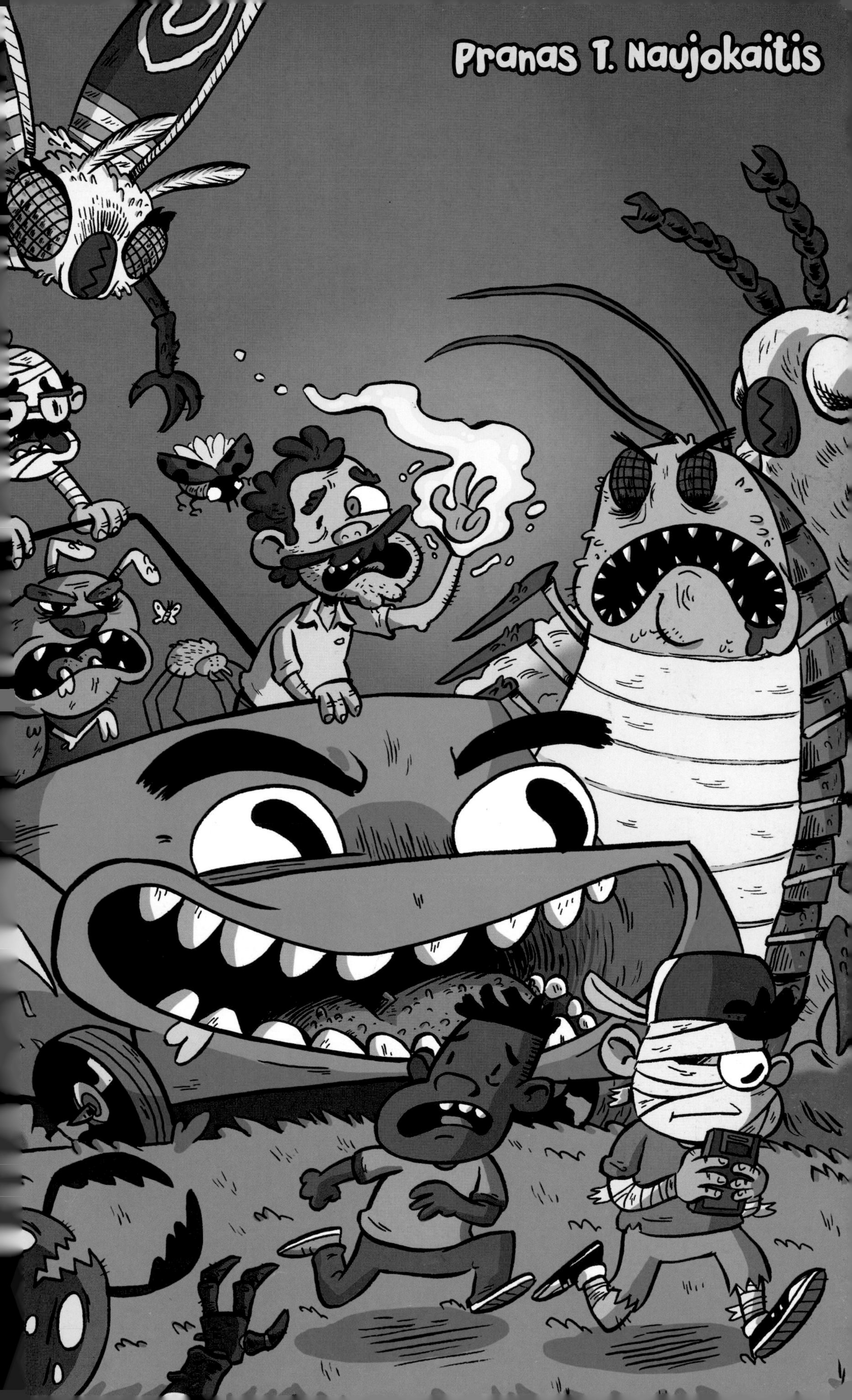

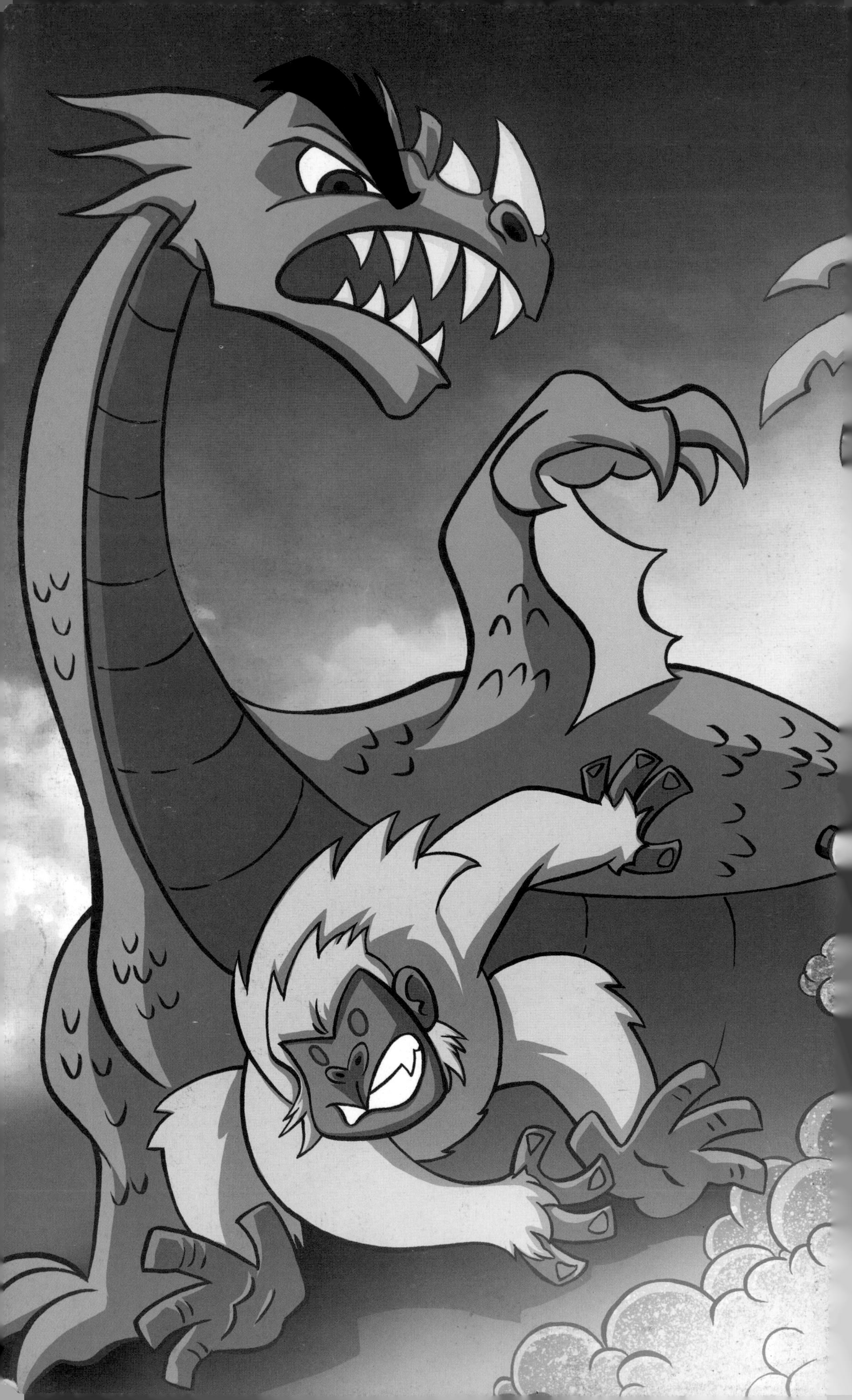

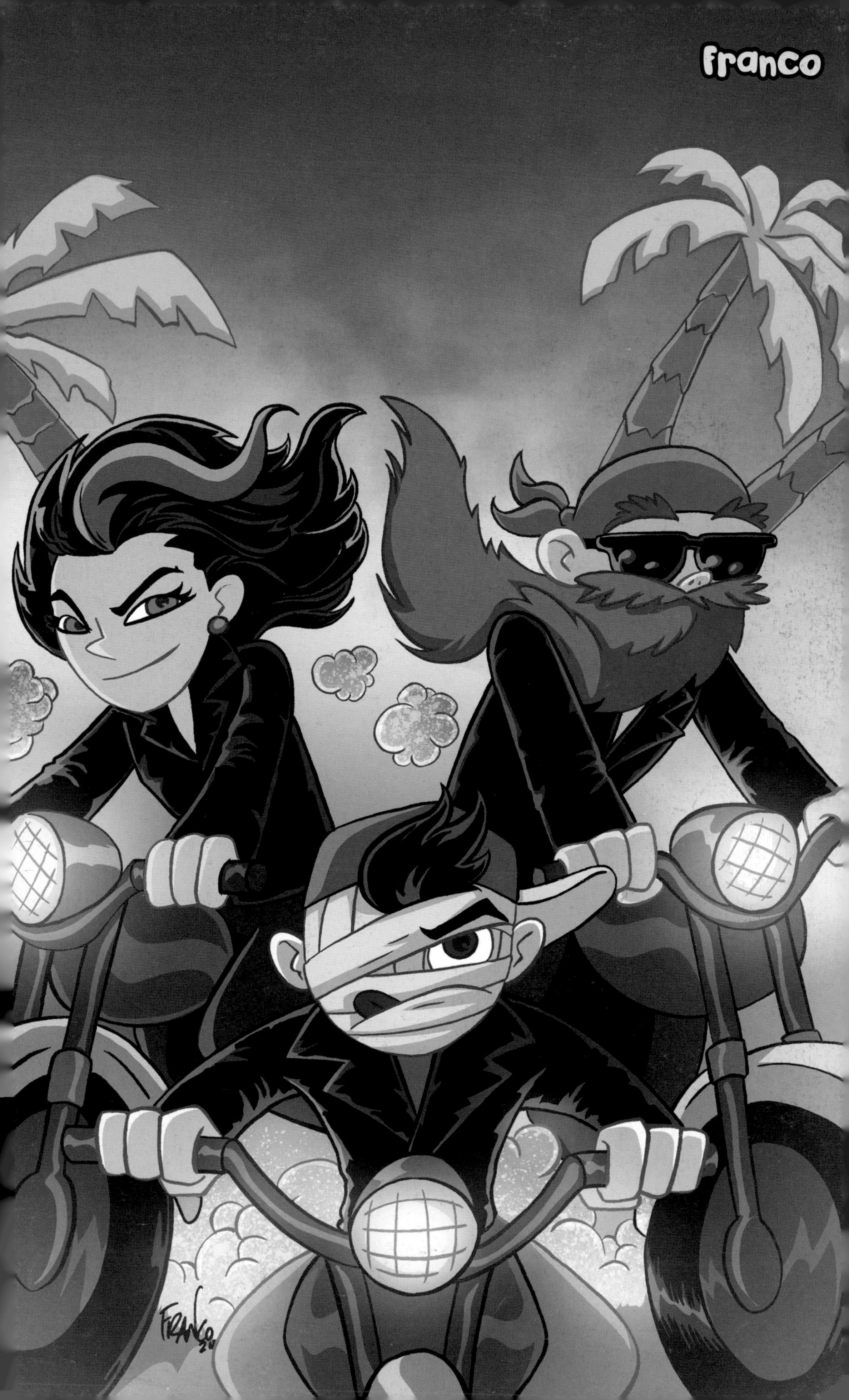
franco

DAVE SCHEIDT is a radical dude from Chicago, Illinois. When he's not writing comic books, he enjoys eating pizza.

SCOOT MCMAHON is the creator behind the all-ages comics Sami the Samurai Squirrel, Spot on Adventure, and a regular collaborator for Aw Yeah Comics. Scoot loves ninjas, superheroes, running, and pizza. Find Scoot at scootcomics.com.

SEAN DOVE lives and works in Chicago, Illinois, where he self-published The Last Days of Danger, worked on Madballs, and cocreated Brobots. His favorite Halloween candy includes those weird Tootsie Fruit Rolls and fun-size 100 Grand bars.